Teresa J Rooney,   Eblana

The Last Monarch of Tara

A Tale of Ireland in the Sixth Century

Teresa J Rooney, Eblana

The Last Monarch of Tara
A Tale of Ireland in the Sixth Century

ISBN/EAN: 9783744622271

Printed in Europe, USA, Canada, Australia, Japan

Cover: Foto ©Andreas Hilbeck / pixelio.de

More available books at **www.hansebooks.com**

áro ríg oeigionac

ná

ceamrac.

sgeul air eirinn anns an seiseaó aois.

noc oo sgríob eblaná.

THE LAST MONARCH

OF

TARA:

A TALE OF IRELAND IN THE SIXTH CENTURY.

BY EBLANA.

REVISED AND CORRECTED BY THE

VERY REV. U. J. CANON BOURKE, M.R.I.A.

ác cliac:

m. h. gíll 'sa mac, 50 sráio sacbill uáccar.

DUBLIN:

M. H. GILL & SON, 50 UPPER SACKVILLE-ST.

1880.

ꝺꞁ́ꝋꝋ́b́ꝛꝋ́ꞁꞁꝋ́ꝗ.

PREFACE.

———◆———

THE following tale of ancient Ireland has been written solely in the interest of this land, and of the Clanna-Gael, at home and abroad; the writer therefore trusts that its shortcomings may be overlooked in consideration of its aim and object. By shortcomings she means the composition and management of the subject. The subject itself; the events recorded; all the principal personages; the religious, literary, civil, and military institutions ¹n all their details; the manners and customs of all classes of the people; their houses, furniture, dress, ornaments, and everything which they used—all these things need no apology; they are all of strict historical accuracy, and in proof of this she refers her readers to the various authorities which she has consulted in the compilation of this little work. They are chiefly: The "Annals of the Four Masters," by Connellan; and by O'Donovan O'Flaherty's "Ogygia;" the "Book of Rights" ("Leabhar na g-Ceart"); the "Chronicles of Eire;" Petrie's "Tara;" Petrie's "Round Towers;" Dunraven's "Irish Architecture," edited by Miss Stokes; O'Mahony's "Keating's History of Ireland;' O'Connor's "Dissertations on ancient Irish History;" O'Curry's "Manuscript Materials of Irish History;" O'Curry's "Manners and Customs of the Ancient Irish;" Bunting's, Walker's, Petrie's, and Hardiman's "Music;" Reeve's "Adamnan's St. Columba (or Columkille); Sir W. Wilde's "Antiquities;" O'Donovan's

"MSS. in Ordnance Survey;" Dr. Joyce's "Irish Names of Places;" the works of the Rev. Dr. Lanigan, Very Rev. Canon Ulick J. Bourke, Miss Cusack (Sister M. F. Clare), Rev. Dr. Colgan, and the Rev. J. O'Hanlon, the eminent author of the "Lives of the Irish Saints." To this last-named learned and painstaking hagiographer, the writer is especially indebted; for not only did his first volume suggest to her the idea of endeavouring to illustrate, in a light form, the lives of some of the saints and heroes of Irish history, but she is also indebted to him for placing the greater part of the above-named works at her disposal. She is also indebted in a particular manner to the Very Rev. Canon Bourke, who read the proofs and greatly improved them. In order to be as correct as possible the writer has also consulted the Ordnance Survey and other Maps, ancient and modern. Specimens of many of the articles described are to be seen in the Museum of the Royal Irish Academy. In describing the glories of the ancient Irish the writer has not omitted their faults, as these ultimately led to their enslavement, and it is profitable for us to take warning by their errors. An eventful period in the life of St. Columkille is introduced. It is much to be regretted that Irish history is banned in Ireland, not only by the foreign rulers of the country, but by the Irish race themselves. They have no idea of what they lose by their wilful ignorance. They are told by their interested masters across the channel that Ireland has no history; that it was a nation of savages until England took pity on it, invaded and civilised it; numbers of them are so debased morally, physically, and intellectually by persecution, that they believe it, without taking the trouble to find out for themselves whether it be true or not. It is enough for them that England says it; it is their duty to believe it; it were disloyalty to doubt. And not satisfied with this, they repeat the calumny, parrot-like, to others, believing that they are speaking the truth. And yet this lamentable state of affairs is not the fault of anyone individually.

It is part of a system, the miserable result of seven centuries of national bondage and its accompanying degradation. The Irish have been taught to look upon their conquerors pretty much as the negroes look upon the whites—as a superior race. But if the people of Ireland studied Irish history, they would know that things were just the reverse of what they are taught to believe. They would know that Ireland was the home of civilisation, sanctity, learning, and worldly prosperity when England was steeped in barbarism, heathenism, ignorance, and poverty; and that, moreover, it was Ireland that elevated England from that terrible condition, and that the latter country owes to the former whatever civilisation and prosperity she now enjoys. But all this is studiously suppressed; and if a stranger arrived here, and visited all the schools of various classes and denominations throughout Ireland, and examined the pupils in history, he would be obliged to arrive at the conclusion that Ireland was a newly-discovered country, lately planted with a purely English colony; or that it was a part of England, like Yorkshire or Surrey, that had, by some volcanic eruption, been separated from the rest of that country by a deep channel of angry waters, but whose people still regarded themselves as purely and thoroughly English in descent, in history, in politics, in aspirations, in everything, and insisted upon having their children taught precisely as the children are taught on the other side of the English Channel. And the stranger would, no doubt, admire the marvellous unanimity of all classes in their anxiety to pose before the world as Englishmen and Englishwomen, as evidenced by the tone of the schools which their children attended, from the Primary School up to the University, and including also all denominations—Protestants, Catholics, Presbyterians, &c.,—each trying to outrival the others in spurning and ignoring the very existence of such a place as Ireland, and trying to make their pupils believe that England is, and ought to be, their country, that they ought to grieve at her misfortune, glory in her triumph, cheerfully give their money, their brains, their blood, their lives in building up

and consolidating her greatness, and be glad to receive in return bare toleration or contemptuous indifference to their rights.
Is it not too true that this is the way in which Irish children are
taught history in Irish schools? Save, perhaps, in a few acade-
mies and colleges, where is the pupil of any of these schools who
can say that he or she has been taught Irish history in any of
these establishments? Where, the student of the Queen's
Colleges, the Queen's University, the Catholic University, or
Trinity College, with whom Irish history has formed part of the
curriculum of his education? Echo answers, Where? where?
The distinguished member for the county in which was enacted
the greater part of the events recorded in our tale stated on one
occasion that, after having passed through the entire of what is
called a university education (which of course included the
histories of all countries except Ireland), he had to *commence* to
study Irish history for himself. It would be very desirable that
every student on leaving the universities would do likewise. It
would be more desirable still if these universities would save
their students this trouble by making Irish history part of the
course, and it would be the climax of desirability if these institutions, together with primary and intermediate schools, public
and private, would sink their differences on other points, and
be as unanimous in encouraging Irish history as they now are
in suppressing it. What a delightful state of affairs! How preg-
nant with hope for the future of the country if the various
educational establishments of divers denominations—Protestant,
Presbyterian, and Catholic—instead of trying to see, as hitherto
many of them have done, which of them is the greatest enemy of
their common country, would endeavour to outrival each other in
instilling into the minds of their pupils reverence and love, and a
thorough acquaintance with the history of their native land; if
the only charge which one denomination would be disposed to
make against the other would be that of failing to turn out of their
hands as good Irishmen as their rivals. This may appear un-

reasonable and impossible, but it is well-known that some of the very best and most patriotic of Irishmen have belonged to each of the denominations that inhabit the country. Whether this will ever come to pass it is hard to say; but it is certain that until it does Irishmen of all colours will have to place all their pride and glory in a country not their own, and be satisfied to shine in the borrowed plumes of another land, even though those plumes had been originally stolen from their own.

It is to be hoped that the following tale will prove acceptable, from a historical point of view, to all hues and shades of Irishmen—for all shades of Irishmen and Irishwomen can say of the country where the scenes are laid,

" This is my own, my native land !"

It is, however, to be regretted that the task was not undertaken by abler and more experienced pens. However, it is not too late for those able and willing to follow the matter up. There are ample materials for the purpose. The present tale is, of course, limited in persons, time, and place, and conveys no idea of other parts of the country, much less of other characters and epochs. Commending it once more to the kind and lenient criticism and perusal of Old and Young Ireland at home and abroad, I beg to subscribe myself

THE AUTHOR.

congmail.

CONTENTS.

───◆───

an céuⱱ cuiⱱ.
Part I.

aⱤⱱ-scoil chluain-iⱤaⱤeⱱ.
THE COLLEGE OF CLONARD.

an cheuⱱ chaibioil.
CHAPTER I.

an ⱱaⱤa chaibioil.
CHAPTER II.

an cⱤeaⱃ chaibioil.
CHAPTER III.

an cheachaⱤmhaⱱh chaibioil.
CHAPTER IV.

———

ᴀn oᴀᴘᴀ cuio.

Part II.

ᴛeamhaiᴘ na ᴘiᴣh.
TARA OF THE KINGS.
ᴀn cheuo chaibioil.

CHAPTER I.

ᴀn oᴀᴘᴀ chaibioil.
CHAPTER II.

Ɒⱀ ⱅⱃⰵⱭⱄ ⱍⱭⰰⰸⰹⱁⰹⰰⱠ:

CHAPTER III.

Ⱝⱀ ⱍⰵⱭⱅⱒⰰⱃⰿⱒⰰⰰⱁⱒ ⱍⰰⰹⰰⰰⰹⰰⱠ,

CHAPTER IV.

Ⱝⱀ ⱍⱊⰹⰸⰵⰰⱁⱒ ⱍⰰⰹⰰⰰⰹⰰⱠ.

CHAPTER V.

Ⱝⱀ ⱅ-ⱄⰵⰿⱒⰰⱁⱒ ⱍⰰⰹⰰⰰⰹⰰⱠ.

CHAPTER VI.

Ⱝⱀ ⱅ-ⱄⰵⰰⱍⱅⰿⱒⰰⱁⱒ ⱍⰰⰹⰰⰰⰹⰰⱠ.

CHAPTER VII.

Ⱝⱀ ⱅ-ⱁⱍⱅⰿⱒⰰⱁⱒ ⱍⰰⰹⰰⰰⰹⰰⱠ.

CHAPTER VIII.

Ⱝⱀ ⱀⰰⱁⰹⰿⱒⰰⱁⱒ ⱍⰰⰹⰰⰰⰹⰰⱠ.

CHAPTER IX.

Ⱝⱀ ⰰⰵⰹⱍⰿⱒⰰⱁⱒ ⱍⰰⰹⰰⰰⰹⰰⱠ.

CHAPTER X.

An Cueas Cuit.

Part III.

se bliaohana oeus 'n oeish.

SIXTEEN YEARS AFTER.

An cheuo chaibioil.

CONTENTS.

ⲁⲛ ⲤⲉⲁⲥⲁⱤṁⲁⲟ Cⲩⲓⲟ.
𝕻art IV.

ⲟⲟⱤchⲁⲟⲁⳋ ⲁⲛ ⳙⲁL ⳙⱤⲉⲓⲛⲉ
(ECLIPSE OF THE SUN-BURST).

cριoch.

END.

ÁRD RÍ̃ DEIʒIONÁC NA CEAṁRAC

The Last Monarch of Tara.

AN ĊEUD ĊUID.
Part I.

ÁRDSCOIL CLUAIN-IRARED.

THE COLLEGE OF CLONARD.

AN ĊEUD ĊAIBIDIL.

CHAPTER I.

An Coizcríoċ ó Ʒreuz.

THE STRANGER FROM GREECE.

T was on a dark, cold night in the month of October, in the year of our Lord, 538, that a lonely traveller traversed the deeply-wooded country which formed part of the ancient kingdom of Midhe.* He had but just lost sight of the light in the house of a BRUGHFER, where he had been entertained and directed on his road; and though he had since travelled a considerable distance, the friendly light had illumined his way, sometimes obscured for an instant by the wood, only to reappear again to cheer him on his journey; but as it gradually became dimmer and more dim, and as no other light appeared to take its place, the heart of our traveller, youthful though he was, began to sink within him. In vain he looked up at the heavens—the moon as well as the stars were completely obscured by black, impenetrable clouds; in vain he looked around—not the faintest

* Meath.

glimmer could he anywhere discern, not even that of the light
which he had but an instant before lost sight of. It seemed
for a moment as if he must pass the night in the wood ; but,
invoking the Divine assistance, he experienced renewed courage,
and proceeded vigorously on his way, using his arm as a shield
against the trees and shrubbery with which his path was beset,
and which enabled him to realise the difficulty of perceiving any
light, had it existed. After a few moments his exertions were
rewarded ; the wood became less dense, and fewer became the
obstacles to his onward progress. He stopped for a moment to
rest, and, raising hise yes, beheld, to his great joy, a faint gleam
of light in the distance, and apparently at a great height, and
at once resuming his journey, bent his steps in the direction of
the welcome beacon ; and soon, emerging from the wood, he
finds himself in a botharin* (bohereen) which appeared to lead
nearly in the direction of the light. However, he determined
to keep on the beaten track as long as possible, as the other
side of the botharin was also wooded. As he trudged along, no
longer feeling any anxiety about the night, he allowed his
thoughts to wander on divers subjects ; now thinking of his far-
off home, his journey, his present plight, and his future
prospects ; then his thoughts would take a devotional turn, and
the beacon-light in the distance would remind him of the star
that five hundred and thirty-eight years before had guided the
Eastern Magi to the crib of the long-promised Messiah ; again
he would be lost in speculation as to whence the light proceeded,
its immense height baffling every attempt at a solution of the
difficulty.

Thus did he while away the time as he shortened the distance
between him and the light, which every moment became larger
and brighter, until, emerging from the botharin into a hard,
well-kept bothar (road), he quickened his steps, as he perceived
that he was opposite to the orifice whence the light evidently
proceeded. This discovery awakened a suspicion as to its
nature, which had escaped his recollection. The road on which
he trod was now illumined by the rays, and as his upturned
gaze was riveted on the cheering beacon, he suddenly stopped,
as what he considered the most delicious music fell upon his
ears. He was both surprised and charmed, as he felt satisfied
that the music proceeded from the same direction as the light—
both descending together like twin spirits ; the one to cheer his
visual organs by her vivifying rays, the other to charm his
sense of hearing with her melody,—both increasing their

---

* (Bohereen), a little road, or country lane.

gratifying attentions as he neared their common shrine, until at length the musical sister ceased her chimes; but the regret which he experienced from this circumstance was of short duration; for as he was beginning to discern the outlines of a tower of gigantic proportions, as the residence of his charmers, there came, wafted towards him by the evening breeze, the deep, bass, mellow tones of thousands of human voices, mingled with the sweet strains of the harp and other instruments. As he turned towards the direction whence they proceeded, he stopped for a moment, when, recognising the solemn strains as of a sacred character, and concluding that it was the Irish chant* of which he had heard, he flung his arms into the air as he exclaimed :—

"Blessed be God! I have at length reached my destination! I am within the precincts of the termoin lands of the far-famed College of Cluain Irared! Yes, here about me in every direction are streets of cells! What a multitude of little houses! And here are some larger buildings! No doubt one of them is the church where the holy monks are singing the Divine Office. I must hasten thither to commence well my career of study by invoking the aid of the Holy Spirit of wisdom and understanding."

So saying, he redoubled his speed until he came to the bank of a river which reflected the light of the tower, and proceeding along the brink, he came to a ceasaigh-droichet (wicker bridge) which he crossed, and then found his way to the church without further difficulty; directed thither by the lights which proceeded from the windows, for the light of the tower had now disappeared, owing to his close proximity to it.

As he entered the church, his first prayer was an act of thanksgiving for his safe arrival. Then he joined his voice to those of the endless rows of monks and students who thronged the sacred building, headed as they were by the holy Finian himself, the bishop and abbot of Cluain Irared—the wax candles on the altar, and the immense twisted rushes which illumined the body of the church, throwing a fitful glare on the countenances of the congregation.

The office over, our traveller posted himself at the door beside the bullán, or holy water vessel, for the double purpose of witnessing the filing out of his future friends and of attracting the notice of the guest-master as he passed.

The students, who first came, eyed him with interest or curiosity; few of the monks saw him at all, but glided on with

* The ancient Irish chant in use before the introduction of the Gregorian chant.

eyes fixed on the ground, so strict were they in the observance
of their rules ; the guest-master, however, whose particular duty
it was to allow no stranger to escape his observation, bestowed
a look of keen scrutiny on the way-worn looking traveller as he
passed him, but could not stop the progress of the monks who
followed him, much less of the abbot himself, who closed the
procession, and whose bent head and absorbed manner extinguished the hopes of the stranger of catching even a
momentary glance from his future master. All had now passed
out, save a certain number of brothers who continued to chant
the psalms, for though the whole community only assembled at
the canonical hours, yet a choir of monks, skilled in psalmody,
continually, day and night, without intermission, chanted the
praises of their Creator in the church of the monastery. This
was easily accomplished without over-fatiguing any, for the
whole body of psalm-singers being divided into companies,
each relieving the preceding one in unceasing sucession, so
that one or other of these companies would be chanting their
psalms while the rest of their brethren were employed in their
respective duties.

No sooner had the venerable prelate passed, than the guest-
master was by the side of the stranger : " My son, thou hast
been travelling, and must need refreshment. Come with me to
the proinn-teach."*

" But, father, I have not yet told thee why I am here, or
whence I came."

" Thou canst do that whilst thou refreshest thyself; but I
think I can guess at thy nationality. Thine accent and appearance proclaim thee a native of the classic land of Greece.''

Here they entered the proinnteach, and the guest-master
ensconsed the stranger at an immense log fire, and placed
at his feet a tub of water, which had been brought in by an
attendant. While availing himself of their attentions, the
youth replied :

" Yes, father, I am indeed a Greek, and having heard of
the fame of your Irish Universities, and of your hospitality
to poor and friendless strangers, I resolved to leave my
native land, once the abode of the arts and sciences, for
this renowned Western Isle. Accordingly, I went on board a
merchant vessel which sailed from the Piræus† to the port
of Baiscui, where we disembarked to visit the Cathair-Conright‡

---

* Refectory.   † The Port of Athens.
‡ The fortress of Oonrigh Mac Daire, composed of huge stones of a
circular form, on top of the mountain between the Bays of Tralee and
Castlemaine, in county of Kerry.

and the Leim-Chuchullain.*   I was surprised to see the
extensive trade which was carried on at that port, and the cities
adjacent.   The splendid cuan (harbour) was filled with trading
vessels from every nation ; and when I had thought that we were
leaving them behind on entering the narrower part of the river
Sionnain (Shannon), I did not expect to find them as crowded
as ever at Luimneach-na-Long† (Limerick of the shipping).
Such, however being the case, we left the merchant vessel for
good, for the greater part of the passengers had arrived at their
destination.   Having spent a short time there, and being fully
refreshed, the remainder of the voyagers, including myself, got
into a smaller vessel, which was bound for Cruachan,‡ which, they
said, was the capital of the Kingdom of Connacht (Connaught).
Thus we sailed down the Sionnain, passing through Loch
Dearg, after which every place of interest was pointed out to me
until we entered Loch Ri,§ where, having been kindly instructed
concerning my route, I took leave of my companions ; and
while they sailed through the Lake of the King to his territory
on the western bank, I stepped on the eastern, when I found
myself on the Sligh-Asail.‖ I had not much trouble in making
myself understood, for, partly in Greece, and partly on my way
hither, I picked up much of your language, and moreover your
people appear used to foreigners, so I was enabled to prosecute
my journey without much difficulty.   Once finally landed on
thine hospitable shores the journey was easy.   Though having
no money, I have not known hunger or thirst, neither have I
been without a night's shelter.   I have been entertained
in all sorts of houses, great and small, as well as
in the biadteachs. ¶   Only a few hours ago I had a
bath and entertainment at the house of a ' brugh,' who pressed
me to stay all night as my road lay through a wood, and the
evening was setting in dark ; but so anxious was I to reach
this monastery, that I declined his kind invitation, and proceeded on my journey. Before long, however, I began to regret

---

* Cuchullan's Leap, from which place that famous hero sets out on his
expedition to attack Conrigh, whom he slew. It is situated on the opposite
shore from Cathair-Conrigh, and is the promontory on south-western point of
the present county Clare. It is incorrectly called Loop Head.
  † Query. When again shall it be called Limerick of the Ships ?
  ‡ Croghan, near Elphin, in the present county Roscommon.
  § The Lake of the King.
  ‖ The western road ; one of the five great roads of ancient Ireland.
  ¶ Biadteachs, houses of hospitality.

my obstinacy when the light from his house disappeared, and I
was left for a few moments in total darkness, until the light from
thine high tower appeared through the trees. Fortunate, indeed, I was in coming from the direction I did, which was
opposite the light, for had I come from any other point, I could
not have seen it, and I must inevitably have been lost in the
wood."

" Not so, my son; from whatever point of the compass thou
camest thou must have seen the light, for there are four orifices
in the top of the cloigteach* pointing to the four cardinal
points, so that the beacon lights which are placed there every
evening, and left lighting all through the night, are distinctly visible to all the country around, and, indeed, travellers
have been thus guided hither from every direction.'

"Well, I am more than ever surprised! That is a wonderful,
dear old tower; it has befriended me in more than one way to-
night, and I shall love it while I live. I must take a good look
at it on to-morrow. But I forgot to tell thee that my name is
Aristophanes, and, like my great namesake, I am a citizen of
Athens."

" Oh! I am not all this time without discovering that thou
speakest the purest Attic dialect of the Greek language ; and
besides, thou didst mention the Piræus as the port whence thou
didst embark for thy voyage hither."

This conversation and the good things which the monastery
provided were discussed at the same time ; the latter consisted
of a plentiful supper of beef, fish, vegetables, bread and cheese,
beer, and new milk.

The Greek, tired though he was, would have liked to ask all
about the music which had issued from the tower ; but as he had
now finished his supper, there was no excuse for detaining the
guest-master longer; so he merely expressed a wish to see the
four lights referred to, before being conducted to the temporary
sleeping-place assigned him in the nearest cell, to which, after
having satisfied his curiosity, the guest-master conducted him,
saying :

"I sent our good Mael to procure a sleeping-place for thee
with one of thine own countrymen, who are here in such
numbers ; but he tells me that they were all fast asleep, and that
he did not like to disturb them if it could be avoided, especially
as one of our native pupils followed him and offered a share of

* Bell-house.

his cell.   However, thou must not let him keep thee awake by asking thee too many questions : there will be time enough for that, and thou needest rest."

Here they entered the cell, and were greeted by the young Ruadhan.   The guest-master having introduced them, and expressed a hope that they would continue good friends, left them for the night.

Notwithstanding this warning, however, the two did talk, until sleep at length overpowered the traveller, and soon, in common with every living thing about the monastery, he was sunk in profound repose.

An ᴅᴀʀᴀ Ċᴀɪbɪᴅɪʟ.

CHAPTER II.

Coɪȝcᴘíoc ᴀȝuᴘ ᴀn ᴄ-Ab.

THE STRANGER AND THE ABBOT.

THE next morning, as Ruadhan was in the act of rising, he was startled by his companion suddenly springing up in bed exclaiming :

"There it is again !   How delightful !"

"What !   What is delightful ?"

"Why, the music that so charmed my ears as I journeyed hither last night, and that seemed to issue from the illuminated tower.   Is that so ?"

"Yes; but they are only five small bells, tuned to the five notes which compose our Irish quinquegrade gapped scale ; they are played with a metal hammer, and are just now calling us to Mass.   Art thou ready ?"

"Yes.   I suppose we must observe silence now till it is over ?"

The church which they entered was built entirely of oak ; was of graceful construction, and highly ornamented.   In a word, the best efforts of the builder, the carpenter, and the goldsmith were lavished upon it.   Although everything in personal use by the monks was of the simplest material possible, yet they spared neither care nor expense in the adornment of the Temple of God. The altar, which was of carved yew, especially was decorated by the hands of the monks. A profusion of beautiful flowers from the garrdha (garden) of the monastery were artistically arranged in vases of gold and silver. Wax candles were set in candlesticks of solid gold, the crucifix and altar plate being of the same precious metal, dug from the mines of Cruachan-Cinnseallagh,* and wrought by the hands of some of the monks skilled in the goldsmith's art. The magnificent illuminated missal was the work of other members of the community who excelled in and taught that particular branch of education. Its cover was of pure gold, sumptuously ornamented with jewels.

The panelling on either side down the whole length of the church was decorated with quaint but beautifully-coloured drawings representing our Lord, the Holy Virgin, the Apostles, the national patron saint, or some scene from either the Old or New Testament. A white linen veil screened off the "iardom" or sacristy, which adjoined the church, and opened also externally.

When the community, the students, as well as the people from the surrounding country who answered, as was their wont, the musical summons from the tower bells, had taken their places, the holy bishop, closing the long procession of monks, ascended the altar-steps, and having been vested in the rich episcopal robes which had been embroidered by the nuns and pupils of Cill-Daire (Kildare), commenced the celebration of the Divine Mysteries, then, with mitre on head, and holding in hand his episcopal staff, he turned to the congregation, delivered a short address, and finished by imparting his benediction. Then all formed again into procession, and returned— the people to their various homes, the monks to their several occupations, and the students to the proinnteach, to partake of the morning meal before commencing their studies. This building, which the stranger had now a better opportunity of observing than on the previous evening, was also composed of wood; it was of quadrangular form, and 30 feet in extent. The pine table extended the whole length of the room, and forms of the same wood were ranged on either side; the walls of panelled oak, having in the centre of each compartment a quaint drawing or painting of some saint, or a representation of some scene from the Holy Bible, executed by the monks or scholars.

---

* Ancient gold mines in the present county Wicklow.

The floor was composed of limestone from Oirghiall,* covered with matting in the centre. In the mensa of the proinnteach were kept the collus, haritorium, biberee, and such ferramenta as pagiones and cultillia.†

When the Greek entered between the guest-master and Ruadhan, and was introduced to his new companions, the latter set up a ringing cheer, and welcomed him with a "ceud mîlé failte," his own countrymen, of whom there were a goodly number, overpowered him with questions concerning their native land, desiring news of all that had happened there since they had left it.

Soon, however, the conversation became more general, and Aristophanes expressed surprise to find that the number of students at Cluain-Irared numbered altogether about three thousand, and amazed at the various nationalities represented ; for, besides the Greeks and the native Irish, there were also students from Britain, Albion,‡ Gaul, Iberia,§ Italy, Germany, and Egypt.

Breakfast over, Ruadhan intimated to Aristophanes that he would escort him over the monastery and its belongings, that he had obtained leave to do so, as it was usual on a new arrival.

The Greek arose to accompany him as the other students filed out to the school, but as the two friends were just outside, the guest-master came up, and desired Aristophanes to follow him to the abbot's house whom he had only that moment found an opportunity of apprising of the stranger's arrival. The Greek accompanied the guest-master to the presence of his holy master.

The abbot's house was at some distance from the others, and situated on a slight eminence ; it was of quadrangular form, and superior in size to all the rest. It was constructed of beams and planks, in form resembling the Swiss Chalet ; it was twelve feet in width, and nine feet in height, formed of rough blocks and planks of oak timber split with wedges. The framework of upright posts and horizontal sleepers, mortised at the angles, the end of each upright post being inserted into the lower sleeper of the frame, and fastened by a large block of wood, or forelock ; the door was provided with a glas (lock) and eochair (key). The roof was flat, and the house of two compartments, one over the other.

The guest-master and the new pupil, entering, passed the two attendants, who were always stationed at the door, awaiting the orders of the abbot ; a third attendant was in the act of

---

* Louth.   † Lanigan's "Ecclesiastical History."
‡ Scotland.   § Spain.

reading to him ; both were seated on wooden benches at a small wooden table, on which were arranged writing materials. Suspended from a hook in one of the joints was a polaire, or leathern satchel, for holding and carrying books.   Two or three pictures, representing sacred subjects, which hung on the whitewashed walls, completed the furniture of this truly monastic apartment; the upper room was fitted out as a bedroom ; but though it contained an humble bed, it was never used, for the holy Finian slept on the bare floor, with a stone for his pillow. He was scarcely past the middle age ; of kindly but firm aspect, and as he was not then engaged in any episcopal function, wore the usual monastic habit, common to all his brethern. Besides the tonsure, he wore a long tunic made of wool, over which was the cuculla or mantle, with its hood, of the same material, the wool being of the natural colour it received from the sheep.   The abbot Finian was deeply absorbed in the manuscript which his attendant was reading to him ; it was a sublime composition by one of his pupils named Ciaran (Kiaran), the son of an artificer.   As he listened, the holy man became overpowered by his feelings ; tears of joy streamed down his cheeks ; he bent eagerly forward, fearful lest he should lose a single word that fell from the lips of the reader.   The latter raised his eyes and suddenly stopped, as he beheld the guest-master and the stranger before him.

Finian, surprised, raised his eyes also, as the guest-master, overcome by what he had seen and heard, fell at his feet, and his example was silently followed by the Greek.   Finian blessed both, and then said: "Is this the young stranger of whom thou hast been telling me ?"

"Yes, venerable abbot; he has travelled all the way from Greece, as so many of his countrymen are doing, to put himself under thy guidance and instruction."

"Come hither, my son ; come to the arms of thy father and thy friend ; thou art no longer a stranger, but a child of my soul and of my heart."

As Finian uttered these words he opened his arms, and the Greek, overpowered by such an unexpected reception, flung himself into them, and leaning his head on the abbot's shoulder, relieved his feelings by a copious flood of tears.   When these had subsided, he related his story, and Finian, stroking him gently, exclaimed: "Now, my child, I hope thou wilt make thyself at home, and if there is any request thou wishest to make, I shall be only too happy to grant it, as far as the rules will permit.   I have a special regard for thy country, once so like our own."

"Nay, father; I came here penniless, attracted by the fame of thy seminary and the generous hospitality which extends so many blessings to less favoured nations; that is more than I could desire. Thy reception of me is in itself sufficient to repay me for all I have gone through during my journey."

"Well, my son, thou shalt have able teachers in every branch of study—sacred and profane—and I am confident thou wilt, by application and perseverance, second their efforts. Thy fellow-students, too, among whom are many of thine own countrymen, thou wilt find friendly and desirous to assist thee. For the first couple of days thou will have enough to do to explore the monastery and its belongings. Ruadhan, who is to accompany thee, will explain everything."

Then turning to the guest-master: "Is he at hand?"

"Yes, my father, I see him yonder; he is studying while he is waiting."

"Well, now, thou hadst better let them commence their rambles: "Beannacht leat mo mhic!" (A blessing with thee, my son!)

The reading was resumed as the two left the abbot's house, and were joined by Ruadhan as soon as he perceived them. The guest-master then left them to attend to his duties, for, his services to Aristophanes were at an end, as the latter was now a recognised *alumnus* of the college.

ᚐᚅ ᚈᚱᚓᚐᚄ ᚉᚐᚔᚁᚱᚑᚔᚂ.

CHAPTER III.

Cloigceach Cluain-Iraireo.

THE BELL-HOUSE, OR ROUND TOWER OF CLONARD.

THE two youths being then left to themselves, Ruadhan asked his companion whether he would like to examine the interior of the monastic buildings first, or to explore the grounds and termoin lands. Then suddenly remembering, added: "Or, perhaps, thou wouldst prefer to examine the Cloigteach first of all?"

"The Cloigteach! Is that what thou callest the round tower with the light and the music?"

"Exactly so."

"Oh, then, the Cloigteach, the Cloigteach, by all means, the first!"

Then looking towards it: "What a majestic structure! How gracefully it tapers towards the summit! How many feet, O Ruadhan, measureth it from the ground to the top of the cross on the conical roof."

"The height, O Aristophanes, is about one hundred and thirty feet, and the external circumference at the base, sixty feet, exclusive of the projecting steps. And before we approach too near, please observe the size of the lower stones, some of which are nine feet long by three feet deep, and they gradually diminish in size until they reach the top. The masonry is Cyclopean, and, rough as it appears when viewed from a distance; yet if thou standst immediately under thou wilt see that it is perfectly smooth and level. Let us mount the steps."

When they took their stand upon the upper platform, they stood close to the Cloigteach, and looked up the side towards the top, Aristophanes exclaiming: "Truly, the architecture is wonderful! Here are a great number of stones, some of them immense blocks, which at a little distance appear as if roughly laid together; and, behold, as I run my eye closely along the surface, the whole length of one hundred and thirty feet is so smooth and even, and so perfectly are all their joints fitted, as to resemble one huge sheet of glass."

"Let us walk around, Aristophanes, until we come to this spot again, and thou wilt see that it maintains the same character throughout."

They proceeded to walk around on the platform at the base of the tower, the Greek running his eye along the surface to the top at every inch until they had completed the circuit, when he again gave expression to his admiration. Then casting his eyes beneath him, he turned to his companion, and said: "By the way, Ruadhan, I presume that this circular projecting base is usual with towers of such great height."

"It is usual, but there are exceptions; this, as thou perceivest, hast three steps or plinths; others of lesser height have only two, or sometimes one; then in some localities they are surrounded by an earthen mound."

"There appears to be seven or eight windows in this tower. Is that the general number in others?"

"Oh, no; they differ in that respect, too, and in many others; there are seven here. Some have more and some less. Let us enter."

A few steps brought them under the doorway, which was

twenty feet above where they stood. A huge strong ladder, firmly secured, reached to it. Ruadhan, assuring his companion that it was perfectly safe and steady, invited him to mount. When they had reached the top, they entered the doorway, which stood open, and only admitted one at a time. When they stood within, Ruadhan called the attention of his companion to the fact that the entrance stood directly opposite to the door of the church. Aristophanes looked, remarking that he had not observed it before, and then stood to admire the fine view which presented itself; but his companion, assuring him that the view would be much finer when seen from the top, invited him to descend the stone steps which led to the bottom or first storey. The floor was of solid masonry. It was lighted by a single aperture; and here Ruadhan pointed out the thickness of the walls at the base, which was five feet, and remarked that it was little less at the door above. Flights of steps lined the walls round about, so that the friends ascended by a different way from that which they took in descending. They find themselves again on the second storey, or that by which they entered, and this floor was composed of wood, resting on joists, which were set in holes in the walls all round.

Ascending then, the flights of stone steps round the interior of the walls, they came to the third storey, which was exactly like that below it, the aperture being nearly as large as the door below. The fourth, fifth, and sixth stories were somewhat similar, save that they became smaller as they ascended, the aperture also diminishing in size. When they reached the seventh storey, Aristophanes remarked that stone hooks projected from the wall, on which hung polaries or book satchels.

"For what purpose, O Ruadhan, are those polaries here, so high up in the Cloigteach?"

"It is in these that the Aistire (artist) keeps his music tablets."

"Oh! is he here now?"

"I do not think he is, but if thou desirest it, he will take the greatest pleasure at any time in giving thee every information. Of course, this is all sacred music—one or other of which he plays on the monastery bells when calling the community, scholars, and people to Mass, or to any of the Divine Offices of the Church."

"Oh, I shall never forget the first time I heard them. Is it taught in the college? I should, above all things, desire to learn it."

"All known kinds of music is taught. Thou hast not yet seen the music-room."

"And are all as proficient as thine Aistire ?"

" By no means. Some are more proficient on the harp,
others on the violin, and so on; but as in all things else,
practice makes perfect. And so our Aistire is the best bell-
ringer in the monastery: in fact it is his special duty."

They had now ascended to the top of the last flight and
entered the Cloigteach (bell-house) proper, and Ruadhan proceeded to explain, as well as he could, the peculiarities of
Irish music, regretting his own superficial knowledge of bell-
ringing and the absence of the Aistire. However, he commenced to play, and Aristophanes protested that he enjoyed it
as much as he did that of the Aistire. When he had finished,
the Greek examined the five bells, sounded each of them separately with the metal hammer; examined the manner in which
they were suspended from the iron bar; and having satisfied
himself, at length turned to look about the apartment. It was
smaller than any of those below it; the height of the walls were
thirteen feet, and from the top of the wall all around rose the
conical roof to a height of seventeen feet, terminating in a point
in the centre above—the total height from the floor being thirty
feet. From an iron hook, fastened in the cone, was suspended
a chain, to which was fastened, just above their heads, the now
extinguished lamp, which the night before had guided the Greek
to the monastery. He now noticed its position exactly in the
centre of the apartment, directly opposite the four windows
which faced the four cardinal points. Then approaching the
southern window, he gazed for some moments at the view
presented, expressing to Ruadhan his admiration, and asking
information about the far-off objects revealed by the morning
sun. Ruadhan pointed out and explained, in turn, the great
monastery founded by St. Brigid, at Cill-Daire, other monasteries and churches, Cloigteachs, resembling the one in which
they stood, palaces, forts, duns, biadtachs, cities. Then at the
western—the most remarkable object among the others was the
palaces, churches, schools, and towers of Cruachan, the seat of
the kings of Olnamact or Connacht.

After admiring the objects of interest and the beauties of the
extensive scenery, they proceeded to the northern window,
where they stopped a considerable time, the Greek admiring all
he saw, and listening intently to the account his companion gave
him concerning all the remarkable places and buildings within
their range of vision and beyond it, dwelling longest on the
history, fame, and glory of the great palace of Emania, the
gorgeousness of its appointments and surroundings, the fame

and exploits of its heroes and heroines, the learning and wisdom of its ollamhs * and filés,† becoming so enthusiastic as to forget everything save the theme of his praise, when Aristophanes, leaning out and looking towards his right, exclaimed:

"Behold, O Ruadhan! yonder to the north-east. What city is that, and what masses of building are those?"

"Oh, that is the Cathair Teamhrach (the city of Tara), the seat of the Ardrigh ‡ of Eire,§ surpassing in power, glory, and letters even Emania itself. Come to the eastern window, and we shall have a better view."

From the eastern window Ruadhan pointed out and explained to the Athenian in as few words as possible the origin, description, and use of the various palaces, duns, forts, schools, churches, and houses of various classes which constituted the royal city. Thence the eyes of the stranger wandered over Magh-Breagh, the "Magnificent Plain," thence to the surrounding country to the kingdom of Laghean or Leinster, in the distance, even to the sea shore, the numerous merchant vessels which crowded its ports appearing like so many specks on its waters, when, his thoughts suddenly reverting to Tara, he said:

"Shall I soon have an opportunity of visiting the chief royal city of Eire?"

"Thou canst visit it at any time, O Aristophanes, by obtaining leave from our holy master; but the triennial feis‖ will soon be held by the monarch Tuathal Maelgarbh.¶ At such times, when all the States of Eire are assembled at Teamhair,** all the colleges and schools break up for the occasion; we are no exception to that rule. Bishop Finian holds a seat in the assembly of the nation, and his pupils know how to enjoy the games and general sports which always accompany it. But the sun is high in the heavens and thou hast seen little yet. Let us go."

"But tell me first, O Ruadhan, are these Cloigteachs used for any other purposes besides calling to prayer and serving as beacon-towers to travellers and pilgrims?"

"Oh, there are several other purposes for which they are used. On clear, starry nights some of our professors come up here to make astronomical observations. Then they are used as ecclesiastical keeps. In some districts where the churches and monasteries have been ravaged, the altar-plate and other valuables were safely deposited in the chambers of the Cloigteach.

---

* Learned men. † Poets. ‡ High King. § Ireland.
‖ Parliament, or Convention. ¶ Thooal Malegarve. ** Tara.

In those cases they are watch-towers, and places of safety, and defence: the doors double, and fastened with locks, bolts and bars, the walls are five feet at base; they are impregnable and proof against fire; they can never be taken by assault; but by their position they command a view of the church-entrance, from which they are distant about twenty feet to the N.W., as thou seest; and missiles can be let fall on the heads of any parties attacking the church. However, nothing of the kind has ever yet occurred in Cluain Irared, and I hope never shall. Still, it is best to be prepared, and in the meantime they are indispensable as bell-houses, and beacon-towers."

"They are most interesting buildings, and in every respect worthy of admiration. I am ready to accompany thee now. Shall we descend by the same way by which we ascended?"

"No; we can descend by the opposite side."

They commenced the descent of the stone steps to the several storeys beneath, until they arrived at the second or lowest storey save one. It will be remembered that it is in this that the entrance is situated. Arrived at the door, they next commenced to descend the ladder by which they had mounted to the Cloigteach: they soon found themselves again on the projecting platform which surrounded the base of the tower; and a moment more and they had cleared the three steps which ran all round the base. The Greek, running a little distance, looked again towards the summit, and coming back, said to his friend:

"Small wonder, indeed, O Ruadhan, that we could see almost the whole country from such a height. The scenery on all sides was truly magnificent."*

---

* Considerable difference of opinion exists as to the origin of the Round Towers. Dr. Petrie, and also Rev. Dr. Kelly of Maynooth, say that they were of Christian origin; while Vallencey, Mr. Beauford, Dr. O'Connor, Miss Beaufort, Moore, D'Alton, Windele, O'Brien, Keane, Giraldus, and others maintain that they were of Pagan origin. The opinions of these various writers are closely examined, and the Pagan theory proved and upheld, with great learning and acumen by the Very Rev. Canon U. Bourke.

αn ceαċαRṁαᵭ ċαɪbɪᴏɪl.

CHAPTER IV.

ꝼoɪꞃᵹneαṁα nα Ṁαɪnɪꞃcɪꝑe.

THE MONASTIC BUILDINGS.

THEY now proceeded to visit the other monastic buildings, and first to the coisteannach, or coitchean (kitchen). This building joined the proinnteach, and was seventeen feet in extent. Many were the utensils for cooking, as the gridiron (craticula), frying-pans (sartago), kettles, pots, (cacabus), the dabhach or hydra (water-pot), lorgna, or skewers, iubhiar (spit), coire, or cauldrons, griddles (gridil), &c. The plata (plates), dabhacha, or tubs, and miasa (dishes), ladara, or ladles were of the simplest material, as wood, or polished stone. The monks, whose duty it was to attend to the creature comforts of the college, were busily engaged just as the two friends entered.

The cóca (cook) was minding an immense coire (cauldron), and his assistants were busy attending to his directions. Then there were the buinnire, or foot messengers. The fuineadoir, pistor or baker, was occupied in making bairgins, or cakes, at a sycamore losaid, or kneading-trough.

Aristophanes and Ruadhan entered into conversation with those functionaries, who began to lead them into all the mysteries of the coitchean, when the rannaire, pincerna, or butler entered from the proinnteach to give directions, and he also assisted in giving every information to the stranger. The latter, being now satisfied, prepared to follow his companion, and as both turned to depart, they were met at the entrance by some of the brethren, laden with large pails of milk, which they had just taken from the cows in the fields of the monastery. They inspected the aith (kiln), which was employed for the twofold object of thrashing (trituratio frugum), and drying ears of corn (ad spicas siccandas). The latter process was conducted by means of a large sieve. Their attention was next attracted by the noise of the brō, or quern, and, as they approached, they perceived, coming from an opposite quarter, some monks, carrying on their backs sacks of corn, which they directly deposited beside the lamhbro (hand-quern). This primitive prototype of the muilinn, or mill, consisted of two flat stones, circular discs, about eighteen inches across, the upper being made to rotate on the lower by means of wooden handles; moreover, the upper was concave, and the lower stone of the quern convex, having a lip or margin called on that account by the significant name potquern. This lip encircles or overlaps the upper stone, while the meal is forced to pass through a hole in the side of the lower. The top millstone was decorated with an ancient Irish cross, carved in relief, the arms of which were enclosed within a circle. This ornament distinguished church querns from those employed for private or public use. The handle holes were placed in the arms of the cross. The whole quern was made of sandstone from Oirghialla, and wrought by the hands of a monk, the son of a quern-maker. All this was explained to the Greek by the brother, who the whole time was occupied in turning the handles, so that he lost not a moment in grinding the meal. This infraction of the law of silence was allowed on useful or necessary occasions like the present. At all other times, and on ordinary occasions, silence was strictly enjoined, in order that, as the brethren worked with their hands, their minds might be fixed on heavenly things.

Ruadhan next led his friend to the sciobōl (barn) close by, an out-office of considerable importance, where the grain when winnowed was stored in heaps until required. Thence they proceeded to the cearda (workshops) of the ceardaidh, or artificers, taking first that of the saor (carpenter). Here they stopped for a while examining the various articles fashioned from the different kinds of wood, as daire (oak), eo (yew), beith (birch), sail (willow), ailm (fir), &c. The articles were many and various, as cups, plates, dishes, goblets, methers, kneading-troughs, bowls, and candlesticks. They were of all shapes and sizes, round, oval, square, formed chiefly of a single piece of wood turned with a lathe. Dishes 20 in. long by 11 broad, and 3 deep, with projecting handles, supported by a reel-shaped piece beneath, extending across each extremity; others 3 ft. long by 21 in. broad and 3 deep. Milk coolers, oval and circular, of a single piece, with perforated handles; tumbler-shaped vessels, methers, or mead-drinking vessels of different kinds, some with one handle, some with two, others again with four handles, prolonged into feet, and decorated with lines and circles, triangular and chequered patterns; tubs and barrels made with staves. All those various utensils, as property special to a monastery, were also ornamented with crosses or other sacred emblems. While some of the monks were engaged in making vessels of this class,

others were engaged in carving or moulding yew or other suitable wood for the decoration of the church. Some cut and
prepared tablets of beith, or birch, for writing purposes, also for
wooden rulers. Others, again, were forming planks and boards
into tables, forms, shelves, and the like, or else preparing posts,
boards, and doors for building purposes. To these latter
Ruadhan observed that they should be ready to erect the cell
for the new comer on the following morning. They next visited
the gobha, or smith, and the ceard umha, or brazier. Some were
shoeing the plough horses, which cocked their ears at the ringing sound of the anvil, and erected their manes as they glared
at the innumerable sparks that shot in every direction ; others
were fusing iron through the ferrementa ; some were fashioning
plates, hooks, and nails of iron ; some were making ploughs
and carts, hatchets, spades, locks, keys, and other articles. The
brazier hammered and worked at various objects, useful and
ornamental. Further on the cearda óir agus cearda airgid,
(gold and silversmiths), worked away at discs, crosses, chalices,
shrines, candlesticks, lamps, book-covers, and other sacred objects. Aristophanes examined carefully these beautiful articles,
as well as the gold and silver ore, and watched with interest the
process of refining, entering into conversation with the monks
to whom that particular branch was committed. He next admired the precious stones, as onyx, amethyst, sapphire, emerald,
carbuncle, cruan, garnet, &c., which were used in ornamenting
the above-named church. Leaving this portion of the building,
their next visit was to the charcoal burner, who in his turn was
continually turning out guail, or charcoal, for the use of those
who as constantly needed it to carry on their operations. At
this moment the tower bells commenced to ring, and the two
friends turned their steps in towards the church, which was soon
filled by the whole community and school, all having left their
occupations for that purpose. Text over, the community went to
their cells, as was their wont, to spend some time in private prayer,
and the students filed into the proinnteach to partake of the good
things which were set before them, being waited on by the
butler and his assistants. After dinner all the scholars returned
to the school-rooms, save Ruadhan and the new comer, who
departed to finish their explorations. This done, the monks
had returned to their occupations. Ruadhan and friend now
turned into the workers in stone, and examined all the objects
made of that useful substance, meeting face to face the fashioner
of the quern, who now exhibited to the Athenian the method of
forming and the manner of polishing the various stone articles,

such as drinking-cups of potstone about four three-eighth inches across the bowl, and five and a quarter over side, which included the handle, and one and a quarter in depth.   They were specially made for placing at roadside wells, to refresh the weary traveller as he passed on his way.   The good brother here informed Aristophanes that so great was the wealth of Eire from A. D. 123 to A. D. 226, during the reigns of Conn of the hundred battles, and his grandson, Cormac Mac Art, that silver cups were placed at roadside wells.   Aristophanes, surprised at this intelligence, declared that he would carefully study the history of Eire from the earliest times.

Other objects formed of stone were next examined; they were cups, bowls, dishes, inkstands, and other articles in use in the monastery.   He specially admired some small limestone salt-cellars.   After this his attention was directed to objects all quite different in kind, as stone coffins, gravestones with sculptured crosses, and inscriptions in Latin and Irish.   Some stones and monoliths inscribed with ogham characters, the meaning of which were duly explained; other tombstones had a cross within a circle, and inscribed in ogham also.   All these were intended to be placed over recently-made graves in the cemetery in the monastery to which the two friends, after watching for a short time the process of stone-cutting and inscribing, had now gained access through a door opposite to that by which they had entered the stone workshop, between which and the church the cemetery lay.   This they now traversed, examining the inscriptions on the tombstones similar to those they had just seen. As many of those interred had been known to Ruadhan, he gave his friend an account of their lives and actions; nor did they leave without offering a prayer to the Great White Throne for those who had preceded them on their voyage to eternity.

Full of those solemn and yet consoling thoughts which a visit to the city of the dead is ever sure to inspire, the two companions left the sacred place by another gate, Ruadhan leading the way to the bronteach (hospital), where the patients, whether monks or students, were tended with constant and unremitting care by the numerous monks, whose particular duty it was, and many of whom were skilled physicians, having made that noble science their principal study, while others of the brethren acted as nurses and attendants.   Here Ruadhan, introducing his new friend to the physicians, nurses, and patients alike, they spent some time in conversing, going from sick-bed to sick-bed sympathising with each sufferer, and warmly praising the care and skill displayed in behalf of the sick : cleanliness being the first and most important thing attended to and enforced, and noting with especial satisfaction the plentiful supply of running water, fed by the river Boinn (Boyne), and so constructed by one of the brethren skilled in such matters as to fill with a continuous flow on one side as fast as it emptied itself on the other. Another remarkable feature in the hospital was the hot-air bath, which was used as a cure for rheumatism, which was very common. Before leaving they witnessed a successful surgical operation, which served to convince the foreigner more than ever that the accounts of Irish scientific skill which had reached his native land had not been exaggerated. On leaving the hospital they directed their steps to the criolaire, or leather-satchel maker. Here they witnessed the various stages of the manufacture of these satchels, of which there were two kinds, the polaire and the tiaga. The former, which were the most elegant, were those in general use by the professors and students for carrying their books from their cells to the school-rooms. Aristophanes, deeply interested, watched the process of satchel-making, first examined the blocks on which they were shaped, and on which were depressed patterns on the sides and top. While he looked the brathair (brother) placed a piece of leather, which he had previously damped and cut to shape, on the block, and pressed it closely into every curve and line of the pattern; He then left it until it dried, and the pattern on the block became indelibly impressed on the leather. When the Greek had sufficiently observed the nicety with which the damp leather was folded on the block, his attention was directed to the next process, and for this purpose he turned to another block on which the leather had dried. This piece of strong leather was 36 inches long and 12 inches broad, and when taken off and folded became transformed into a six-sided case 12 inches long, $12\frac{1}{2}$ broad, and $2\frac{1}{2}$ thick, having a flap which doubled over in front. The brother now went to a table on which were a lot of leather straps, which had been carefully cut, and selecting two of them, commenced to stitch them on the upper corners of the sides with a leathern thong. These were for the purpose of slinging the case from the shoulder. The next thing was to fasten on a lock which had been brought from the smithy, which the Greek had already visited; then eight staples were admitted through perforations in the flap for short iron rods to enter and which met at the lock. When the whole was completed, Aristophanes took the polaire into his hands to examine the embossed work more minutely. The ornaments consisted of trigretra, interlaced cross of two ovals; the cross formed between

four segments of circles within a circle, as well as several
varieties of the interlaced tracery forming crosses. He next
examined other cases which had been formed on other blocks,
and, with the help of the brother and Ruadhan, examined the
basso relievo, which differed from the other, this one consisting
of circles, having within them three animals interlaced in different forms in each, curious animals, having their tails interlaced
with diamonds, knots, and crosses.   The bottom of this case is
ornamented with triplicate, pear-shaped ornaments.   Having
examined several other polairidh formed after the same manner,
but differing as to ornamentation, the Athenian now turned his
attention to a monk who was making satchels after a very
different manner, having before him a great number of flat bands,
which he interlaced until they formed a polaire, and then
finished.   Aristophanes, on examining it, perceived that a line
ran down the centre, and that there were five small circles, which
the brother proceeded to ornament with the bead.   The straps,
staples, iron rods, lock and key, having been all fastened on,
this kind of satchel presented a very pretty appearance.

A third method of making polairidh was now shown to the
Greek, who found himself beside a monk who had spread out
before him a skin which he had just cut out to the proper shape,
and had commenced to carve in very low relief or "grave en
creux."   Having attentively looked on for some time and admired the perfection of the workmanship and the facility with
which the monk fashioned such endless varieties of fanciful
designs, his companion called his attention to another of the
brethren who was engaged in making the tiaga.   These leathern
receptacles were somewhat similar to the polairidh, but of a
larger and rougher construction.   They were also used for the
carriage of books and other articles as well.

As they were leaving, they were recalled by the monk to
whom they had first spoken on entering, and Aristophanes was
informed by him that he was entitled to a polaire, and that he
might take his choice.   Aristophanes thereupon chose one of
those ornamented with the curious animals, and then left it to
the care of the brother until his cell should be erected.   They
now turned into the greusaidh, or shoemaker, and the harness-
maker, who were busy plying at their trades.   Next they visited
the monk whose special occupation it was to prepare parchments
for writing.   From this they proceeded to the halla ceachd
(lecture halls), in one of which a fear-leighin (professor) was
delivering a lecture on metaphysics to his pupils; thence to the
music room, where instruction was being given in singing and

in playing on the different kinds of musical instruments, as the
cruit (harp), ceis (small harp, lit charmer), the tiompan (another
kind of harp), cloga (bells), córn (horn), clairseach (another
kind of harp), cinnárd cruit (the high-headed harp), crom cruit
(the down-bending harp), the ceiruin (a portable harp used for
religious purposes), the fidiol (violin), stoc (a horn), cuisle ciuil
(the musical pipe), and adharca ciuil (musical horns). They
traversed the airdal (room), looking at these various instruments,
looking attentively at the performers, and examining the piles
of music tablets suited to the different instruments. Leaving
this department, they entered another building called the teach
scriopta, or house of writing and drawing, where numbers of
monks were engaged in transcribing and illuminating manuscripts. They were called scriobaidh (scribes), and scribneoiridh
togaidhe (choice scribes); while some were multiplying such
works as the Holy Bible, the Four Gospels, the writings of the
Fathers and Doctors of the Church, the compositions of native
and foreign authors, in the most finished caligraphy; others,
with exquisite skill, traced fanciful and curious designs of endless variety, and filled them with the most chaste and gorgeous
colouring, sometimes brightening the effect by the application
of gold and silver. The chimes now pealed for None; they
entered the eglais (church), and on coming out when the Divine
Office was over, Ruadhan informed Aristophanes that the monks
were about to break their fast for the first time that day, it being
Diaceadaoine (Wednesday), which, as well as Dia-h-Aoine
(Friday), was always strictly observed. Before partaking of
their frugal meal, they chaunted the long 118th Psalm and the
"Magnificat" standing.

---

an ċuigṁaḋ. ċaibroil.

CHAPTER V.

Ταlτa an Ċoláiroc.

THE COLLEGE GROUNDS.

CROSSING a faitche (a green or court), they bent their steps
towards the pasture and tillage lands; passing along through
various sraida, or streets of botha (small houses or cells) of the
brethren or students.

These were of wickerwork, round, with a cup roof, and
simply furnished. They looked at several; they were the same
as that inhabited by Ruadhan, and occupied temporarily by

Aristophanes, to whom his companion explained that he should the following morning see for himself the way in which they were built at the erection of his own cell.

These cells formed streets on every side round the monastic buildings, all diverging from the sráid-mhōr, or great street, which was lined by the larger buildings, already described, the whole combined to form a city in itself.

After traversing several of these streets, they found themselves in the agricultural part of the monastery; looking in at the seasmhach (stables) for the horses and carts, and at the buailidh (booleys) for the ba (cows), caoire (sheep), and muca (pigs), which, however, were not at the time in their sheds or quarters: the two former grazing in the fields, and the latter grunting in a muclach, an enclosed place hard by. And now, as they turned their backs upon these ungainly though useful creatures, and gazed before them, another hive of industry presents itself to view. Hundreds of monks are engaged in various agricultural avocations, and the high state of cultivation of this immense tract of land bears ample testimony to their unremitting toil.

As the two friends walked through the ceapach (tillage lands), watching the labourers at their work, Aristophanes asked many questions of his companion, and sometimes of the brethren. He was thus made acquainted with the names of all the various vegetables then known. The lus lubhgort, or garden vegetables, were meacons, or parsnips; cabaiste, or cabbage; uiniuin, or onions; lus-na-bhfrancach, or tansy, &c. Immense fields of tiuriund or crainneacht (wheat), seagal (rye), eorna (barley), coirce (oats), &c., spread before him. They were separated by thick, well-trimmed, quick-set hedges of truim, or elder; sceach, or hawthorn; ubhall-fiadhain, or crab-apple.

The monks who acted as labourers in the various branches of agriculture were evidently scrupulously exact in bringing everything of which they had charge to the greatest possible perfection. The capala (horses) belonging to the farm were all in the best condition. The carts to which they were yoked were a kind of sleigh, without wheels, and were called carra.

Before proceeding any further, they turned to the right, and entered the abhal-ghort, or orchard, which abounded in all the native fruit, including the vine, which was at that time cultivated in Eire. Having eaten some abhala, or apples, and other fruit then in season, and having conversed with the monks, to whose care the abhalghort (orchard) was committed, they left it, and immediately came to the corcōga, or beehives, with their swarms of beacha (bees). They were carefully tended, their honey

being used in the proinnteach as an article of food, and in the
oron-teach (hospital) as a medicine, and their wax for many
purposes, as making wax candles for the altar, waxing tablets,
polishing wood, &c. Passing this, they entered the garrdha
(flower garden), which was beautifully laid out in beds and walks by
the religious labourers, and in which were groves of trees, hedges
of àirne (sloe), sceach (whitethorn), or droighean (blackthorn).

Special attention was paid to the horticultural department,
great taste and skill being expended on the rearing of all known
kinds of flowers, these beautiful natural objects being constantly
required for the floral decoration of the altar—the monks ever
bearing in mind the words of the Psalmist, "Lord, I have loved
the beauty of thy house, and the place where thy glory dwelleth."
It was besides useful for instructing the scholars in the science
of botany, as then known. A number of students were assembled
for that purpose as the two friends entered.

Leaving this, they traversed a muine (a brake or shrubbery),
which led them past cruacha, or stacks, or ricks, to a tamhnach
(tawnagh) a green field, where the cattle rest, when next they
found themselves at the ingheilt, or pasture lands, where
thousands of damha (oxen), ba (cows), and caoire (sheep), all in
admirable condition, grazed or ruminated in every direction.
The cattle were tended by the buachailla or cow-minders, the
sheep by the aodhairidh, or shepherds.

The two friends walked over a considerable part of the pas-
turage, until they came to the termoinn or boundary, when they
wheeled round to the right, and came on a soft meadow land,
where Ruadhan showed his companion another kind of cart called
the carr-sleamhnain, or sliding car. It consisted of low narrow
framework, with two low wooden tympana, or solid wheels. It
was more suitable for meadow lands than the car above named.
Continuing their course they soon came to a geartha (gairha) or
woodland overgrown with underwood, and emerging from this
they found themselves on the banks of the amhain (river) Boinn,
or Boyne. Here several of the brethren were fishing for the use
of the monastery, this famous river abounding in various kinds
of iasg, or fish. It was the termoinn of Cluain-Irared, which
was situated on its left bank. Following its course, they came
to its confluence with the Amhain-dhu, or Blackwater. Here
the Greek obtained a good view of the surrounding country,
which, though a dead flat, presented a delightful and varied
scenery. On the two rivers curachs and cóca glided along;
beyond, as far as the eye could reach, could be seen dotting the
country the churches, palaces, towers, forts, duns, and private

houses, rich and poor, with their gardens, farms, race-courses, rivers, and mountains. At one side, a dense forest; at the other the monastic buildings, and the city of Cluain-Irared. Turning towards the direction whence they came, they beheld in perspective all that they had already seen in detail. Aristophanes, charmed with the scenery, expressed his admiration to his companion, who informed him that up to the time that the abbot Finian arrived here the immense tract of highly cultivated land, as well as the ground on which now stood the city of Cluain Irared,* was one vast fasach, or wilderness, called Ros-Fionnachuie.† The holy man, however, with his small company of brothers, at once commenced to cut down the trees and build the church and cells, and from this small beginning grew the present gigantic establishment, the fame of his learning and sanctity drawing under his wing countless multitudes of monks and students; first from Midhe (Meath) and the surrounding districts; then from the other four kingdoms of Eire; and, finally, as he could see, from every country of Europe, and even from sunny Africa. Ruadhan continued to explain that it was a type of many other such monasteries spread throughout the land and increasing every day.

They continued to converse as they walked along the river bank until at length they relapsed into silence, both being impressed by their surroundings, and the feelings, recollections, and surprise it evoked. As they pondered, they bent their heads towards the river flowing at their feet, rippling of which murmurs a purring accompaniment to the songs of the birds; to the evening hymns of the bádoiridh, or boatmen, as they glided along in their corachs, as well as to the deep, solemn voices of the choirs of monks who chanted perpetual praise in the college church, and which were borne towards them on the evening breezes, mingling strangely with the noise of the bro, of the implements of husbandry, of the ringing anvils, and other tools of the busy workmen in the various workshops; the baial, or axe, of the brother, who could be heard cutting firewood at a little distance in the thicket; the lowing of the cattle; the soft breathings of the

---

* Clonard is situated at the confluence of the rivers Boyne and Blackwater, in the present barony of Upper Moyfenrath, in county Meath, being twenty-six miles from Dublin. Vallency and Sir James Ware say that Cluain-Irared means "The Retirement on the Western Height;" that is, cluain, a lawn; iar, western; and árd, a height; but Colgan and O'Donovan maintain that the meaning is "Irard's or Erard's Lawn or Meadow," Iar-árd being the name of a man, and not of a place.

† (i.e.)—The wood or shrubbery of the white hazel.

wind through the crainn (trees)—all mingling together as the two friends stood there in silence, scarcely conscious of each other's presence, unmindful of the fast-falling shades of even', oblivious of all, save the witching influence of the charmed spot and of the strangely commingled sounds which fell upon their ears. There is no knowing how much longer they would have remained there had not another sound suddenly broken the enchantment, causing them to start from their reverie, the Greek exclaiming:

"Hark! the monastery bells! It is the hour of vespers. Let us to the church."

"Look, O Aristophanes," said Ruadhan, as he looked towards the tower, "the cloigteach is illuminated."

"Ha!" exclaimed the Greek, "the sisters are again united. My first friends, they shall be dear to me unto the end."

Locked together, the two companions moved at a brisk pace towards the eglais (church) by a different way from that by which they had come. They could see the brethren flocking from all directions towards the same spot; the horses and "carra" were stabled; the pastures were emptied of their occupants for the night; every one had left off work for the day to devote himself wholly to prayer and contemplation. The companions soon came to the ceiseog-droichet, or wicker bridge, which Aristophanes had crossed on the previous night, and which had been one of the first erected by the earliest monks on their taking possession; passing the cloigteach, from the uppermost storey of which the bells still pealed, they soon were inside the church, together with the entire college—clerical, religious, and lay. The perpetual choir having been joined for vespers by the entire congregation in singing the psalms, as was usual, all again left for their cells to spend the remainder of the evening in prayer, reading, and contemplation: the only difference being that the choir which had been previously singing were now relieved by another company, which would be, in like manner, relieved at a later hour, thus keeping up a perpetual round of prayer and praise. The students having partaken of their evening meal in the proinn-teach, afterwards spent some time in recreating themselves before retiring to their cells to study until called to the First Nocturn at nine o'clock, when all again assembled as they had been on the previous night at the hour at which Aristophanes first made their acquaintance. This over, all retired to their beds, the Athenian again sharing Ruadhan's cell. At intervals until morning the bells rang for second and third Nocturns, the monks and many of the students rising each time to assist at the devotions, the perpetual choir relieving each other by night as well as by day.

The next morning, Ruadhan and Aristophanes assisted at
the Divine Office. The former procured the assistance of the
saor, or carpenter, to build the cell for the Greek, according to
the orders of the abbot. The materials were all carried to the
sraid na Greugac, or street of the Greeks, which ran parallel to
the sraid na Galla, street of the Gauls, and at right angles with
the sraid na Sassenach, or street of the Saxons. Having first
carefully cleared the ground, the brother, with the assistance of
Aristophanes and Ruadhan, planted a taircadh, or stout post,
firmly in the spot which was to be the centre. Then each, taking
a pole from a number of slighter dimensions which lay on the
ground, proceeded to plant them in the places pointed out by
the brother. When these were secured, they proceeded in like
manner with the remainder of the poles, until they formed a
circle at equal distances round the central post, which towered
a considerable height above them. The next operation was to
take rods of coll, or hazel, from a heap which had been previously
cut and carried to the spot. With these they commenced to fill
the interstices between the poles, in the form of wicker or basket
work, until it reached the required height of the walls. This
done, and the structure now able to bear their weight, they
climbed to the top of the wall, and inserted by means of mortise
and tenon, a number of rafters which descended slantingly all
round from the tuircadh in the centre to the tops of the upright
posts of the walls. As the distance between these rafters necessarily increased as they radiated from the centre, cross-pieces or
beams were inserted between them as often as needed, until at
last a regular shield roof with a sharp pitch was formed above.
Across the rafters and ribs thus inserted were then laid bands
or laths, or narrow strips of wood, which were fastened with
pegs or with gads or twisted withes, forming a regular net-
work from the top of the roof-tree to the walls. On these again
they fastened, at short distances, a sheeting of rods and branches
of trees stretching in like manner from the roof-tree to the walls.
And now, having completed the shell of the house, they thatched
it with rushes, which they neatly fastened down with scolba, or
scollops. This done, they staunched the walls with moss,
forming a complete lining with it on the inside. An iron hook
was fastened to one of the rafters on the inside, on which Aristophanes could hang his polaire, or leathern satchel, which he
got from the criolaire. This pavilion-shaped house was next
furnished with a small round table, on which was placed a
wooden or stone candlestick for holding a candle made of
twisted rushes dipped in oil; a wooden box, which served also

for a seat; a simple wooden bedstead, provided with a pallet filled with straw, and a gamme, or cushion of chaff, and coverlets of ollan, or wool, which completed the appointments of the wicker house, being precisely similar to the many thousands of others which surrounded it. It was then handed over to Aristophanes as his special habitation. By this time the cloigha (bells) began to ring for the morning Affrion (Mass), and all proceeded to eglais na mainistirè (church of the monastery.) After the Holy Sacrifice had concluded, all again came forth; the monks to their respective duties, the students to the proinnteach for ceud proinn, or breakfast, after which they retired to their respective houses or cells to prepare for their studies. Ruadhan intimated to Aristophanes that they would now visit the leabharagan or library, and suggested that Aristophanes should bring his polaire to avoid having to go for it afterwards. For this purpose both went to the new house, and the Greek, taking his polaire, which was as yet empty, from its hook, accompanied his friend back to the monastery.

ⱱn ⱦ-séⱦⱥⱱ ċⱥibⱱⱱil.

CHAPTER VI.

ⱱn leⱥbⱥpⱥⱨⱥn.

THE LIBRARY.

foⱨlⱥm eⱱreⱥnn pⱥⱨⱥnⱦⱥ.

IRISH PAGAN LITERATURE.

ON entering the leabharagan (the library), Ruadhan conducted Aristophanes to the leabhar-coimhedach, or librarian (custos librorum), who was arranging some manuscripts near the entrance; looking up as Ruadhan addressed him:

"Oh, Conan, leabhar coimhedach, I bring to thee a new pupil of our holy abbot, Aristophanes, a Greek, from Attica. Before entering on his studies, he desires to be made acquainted with the contents of the leabharagan, of which accounts had reached him in his native land."

Conan, addressing the Greek—"My young friend, thou art welcome. I know that Ruadhan has been escorting thee all over the monastery, and I have been expecting a visit to myself. I am always most happy to be of service to any who present themselves, but it is especially gratifying to meet with one who is capable of appreciating the particular department under my charge, as those coming from thy beloved and classic Achaia always do."

Aristophanes—"Oh, sir leabhar-coimhedach, thy kindness confuses me. I must take thy compliments as referring to my country rather than to myself, and they are not undeserved. Greece, once so great and glorious, and so renowned for learning and civilisation, has sadly deteriorated, owing to the jealousy of her enemies, and still more to the internal dissensions and domestic strife of her own children. There appears to be a wonderful similarity in laws, manners, customs, and institutions between Greece and Eire; so at least I have heard from those who spent some time in this country, and travelled through every part of it. I hope this second Greece will take warning by its eastern prototype."

Ruadhan looked grave, but Conan shook his head, as he observed:

"I fear there is a similarity between the two countries in more ways than perhaps is fortunate for either."

The leabhar-coimhedach then proceeded to show the Athenian through the leabharagan, which resembled in form and size the proinnteach, having tables running down the centre, at which were seated numbers of students, so deeply absorbed in reading, for purposes of composition, that they heeded not the short conversation which had just taken place. On these tables, at hand for the accommodation of the students, were strewn all sorts of books and manuscripts, as well as maps, charts, and globes.

The walls were lined with shelves, on which were arranged, in admirable order in sections, thousands of manuscripts of various ages, some quite discoloured with age, while others appeared quite new; some were written on tablets, and some on parchment.

Commencing at the entrance to the left, Conan first pointed out the works of the ancients of other lands, among which Aristophanes recognised the Greek and Roman classics; also all the known works in history, poetry, philosophy, astronomy, physics, theology, &c., of the pre-Christian period; all those again were divided into two sections, viz., those in the original languages in which they were composed, and the translation of those various works into Gaodhalic, by the monks and students of the college.

Further on they stood before the sections containing the ancient pagan literature of Eire; and Conan, reaching for some very shabby-looking, discoloured old tablets, handled them with the greatest care and respect, as he turned to the Greek, and said:

"Here, O Aristophanes, on these old tablets, nearly decayed with age, are inscribed the writings of the Tuatha-de-Danaans. They are the earliest record we have of Irish literature written in this country. Those first are the works of Dagda, King of Eire, in the year of the world 2804, or 1200 years before Christ. The next are those of Ogma, who lived a little later. He was the inventor of that occult and mysterious method of writing called Craobh-Ogham (i.e., Virgean characters), of which these are curious specimens. In their proper places I will show thee a collection of this kind of writing by succeeding authors, both Danaan and Milesian, but all alike acknowledge Ogma as the inventor. Following next in order are the writings of Etana the poetess, mother of King Dalboet, Anno Mundi 2884, while Samson was yet Judge of Israel, or 1120 years before Christ; those of Cairbre, the poet, son of Etana; of Dannanna, the poetess, daughter of King Dalboet; and Brigid, the poetess, daughter of King Dagda. It is needless to observe, O Aristophanes, that there must be a great deal of the works of the Danaans lost through the lapse of ages, and the many conflicts they had with their Milesian conquerors, and for the same reasons must we be deprived of the names of many more composers. But turn we now to their supplanters. And here, O Aristophanes, on those venerable tablets are inscribed the writings of the first Milesian Ollamh,* philosopher and bard of Eire—Amerghin,† the son of Milesius and Scota, the brother of Heremon, Heber, and Ir. These we consider great curiosities: they consist chiefly of poetry, philosophy, and law, written in the purest Gaodhalic."

Aristophanes—"Is it not strange that so many ladies distinguished themselves at so early a period of your history, and that their names should have been so well preserved?"

Ruadhan—"No; nothing strange about it. Our Irish laws proclaim woman the equal of man. God and nature proclaims it as well, and we are too religious and too chivalrous a nation to deny it, or to seek to suppress the truth merely for the sake of shining at the expense of our countrywomen, the crowning work of creation. We Gaodhals yield to no other nation on earth in chivalry; it is a part of our education, our morals, and our religion."

* Learned Man, pronounced Ollav, from " oll," all, complete, whole, and " lua," uttering, eloquent, free, ready,—a man ready to speak on any subject— or, " oll," and " lain," *hand*, a " complete hand," on any point.—*Canon Bourke*.

† Averean.

Conan—"We had better return to Amerghin and his works, lest you quarrel, and we shall have to bring our future king to read a lesson to Ruadhan, they are such good friends."

Ruadhan—"Oh, thou speakest thus because thou knowest that we never can agree; but Diarmaid is not king yet."

Aristophanes—"And who is this mighty Diarmaid, O Ruadhan?"

Ruadhan—"Dost thou not remember, O Aristophanes, a haughty, distinguished-looking youth, whom I pointed out to thee in the refectory, and who I told thee was Prince Diarmaid MacFergus MacCearbhall, who calls himself heir to the monarchy, and even its rightful king."

Aristophanes—"Ah, I think I remember; but there were so many haughty, distinguished-looking youths there that I am not quite sure that I would again recognise him."

As he said this, he scanned Ruadhan with his eye from head to foot.

Now, Ruadhan, though young, was exceedingly tall and majestic-looking; he had already reached six feet, and had not yet done growing. Not appearing to notice this, he said:

"Prince Diarmaid has as many airs as if he were already Ardrigh."*

Aristophanes—"A haughty, distinguished-looking presence is sometimes the sign of greatness."

Ruadhan—"It is much more frequently its substitute."

Conan—"But Diarmaid is making rapid progress in his studies, and I have no doubt before long he will be a great proficient. He studies unceasingly; himself and young Columcille are the most industrious and studious in the whole college, carrying their zeal so far as frequently to break through the rules which the abbot has established for insuring sufficient rest and recreation."

Ruadhan—"But there is this difference between Diarmaid and Columcille: Columcille studies with the intention of devoting his talents at some future time to the glory of God and the interests of the Church. Diarmaid, on the other hand, only thinks of qualifying himself for the throne which he is determined one day to fill, but for which he is utterly unfit, being but half a Christian."

Conan—"Oh, come, come, my son, thou must not be uncharitable. Diarmaid's life has been swayed by circumstances which have never influenced thine; and thou oughtest to be

---

* High King or Monarch.

grateful, instead of making uncharitable remarks on thy neighbours' shortcomings."

Ruadhan—"But could he not be like Columcille, who, though as likely to inherit a throne as he, is yet as gentle as the bird whose name he bears ?"*

"Save when his hot Hy-Nial blood is up," exclaimed a voice behind them.

On looking round at the sound of the well-known voice, Prince Diarmaid himself stood before them ; and Conan exclaimed :

"Ha, Ruadhan, thou art caught this time. When will you two learn to evince common Christian charity and mutual respect towards each other ?"

Diarmaid—"I cannot stand his constant taunts and sarcasms consistently with my self-respect."

Ruadhan—"Nor can I stand his seditious language and druidical superstitions, consistently with my loyalty to my king and my duty to my Church."

Diarmaid—"Thy 'lawful' king stands before thee ; and thy Church, which is also mine, does not acknowledge thy right to judge thy neighbour."

Ruadhan—"Thou wouldst make everyone as disloyal as thyself."

Diarmaid—"Since thou preachest so much of loyalty, thou oughtest to practise at least a little respect where thou wilt one day have to render homage."

Ruadhan—"I shall never pay thee homage, O Diarmaid."

Diarmaid—"Then thou shalt take the consequence, O Ruadhan."

Saying which the young prince turned on his heel and faced Conan, who, by a sign, checked the rising anger of Ruadhan, and beckoning to Aristophanes, who had been a silent spectator, thus addressed him :

"My son, thou must not think worse of these young gentlemen for the scene which thou hast just witnessed ; but we Gaodhals have an unfortunate propensity of quarrelling amongst ourselves ; and as I fear that Ruadhan will not introduce thee to the prince, that duty now devolves upon me."

Conan then introduced Diarmaid and Aristophanes, who shook each other warmly by the hand—the prince asking the Greek many questions, and was about leaving, when Conan asked him whether there was anything he could do for him, but

* Columb is the Irish for dove.

Diarmaid replied that it would do another time, as he was now too agitated. He then left, and Conan, Aristophanes, and Ruadhan at last resumed their examination of Amerghin's works, which had been carefully preserved down to that time, i.e., over 1,500 years, though, as Conan told them, the greater part had been long lost."*

After these curious writings had been duly examined, Conan carefully replaced them, and then pointed out other works of succeeding ollamhs, filés, lawgivers, and kings, including Lughaidh,† the son of Ith, and nephew of Milesius ; these formed a very considerable collection, and after explaining the nature of their contents, he said :

" And here are the celebrated works called the 'Feneachus' (or what the Romans would call jurisprudence), containing a collection of civil laws, compiled by Ollamh Fodhla,‡ the famous legislator, who reigned Ardrigh of Eire seven centuries before the birth of our Saviour. He was assisted in this great work by the brehons, ollamhs, and sages of this country. It consists of judgments of all possible cases, which occurred to them, according to the unerring line of equity and justice. These they promulgated for the use of the Breithemhne§ and Muinter.‖

Aristophanes—" Then this great body of laws are over 1,200 years old ?"

Conan—" Yes, they were compiled about the time of the destruction of the first Assyrian Empire, and the formation from its ruins of the three separate kingdoms of Nineveh, Babylon, and Media."

Having noticed the productions of various succeeding poets and legislators, they next came to a collection of works on history, science, law, and other subjects, which were written by various learned persons in the reign of Cimbaoth,¶ the great restorer of the Irish Constitution, and the liberal patron of literature, science, and art, who flourished 350 years before Christ.

Next in succession came the literature of the reign of Ugoni (or Hugony) the Great, who flourished fifty years later, and was also remarkable for the encouragement he gave to learning. Next after these, the commentaries on the laws of Ollamh Fodhla, written by King Hugony's son and successor, Roigny

---

* Twenty-four of his poems are still extant.

† At least one of Lughaidh's poems is still extant. It was written in honour of his wife, and is an example of the modesty of Irish women in those far off pagan times.   ‡ Ollav Folla, i.e. Sage of Ireland.

§ Judges.   ‖ People.   ¶ Kimbath.

Rosgadach,* as well as works on various subjects by eminent persons in his reign.

When Conan had shown an innumerable collection of the works of the three succeeding centuries, he said:

" During the century preceding the birth of Christ, owing to internal commotion, the filés, with the assistance of the Druids, were enabled to corrupt the laws, rendering them occult and cabalistic. About the opening of the first century they, by their bad effects, drove the people to desperation, and in the torrent of popular fury, making no distinction between Use and Abuse, Good and Bad alike were driven by the people of Lagheant and Mumhant out of the Heberian and Heremonian provinces. In their deep distress, those learned engrossers of law fled to the Court of Eamhain,§ in the kingdom of Ulladh,‖ where they were received with honour by King Concobhar (Connor) Mac Nessa, one of the wisest and most valiant princes that ever reigned in Eire. That great prince, conscious of the danger, set the most learned of the filés to work, and the result was the production of a code of laws, at once simple and intelligible, giving judgment of all cases so clearly that any person of fair education could be a tolerable judge of his own case; and the principal among the compilers, namely, Forchern, Neid, and Atharni, of Ben Hedar,¶ gained immortal renown, and the Order of Filés were again admitted to credit with the people, which has continued ever since."**

Aristophanes—"Was this the same king who died on the day of our Lord's crucifixion, after having been granted a knowledge of the great mystery which had just been consum-mated, and grace to commend his departing soul to the Crucified One ?"

Ruadhan—"The same."

Conan—"Here are the various sections of that great work, and here (showing other volumes) are the Axioms, to which succeeding filés reduced it. They are called Breatha-Nimhe,†† which name they obtained from the supposition of having been compiled with so much equity and wisdom as to receive the approbation of heaven, and to be unalterable."

Ruadhan—"Here, O Aristophanes, is one of the sections of that great work, the name of which has been lost. It relates specially to the Laws of Poetry ; lays down rules for Panegyric

---

* Royne the Poetic. There is a poem of his still extant, which describes the peregrinations of the Gadelians.

† Leinster.　　‡ Munster (Mooan).　　§ Emania.　　‖ Ulster.
¶ Hill of Howth.　　** O'Connor.　　†† Celestial Judgments.

and Satire; and prescribes penalties against licentious poets
and libellers. This part was begun by Atharni, and had several
additions from the hands of Ailgerach and from several others."

Conan—"Here now is another work, called the Uraiceacht-
nan-eagios (or the Precepts of the Poets), containing a hundred
kinds of compositions, written about the same time by Forchern.
And this collection here are all the known works of several
poets: their names were Sencha, Fachtnas, Ner, and Man-All-
Knowing, the poets.

Aristophanes—"Man-All-Knowing! Was that his name?"

Conan—"It was either his name, or else a title given him
on account of his learning and extensive acquirements. At all
events, it is the only name by which he is now known. Then
these next to Man-All-Knowing's are the works of Ethnea, the
poetess, the daughter of Amalgaidh. And here are a collection
of anonymous authors of the same time, and a miscellaneous lot
of the imperfect works of others."

He next showed the writings of various judges and filés, and
amongst others those of Moran, the son of Carbrie, King of
Eire, and celebrated chief judge under Feredach the Just, A.D. 85.
Also those of King Feredach himself, together with the literature
and poetry of the following century, among others the " Meill
Bhreatha," by MacFalban.

" And here, O Aristophanes, said the leabhar-coimhedach,
is a book called Teagasc-na-Ri (or the Institutions of a Prince).
It was written by King Cormac MacArt, who died A.D. 266, and
contains admirable maxims on manners, morals, and government; and here is another book, or law tract, called the Book
of Acaill, by the same author; and all those here are the
writings, on divers subjects, of Cormac himself, as well as the
learned men of his time. But here is the most remarkable of
all the works of that great king; it is called the Saltair of Teamhair, and was compiled by him and his seanchaidhe,* the
principal of whom were Fintan, the son of Bochra, and Fithil,
the poet and judge."

Aristophanes—I have often heard of the great king Cormac,
and have heard the Saltair of Teamhair mentioned, but I have
never been fully informed of the subjects on which it treats."

Conan (reading)—"Cormac assembled the ollamhain† of
Eire, and ordered them to collect the chronicles of the country
to Teamhair, and to write them in one book (the same which
thou now beholdest). In it were entered the coeval exploits
and synchronisms of the Kings of Eire with the kings and

* Shaanachy (Historians).   † The learned and wise.

emperors of the world, and of the kings of the provincial kingdoms with the monarchs of Eire. In it were also written what the monarchs of Eire were entitled to receive from the provincial kings, and the rents and dues of the provincial kings from their subjects, from the noble to the subaltern. In it also are described the boundaries and mearns of Eire from shore to shore, from the provinces to the cantreds, from the cantreds to the townlands, from the townland to the traighedh of land."

Then reaching for another MS., and opening it at a certain place, he said :

" And here is a work of a later date, called the Uachonbhail, which describes the Saltair of Teamhair thus :"—

He then read :

" A noble work was performed by Cormac at that time— namely, this compilation of Cormac's Saltair, which was com- posed by him, and the synchronisms and genealogies, the succession of their kings and monarchs, their battles, their contests, and their antiquities, from the world's beginning down to that time were written ; and this is the Saltair of Teamhair, which is the origin and foundation of the historians of Eire from that period down to this time."

Ruadhan—"Cormac was the inventor of this kind of chronology."

Having looked over the Saltair and the Uachonbhail, both were again put into their respective places, and Conan pointed to other manuscripts, saying :

" Those are the Celestial Judgments, written by Caribre Liffe-car, Cormac's own son and successor."

Ruadhan—" He was called Liffe-car because born on the banks of the Amhain Liffe."*

Conan—" Here are other works under the same title, written by Fathil, judge to King Cormac ; and here again are other Celestial Judgments, as well as romances and poems, by Finn Mac Cumhaill,† that king's son-in-law, and general of his army."

Aristophanes—" I have heard O Conan, that poetical qualifications are a necessary condition of obtaining admission into your Fenian Army. Is that true ?"

Conan—" Oh, most certainly Ruadhan, repeat in the exact words of legal military regulations, the second of the ten condi- tion for admission into the Fianna Eirionn."‡

Ruadhan—" No man can be admitted into the Fianna until he has mastered the Twelve Books of Poesy."

* River Liffey. † Oool. ‡ Fenians of Ireland.

Aristophanes—" Have you the Twelve Books of Poesy here ?"

Conan—" We have; here they are in this very section. They are selections from various very old MSS., some of which you have seen, and some of which are now lost. But we do not train youths here for military pursuits; we are men of peace, and leave those affairs to the various military schools throughout the country, the chief of which is the military department of Mur Ollamhain of Teamhair, which comes down from remote pagan times though now modified and Christianized. Finn Mac Cumhaill* was a most famous Fenian hero in Cormac's time, and his learning, bravery, and exploits are the favourite themes of our bards. And this range here are the works in succession of Fachtna, Seanched, Nerea, Eogan, Mac Duthreacht, Achay, Mac Luchla, Modon, Mac Falban, and Conla, Judge of Connacht. They treat on a great variety of subjects, principally philosophy and law. Here again is the Fiondsuith, by Fiatach, a Temorain civilian, in the reign of King Cormac, A.D. 260. The Teacht-Bhreath, a miscellany of several laws, the Fuigheal-Bhreath, a supplement to the laws; the Fothamor, showing the true office of a judge, and the errors which subjected him to a privation of his magistracy; the Fotha Beag, or book setting forth the Laws of Partition; Aid-Bhreathe, a law book treating of theft; the Corrasfinnes, a book prescribing proper rules for regulation of disputes in dynastal tribes or clans; the Book of Cain, or Mulcts in four parts; the first relates to mulcts of all kinds; the second to murders and other vices; the third to securities, pawns, and forfeits; and the fourth to witnesses and testimonies. To this work is added an appendix entitled Eidgheadh, a book treating of crimes against the laws. Here is a book called the Cain Fuitribhe, which treats of the laws of prescription and possession. Faidh Fenechais, a miscellany of all laws; the Cain Borachta, or property in herds and flocks. And here—what ! what are these ? why, here are the Fenian poems of Oisin,† Fergus, Caoilte, and others. Who put them here ? They should be with those of Finn Mac Cumhall and the other Fenian poets. Ruadhan, dost thou know who placed them here ?"

Ruadhan—"I do not know, O Conan, except it be that idiot, Bec Mac De, who—oh ! oh !! oh !!! "

This exclamation from Ruadham was caused by the object of his slighting remark springing up from a seat behind him,

---

* He is the Fingal of MacPherson.

† It was on these poems of the Irish Oisin (Ossian) that MacPherson founded his celebrated Scotch forgeries.

and pulling vigorously at both his ears. Conan and Aristophanes turned suddenly round ; but the students, who were dispersed through the leabharagan reading at the tables, rose to their feet and gave a ringing cheer for Bec Mac De, who cried:

"Callest thou me an idiot, oh, thou loyal subject of Tuathal Maelgarbh. I, who am to be poet, philosopher, and friend to Ardrigh Diarmaid MacCearbhall."

Ruadhan—"Thou! ha, ha; thou mayest be his friend, but thou art more likely to be his fool and his jester than either his poet or philosopher. But, in truth, O, Bec Mac De, I did not know that thou wert in the leabharagan, else I should not have spoken of thee at all."

Bec Mac De—"Well, the next time thou wantest to speak of me only to call me an idiot, I would advise first to look carefully around thee on every side. And listen, O Ruadhan, when I am installed with Diarmaid at Teamhair,* thou wilt then know whether I am his fool and his jester or his poet and philosopher."

Ruadhan—"Well, perhaps by the time that Diarmaid is Ardrigh of Eire, thou wilt be both a poet and philosopher."

Bec Mac De—"Thou speakest in irony; but thou shalt see."

So saying, Bec sat down and resumed his reading. The other readers who enjoyed the scene also resumed theirs. Ruadhan, turning, noticed a grave expression on the face of Conan, while a scarcely expressed smile played about the features of the Greek.

"Wert thou laughing, too, O Aristophanes ?"

Aristophanes—"I assure thee, O Ruadhan, I was not laughing at thee, but felt very sorry; but I could not help admiring the pluck and spirit of thine idiot and prince Diarmaid's philosopher."

Ruadhan—"And what dost *thou* admire, O Conan, thou lookest grave ?"

Conan—"Were I a man of the world I would admire what Aristophanes calls the pluck and spirit of simple Bec Mac De, who is so much weaker and younger than thyself. But as a monk, I admire neither thine ungenerous slight nor his pugilistic mode of redressing his fancied wrongs. Were our holy abbot here he would be very much displeased with both. And now, Ruadhan, I hope that this will be the last quarrel, at least for this day."

Aristophanes—"And are these all Fenian poems, O Conan ? What an immense collection !"

---

* Tara.

Conan—"They are Fenian poems and tales. These are divided into four classes. The first consists of poems ascribed directly to Finn Mac Cumhaill; to his sons, Oisin and Fergus Finnbheoill (the Eloquent); and to his kinsman, Caoilte. The second class consists of tracts made up of articles in prose and verse, ascribed to some of the same personages, but related by a second person. The third class consists of miscellaneous poems, descriptive of passages in the life of Finn and his warriors, but without any ascription of authorship. The fourth class consists of certain prose tales, told in a romantic style, relating to the exploit of the same renowned captain and those of his most distinguished companions. And all that thou seest here, to the end of this section, are the works on divers subjects (of various authors down to the arrival of St. Patrick, whose advent gave a new turn to the literature of Eire. He began by purging the Fenachus of all laws relating to Druidism, and then was compiled the Code Seanchus Mor, or the Great Antiquity. This work is tripartite, and contains a summary of all laws—civil and ecclesiastical. It is, however, regretted by many that the saint, in his great zeal, burned no less than 180 volumes of Druids' books at Teamhair. Now, there can be no doubt that there were many shocking things in them which deserved to be burned; but there were thousands of persons well qualified to revise those ancient works and retain all their beauties, while they rejected whatever was inconsistent with the Christian religion."

Aristophanes—"Well, I am very much surprised, indeed. In other countries the missionaries have ever been most careful to guard the ancient native Pagan literature in consideration of their intrinsic merit, though none of them all could compare with the genius, learning, and refinement of thine ancient Gaodhilic scribes."

Conan—"Our literary men deeply deplore the loss of such valuable MSS., even while they pay a high tribute to the sanctity of the Apostle and to the very zeal which induced him to destroy so many memorials of Eire's ancient glory, that it might redound to her spiritual advantage. These here are the Cain Drubhartaigh Bearra, which treat on commercial and maritime affairs; the Cain Lanambhna Mor and the Cain Lanamhna Beag, which shows the sacred relations of society and how equals of all denominations might compose disputes and live in harmony. Here is the Cuilmenn; the Book of Cuana; the works of Congal, the son and poet of King Eochy Feilach; and a host of other works."

Aristophanes—"What large volume is this?"

Conan—" ' This is the Cin Droma Snechta or the Book of Invasions of Eire, from Magog, son of Japhet, from whom Milesius, down to the year in which it was written—to wit, A.D. 365—by Ernan MacDuach, son of the King of Connacht, an ollamh and a prophet, a professor in history and a professor in wisdom.' "

Ruadhan—" It was he that collected the genealogies and histories of the men of Eire in one book—this Cin Droma Snechta."

Conan—" Thou seest here, O Aristophanes, the poetical works of that most eminent bard, Torna Eigeas (or the learned), chief bard to King Nial Naoi Gialliagh.* And here beside them are those of the famous Dubthach Ua Lugair, who was arch-poet to King Leoghaire;† these, however, are only the poems he wrote while still a pagan."

Aristophanes—" This next division is smaller than the others. What doth it contain?"

Conan—"That is entirely devoted to ogham writings. They are the works of various authors, both pagan and Christian, from Ogma himself, who invented it, down to the present day."

Ruadhan—" See here these staves. Wouldst thou ever think, O Aristophanes, that these contained writing in prose and verse ?"

Aristophanes—" Never, indeed. I should rather think they were square walking-sticks."

Conan—" Precisely, and so they are ; but they serve a double purpose. They are known by different names—as Tamlorge Filid (or staves of the poets) ; Taballorga (tablet staves) ; Tabli Fili (tables of the poets) ; Fleasc Fili (the wand of the poet). This, indeed, was the form of the ancient Gaelic tablet. The old poets and historians always carried one of these wherever they went. It served as a staff on which to lean ; and when they wished to write, which they could do anywhere, even on the roadside, they had nothing to do but to open their staff, thus."

Aristophanes—" How curious ! Why it is now a regular fan."

Conan—" Yea, it is now a fan-shaped tablet ; and as thou mayest see, neither pen nor ink was required. The scribe need never be at a loss for writing material so long as he carried a square staff in his hand and a knife in his pocket."

Aristophanes—"It is indeed truly wonderful ; and it is all covered with writing. Is that the ogham character ?"

Conan— " Yes ; that is ogham, and is an excellent specimen of that method of writing. We have here but a few of these tablet staves, but there are many of them in the Mur Ollamhain, of Teamhair, and the other ancient schools of Eire."

* Nial of the Nine Hostages.   † Leary.

ᴀn ᴄ-seᴀċᴛṁᴀᴅ́ ċᴀɪbɪᴅɪᴌ;

CHAPTER VII.

ᴀn ᴌeᴀbᴀpᴀɣᴀn.

THE LIBRARY.

ᵹoɣᴌᴀm eɪpeᴀnn Cpɪopoᴀɪᴅe.

IRISH CHRISTIAN LITERATURE.

As they came to the next division, the leabhar coimhedach said: "And now we come to the Christian section, which dates from the arrival of St. Patrick, about a hundred years ago, with the exception of these few compositions of isolated Christians scattered throughout the country before that time, and which are all here together on this shelf, and amongst them those of St. Ailbhe, of Imlaigh (Emly). These thou seest here, O Aristophanes, are the Confessions, Epistles, and Canonical Decrees of St. Patrick, and next to these are his hymns, amongst which are his Feth Fiadha or Lorica, the hymn which he composed and sung on his way to Teamhair. Now, here is a work on the life, virtues, and miracles of St. Patrick, by his successor, St. Benin ; and here is the celebrated Leabhar-na g-Ceart (or Book of Rights) by the same writer."

Aristophanes—"What doth the Leabhar-na g-Ceart contain ?"

Conan—" It containeth an account of the rights, privileges, restrictions, and prohibitions of the kings and princes of Eire."

Ruadhan—" Are not these, O Conan, the Christian works of Dubthach-Ua-Lugair ?"

Conan—" Yes ; all these he wrote after his conversion. Among them are some most elegant verses praising the Omnipotent Creator and commemorating his saints. Here are his celestial Decrees and his other prose works ; and here is the Seanchus Mor, which I told thee, O Aristophanes, St. Patrick purified. Well, Dubthach was one of those St. Patrick engaged to revise and improve these old statutes of civil law—the Phenechus. Here is a hymn of thirty-four distichs or ranns, on the Acts of St. Patrick, by the holy Fiac, late Bishop of Sleigthi (Sletty) ; he was a disciple of Dubthach. Here also are the numerous works of Sedulius, the accomplished poet, orator, and divine ; the prophecies of Cathal, our Irish Bishop of Tarentum,

in Italy ; a Life of St. Patrick, by St. Cianan, Bishop of Daimh-
laig (Duleek) ; the Exhortations and Treatises of St. Fridolin,
the son of one of our kings ; the works of St. Jarlath, Bishop
of Tuaim-da-ghualaiun (Tuam) ; and of several minor authors.
And all these here are the works of St. Brigid, including her
Epistles and Poems ; among the latter is a poem on the virtues
of St. Patrick ; also a Rule for Nuns ; and a book called the
Quiver of Divine Desires."

Aristophanes—"How long is St. Brigid now dead, O Conan?"

Conan—"She is now dead thirteen years, but her fame, her
virtues, and her example will live for ever. Then there are
writings of her chaplain, St. Ninnidh Lainidha, including several
hymns as well as a panegyric of St. Brigid. And here is another
panegyric of St. Brigid, by Brogan Cloen ; and her Life, by
Cogitosus. Following on these are the numerous works of
several holy virgins, including SS. Fanchea, Ite, &c. &c."

Aristophanes—"What great tome is this ?"

Conran—"Oh, that is an old work which has also been revised to suit the altered state of things ; it is called the Dula,
and is in three parts. The first: Political subjection and
measures of Obedience to Kings ; of Wardships, Patronages,
and Privileged Places ; of Punishment of Offenders in case of
Blood ; and of the forms in which all sorts of Pacts, Contracts,
and Treaties should be reduced to writing; second part: Ecclesiastical Affairs, by Comin Fodha, and the rest of Laws, by Sea
and Land, by Cormac and Lifficar ; and third part: of what
Honours are due to Kings, Bishops, filês, &c., and what reparation to be made for injuries done to them. This last part was
one of those composed by Roigny Rosgaidhach, 300 B.C., and
is in separate form among his other works, which I showed to
thee in one of the pagan sections. Here, again, are the compositions of the distinguished poet Gemmen ; and here is a
Psaltar commemorating 52 Irish saints, by Diarmaid the Just,
abbot of Inis Clothran; the Canons of the Blessed Frigidian,
our Irish bishop of Lucca, as well as the works in prose and
verse of St. Cailin, bishop of Down and abbot of Fenagh.* And
the remainder of this section are a miscellaneous collection of
MSS. treating on divers subjects, too numerous to mention.
They are civil, ecclesiastical, historical, poetical, and mytho-
logical ; they are by bishops, abbots, priests, monks, nuns, poets,
philosophers, ollamhs, brehons, &c."

The leabhar-coimhedach then pointed out to Aristophanes
the works of contemporary eminent living authors.

* Rev. J. O'Hanlon.

Conan—"All of this collection are the works of our holy abbot Finnian himself. Those which follow next are the writings of blessed Comgall, at present presiding over the great college of Beanchor; these again, are those of the abbot Finnian, of Maghbhele (Moville), &c. &c."

Then Conan showed to the astonished Greek the youthful efforts of some of the pupils of Beanchor; the Columbans and Columbanuses; the Mochoenocs and the Molnas; the Blaans and the Carthaigs; the Galls and the Dichels; the Fintans and Fegnarnachs, and many other young scholars of Beanchor; and also of other colleges whose early effusions gave promise of future glory. And after examining the various kinds of contributions which daily flowed into Cluain-Irared leabharagan from every part of the kingdom of Eire, Conan said:

"And this division here, O Aristophanes, is especially set apart for the approved compositions of the students of our own college—thy future comh-alta (fellow-pupils); and I must say that they are in no way inferior to those of any other scoil (school) in the righeacht (kingdom). Here, for instance, are the essays and poems of <u>Brendan</u>; the two Columbs—that is, Columcille and Columb Mac Crimthan; of Canicus (or Kenny) Ninnidh and Nathy. Here are those of Lasrean and Ciaran, who has just written another work of a most sublime character, and which I hear has delighted the heart of our holy abbot."

Aristophanes—"Oh, I now remember; on my introduction to the abbot in his own house his minister was engaged in reading to him that very work, and he was so deeply absorbed and moved that he did notice our presence, his minister was the first to observe us. I shall never forget that scene."

Conan—"Here again, are the productions of Colman, or as we generally call him, Mocolmoc, the nephew of our abbot; and here, O Aristophanes, are those of thy friend, Ruadhan—nay, Ruadhan, do not be a coward; stay where thou art, I have something to show thee. Hast thou ever at all seen the compositions of an idiot? Look!"

Ruadhan—"Whose are these compositions, O Conan?"

Conan—"Dost thou know any idiot in Cluain-Irared?"

Aristophanes—"We had better speak softly, lest we get our ears pulled."

Conan—"He is gone, and will not hear Ruadhan's praises."

Ruadhan—"Who is gone? It cannot be! Whose are these?"

Conan—"Thou knowest well, O Ruadhan, to whom I refer. These are the writings of Bec Mac De."

Ruadhan—" Bec Mac De! Impossible! I can never believe it. In all my life I have never met so simple a boy. Why, the subjects of these pieces are far above him."

Conan—" Nevertheless, he has written them, and moreover they have undergone the keen scrutiny of one of our professors as well as of our holy abbot himself; but perhaps they will not bear *thy* criticism."

Aristophanes—" After all, I am afraid that Prince Diarmaid is a better judge than thou art, O Ruadhan."

Ruadhan—" But why was it kept so secret from me?"

Conan—" Because Bec Mac De feels too keenly thy slights to wish to undeceive thee. I am acting against his wishes in informing thee of the matter at all."

Aristophanes—" But that is all pride. Is it not?"

Conan—Well, perhaps it is; but in so young a boy it is excusable. And then Ruadhan is so hard on him."

Ruadhan—" My quarrel with him is less on his own account than because of his intimacy with Diarmaid, and his adoption of the prince's opinions."

Aristophanes—" Purely political."

Conan—" I wonder what will be the end of all this."

Aristophanes—" Nothing good can come of fraternal strife."

Conan—" Now it is growing late. Let us finish. Here is a large collection of the recently received works, in prose and verse, of eminent living authors; of bishops, abbots, nuns, monks, filés, ollamhs, philosophers, brehons, bards, and private persons from every part of the nation ; all of which must undergo strict examination before we can admit them; they include some of our former pupils, as Ciaran, the new bishop of Saighir (Sair), Brendan, the navigator, and others. And now we come to the section which contain the scientific works of our nation, ancient and modern, including a great collection of medical works by native physicians ; works on astronomy, geometry, painting, music, and all the known arts and sciences. All these are placed here together for greater convenience, being constantly required in the school-rooms. And here now is the foreign Christian section, and first the sacred Scriptures, the first five books of which, as thou knowest, O Aristophanes, was written by Moses, Here, then, are several copies of the Holy Bible, Old and New Testaments. Following in order are the writings of the fathers and doctors of the Church, and a general collection of foreign literature in the various languages in which they were composed. And here in the next compartment are the translations of those works into Gaelic by the monks of the college, assisted by many of the students. The last section contains only illuminated MSS. Here, again, are some copies of the Holy Scriptures, also translated into Irish, and, as thou seest, gorgeously illuminated in gold and colours. Their covers are of pure ductile gold, finely chased and studded with gems, all—from the preparation of the skins—the work of our college."

Aristophanes—" I have never seen anything so beautiful ; all the workmanship in every department is simply perfect. Ruadhan has led me into all the various departments where these works are carried on, and I have seen them in working order, but until now I could not imagine the result of their combined efforts."

Conan—" Here are other and different kinds of work. The Four Gospels, books of psalms, hymns, and other compositions and translations, magnificently illuminated and bound in gold or silver, or sumptuously ornamented with these metals or with jewels. Besides these books here are great numbers of single tablets, containing short hymns or passages and proverbs from Scripture, the work of the younger pupils, also illuminated with more or less elegance and ingenuity."

Aristophanes—" What a delightful art ! I must apply myself diligently to its acquirement."

Having spent the day in taking a cursory glance at the most remarkable of the very large collection of MSS. in the leabharagan they found themselves again at the entrance on the opposite side of the door from which they commenced.* They then went to the tables, which ran along the centre of the room, and looked at the various books with which they were strewed; they were similar to those which he had seen on the shelves, and were only taken down for the use of the students who required them, but who had by this time nearly deserted the leabharagan.

Mingled with these were maps, and chartes of various countries, besides maps of the existing Irish Pentarchy, maps also of the more ancient Eire under the various names by which it had been known to the ancients.

Maps of the various divisions of Eire under the different colonists, viz., the Partholanians, Nemedians, Fomorians, Belgians, Firbolgs, Tuatha-de-Danaans, and Milesians.

---

* Although all this mass of literature is necessarily described in English, it must be remembered that no such language then existed even in Britain. In Irish *alone*—the spoken language of all Ireland at that time—were all these works written. There were, of course, numerous works in Sanscrit, Greek, Hebrew, Latin, and others, but especially Latin. Irish however predominated in literature as in all else.

Maps showing the twenty-five divisions of Eire under Ugoni the Great. Others showing the two divisions of Leath Cuinn and Leath Mogha, of later times. Finally, the curious old maps of Eire, by Ptolemy the great Greek geographer.

Then there were separate maps of the several kingdoms and principalities into which the country was divided.

Aristophanes having expressed himself highly delighted with all he had seen and heard, returned hearty thanks to the leabhar-coimhedach for the treat he had given him, was about to leave, expecting Ruadhan to accompany him, when the voice of Conan arrested him:

"Stay, O Aristophanes, I am not done with thee yet. Where is thy polaire?"

Ruadhan—"Here it is on the floor, where he let it slip on his entrance."

Aristophanes—"I had quite forgotten it."

Conan took the polaire from the hands of Ruadhan and went again to the shelves. Ruadhan went after him and offered to hold it. Conan consented, and then proceeded to take a book from this place and another from that, going round the room again. Ruadhan following, holding the polaire open until they came again to Aristophanes, who had sat down, when the leabhar-coimhedach, taking the well-filled polaire from Ruadhan, presented it to Aristophanes in the name of the college. The Athenian, overpowered with gratitude, was more profuse than ever with his thanks, and promised to be very careful of these valuable books.

Conan—"Be careful of them by all means; but remember, they are thine own. Thou hast here in this polaire all things necessary for the curriculum of the college, thy daily studies in every branch of literature and science, and thou hast also the entire leabharagan at thy disposal. I hope that thou wilt make good use of it."

Aristophanes—"Thou needest not fear for that, O Conan; my teachers shall find me a diligent student, and thou a frequent visitor to thy leabharagan. Neither shall I be wanting in gratitude to my benefactors."

Conan—"If thou doest all that thou sayest, we shall be amply repaid. It was for the diffusion of religion and learning that our institution was founded by the blessed Finnian, and we are following our vocation to the best of our ability. We look for our reward in another world."

Aristophanes—"And great shall be the reward of such self-sacrificing zeal and universal beneficence."

Conan—"Beannacht leat mo mhic."

The two friends emerged from the leabharagan, and as they did so the bells chimed for vespers. Soon again the church was filled; soon another day was o'er; and the third night of his stay at Cluain-Irared saw Aristophanes safely lodged in his own cell—his independence, however, not unmingled with regret for the loss of the nocturnal society of his already dear, though captious friend.

ᴀn ᴄ-oċᴛṁᴀⱶ ċᴀɪbɪⱱɪl.

CHAPTER VIII.

ᴀn Sᴄoɪl ᴀ5ᴜꜱ ᴀn Ⱞᴀɪnɪꞅᴄeꞅ.

THE SCHOOL AND THE MONASTERY.

THE next morning, at the usual hour, thousands of students with their polaires slung across their shoulders, emerged from the different sraida (streets) which surrounded the monastic buildings. They were of many nationalities—Gauls, Saxons. Albanians, Iberians, Italians, Helvetians, Egyptians, and Greeks—but by far the greater number were, of course, children of the soil, representing not Midhe only, but the other four provincial States of Eire as well. Ruadhan had visited Aristophanes, gave him some injunctions, taught him how to arrange his polaire, and finally bore him company from his cell to the school. As they joined the crowd, which thickened on every side, and made their way into the school rooms, which were soon filled, Aristophanes exclaimed :

"What a din ! I thought all were bound to silence."

Ruadhan—"Silence, indeed! The monks are bound to silence, as far as is consistent with their several avocations; but the students——"

Aristophanes—"It is not so easy to impose silence on so many thousands of school boys."

Ruadhan—" No; the abbot Finian has worked many wonderful miracles, but that is one he has never been able to accomplish. However, once they are fairly settled down to the day's business they will not be so bad until it is time to break up again. Lo! here come the feara-leighene (professors), with the abbot at their head. See, he approaches Ciaran Mac-an-t-Saoir."*

---

* Macanteer.

Aristophanes—"Is that he whose compositions so much delighted the abbot?"

Ruadhan—"The same, O Aristophanes, and now he embraces him; he is also speaking; but, with the noise, we cannot hear. Ah, now they are aware of Finian's presence; the din subsides; but we are late: he is now about to bless him. Yet, listen."

Finian was in the act of raising his hands in benediction over the bent head of Ciaran, and the whole school could now hear the last words of the abbot.

"And further, O Ciaran, thou shalt be the spiritual father of a numerous progeny, and half the monasteries of Eire shall receive a rule from thee, and may the blessing of the Most Holy Trinity—the Father, the Son, and the Holy Ghost—descend upon thee and dwell with thee for ever."

These prophetic words fell from the lips of Finian amidst universal silence, and stamped thenceforth a new character upon the happy Ciaran; for all knew from experience that the prophecies of Finian were sure to be fulfilled."

The abbot then proceeded to make his usual morning inspection of the opening of the school.

At last, on perceiving Aristophanes, he advanced towards him and shook him warmly by the hand, and then proceeded to introduce him to his future oididh (tutors)—the caogadacha, or fifty men who had only to chant 150 psalms; the foglaintidhe, or professors of the fochaire or native education, who taught ten out of the twelve books of the college course; the staraidh, or historian, who had also, besides history, thirty lessons of divinity in his course; the foir-cetalach, or lecturer, who professed uraicecht, or the grammar of the pupils, orthography, criticism, enumeration, the course of the year, and the course of the sun and moon (i.e., astronomy), and general science; the saoi canoine, or professor of divinity, who taught the Canons and the Gospel of Jesus, that is the Word of God in the sacred place in which it is—that is, who taught the Catholic canonical wisdom; to the feraleighen, or professors of Greigis (Greek), Eabrais (Hebrew), Laidion (Latin), and Gaoidilge (Irish); the aos ealadhan, or men of science: the drumchli* or chief head, a

* "Druimcli, i.e., he who has (or knows) the top ridge (or highest range) of learning, compounded of Druim, the ridge of a hill or the ridge of a roof of a house; and cli, a form of cleit, the column or tree which in ancient times supported the house; and the man who was a druimcli was supposed to have climbed up the pillar or tree of learning to its very ridge or top, and was thus qualified to be a ferleighen—a professor or man qualified to teach or superintend the teaching of the whole course of a college education."—O'Curry.

master who knew the whole course of learning* "from the greatest book, which is called Cuilmein, down to the smallest book, called the Ten Commandments, in which is properly arranged the Good Testament which God prepared for Moses." Thus the fera-leighin, drumchli, or chief master, was obliged by law to be master of the whole course of Gaodhælec literature, in prose and verse, besides that of the Scripture, from the Ten Commandments up to the whole Bible, as well as the learned languages.

Finian having introduced Aristophanes to all the feraleighena (professors), in turn, then said :

"Here, then, O Aristophanes, is the pedigree of the scholar :
Schoolboy, son of Lesson,
Son of Caogadach,
Son of Foglaintidh,
Son of Professor of (profane) Letters,
Son of Professor of the Canons,
Son of Druimcli,
Son of the Living God."

Aristophanes—"A curious pedigree, truly. I never heard the like of it before. I shall not forget it easily, O father abbot."

Finian—"I am sure thou wilt not, my son; and thou shalt pass under all these gradh egna (grades or professors of know-ledge and wisdom), and every care shall be taken to instruct thee in the whole circle of the sciences, but thou thyself must, by diligence and industry, second the efforts of thine oididh (tutors); and now, my son, I must attend to other duties for a little while, and the Master Regent, will examine thee to find what progress thou hadst made in the great school of Athens, and he will then know in what classes and under what fera-leighein to place thee. Thine Athenian birth and education is a great advantage to thee. I have never heard any of thy countrymen speak in purer Attic dialect. Here comes the Master Regent; farewell, my son, for a little while."

The Master Regent then proceeded to put Aristophanes through his facings in every conceivable branch of foghlaim (education), and found him more advanced than he had ex-pected even from an Athenian.

He therefore placed him at the outset in an honourable place in the school, and thus the latter commenced his career of hard study, where so many of his countrymen, as well as foreigners of other nations had already done, and continued to do for many

* O'Curry.

centuries afterwards ; for Clonard was indeed a second Athens, but of far more holy descipline and enlightened morals; the closet of all wisdom and holiness; the clear spring which flowed through all Eire and all Europe ; the healthful life-giving waters of mental cultivation and spiritual regeneration—the tree which spread its branches over all the neighbouring states—the nursery from whence issued the Twelve Apostles of Eire, to found similar institutions for the diffusion of piety and learning, and which in their turn became the parent-houses of yet more numerous progenies, destined to shed light and lustre not only over the land that gave them birth, but over the less favoured nations of the earth, and which obtained for Eire the proud titles by which for many centuries afterwards she was known— " the University of Europe," " the centre of light and learning," " the tranquil abode of the arts and sciences," " the island of saints and scholars," and " the prime seat of learning to all Christendom."

Thus flowed on smoothly and evenly, day by day, monastic life at Cluain-Irared—work, prayer, and contemplation follow- ing in unceasing succession.

At early dawn the monastery bells called forth the whole city of Cluain-Irared to a new day of labour, prayer and praise ; the divine offices, the holy Mass, the hour of solitary contem- plation—each at their proper time.

These morning duties over, the whole community dispersed to their several occupations—some went to the schools to fulfil their duties in the various degrees of professorships, already alluded to, as teachers, readers, or lecturers in the many branches of science, literature, and art. Some went through the country to missionary labours, preaching and administering the Sacraments—some to the church for a day of meditation— good psalmodists to relieve the perpetual choir—some to the proinnteach to give alms, and to attend to visitors and travellers—good transcribers and illuminators to the leabhar- screptra (scriptorium)—the leabhar-coimhedach to the leabhara- gan—some compiled the civil and ecclesiastical annals of the country (and to their laudable diligence must be attributed the fact that no country in Europe has a more ancient and authentic history than the Irish) ;* those skilled in medicine went to the hospital—the butler, baker, cook, attendants, and messengers went to their respective duties—those skilled in the various trades went to their workshops—some went to fish in the rivers,

* Cogan.

others to bring the cattle, sheep, and pigs to the fields—some to yoke the horses to the ploughs and carts—some went to the flower-garden, some to the kitchen-garden, others to plough and harrow, and thrash, and winnow, and many to other agricultural pursuits—all were incessantly employed from morning till night, interrupted only at intervals by the chiming notes from the cloigteach, calling them to the eaglais (church), to recite the canonical hours, or to the proinnteach to partake of their frugal meal, and to return with renewed strength to their respective occupations.

However, the recitation of Prime, Tierce, Sext, and None did not take long, containing only three psalms each; consequently they were not over-loaded with long offices, and, though bound to work at their various callings every day, except Sundays and holidays, they had all, without exception, leisure enough for study and attending the instructions of their brethren, the professors and lecturers, and were also allowed a certain time for reading; for, owing to their great numbers and the admirable order and discipline established by their holy founder, all this could be accomplished without any inconvenience, loss, or disorder; all the various branches of industry being pursued for a certain number of hours each day, and every department kept in the strictest order and continually improved; for the holy abbot ever active, ever on the alert, visited in turn everybody and everything under his sway.

Now he would glide from one workshop to another, instructing, consoling, and encouraging the artificers: again he would flit through the fields and mix among the labourers, gardeners, and shepherds; next he would be in the hospital consulting with the physicians, or supporting, by his exhortations and sympathy, the sufferers, going from bedside to bedside in turn, shaping his words to the peculiar circumstances of each; he was infirm with the infirm, wept with those that weep, was all things to all men.

His presence each day was eagerly looked forward to by the patients; his very appearance was in itself a consolation; he healed their souls, and in many instances he was known to heal their bodies also, so as sometimes to astonish the physicians, who, though holy monks themselves, were not equal in sanctity to their revered abbot.

He would next be amongst his pupils and their teachers in the school, reading-rooms, and lecture-halls, teaching, reading, and lecturing on many subjects, and expounding the Holy Scriptures.

This latter occupation took up the greater part of his time, and so great was the fame of his learning, both sacred and profane, that he was known by the title of Reader to the Saints of Eire (Ireland), partly from being invited by several saints, male and female (among the latter St. Brigid), to instruct their communities, and partly from the great number of saints who, during many years issued from his schools, to be in turn founders of other monasteries, famous as his own.

Then he would visit the leabharagan, or he would sit in his own humble house reading or writing, or sometimes listening to his minister reading to him, as on the occasion when Aristophanes was first introduced to him.

But having founded other monasteries as Inisfallen and Achonry, he was obliged sometimes to visit them, though he took care to place them under proper management. When thus leaving his principal residence at Cluain-Irared for a time, he would appoint his fer-tighis, or prior, who always assisted him when at home, to take his place when abroad.

These were times of sorrow for his community and pupils, but it only served to intensify their joy on again beholding him. He was beloved by the whole monastery, to whom he set an example of the highest Christian perfection ; he was the strictest and most fervent observer of the rules which he laid down for the guidance of his brethren.

Their fare was of a very simple kind, consisting of herbs, farinaceous substances, mixed with water, and a small allowance of biscuit.

Their meal was late in day, but although scanty and such as to render every day a sort of fast day, it was sufficient for the necessities of nature, without injuring the health or impairing the strength of the body, or preventing the monks from fulfilling their duties of praying, working, or reading.

They were not allowed to eat anything before None (three o'clock in the afternoon) on Wednesdays and Fridays throughout the year. The great fast of Lent did not begin till the Saturday previous to the first Sunday in Lent.

They abstained at all times from flesh meat, but were allowed to eat fish and eggs even in Lent. Their usual drink was milk and water.

On Sundays, however, their fare was improved, even the blessed Finian allowing himself on these and other holidays a little fish and a cup of beer or whey. On all other days throughout the year confining himself to bread, herbs, and water,* in which

* Dr. Lanigan's " Eccl. Hist."

his example was followed by many of his disciples; for though
he laid down strict rules as to diet for his brethren, and which
he inexorably enforced, except in case of sickness, yet he always
took care to set an example of greater mortification, self-denial,
and labour in his own person than any which he imposed on his
followers. This, as was to be expected, resulted in the voluntary imitation, by many of his disciples, of the virtues and
austerities of their holy founder. He was also considerate in
other respects; thus while his community slept on humble beds
with straw pallets, he laid himself down on the bare floor with a
stone for his pillow; also, in the matter of the canonical hours,
according to the office prescribed for each day, for though all
were obliged to answer promptly the summons to Matins, Lauds,
Prime, Tierce, Sext, and None, Vespers, and Complin, as well
as the three Nocturns during the night, yet they were so
arranged as to render them as easy as possible; thus a much
greater number of psalms was read in the morning than during
the night or even during the day.

Saturday night, however, was an exception, as, coming so
near to Sunday, a much greater number was read on that night
than on any other. The First Nocturn was said at night; the
second at midnight; the third at the crowing of the cocks, and
the fourth early in the morning.

Then, again, when the nights began to grow long, the
number of psalms were augmented, and so proportionally until
they reached their greatest length, and diminished as the nights
became shorter.*

On Sundays and festivals, days on which they rested from all
labour, they gave themselves up wholly to psalm-singing, prayer,
meditation, and celebrating the Divine Mysteries.†

The students, however, were allowed more latitude. They,
too, rested on Sundays and holidays. There was no school, no
studies on those days; they spent more time in the church on
those days; more time in reading the Scriptures and other
books of devotion; but they also spent a portion of the day, at
intervals, in innocent recreation, for none knew better than the
abbot Finian that old heads could not with prudence be placed
on young shoulders, and he had too much respect for those
days dedicated to God or the saints to permit them to be made
disagreeable or irksome, to appear too long, or to be in the least
degree dreaded by even one among the multitude of youths of
various nations, and divers characters and idiosyncrasies who
were committed to his charge.

* Dr. Lanigan's " Eccl. Hist."   † Ibid.

Their diet also was as generous as it could well be—everything that the monastery produced was plentifully supplied to them—beef, mutton, veal, pork, bacon, poultry, fish, vegetables, fruit, wine, and ale. Every care was taken of their health, the ablest physicians were always at hand ; in fact, they had everything needful for soul, mind, and body ; for, owing to the liberality of the kings, princes, and prime families of Eire, the monks were enabled to supply their numerous scholars (free of charge) with food, raiment, and lodging, books and education of the very highest class, embracing the whole circle of the sciences, arts, and languages; and when it is remembered how precious those MSS. then were—just a thousand years before printing was discovered, when books could only be multiplied by the incessant labour of the monks—we shall be able to appreciate the inestimable blessings which this nation conferred on the other kingdoms of Europe; for Clonard was but a type of similar institutions which already dotted the land, and which continued to increase and multipy, sending forth myriads of pupils who were destined to shed eternal lustre upon the Irish Church and nation, which at the time of which we write was already an Island of Saints and Scholars, but was destined to reach the meridian of her glory towards the close of the following century, and continued thenceforth the bright luminary of the world for many ages, until at length, first the Danish and then the English vandals casting their greedy eyes in turn upon this rich fertile little island, which was able to feed, clothe, and educate (gratis) the other nations of the earth—conceived the diabolical plan of robbing their benefactors of their natural inheritance and reducing to slavery their former masters ; for it is a remarkable fact that, next to the native Irish themselves, perhaps no nation under the sun profited so much from Irish liberality and culture as the barbarous Saxons of Britain. They thronged our shores in great numbers, and in time returned to their own country transformed from ignorant savages into civilized, educated men. Little dreamt the Irish princes and monks that the result of their generous hospitality would be the destruction, enslavement, and utter demoralisation and humiliation of their beloved Eire. Oh! that they could have forseen the hordes of Saxon and foreign vipers springing in thousands on their shores, with death-dealing weapons in their hands and hate and fury in their countenances, a murderous-looking monster with trembling frame and blood-shot eyes at their head, armed with a canting, hypocritical, cruel "bull" from an English pope, flying in all directions through this unhappy land; burning, pillaging, and razing to the ground churches, schools, and monasteries; torturing, outraging, and murdering their helpless, defenceless inmates; burning and destroying piles of books, MSS., and precious and beautiful works of art, especially such as treated on Irish history, that the name and memory of the Irish nation might be swept from off the face of the earth; the bandit English king granting away by wholesale, thousands of acres of fertile Irish provinces to his hungry, ravenous followers;* stripping the Irish chiefs and princes of their lawful inheritance, devoting them to poverty, exile, and death; reducing their country to pauperism, slavery and ignorance; making her for the space of seven hundred years the by-word and scorn of all Europe; plundering her of her riches and then despising her for her poverty; making it a crime against the laws to teach her children, and then holding them up to ridicule for their ignorance; creating crime by infamous blood-stained laws, and then defaming the fair name of a virtuous, justice-loving people. Such was the idea of civilisation at those times in the minds of the forefathers of Englishmen of the present day.

What an ungrateful return to the descendants of those who spared no labour or expense to raise the ancestors of these foreign pirates from the abyss of ignorance and barbarism in which they were engulphed, and bestow on them the inestimable blessings of knowledge and civilisation. But the ancient Irish knew nought of all this; and, unconscious of what the future would bring forth, they continued with unabated zeal their charitable labours at home and abroad,† leaving behind many monuments all over the world to prove to posterity that

---

* One of the first acts of Henry II. in carrying out his mission of converting the Irish was to grant (?) to Hugh de Lacey the entire kingdom of Meath, containing 800,000 acres, which he robbed from its lawful owners. The remainder of Ireland shared the same fate according as it fell a prey to the English.

† The Irish monks, not contented with what they could do at home, also embarked from Eire to evangelise the other nations of Europe, founding churches, monasteries, and schools, many of which remain even to this day. It has been calculated that the ancient Irish monks founded 13 monastic foundations in Scotland; 12 in England; 7 in France; 12 in Armoric Gaul; 7 in Lotharingia; 12 in Burgundy; 10 in Alsatia; 9 in Belgium; 16 in Bavaria; 6 in Italy; 15 in Rhetia, Helvetia, and Suevia, besides many in Thuringia—*Apologia*. Further, in Germany 150 Irish saints are patrons of churches, and of these 36 were martyrs; in Gaul 45 Irish saints, of whom 6 were martyrs; in Belgium 30, of whom many were martyrs; in England 44 Irish saints and patrons of churches; in Italy 13; in Norway 8; and in Iceland the same number. The number in Switzerland is not exactly known, but they were many; and a whole Canton (that of St. Gall) took its name from one of them.—*Apologia*.

Ireland is the best fitted of all other countries to be a separate independent nation—the home and inheritance of the Irish race—instead of giving, for centuries her intellect, her riches, and her blood in building up the greatness of her once dull pupil and her now most inveterate foe.

ᴀn nᴀoimᴀᴅ ᴄᴀibᴅoil.

CHAPTER IX.

ᴎeíᴄe ʟe ᴄeᴀᴄᴄ.

COMING EVENTS.

The students spent the earlier hours in close application to study, save when they answered the summons of the cloige-na-mainistire. Their hour of recreation has come, and now they pour out of the school-rooms, and lecture-halls, and library in shoals, and disperse in groups to amuse themselves as they list; some remain on the faitche and play various games, as hurling, &c.; others run down to the amhain (river), where a great number of corachs (boats) lie waiting for them, these they enter, and ride gaily on the water, or get up a boat race; others, again, roam into the neighbouring woods; some traverse the streets of Cluain-Irared, and emerge at the end of the city opening into the country at the opposite side; others dispose of themselves in the various fields belonging to the monastery, where they divert themselves in many ways.

In one field a group were preparing for a hurling match; among them was Ruadhan, who, while in the act of stooping, felt his shoulder touched by some one, and looking up, he beheld Aristophanes, who exclaimed:

"Ho, Ruadhan, I have found thee. I did not know what had become of thee. Canst thou tell me what they are doing in yonder field?—they are hauling some large objects."

Ruadhan, looking in the direction indicated, said:

"I am sure I do not know what it is all about; but I fancy I see Prince Diarmaid among them; he appears to be directing their movements."

Aristophanes—"Then thou dost not care to go over there?"

Ruadhan—"I much prefer staying here and playing hurley with these gentlemen."

Aristophanes—"Then I shall help thee, O Ruadhan."

They then commenced to play, but after the first game, Aristophanes exclaimed:

"Look, O Ruadhan, who is that elevated in the centre of a crowd of youths like a king on his throne?"

Ruadhan, laughing, "Why, I declare Prince Diarmaid is holding a mock court. He is turned from us, so we can approach without being perceived by him."

"Where has he obtained the royal outfit, even to the crown?" asked the Greek, as the two had approached sufficiently near to obtain a good view of the prince.

Ruadhan—"All are his own save the crown, and—let me see—why he must have obtained a number of gold ornaments from the goldsmith yonder, and formed them into a crown. It is not exactly like the asion or the "mionn," which our kings wear, but under the circumstances is very ingenious."

Aristophanes—"And look at the throne."

Ruadhan—"Ay, that is formed of the objects we saw them carry; the steps are trunks of trees, a small table from one of the cells; on top is an unfinished carved chair which the carpenter is making for the abbot; it is ornamented with some of Diarmaid's own jewellery, as well as some gold and jewelled ornaments procured from the same monk who lent him the materials for the crown; it is covered with one of his own scarlet mantles. Then, again, behold his court; they are so disguised in their various characters that I scarcely recognise them, but I think that is Brendan in the robes of a brehon (judge). Ninnidh in those of an ollamh (learned man), Columcille is easily recognised in the character of chief bard, and Columb Mac Crimthan is that of herald bearing the spear of state; but who is that in the hood of a filé (poet and philosopher), I cannot see his face?"

Aristophanes—"Why, that is thy friend, Bec Mac De."

Ruadhan—"Ah, indeed! Well, at all events, I believe the ten principal officers of state are complete: there are the bishops, and the high steward, and the attendants, and all the hundreds of silly boys who surround the prince, seem to think that all is reality. If King Tuathal Maelgarbh appeared upon the scene, he would soon spoil all their sport."

Aristophanes—"Who is that in the garb of a prince?"

Ruadhan—"Ah, that is Maelmordha Mac Argeadan, Diarmaid's step-brother, who is taking the part of Righdamhna."*

Aristophanes—"Look, look! O Ruadhan look at the miniature army approaching in perfect military order; they do honours to their king, and a certain number form themselves into a body guard. What are they called whom they represent?"

---

* Heir Apparent.

Ruadhan—"The Fianna Erionn.* Hark! what is that ?"

The exclamation was taken up by the crowds of young men and boys, who by this time had assembled at the scene of the improvised court. Many of them now rushing in one direction, exclaiming:

"To the river! To the river!"

The two friends ran with the rest towards the river Boinn (Boyne), but were obliged to look over the shoulders of those who had gained it before them, and were now lining its brink, cheering and clapping and welcoming with many "ceud milé failte." The cause of this excitement was soon known to all. It was nothing less than about a dozen boats' full of woe-begone looking Saxons who had come to seek admission to the schools of Cluain-Irared.

The manner of their reception seemed to reassure them, and with the assistance of their new friends, they were soon landed on the monastic grounds; but one of the mischief-loving youths, from which even Cluain-Irared was not free, bethought him just at the last moment of turning this unexpected event to account ; so running with all his might towards where the prince and his mock court were stationed, and knowing that though they must have heard the noise, they were too far away to learn its exact nature, he forced his way through the crowd surrounding the "throne," and falling on one knee before Diarmaid, exclaimed, with mock gravity, and panting for breath :

"O King! a Saxon invasion! Quick, quick to arms. Send, O King, thy redoutable Fenians against——Quick, oh, quick ! they come! they come!"

Though this event was then unexpected, it was by no means unusual, so Diarmaid never for a moment lost his presence of mind, and rising up from his seat, and waiving his hand with an air of command, he cried :

"To arms! to arms! O Fianna Erionn, go, hurl the invaders from our shores. Go, officers, order your men into battle aray. I will myself lead you to victory. Ho! there, my armour."

By this time the miniature regiments above-named commenced to march in order of battle, facing towards the river.

They had only gone a few steps, however, when they saw the "invaders" approaching. On beholding them the "army" recoiled in disgust, their chief officer approached Diarmaid just as he was about to descend from his throne to head them, and cried out:

* Fenians of Ireland.

" O King, thou hast been deceived; no army threatens thy throne.   Sendest thou thy brave Fenian army against a horde of unarmed, defenceless, and half-naked savages ?"

Diarmaid—" Oh ! horror, horror !   Sayest thou truly, O——. Back, back, O Fianna Erionn.   Let the Saxons approach our throne in peace."

The bewildered Saxons approached, scarcely knowing what they were doing, and looking in wonderment at all they saw.

Diarmaid again seating himself on the "throne," interrogated them :

" Whence came ye, O strangers, and whither ?"

" We came, O King," answered one who acted as spokesman, " from Britain, our native land, to seek instruction in the famous schools of Cluain-Irared."

Diarmaid—" Then ye came not as spies or enemies of our Irish throne ?"

The Saxon—" I assure thee, O King, we have not come, nor were we sent for such purpose; but if we knew that the great King of Eire were here we should have delayed our voyage."

Diarmaid—" In what, then, have the Kings of Eire ever harmed thee, or those of thy nation ?"

The Saxon—" In nought have they ever done us anything but good."

Diarmaid—" What way didst ye come ?"

The Saxon—" We landed at Inver Colpa* and sailed up the Boinn (Boyne)."

By this time the prince realised the absurdity of the situation and could stand no more.   He remembered that they were foreigners, and also their pitiable plight, as well as the suddenness of their appearance on the scene, and at once his better nature mastered his youthful folly.

The other students arrived at the same conclusion in a moment, and one of the Saxons who was some years at the college, said to his young countrymen :

" You fools, do you not see that it is all a play ?"

The young strangers now began to realise that it was. They brightened up, and one of them said :

" Oh, what a jolly place we have come to."

" I thought it was all a reality," said another.

" So did I," said a third; " but I was not afraid, for I knew we were in the monastery ground."

" We shall have fine sport," said a fourth.

* Drogheda Bay.

And so they went on talking.

Diarmaid—"Hark ye, guards, escort with honour these Saxon knowledge-seekers to the presence of our trusty liege, the abbot Finian."

"So I am thy trusty liege already, O Dairmaid."

Diarmaid turned round, and to his shame and dread beheld the abbot himself, and by his side the guest-master; but another look convinced him that all was right, as he saw the good-natured, amused expression with which Finian and his companion viewed Diarmaid and his surroundings. However the prince stammered :

"Oh, father abbot, I did not know that thou wert there, and we were only playing."

Finian—"I am aware of all that, my son, and am not displeased; but had the joke been carried any further with the foreigners, I should have been very angry. God bless you all."

Then turning to the young strangers he said :

"Come with us, my children; we have come out specially to meet ye, having heard of your arrival."

Finian, the guest-master, and the newly-arrived Saxons then proceeded towards the monastery, the latter to be bathed, rehabilitated, and refreshed.

The students resumed their amusements, Diarmaid continued to play the king; Maelmordha, the Righdamhna, Columcille discoursed sweet music on the harp, the heralds blew the trumpets, or flourished the spear; the ollamhs tried to look as wise as they could, and the abbots, brehons, stewards, Fenians, and others all played their parts, and thus displayed wonderful powers of imitation.

Some of the youths only looked on, while others again paid no attention, but amused themselves at running, leaping, hurling, or otherwise, as they thought fit.

Many chatted in groups, or walked about. Among the latter were Ruadhan and Aristophanes, arm in arm, chatting on some subject, about which the new arrivals had evidently something to do, for the Greek is heard exclaiming :

"How can it be possible, O Ruadhan, that those wild, uncared-for looking foreigners are the countrymen of the Saxons of Cluain-Irared, who appear to be as civilised as the natives of more advanced countries, even of those of Greece or Eire ?"

Ruadhan—"Oh, there is nothing easier of explanation. The Saxons here were just as barbarous-looking on their arrival as those we have just received, and many of them even more so; they were steeped in paganism; they knew absolutely

nothing, had no idea of the commonest requirements of civilised
beings; but that condition of things could not long continue
in any part of Eire, and certainly not in Cluain-Irared. They
almost invariably commence at the very lowest place in the
school, but rise by degrees to honourable distinction. Indeed
the monks bestow more care and time on them than on any of
the other students, native or foreign, owing to their near neighbourhood to our own isle, and their extremely backward condition, socially, mentally, and spiritually."

Aristophanes—"And yet, they are fair of aspect, and of
goodly presence; it is, indeed, a pity that they are so low in the
scale of humanity, but perhaps a bright future is in store for
them."

Ruadhan—"I sincerely hope so. Thou seest what can be
made here of even the most unpromising materials. In a short
time thou wilt not know the young savages who arrived here
to-day."

Aristophanes—"I can already guess at the transformation
which will be effected, if I can judge of their countrymen who
preceded them. But of this I am convinced, that whatever
glory, prosperity, or greatness may be in store for Britain, she
will owe it all to the charity, learning, and generous hospitality
of the Irish Nation."

Ruadhan—"I trust that when Eire shall have finished her
glorious work in regard to Britain, the two countries shall continue in mutual friendship for ages yet to come, and our kings
find faithful allies and friendly neighbours in the future
sovereigns of Britain."

Aristophanes—"I hope so; but it is hard to say what the
future may bring forth. I trust the future inhabitants of Eire
will never have cause to regret the beneficence and hospitality
of their ancestors. But there is one thing which has just
occurred to me, O Ruadhan; while yet in Greece I have heard
that Eire was full of Saxon slaves. Is that a fact? and if so, is
it any cause of offence to the neighbouring island?"

Ruadhan—"It is a fact; but, as for it being a cause of
offence, it is all the other way. Saxon parents sell their sons
and their daughters to our people, and they think themselves
the gainers by the bargain. Besides, we are not the only pur-
chasers; for Saxon children are in every market in Europe;
though they are the most numerous in this country."

Aristophanes—"I suppose they could not be done without?"

Ruadhan—"Never; for notwithstanding the subjugation of
the Aitheach Tuatha (Attacotic) race, Eire herself could not

supply the fortieth part of the numbers required for servitude. Foreign slaves we must get, and none so ready as the Saxons to supply our demands; besides, they are better off under Irish masters and mistresses than under Saxon parents. They are converted to Christianity, and have the benefit of education and civilised life, moreover they are kindly treated, and made capable of rising themselves if they desire it."

This dialogue was carried on while the two friends walked a considerable distance round the grounds of the college. They had returned within sight of the field where Diarmaid was playing the king, when Ruadhan said :

"The 'court' is not broken up yet."

"What is the prince doing now ? He is standing on the platform under his royal chair, and appears to be making a speech."

"Oh, yes; he is addressing his council on some affair of State, I have no doubt."

"Airing his oratorical powers ?"

"Yes ; and showing in every way how fit he is to reign."

"I know nought of his rights or his pretensions, but I affirm, O Ruadhan, that he looks every inch a king, notwithstanding his youth and the mockery of his present situation."

"No doubt he has a regal presence, and it is enhanced by his present rich attire and graceful gestures."

"Dost know, O Ruadhan, he reminds me of a tradition of Greece, which tells us of an Irish chief named Abaris, who was sent there as ambassador from this country many hundred years before Christ, and was present at a Council of Athens, having his majestic figure set off to great advantage with the most costly dress, and his language, wisdom, and prudence as a statesman, orator, and courtier held forth for the admiration of all the Grecian States."

"Yes; Abaris upheld the honour of his country abroad; and since Prince Diarmaid is so like him, it would be well if he were sent as ambassador somewhere, just to keep him out of mischief at home."

"Look at him now. His chief brehon, Brendan, is writing something on parchment at his dictation."

"No doubt it is as important as the rest of the business; now he is sending off a courier at full speed."

"And now the courier is returning with Ciaran Mac an t-Saoir."

"Ciaran Mac an t-Saoir ! Can it be ? Is he going to take part in the foolery too ? Why, see; he is actually going to do homage to Diarmaid !"

"Are they always good friends ?"

"Oh, yes ; Diarmaid and Ciaran are always on the best of terms. Now the important document is completed, and Brendan hands it to Diarmaid, who looks at it and hands it back to Brendan who begins to read it aloud. I would we were a little nearer that we might hear. Now it is eagerly discussed by all three. Diarmaid orders Brendan to make some alterations. These are made, and again Diarmaid and Ciaran converse."

"Brendan is now reading the parchment again and it appears to be satisfactory, as he once more hands it to the Prince ; and look, Ruadhan, he now invites some of the members of his court to sign it. Now he signs it himself and presents it with all due formality to Ciaran. Canst thou guess what it is all about."

"Not I. I am sure it is all nonsense, like the rest of the performance. Diarmaid likes to rehearse the part of a king, for which honour he has a great ambition, and which makes him forget the allegiance due to his lawful sovereign."

"He fancies himself the lawful sovereign, I understand ?"

"But his fancy is treason and sedition."

"There appears to be a difference of opinion on the subject among thy countrymen, O Ruadhan. I already know that many of the students here, and, no doubt, all of those now surrounding the Prince, would call King Tuathal Maelgarbh an usurper."

"No doubt Diarmaid has a strong party, not in Midhe only but throughout all Eire. The native students here represent the opinions of their parents and friends."

"Dost thou not fear that all these mutterings may be like those of the volcano of which any day may witness the eruption."

"It will not be Diarmaid's fault if our beloved Banba* is not some day transformed into a political Etna or Vesuvius ; but forewarned is forearmed, and King Tuathal, though aware of his pretensions, so little fears him that he will offer no opposition to his entrance into Mur Ollamhain."

"Where or what is Mur Ollamhain ?

"It is the chief university in the kingdom."

"A college like this ?"

"A college, but not like this ; for though both are educational institutions, it is scarcely possible to imagine any two institutions so dissimilar. This College of Cluain-Irared and other similar colleges throughout Eire are the result of the introduction of Christianity."

* A poetical name for Ireland.

"Then how comes it that they are so different from and superior to similar institutions in other countries where Christianity prevails ?"

" Well, that is because Christianity, besides converting the people of those countries from paganism had to commence the task of their education, and a difficult, tedious task it necessarily was ; while the Gospel found its immediate universal reception in Erin, favoured by the splendid literary attainments and time-honoured intellectual life of its people."

" Then what meanest thou, O Ruadhan, by saying that these Christian colleges are the result of the introduction of Christianity ?"

" Well, I will explain. For many hundred years before Christ, colleges and schools, wherein were taught all the known arts and sciences, abounded throughout all Eire ; but the chief and principal of all these was the famous Mur Ollamhain of Teamhair. These pagan colleges continued down to the time of St. Patrick, and still continue in their modified and Christianised form ; but it was found that they could not, without entirely destroying their character, undertake the additional duties inseparable from the changed order of things, so the holy men who sprung up in such numbers after the arrival of St. Patrick conceived the plan of founding such institutions as this, thus blending religion and nationality in happy unison. In fact when Christianity crossed the sea and became wedded to Irish literature, the result proved beneficial to both, for while Christianity elevated and ennobled the intellect of Eire, the latter, in turn, enriched with the brilliancy of its genius, and showed to the world, through the mirror of mental illumination, the amiable qualities and heaven-born attributes of its fondly cherished partner ; and following the natural order of things, the Christian colleges of Eire bear an unmistakable family likeness to both parents."

" I understand the matter perfectly now. It explains what was before to me quite incomprehensible. But there is another thing that I do not quite understand. Thou hast said that the king had so little fear of Diarmaid that he would not oppose his entrance into Mur Ollamhain, the chief university. Now what wants Diarmaid there ? Is not the splendid curriculum of Cluain-Irared sufficient for even a prince who aspires to a throne ?"

" As I said before, there is not a particle of similarity between the monastery and the university. Prince Diarmaid, be his pretensions ever so just, his rights so indisputable, and his

6

qualifications ever so many, or so brilliant, could never ascend the throne of Eire until he had taken out his degrees at Mur Ollamhain, and that law is enforced, not only on candidates for the Crown, but for those of every other office of trust, emolument, or dignity in the kingdom. Diarmaid has been to Mur Ollamhain already, having entered it at the age of seven years, and gone through the minor degrees in the various branches taught there during seven years more; but he left it, as is now the custom, to spend some time in a Christian monastic school, and he chose Cluain-Irared, only to return to complete his scholastic course in the prime university of the nation."

"And when does Diarmaid leave Cluain-Irared for Teamhair?" asked Aristophanes.

"Eight months hence, and on his arrival at Teamhair he will first visit the royal palace to pay his respects to his sovereign and rival, King Tuathal Maelgarbh."

"And has he no fear of the King?"

"None; nor need he, so long as he conducts himself; but I fear——ho! Brendan, come hither, is the court broken up? What a solemn-looking brehon thou wouldst make. I had thought thou wouldst choose the Church as thy portion."

"So I intend, O Ruadhan, as well as thyself, answered Brendan; "but that is no reason why I should not humour the prince. We might as well play at that as at anything else."

"What didst thou write upon the parchment which Prince Diarmaid gave to Ciaran Mac an t-Saoir?"

"Oh, that was no play. It was the only real thing in the whole game."

"What meanest thou, O Brendan?"

"I mean, O Ruadhan, that Prince Diarmaid has granted to Ciaran Mac an t-Saoir, as a free gift for ever, for the purpose of monastic foundations, the Isle of Inis Aingin* and the lands of Artibra,† which thou knowest, O Ruadhan, form part of Diarmaid's own private patrimony."

"I know; but has he really granted those places to Ciaran?"

"Really and truly."

"But of what avail is a grant made in such a manner?"

"Oh, it will be all right. It will be duly witnessed and legally transferred to Ciaran."

"Well, after all, I am not surprised. Ciaran and Diarmaid are old and fast friends, and the prince heard the prophecy of Finian anent the future greatness of the son of the Saoir."

* In the river Shannon.   † In King's County, now Clonmacnoise.

" Here," said the Greek, " cometh Columcille, with his harp, one of the witnesses of this never-to-be-forgotten grant."

"Oh," said Columb, coming up, " that was only for the sake of the play. It will be properly witnessed before it is duly tendered to Ciaran. I see Brendan has been telling ye all about it."

" It looks," said Brendan, " as if Prince Diarmaid meant to befriend the Church."

" If ever he becomes Ardrigh he will, I have no doubt, amply endow monastic establishments."

" Then thou thinkest, O Columb, that it is not merely personal friendship for Ciaran to which Eire will owe the new colleges that Ciaran will, no doubt, establish ?"

" I think not, O Ruadhan ; though Diarmaid loves Ciaran well, he loves learning, and the welfare of his country better."

" Yet thou quarrelest with him sometimes."

"I do. Our tempers are both very hot ; but we make it up again ; and I say what I believe, O Ruadhan."

"And what thou sayest must be true, O Columb. Here, O Aristophanes, is a young gentleman who is wiser than his master."

" Indeed ! In what then doth his wisdom excel that of Finian ?"

"When first he arrived here, after having passed under Finian of Magh Bhile (Moville), and Gemmen of Laighen (Leinster), our abbot directed him to build his cell at the door of the monastery. Well, Columb obeyed the first part of the order, but failed to the second ; so that he built his cell which thou seest yonder, not at the door, but a long way from it."

" Why, that was disobedience."

" Nay, Aristophanes," said Columb, " I meant it not as such, but I knew, no matter how, that the college would extend."

" Ay," said Ruadhan, " when the abbot saw where his docile pupil had built his cell, he asked to know the reason of its not having been built at the door, to which our friend here replied : ' True, O Finian, it is not, but the door will be at this place hereafter.' "

"Well," said Columcille, " I am not so very long here, and behold already my words have been in part fulfilled ; for since I built my cell the scholars have increased, and behold there the new lecture-hall which it was found necessary to build, and as it happened that that part of the college, nearest to my cell, was the most suitable place for it, it filled a considerable space between the other monastic buildings and my cell, which even now is nearer to the door than when I built it."

"It is singular ; but still, it is not at the door."

" But it will be, O Ruadhan."

Saying which, Columcille and Brendan tripped off to the school-rooms, whither all the students were now repairing, their playtime being up.

Ruadhan and Aristophanes followed, remarking on the singularity of the prediction of Columcille respecting the college, Ruadhan repeating to his companion many other curious instances of early indications of future greatness in the young "Dove of the Cells."

Again the school-rooms and lecture-halls were thronged with the students, who poured in from the fields, the rivers, and the surrounding country. Lessons and studies were resumed until again interrupted for purposes of prayer, refreshment, or rest, as the case might be. And even when the library, lecture-halls, and schools were deserted at close of day, the scholars, after they had retired to their cells, continued to study their lessons by the light of a large thick candle of twisted rushes dipped in oil, which stood in the candlestick on the little round table which was placed in the centre of each cell, and they studied diligently until time for retiring to rest ; and at early dawn again resumed the rehearsal of their lessons in the intervals between church hours and breakfast, until the opening of the school.

And thus sped day by day in prayer and study, work and play, in the college of Cluain-Irared; and thus were prepared for the struggles and duties of life, in Church or State, the multitude of youths, native and foreign, of every grade and condition who daily thronged its halls and there drank deeply of the Pierian springs of Classic Lore, and of the divine fountains of Eternal Wisdom.

END OF PART I.

an oara cuio
Part II.

ceamain na Ríg,
TARA OF THE KINGS.

an ceuo caibioil.
CHAPTER I.
Ceamaiṁ na Ríg.
TARA OF THE KINGS.

THE ancient kingdom of Meath comprised, besides the present county of Meath, that of Westmeath, also parts of Dublin, of Kildare, and King's County, parts of Cavan and Louth, and the greater part of Longford. The capital of this Righeacht Midhe (kingdom of Meath) was Teamhair or Tara, the royal seat of the supreme monarch of all Ireland. The Hill of Tara was situated in the centre of the regal city; and this in turn formed part of Magh Breagh,* or the Magnificent Plain, a portion of the Meathian kingdom comprising the greater part of the present counties of Dublin and Meath.

The " five great roads to Teamhair's royal seat" were the great highways of intercommunication between Tara and the more remote parts of the kingdom of Eire (Ireland). The northern road was called the Slighe Miodh-Luachra; the western road, Slighe Asal; the eastern road, Slighe Cualann; the southern road, Slighe Dala; and the largest of all, the Great Western Road, or Slighe Mór, defined by the Eascair Riada, a line of gravel hills extending from Dublin and Kildare to Galway Bay and to Mayo, and which, calculating roughly, divided Ireland into two almost equal parts. At these five approaches to the palace, 1,050 soldiers mounted guard every day, to point out to the public, with great dignity, where the monarch resided. These great roads, which were constructed in the second century, were paved with large blocks of stone, somewhat resembling the old Roman roads. Intersecting these, in all

* Moy Bray.

directions, were a great number of inferior roads of various
sizes, all of which were kept clean and in repair, according to
law.   The Cathair Teamhrach (City of Tara) was composed of
seven duns or enclosures, each containing 140 houses and 700
warriors—that is to say, nearly a thousand houses and 4,900
warriors in the whole city.   Then the seven bailes, or townlands, of Tara contained altogether grazing land for 2,100 cows,
besides horses, sheep, swine, and deer, and the ploughing of
forty-nine ploughs for the year.   Poultry, as well as bees,
abounded.   The houses of the people were very varied.   Every
house of the wealthy, and even of the humbler classes, contained slaves who were, for the greater part, foreigners, and
of these the majority were natives of Britain ; but of the
general native Irish population, the poor occupied small, round
huts of mud, whitewashed outside and inside with lime, and
which were outside the city at one side.   The farmers of various
classes occupied houses according to their means.   Some were
of wicker-work, like those of Clonard, but larger, and fit for a
family.   Some were log-houses of two stories, like the Swiss
Chalet, with flat roofs.   Houses were built of " gius," or deal, of
" dair," or oak, and other kinds of wood ; they were round and
conical, or long and flat-roofed ; they were dashed, painted, or
polished, or thatched with skin or feathers ; on the inside they
were matted, stuffed with feathers, or panelled and polished.   Most
of the middle-class houses were oblong buildings, divided into
three parts by two rows of pillars which supported the roof.
The fire and candelabrum were in the central division, which
was about two-thirds of the whole length.   In the recesses
between the pillars, and in the side divisions, were the imdai,
or couches.   The furniture differed with the houses.   Those
of the more pretentious farmers and citizens were furnished
with couches, chests, tables, shelves, &c., all polished and
sometimes carved.   All houses of every class had more or
less land attached. Persons in comfortable circumstances
generally five houses each.   The biadteachs, or houses of
hospitality, were very large buildings, sometimes two hundred
feet in diameter, and having immense tracts of land attached for the free entertainment of the poor and sick,
also travellers, strangers, pilgrims, and persons of all classes,
rich and poor.   There were about 5,000 of them all over
Ireland, and about fourteen in the city of Tara.   The biadteach was generally composed of seven large buildings, including a mill.   There were many doors to the great dining-
hall, which could be opened or closed at pleasure.   There were

in the kitchen—besides coires, or chaldrons, capable of holding an entire ox and pig whole, and all other kinds of cooking utensils—great cooking machines, one of which contained thirty spits for roasting. This great accommodation was necessary, as the owners of these establishments were obliged to have always ready, for all comers, all kinds of cooked beef, mutton, veal, fish, poultry, soup, bread, fruit, milk, ale, honey, &c.

The traders and artificers were held in high esteem, some of them ranking with the highest of the gentry. Their houses and lands were in keeping with their state. There were sciathaires, or shieldmakers ; makers of all other military weapons ; leather bottlemakers, leather-satchelmakers, shoemakers, saddlers, braziers, gold and silversmiths, chariot and cartmakers ; workers in bronze, stone and wood ; turners, carpenters, manufacturers of fancy furniture ; builders of wooden houses and churches ; builders of stone houses, raths, fortresses, churches, &c. ; smiths and engravers ; dealers in feathers, skins, furs, parchments, &c. ; manufacturers of linen, wool, silk, and satin ; dyers, embroiderers, and upholsterers.

The citizens of Tara traded with the other cities of Eire, and with foreign countries. Merchants from all parts of the world were constantly traversing the streets of Tara. The seaport towns of Ireland were full of the shipping of her own and other nations, and from these various havens goods passed by road or river to Tara, and back from Tara to the coast.

There were seven degrees of nobility : they were called Flaiths or Aires ; they held various offices in the State, and each had his own court, over which he presided, except the Aire Echtai, who was the military commander of a district. The Aire Ard was the Maor, or High Steward of the king, and the Aire Forgaill was the Lord High Chancellor. Their houses were raths or duns, and were sumptuously furnished. They kept retainers, hunters and hounds, chariots,, and race-horses. The higher nobility resided in raths. The ruins of two of these raths are still to be seen—the Rath Miles, about a mile to the north of Tara Hill, and the Rath Meabhe, about a mile south-east of the hill. Besides the other officials of the Ardrigh, or High King of Ireland, which were a goodly number, there were ten principal who never left his presence. These were a prince, who was the companion and champion of the king, a brehon or judge, a bishop or priest (in pagan times a druid), a physician, a bard, a musician, a historian, and three stewards ; he had also his bodyguard, besides the attendance of a detachment of the Fenian army.

The Ardrigh and Ardrighan (supreme king and supreme queen)
with the royal household, officers and servants, resided on Tara
Hill. Drs. Petrie and Keating describe the various buildings
situated on the royal hill. The principal of these were the Teach
Miodchuarta, the House of the Conventions and of the
Banquets. The full length of this great house was seven
hundred and fifty-nine feet, and the breadth ninety feet. That
part of it called the Convention, or Banqueting Hall was three
hundred feet long, eighty feet wide, and nearly fifty feet high.
It had fourteen doors—seven to the east and seven to the west.
It was built of solid oak, the walls divided into panels, and
highly polished, and on them hung the shields and arms of the
warriors, and decorated with the horns of the elk. The cornices
and ornamentation were of iubar dearg, or red yew, quaintly
carved and well polished. The ceiling matched the walls,
being of pannelled oak, ornamented with yew likewise, and
from these beautiful polished carvings depended at intervals of
this long hall seven great brass chandeliers of the most elaborate workmanship; in the evenings these were lighted up with
myriads of wax candles. In this hall were tables and imdas, or
couches of polished oak and yew, the couches and seats stuffed
with feathers and covered with silk. Gold and silver plate
abounded, as well as vessels of glass, horn, and bronze. Oxen,
sheep, hogs, fish, poultry, fruit, wine, ale, honey, and butter
were served in immense quantities every day to one thousand guests, besides princes, orators, and men of science,
engravers of gold and silver, carvers, modellers, lawyers,
physicians, nobles, professors, and judges.

Besides this great hall, which was at once the Banqueting
and the Convention Hall, the royal residence of the monarch was
divided into several divisions. There were in it one hundred
and fifty splendid apartments capable of containing sixty
persons in each, and one hundred and fifty others of less
pretensions, and used as barrack-rooms. But the state bedchamber was the most magnificent portion of that great house.
The floor was covered with ornamental matting, the walls
draped with crimson satin, elaborately embroidered with gold
thread and silk of many colours; the windows and their
shutters beautifully carved, and having bars of gilt bronze on
the outside; the highly wrought brass chandelier was lit up at
night with many wax candles, which burned all through the
night, and were reflected in the polished ceiling, with its rich
festoons of varnished yew, as well as in the scadieres, or mirrors,
which here and there relieved the dark, rich-coloured tapestry on

which they hung. But, perhaps the state bed itself reflected most of all the light of the wax candles. It was a great, square couch, ornamented with plates of silver, and having four great posts of red bronze, with gilding of gold on their heads, and inlaid with gems of carbuncle, "so that day and night were of equal light in it." There was a plate of silver—i.e., a kind of gong in the canopy—reaching to the roof of the royal chamber. this the monarch struck with his wand whenever he wished to impose silence on his attendants. The royal couch was provided with great soft, downy feather-beds and pillows ; these were covered with linen sheets and woollen blankets, and, over all, beautifully embroidered and ornamented coverlets ; the head was to the wall, the feet towards the fire. On porphyry tables, inlaid with silver, were necessaries for the toilet, beside them hung tiagas, or ornamental leather bags, gilt and bejewelled ; in these were kept such of the jewellery and ornaments as were in ordinary use ; the rest were safely stored away in chests of bronze (ornamented like the bedposts), which adorned other parts of the chamber.

Then there was the house of the women, who fulfilled the various duties necessary in the palace. There were twenty-seven " coisteannacha," or kitchens, in which were "one hundred and fifty stout cooks ;" there were nine cisterns for washing hands and feet. The diameter of the surrounding rath was nine hundred feet square. This enclosed the Teach Miodchuarta. The Rath Na Righ was formed of two murs, or parapets, having a trench between them ; the great or external diameter of the outer walls is eight hundred and fifty-three feet, having a fosse four feet deep from the ground running between them ; it encircled the southern brow of the hill. Within the Rath Na Righ were three decra inganta, or wonderful monuments ; the first of them was the Teach Cormac, or House of Cormac, in the south-east of the rath. This house, which had been built by King Cormac Mac Art, about A.D. 210, retained his name. It was of circular form, the internal diameter every way being three hundred feet, or nearly nine hundred feet in circumference. The windows lit the house at intervals all round the building, secured on the outside, as was usually the case, with bars of ornamental bronze ; the shutters and doors were of polished and carved yew ; the walls between the windows were draped with a sort of hanging made of the wings and feathers of white and coloured birds. About the distance of sixty feet from the walls all round were pillars of polished oak, inlaid with silver ; this inner circle was about five hundred and forty feet in circumference, the spaces between the pillars being furnished with imdas, or couches, which also ran round the walls. The floor was covered with ornamental matting, on which were placed here and there large skins of various animals; on pedestals between the windows were busts and statues of famous kings, warriors, poets, statesmen, and orators; from various places in the conical roof hung chandeliers of wrought brass—the largest being in the centre; between the festoons of the ceiling were ranged mirrors, which reflected everything and everybody in the house. In the centre, right under the great chandelier, stood the most conspicuous object in the building—the throne of the Ardrigh and Ardrighan. It was composed of pure gold, magnificently wrought, and studded with emeralds: it was covered with crimson satin fringed and bordered with gold, as were also the steps and the canopy; from the latter, which, was circular, hung the craoibh ciuil, the musical branch, or branch of peace; it was a sort of crescent, having three apples, or balls of red gold, upon it; whenever the spirits of the courtiers rose too high, the monarch shook his golden branch, and immediately it produced peace and silence, and " sweeter than the world's music was the music which the apples produced." The Gal Greine, or Sun Burst—the national flag of Ireland—hung behind the sovereigns over the cathair rioghda (royal chair). This palace of Cormac continued to be used by every succeeding royal couple for all the purposes of a throne-room. The second object of interest within the Rath na Righ was the Foradh, where the people sometimes assembled. It extended three hundred feet to the west, alongside the House of Cormac. The third was the Mur Tea, which lay between the two preceding on the south side; it was sixty feet in diameter, and had been erected over the queen who gave her name to Teamhair.

There were besides three other buildings within the enclosure of the Rath na Righ—first, the Dumha na Bo, or the Mound of the Cow, forty feet in diameter; second, the Dumha na-n-giall, or Mound of the Hostages, where prisoners of war were kept, sixty-six feet in diameter; and third, the Lia Fail, or Stone of Destiny. On this stone the monarchs of Eire, both pagan and Christian, were for many ages inaugurated : it was composed of granular limestone, was about eight feet above the ground and four below it. The mill was situated on the well of Neamhnach, adjacent to the Rath na Righ. Then there was the Rath na Seannaidh, or Fort of the Synods, where great ecclesiastical meetings were held; it had two external fosses, and within two raths or mounds; the larger was one hundred and sixty feet in diameter, the smaller thirty-three feet. These synod houses were plainly-furnished buildings, having great numbers of long seats, or forms, of polished pine for the accommodation of the bishops, abbots, and clergy who met there from all parts of the kingdom for the regulation of Church affairs. Adjoining these was the church, a beautiful wooden structure, somewhat like the Church of Cluain-Irared, but more gorgeously decorated. Here it was that the royal family, officers of state, literati, and the guards, attendants, and servants in general of the Royal Hill fulfilled their religious duties.

The Rath of Laeighaire (son of Nial of the Nine Hostages) is by the side of Rath na Righ to the south. There are four principal doors in it facing the four cardinal points; it was occupied by the High Steward of Tara, and was furnished with the usual magnificence—oak and yew, silver and bronze, skins, furs, and silk.

The Tur Trean Teamhrach, or Strong Tower of Tara, was a fortress of cyclopean architecture composed of great stones without cement, but of admirable architecture and of circular form, about two hundred and eighty feet in internal circumference; the walls about twenty feet in height and fourteen feet in thickness, with a doorway leading inside. A broad, deep fosse surrounds this building on the outside; here the ammunition of war was kept, and armour of both men and horses; it was always guarded as the battlement of Tara. From the summit of this, as well as of the royal palace, floated in the breeze the Gal Greine, or Sun Burst. To the north-east was the Mur Ollamhain, or House of the Learned, in which resided the brehons, ollamhs, fillés, seanchaidhe, and other learned men. In it were the highest of the Irish law courts; the great Literary Committee for the Supervision of Letters, and the celebrated schools; the Roll of Tara, which took cognisance of all legislative enactments, and everything connected with the great Triennial Feis, or Parliament of the States of Eire, assembled at Tara; and, lastly, the Royal Gymnasium and Military Institute, in which were trained in military tactics and feats of arms the celebrated Fenian army and the other male youth of Ireland. There were similar institutions attached to the other royal courts of the provincial kingdoms, but the Mur Ollamhain of Tara was the first and chief. Beside it was the bronnteach, or hospital for the sick and wounded. Then there were for each of the provincial kings and their families a royal palace on the Hill of Tara, appropriated for their exclusive use on occasions of their visiting the capital of Eire on pleasure or business. Thus, the King of Leinster had the Long Laighneach (Long

Loynagh), or Leinster House; the King of Connaught, the Coisir-Connactach (Coshir Connaughtach), Connaught Banquet House; the King of Munster's residence was called the Long Muimneach (Long Mueenagh), or Munster House; and the King of Ulster dwelt in the Echrais Ulladh (Aghrish Ulla), or Ulster House. These four palaces were in every way fitted to receive their royal occupants. But surpassing all these buildings was the Grianan-na n-Inghin, or the Sunny Palace of the Ladies. It was here that the queens, princesses, and ladies of the court resided. It was encircled on the outside by a mound; the dun was erected within; over this was the Grianan, from which they had a full view of the surrounding country. The outer roof and walls were covered with the wings of coloured birds, wherever the multitude of " lightsome windows " with their bars of bronze did not interfere. The bedrooms were furnished as became their occupants; but the great " Sunny Chamber," common to all the ladies was the most delightful apartment of the royal eminence of Tara. Its great dimensions, elevated position, and circular form, lit as it was all round about with innumerable lightsome windows, rendered it worthy indeed of its name, besides affording to its fair occupants a most magnificent view in every direction. The beautiful variegated floor matting was hid in many places by the rich furs and skins which were laid here and there as rugs; the walls between and over the windows were thickly covered with the wings and feathers of many coloured birds: the ceiling, with those of peacocks, so arranged as to diverge from the centre in a round fan-like form, the interstices, as they widen towards the walls, filled up with such care and precision, that, while the whole ceiling was covered, it appeared as if each tail extended from the central point to the wall, widening as they diverged all round. This produced a most charming effect. From this central point hung the grand chandelier. The *imdas*, or couches of polished yew, inlaid with silver, were covered with green *sroil* (satin), embroidered with *orsnath* (or gold thread), and were scattered here and there through the apartment, and could be moved to the windows if desired. The window curtains, which hung in ample folds at each window, matched the coverings of the *imdas*. Between each of the windows hung a mirror; above or below, a painting. On small ornamental tables of jasper and porphyry, inlaid with gold, were placed vases of richly chased gold, others of carved horn, with stands and mountings of gold; these were filled with beautiful flowers from the well-kept gardens hard by, which caused a delicious scent ever to pervade the atmosphere of the Sunny Chamber; they were placed in some of the windows, in the recesses between, or dispersed through the apartment. Various other ornaments adorned other tables; among the rest were marble statuary, harps and charmers set with precious stones, backgammon-boxes, inlaid chess-boards, and many beautifully illuminated MSS. These MSS. were either the standard works of the time, in prose or verse, or were recent productions of contemporary authors, and not unfrequently the compositions of the ladies themselves, who never failed to do credit to their religious teachers in the various convents throughout the country, and notably that of St. Brigid's, of Cill-Daire (Kildare). The covers of these books were of great variety—ivory, mother-of-pearl, silver, and even some of solid gold and studded with gems.

It was in this "Sunny Chamber," the Royal "Grianan-na-n-Inghin" of Tara, that the sovereign queens and princesses of successive monarchs of Ireland basked for ages. There were numerous other buildings and monuments on Tara Hill which the late Dr. Petrie fully describes, but which are not necessary for our tale.

Such of the buildings as were called cathairs, or duns, were composed of immense blocks of stones, laid together without cement, but as evenly as glass, and of great strength. Those called raths, dumhas, murs, or mounds, were formed of fine clay, not unlike that of the ancient Germans, of which Tacitus speaks so highly, and which he describes as an earth so pure and splendid as to resemble painting. Then, those buildings called teachs, longs, &c., were of oak from the forests of Cill-Daire (Kildare) erected with no less taste and skill than the wooden architecture of ancient Greece, and, indeed, it was to this class that the Great Convention Hall, as well as the luxurious family apartments on the Druim Aobhin (Beautiful Ridge), for the most part belonged. The roofs of all the buildings were painted in many colours, and had a very beautiful effect. Towering over all waved the Gal Greine, or Sun Burst, the Irish national banner.

The beautiful flower-gardens, with the "groves of fair trees," stretched out from the Grianan. The entire group of buildings was surrounded by nine great ramparts, which completed the whole and gave a finished appearance to the "beautiful hill." In fact, from whatever side Tara was viewed, it presented a most splendid and imposing spectacle, much of which it owed to the celebrated king, Cormac Mac Art, who resigned Ardrigh of Eire in the third century, and was the most celebrated of Irish kings for munificence, learning, wisdom, and valour.

ᴀn ᴅᴀʀᴀ ᴄᴀɪbʀᴏɪʟ.

CHAPTER II.

Coṁ-ᵹʀᴀᴏᴜɪᵹᴄᴇᴏɪᴩɪᴏ.

THE RIVALS.

IT was the morning of St. John's Eve, something more than eight months after the opening of our story. The mid-summer sun shone resplendant in the heavens, as it looked down on the thriving Cathair Teamhrach, and its prosperous inhabitants, who had entered on another day's round of work and business.

The thoroughfares were already full of pedestrains, horse-men, and all kinds of chariots, cars, and waggons, when suddenly a courier on horseback appeared in their midst.

His presence did not excite any surprise, as couriers with messages for the high king frequently came from all points of the compass. The people made way for him, and his panting steed. He rode towards Druim Aoibhin (the Beautiful Hill), and having reached the outer rampart, where the sentries on guard were stationed, exclaimed:

"Ho! there, guards, a message for the Ardrigh Tuathal Maelgarbh."

" Whence comest thou?" asked one of the officers on guard.

"I bear a letter from Prince Diarmaid Mac Fergus Mac Cearbhall," answered the courier, boldly.

"Prince Diarmaid! Ah! Pass on, then; so long as 'tis not the prince himself."

"Where is the Ardrigh?"

"The Ardrigh is holding council in Teach Miodhchuarta."

At the door of Teach Miodhchuarta the courier jumped from his horse, and passing the janitors, one of whom announced him; he proceeded to the feet of the Ardrigh, who was surrounded by his Airlighe ar da cleth, chief, or highest advisers, the members of his council, and on his knee presented the sealed letter.

King Tuathal Maelbharb was rather a young man, though his head was nearly bald, which looked odd, at a time when men of all classes wore their hair long and flowing.

He was, however, good-looking and very stately, and majestic in his bearing. He was attired in triuibis, or pantaloons of tartan satin of seven colours; *assai*, or shoes of purple leather, highly ornamented and jewelled ; a vest of purple, embroidered with gold, and with gold buttons ; a long flowing cloak of emerald green, richly embroidered also with gold thread and fringe, and buttoned and clasped at the throat with the Roith Croi, or hereditary, wheel-shaped brooch of solid gold.

His sword was sheathed by his side; rings and jewels adorned his fingers. He wore on his head his diadem, and was engaged in serious conference with his council when the courier arrived.

King Tuathal having read the message, thus addressed his council :

" This letter, oh, most noble counsellors, has been sent to us by our cousin, Prionsa Diarmaid Mac Fergus Mac Cearbhall, and his brother, who crave permission to pay to us their respects, before entering Mur Ollamhain. What sayest our Airlige ar da cleth ?"

The Aire Forghaill says :

" O illustrious Ardrigh of Eire, my advice would be to forbid the palace to Prionsa Diarmaid and his brother. The designs of the prionsa on the throne are well-known, and his coming bodes no good for those politically opposed to him."

The Aire Ard—"I concur in the opinion of the Aire Forghaill ; but I would go further, and exclude him not only from the royal presence, but from Mur Ollamhain itself. If he is bent on mischief, Mur Ollamhain is sufficient for his purposes owing to its close proximity to the Royal Palace."

The Ard Brethmne*—" Thou forgettest, O Aire Ard, that there is no law to prevent the prionsa, or any other youth, however exalted, or however humble, from taking advantage of the high education obtainable in Mur Ollamhain ; on the contrary, were Prince Diarmaid, so unlike his countrymen of all ranks, as to refuse, or neglect to do so, it would be the duty of the law to enforce his attendance thereat."

The Ard Ollamh †—"The Ard Breithmne is right. The brothers must enter Mur Ollamhain ; there is no use in discussing that question any further. It only remains to be seen whether it is expedient to allow them access to the Royal presence."

The Ollamh re Seanchaide ‡—" I do not see what harm can come of it. Our illustrious monarch is in possession of the throne, and he reigns also in the hearts of the majority of the

---

* Ard Brehon (chief judge).   † Ard Ollav (chief doctor.)
‡ Doctor of History.

nation. The Prince's party are hopeless and disheartened ; and their hero, at best, is but a stripling, and has to take out his degrees at Mur Ollamhain before his claims, were they ever so just, could be fully recognised. Now, that will take some years, and there is nothing to prevent the Ardrigh from being prepared for the worst by that time, and meanwhile, should any overt act be committed by Diarmaid, his brother, or any of his followers, or any seditious language made use of, the law gives power to the Ardrigh, or his chancellor to order the arrest, or the expulsion of the offender, even from Mur Ollamhain."

The Aire Tuisi*—" I agree with the Ollamh re Seanchaidhe, but I cannot help wishing that the law gave more power to the ard-righ in such emergencies. I would that such dangerous personages could be excluded altogether from the Kingdom of Midhe."

The Ard-righ—" I heartily wish so, too ; but there is no time now for idle speculation as to what might, or ought to be ; we have only to deal with things as we find them ; and while we are trying to discover what we ought to do, the subject of our discussions and our fears is on the way to our palace."

The Aire Tuisi—" When, O King, is the Prince to arrive ?"

The Ard-righ—" He may be here at any moment."

The Aire Forgaill—" What! so soon ? He asks a favour, and gives thee scant time, O King, to refuse it. I like not—but what is that ?"

At this moment an officer of the guards entered with the information that Prince Diarmaid, his half brother, and suite, were at the gates, but were not permitted to pass them. What was to be done ?

Ard-righ—" Admit the two princes to our presence, and set an additional guard without, and, see, let the suite be dismissed."

The officer bowed, saluted, and then disappeared.

In a moment afterwards horses were heard galloping up to the Teach Miodhchuarta, where they suddenly stopped. Their riders dismounted, threw their bridles to the royal grooms who were at once in attendance, and entered between two officers of the household.

Though only half brothers, they had a remarkable resemblance to each other, displaying the same fair complexions, glowing with health, and considerably heightened by their late ride ; the same large brown eyes, the same intellectual expression, the same nut-brown silky hair, falling in ringlets over their

* A military commander.

well-formed shoulders; the same graceful presence, and mutually affectionate demeanour towards each other, which never failed to strike even the most casual observer.

They were dressed alike. Triuibis of vivid yellow, embroidered *assai* of same colour, vests of green silk, embroidered with gold thread and buttons ; the mantles of royal purple, bordered with white feathers, and clasped at the throat with brooch of gold ; they held in their hands their *barreads*, or caps of black satin, bordered with small white feathers.

Approaching the throne, which was situated in the centre of the great hall, the royal princes saluted the monarch, who exclaimed :

"Welcome to Teamhair, oh, noble youths. No doubt your arrival here is due to the most laudable purposes—the desire to become masters of the whole curriculum of Mur Ollamhain ?"

"None other, O King," replied Diarmaid.

"Thy courier, doubtless, delayed on his journey, else thou wouldst not have followed so soon on thy letter ?"

"Nay, O High King, our courier lost not a moment ; but I conceal not the fact that we so timed the despatch as to leave the least possible time for deliberation.

"Thou art candid, O Diarmaid."

"I deprecate thy displeasure, O Ardrigh ; but I feared a refusal."

"We can understand thy fears, O Diarmaid. There is just cause for them, and for which thou thyself art to blame ; and we would excuse thy haste had we even time to consult with the partner of our secret thoughts."

"It the partner of thy thoughts and of thy throne, O King, have aught to fear, it will not be the fault of Finian Mac Fintan, the bishop and abbot of Cluain-Irared."

"Ah ! How fareth it with the blessed Finian ?"

"Our late master is well, and commends himself to the royal couple who sway the sceptre of Eire."

"May we hope that, coming as you do from under the guidance of so learned and holy a master, you will accept accomplished facts and refrain from political agitation, which can only result in misfortune and misery for our dear country ?"

"The abbot Finian has not allowed us to escape without a long lecture concerning our duty to those among whom, for some time to come, our lot will be cast ; but I confess that part, at least, of the advice was very unwelcome, for my claims are undisputed ; but as I have been unfortunate, owing to my tender

7

age at the time of thy accession, O King, I am convinced that it is next to useless to press my claims any further."

"That is sensibly spoken, O Diarmaid. Nobody blames thee for wishing that the throne of thine ancestors had come to thee. It is but natural that it should be so. If thou hadst had no claims at all, thou shouldst have no trouble in coming here, and we no fears. As it is, heaven has recognised our senior claims."

"The Bishop Finian has also impressed that upon me, and many other things as well. Disagreeable as some of his words were, I know at least that he spoke with a conscientious regard to what he believed to be his duty, and he has always been kind and forbearing, notwithstanding that I have ever been the blackest of his black sheep."

"Candidly spoken again, O Diarmaid. And thou, O Mael-mordha, wert thou another black sheep?"

"Undoubtedly I was, O King," replied the younger prince.

"My brother's greatest crime, before some of the students of Cluain-Irared, has ever been his love for and devotion to my-self," protested Diarmaid.

"Well, well," said the Ardrigh, "before ye have entered on the books of Mur Ollamhain, ye shall have a little grouse shooting and boar hunting, and there will be a reception in your honour at Rath na Righ in a few days. For the present the steward shall attend to your refreshment, and we shall expect ye to sup with us this evening."

The two princes bowed, and Diarmaid said :

"We desire to pay our respects to the Ardrighan."*

"The Ardrighan is in the grianan, and ye shall there find her, when the steward has attended to ye."

The princes again bowed, and attended by the steward and two officers of state, backed out of the royal presence, and leaving the Ardrigh and the Airlighe ar de cleth to resume the business which had occupied them previous to the receipt of Diarmaid's letter, the latter and his brother were attended to by the steward and his waiters, after which the two young princes proceeded to the royal grianan, and entering the dun, mounted the staircase, announced by an usher.

Before entering the dun they heard distinctly the sweet strains of a cruit (harp), to which a female voice of surpassing richness accompanied a soul-stirring Fenian song.

But their sounds had died away as they reached the foot of the staircase, and on approaching the top they heard another

*High Queen (pronounced Awrd Reean.)

voice reading, which ceased immediately on the usher announcing the visitors.

On entering the regal apartment the quick eyes of the royal youths took in at a glance the situation.

The Ardrighan, who was surrounded by her ladies of honour, welcomed them with a gracious smile, but beneath which, the youths were not slow to perceive an ill-concealed expression of alarm and bewilderment on the fair, pale features.   She was attired in a long, flowing robe of bright green satin, richly embroidered with *ór snath*, or gold thread ; around her waist was a girset, or sash, also of satin but of cross-bar pattern, embracing the whole seven colours allowed only to the occupants of a throne. A scarf of white satin, bordered with beautiful small green feathers, was thrown over her shoulders ; on her feet were sandals of golden net work ; her wrists were clasped with dorn-nascs, or bracelets of gold, set with emeralds ; on her fingers were golden ornasc, or finger rings ; round her neck was a fiam, or chain of gold.

Au nasc, or earrings, depended from her ears ; round her head, a little back from the forehead, was a niamh land, or radiant leaf of gold.   It was a splendid flat crescent of gold, broad and high immediately over the head, and diminishing gradually as it came behind the ears, until it met in two points under the hair behind the neck, where it was fastened, and kept in proper place the wavy flaxen hair.

This beautiful ornament, especially in such an advantageous place as the grianan, which was nearly all window, gave the impression of a glorious nimbo, surrounding the head of a saint. It also added to the height of the already queenly figure.

Her ladies were attired in the same fashion, and with scarcely less magnificence for the most part, besides differing in the arrangement of colours.

They were seated on the many imdas which were scattered through they sunny chamber, and were variously occupied— some reading, some writing either compositions or correspondence, some engaged in embroidery, &c.

The high queen having introduced to them the two brothers, the latter perceived that they were as disturbed and anxious-looking as their mistress.

The fact was they had all seen what was going on from the windows.   They had first witnessed the arrival of the courier, but did not much mind that, but the arrival of Diarmaid and his party sent through them a thrill of astonishment and all but consternation.

The Ardrighan was on the point of descending from the grianan to seek the Ardrigh in Teach Miodchuarta, but one of her mna-uasala (ladies), represented to her that it was now too late, and that it was best to put a good face on the matter, as most probably the princes would visit the grianan as soon as they had seen the Ardrigh.

The Ardrighan felt that this was, under the circumstances, the best course to take, and complied, awaiting results.

Now that the youthful, though dreaded, rival of the Ardrigh was here to account for himself, the noble ladies listened intently to the conversation which passed between the Ardrighan and Diarmaid, and which was in substance, the same as that which he had already held with the Ardrigh.

All the while Maelmordha, who said little, was engaged in marking its effect on the fair listeners, as he had previously done with their fathers, brothers, and husbands in Teach Miodchuarta, while his brother held converse with the Ardrigh; for Maelmordha was a good reader of the human countenance, and often learned more therefrom than could ever be learned from letters or conversations.

By the time the explanations came to a close, Maelmordha flattered himself that he knew exactly the diverse feelings it excited in the breasts of the listeners; diverse, indeed, he thought, as the colours which they wore; for though all felt it their duty to be loyal to the powers that were, yet the strife of party politics and the plausible arguments frequently dinned into their ears by the princes' party, together with his acknowledged descent from their former kings, added to which his handsome appearance, majestic presence, and focail samhasach, or polite address and gentle conversation—all conspired to make them wish he had not come, for they felt it difficult to reconcile these feelings with the scruples of their consciences; but the noble maidens felt most guilty of all, for the last-named qualifications of the prince and of his brother drove politics completely out of their minds.

All this, and much more, did Maelmordha read, or fancy he read, in the fair faces before him, and this he managed without leaving on their minds any impression of rudeness or offensiveness. In fact, he would have sacrificed any information his talent could give him, rather than give the least offence or cause the slightest confusion to any, even the lowliest of the opposite sex.

When the Ardrighan was satisfied, or appeared so, she changed the subject to lighter and more agreeable topics, in which the ladies joined.

It was now that the brothers appeared to most advantage; and after every available subject was discussed, the cruit and ceis* were taken from their places where they formed beautiful ornaments, and by the desire of the Ardrighan several songs were sung to those charming accompaniments.

Diarmaid and Maelmordha contributed their share to this delightful amusement, and such was the result, that the maids of honour felt convinced that the two princes were paragons of human perfection.

After a game or two at fitcheal, or chess, for which the gem-set chessboards, with their mother-of-pearl men, were put into requisition, the two brothers took leave of the high queen and her brilliant band of ladies, left the grianan, and, ordering their horses, they set out for a ride through the city and part of the Magnificent Plain.

The animals which they rode were two beautiful black young steeds of high mettle. The saddles were embossed and ornamented, with golden bridles. On the necks of the steeds were mael lands of silver, with little bells of gold.

On emerging from the precincts of the palace, the officers and servants of which were scattered about in groups, full of curiosity and amazement, the two brothers were not a little surprised to find themselves objects of curiosity and speculation to the citizens as well.

This they were not prepared for so soon; but sudden as their arrival was, and in a city, too, where distinguished strangers were not an uncommon sight, they were at once recognised, and the news spread like wild-fire all over Magh Breagh.

The consequence was that there was nearly a cessation of business when it was rumoured that the princes were coming; every one ran to the doors of their houses; those who could, filled the streets.

All classes were full of the importance of the event which had so suddenly come upon them. They chatted in groups, friends and foes alike, though with very different feelings.

The princes rode on, watching the effect of their presence on the people, returning salutes where they met them, and appearing oblivious of manifestations of a contrary nature.

The well-wishers of the royal youths, however, evinced great prudence, and refrained from demonstrations which might bring themselves or the objects of their regard into trouble; for Tuathal's Fenians were everywhere, and not likely to over-

* The harp and the charmer.

look any disloyal demonstrations from whatsoever point it proceeded.

Thus, Diarmaid and his brother rode on until they left the city behind, and with it the hurry and bustle of commerce and trade, and emerged into the country parts.

The chariots, cars, and waggons were exchanged for the hunting and shooting parties, whom they now frequently met, and whom, for the most, they contrived to avoid or pass unnoticed, leaving the sporting gentlemen to make the discovery only on their arrival at their respective homes.

They were not, however, always so successful, for many of all classes recognised them everywhere they went; and not the least demonstrative on those occasions were the groups who here and there were engaged in constructing the heaps which were to compose the bonfires in the evening.

Aɴ cReAꝶ ċAɪbɪ́oɪl.

CHAPTER III.

Aɴ c-Aᴘꝺ Ríꝼ Aꝼuᴘ Aɴ Aᴘꝺ Ríꝼáɴ.

THE HIGH KING AND THE HIGH QUEEN.

MEANWHILE, though the royal pair saw each other frequently during the day, there was no opportunity for any conversation between them until coming towards evening, when the Ardrighan was again in the grianan, having only a few of her ladies about her, the Ardrigh found leisure to visit her.

On his entrance the Ardrighan advanced to meet him, taking care to lead him to that part furthest removed from her ladies. They, knowing the situation, discreetly moved further away, completely out of hearing, and chatted away at the window next to them.

The royal couple, on thus meeting alone, exchanged glances of intelligence, inquiry, and concern. The Ardrighan was the first to speak, and said:

"What a dreadful business, O Tuathal! What on earth is to be done?"

"Done! There is nothing to be done but to submit to the inevitable."

"What words from an Ardrigh! Submit to Diarmaid Mac Cearbhail!"

" Not to Diarmaid Mac Cearbhaill, but to the law."

" The law ! Does the law then compel thee to receive in thine own palace whosoever listeth to intrude upon thee ?"

" Not exactly; but Diarmaid sent a courier with a letter asking my permission to pay his respects to myself and to the partner of my throne."

Here the Ardrigh bowed.

" And couldst not thou have refused ?"

" Well, that was the very thought that first suggested itself; but Diarmaid arrived before my council, whom, of course, I consulted had come to any resolution on the subject."

" And pray why didst thou not consult me ? Tuathal Mael-garbh, thy crown and thy throne are also mine, and thou hadst no right to endanger their possession without first consulting me. Thy council, indeed. Had Diarmaid been chosen king instead of thee, thy council would now be advising *him.* But what sayeth thy council ?"

" Well, they were divided in opinion ; and it is hard to say what conclusion would be arrived at had not Diarmaid and his brother settled the question by arriving too soon; and that is also my answer to thy question as to why I had not consulted thee."

" But why didst thou not keep him away by force, when it could be otherwise done ?"

" Thou forgetest, mo mhuirnin,* that the business of the royal brothers to Teamhair is to enter Mur Ollamhain, there to com-plete the education which the law exacts ; and it would not look well either for them or for us if they were excluded from the palace."

" A's mo ghradh,† couldst thou not exclude them from Mur Ollamhain itself ?"

" I have no power to do so."

" No power ! And thou callest thyself a Righ and an Ardrigh, too."

" But even an Ardrigh is not above the law, and the law makes no excuse whatever for any youth of any position to fail in acquiring the many branches of education which it has laid down for them, nor does it permit anyone, however exalted, to interfere with them or throw any obstacle in their way."

" I am aware of that; but surely in such a case as the pre-. sent something ought to be done to prevent Prince Diarmaid from taking advantage of his position as a student at Mur Ollamh-

---

* My passionately beloved one—my darling.   † And my love.

ain, to sow the seeds of disaffection to our throne by ingratiating himself with the people."

"I do not think thou needest have so much fear of Diarmaid; for, singular as it may appear, I have a greater fear of his brother, Maelmordha."

"Maelmordha! Oh, I do not think of him at all, much less fear him. He counts for nothing. He is but Diarmaid's halfbrother, on the mother's side, and consequently cannot inherit from Fergus Cearbhall, Diarmaid's father, through whom alone Diarmaid claims the right to the throne."

"That is all true, a mo cheile*; but still, since Maelmordha's coming, I have felt an unaccountable dread of him, though I know it is foolish, and perhaps wicked, to harbour the thought that flashed through my mind, but it was quite involuntary."

"Is dilse"† exclaimed the Ardrighan, throwing her arms round the neck of the Ardrigh and embracing him affectionately, "can it be that thou thinkest that THAT is in peril, which is dearer to me than crown or sceptre?"

The Ardrigh, kissing her, "Do not be alarmed, a chuisle agus a stoir mo chroidhte‡; there is no danger of that from the pupils of the holy Finian of Cluain-Irared."

"Ah, but they said something about being the black sheep of Finian, whom with all his sanctity and disciplinary skill he found it difficult to manage."

"Well, well, at all events the moment that any overt, seditious act is committed, we can legally banish them, not only from Mur Ollamhain and from Magh Breagh, but even out of the righeacht Midhe (kingdom of Meath)."

"Well, be it so, since there is no help for it; and I suppose we must treat him in every way as if he were our greatest friend, just to save appearances."

"There is no doubt of it. After all, they are royal princes, and we must show them the honour which is their due. I confess I do not quite like it, but perhaps it is best. It will show that we do not fear them, and that we can afford to treat their pretensions with contempt."

"Yea, yea; I like that. Thou hast now put the matter in its proper light. We shall spare no pains to do honour to our dear guests, especially for the few days that must elapse before their entry into Mur Ollamhain. We shall each do our respective parts; so between hunting, shooting, racing, hurling, sports,

---

* Oh, my spouse—wife.   † Most fond and faithful.
‡ Oh, pulse and beloved of my heart.

banquetting, receptions, reviews, &c., we shall convince the people that there is an excellent understanding between us: even the opposite party will think it useless to any longer resist the established order of things, and perhaps in the end the princes themselves may be won over by gifts which will make them the richest men in all the kingdom of Eire."

" Sell their birthright for a mess of pottage ?"

" Their birthright, Tuathal !"

" Ay, their birthright—at least Diarmaid's birthright. He is descended in the same degree as myself, from Nial Naoighillaigh,* whose two sons—our two grandfathers—also reigned in turn."

" Well, ye are the same in that respect, but thou hast the senior claim."

" The thing is, though, to get Diarmaid to acknowledge that."

" Well, we shall do our best—but look, Tuathal, the princes have not yet returned from their ride. I have no doubt that they were recognised ; and, there, oh ! Tuathal—there are bonfires in their honour ! See ! all Magh Breagh is ablaze with them ! Look ! in every direction !

With this the Ardrighan literally dragged her husband around the great curtained apartment, to many of the windows in succession, drawing the curtains wherever they obstructed the view.

The Ardrigh looked bewildered for a moment, and then coming to himself, said :

" Mo cheile is mhilse,† thy fears have got the better of thy memory. Knowest thou not that this is the Eve of St. John, and that those bonfires would blaze away had Diarmaid Mac Cearbhall never been born ?"

" Ah, I had forgotten. But is it not rather early ? It is not yet dark ! And behold all the people—what crowds ! It would appear as if every inhabitant of Magh Breagh were abroad. Who can they be going to meet ?"

" Ah, mo ghradh,‡ that is as usual an occurrence on an evening like this as the bonfires themselves. Thou wilt find that it is all right."

" I hope so ; but every circumstance now appears ominous. But here cometh the princes, we must prepare for supper."

" Slan leat, mo shearc."§

" Slan leat, a chuisle mo chroidhe." ‖

---

* Nial of the nine hostages.   † My sweetest wife.   ‡ My love.
   § Safety with thee, my affectionate one.   ‖ Pulse of my heart.

an ceaċarṁaḋ caibidil.

CHAPTER IV.

Comḋail.

THE RECEPTION.

THE royal pair here separated to prepare for the entertainment
of their unwelcome guests, and when at night they retired to
rest, it was with the hope that the course of conduct which they
had resolved upon and inaugurated that evening would not be
without beneficial results.

The next day, being the Feast of St. John, everyone, including the newly-arrived princes, were present at the celebration of
Mass in the royal church adjoining the palace ; the rest of the
day was spent befitting a great feast, as it was the custom for all,
even the laity, to attend the divine offices of the Church, at the
canonical hours.

The next few days were spent in following the red deer and
the wild boar through the forests of Midhe ; in partridge and
woodcock shooting ; in horse racing, and boat racing ; in hurling
matches, and various out-door games ; in chess playing and back-
gammon playing ; songs and music by the bards and musicians
of the palace, headed by the Ard Filé ; stories by the Seanchaidhe, or story-tellers, who told tales of the times of old,
of Fenian prowess, and Red Branch chivalry. The satirists,
the jugglers, and the clowns contributed their share to the general
amusement. All this continued until the day on which the reception in honour of the princes was to take place.

Accordingly, as the hour appointed drew near, the gorgeous
chariots of the Ard Arcon (high nobles of the State) could be
seen dashing along from different points in the direction of the
Tulach Aoibhin (beautiful hill).

The citizens were astir watching the gay equipages and their
gayer occupants, as they sped past. Foreigners also filled the
thoroughfares, full of curiosity, and making inquiries as to the
names and offices of the owners of the various carbads.

These carbads, or chariots, though alike in construction,
differed considerably in colour and ornamentation. The
bodies were all highly polished, and in some instances carved.

The colour of the curtains, seats, and canopies differed in different vehicles. Some were all of one colour, some striped, or barred, some speckled, or plaided. The top of the canopies were all decorated with plumes.

The gilding was most elaborate. The poles were of gilt bronze, or, in some of the highest, were overlaid with silver plate. The harness and bridles were golden or silver, or ornamented cruan. Round the horses' necks were the " mael land " of silver, with their golden bells. The horses themselves, of which there were four to the highest class of carbads, were of the finest breed, and quite in keeping with the splendid equipages which they drew.

The araid, or charioteers, wore the cocul, a short cloak or cape, with sleeves reaching only to the elbow, or in some cases covering the whole arm. Sometimes it had a smaller cape over. They were of various colours. Belonging to them, but not always attached, was a cennid, or conical hood, sometimes of the same colour as the cape, and sometimes of a different one, and bearing a tassel at its apex.

The cape had a kind of band or collar, ending in long lappets, tied across the breast. They also wore woollen triuibhis or pantaloons, and shoes of embossed leather. On their heads they wore a gipne, or band or crescent of red gold, to keep the hair down in its proper place on the forehead, and also as a distinguishing mark of their profession.

As each chariot drew up in the courtyard of Rath na Riogh, and deposited its occupants, fair and brave, before the grand entrance of Teach Cormaic, or the House of Cormac, the ara, or charioteer, at once drove the equipage off to the Fan-na-g-Carbad, or Slope of the Chariots.

The order was strictly enforced, for but one chariot was allowed in the courtyard at a time, in order to prevent confusion. Thus by the time the Teach Cormaic was full of aires, the Fan-na-g-Carbad was lined with their chariots.

The assemblage which now thronged the Teach Cormaic was a very brilliant one. All the grades of aires were there ; all the Gradh Gasgaidh (Orders of Chivalry); the Chain Knights; the Knights of the Golden Garter ; the Curadhes Craoibh Ruaidh, or Red Branch Knights; the Fenian warriors, or Fianna Erionn; the Clanna Diaga, and the Clanna Morna ; all the highest officers of the various regiments ; the great officers of state, and of the Household ; all the ollamhain, the breithmac, or judges of every degree; the ollamhs, or learned men ; the orniths, or sages ; the seanchaidh, or historians ; the fileadh, or poets, and philosophers;

all the foreign ambassadors, accredited to the Court of Team-hair, were there, and the wives, sisters, and daughters of all these classes.

The mna aisle oga* generally wore dresses of pure white siraic (silk), or sroil (satin), though sometimes it was relieved with a narrow stripe of green, blue, or pink ; round their waist a girset of plaid, containing four or five colours, generally five ; a sash matching in colour the stripe or the spot, when any, of the dress ; a small gold or silver brooch was fastened at the throat ; round their necks were necklaces of pearle (pearl), or partaing (coral), bracelets or armlets to match ; another string of pearls, or of coral bound their hair, which hung in ringlets, though sometimes they wore instead a small narrow niamh land, or golden crescent, from which hung the meirge or silken veil, generally of white, sometimes to match the colour of the scarf, &c.

Sandals of gold network were on their feet, beneath which the white silken stockings appeared.

Their mothers and married sisters were more gorgeously attired. Richly coloured silk or satin robes of any of the pre-vailing tints, or else black or white, elaborately embroidered with gold or silver.

Sometimes these dresses were santbrecc, or beautifully speckled ; in some cases, again, they were srebnaide sroil, or striped satin, in which were two, three, four, or five colours ; others were tartan or plaid.

Scarves matching or contrasting, and bordered with a curther or fringe of gold, or sometimes with white or coloured feathers ; golden network sandals, in which were inserted precious stones.

Veils of light silk, spotted with gold or silver ; niamh landa, or radiant leaves of gold of large size ; muinche torcs of the same precious metal round their necks, or sometimes fiams or gold chains, with a cross or other pendant ; magnificent gold brooches set with various gems—the Tara brooch prevailed— dornascs or bracelets, and geugau, or armlets, to match ; finger and thumb rings—ornasc and ordnisa, set with gems ; grace-fully carved cior (combs) of silver or mother-of-pearl adorned the head, while the plaited hair terminated in two little caskets or balls of gold called mella ; and au nascs, or earrings.

The officers of the army were in the uniforms of their various regiments, and were distinguished by colour and device. They wore triuibhis, or pantaloons, of the finest woollen

* Young ladies.

texture ; fillans, or vests, of different colour, and embroidered with gold or silver, with gold buttons down the front. Over this they wore the diallait oenaig, or assembly cloak, which was in five-folding fuam. It was generally of tartan, bordered with a golden border or fringe, and clasped at the throat by one of the great variety of dealga, or brooches, which prevailed. Their fingers and thumbs were also adorned with gem set rings ; on their feet were assai of findruine, or of silver, embossed with gold, and generally studded more or less with gems. Their swords and spears were very various, every regiment having a different device on them, as well as a different colour on the blades. The helmets were in keeping with the rest of their outfit, being ornamented with precious metals.

The Gradh Gasgaidh, or Orders of Chivalry, besides all just described, had the distinctive marks of their several orders, thus : the Knights of the Golden Garter—Nasc Niadh—were distinguished by a golden fillet-ring or garter, worn on the leg.

In order to obtain this badge of distinction, the wearer was obliged to establish his title to it on the field of battle, sword in hand.*

The Curradh Craoibhe Ruaidh, or Red Branch Knights were known by their golden lion.

The Curradh Fiam, or Chain Knights displayed the ornament which gave them their title, and which as well as the Red Branch Knights, they won in many a hard-fought field.

The Clanna Morna had fought and earned the red gold rings, which King Fail-dearg-doid invented as a reward for bravery in the year of the world, 3882.

The Clanna Deaga had helmets, with the necks and fore-pieces all of solid gold.

The Ollamhain, including the ollamhs proper, brehons, seanchaidhe, filés, and learned professors, generally wore the canabhas and long flowing robes of the very finest texture and of the six colours. They wore on their heads a kind of barread, or cap, peculiar to themselves, resembling a turban, and having a tassel at the point. They wore gold and silver also, but the rings on their fingers were prizes and marks of distinction for pre-eminence in their respective sciences.†

---

* O'Curry, who also remarks that in those remote and what our enemies call, barbarous times, the fawning on Prime Ministers was but a poor way to obtain decorations and dignities.

† It was Aildergoid, King of Ireland in 3705, A.M., that first bestowed gold rings on such as were pre-eminent in any science.

When all had assembled, and were either seated upon the luxurious imdai which ran all round about the great circular hall, or else promenaded backwards and forwards, or all round, they conversed freely until the arrival of the sovereigns, discussing many subjects, but the prevailing topic was the late royal arrival. As might be expected, a great diversity of opinion existed, and as the time drew near, expectation and excitement became more and more intense.

At length a flourish of trumpets was heard and all relapsed into silence, while the royal procession entered Rath na Riogh, and filed into Teach Cormaic.

The royal bodyguard, the officers of State, and the "ten," attended the steps of the royal pair, who were accompanied by Diarmaid and Maelmordha. All rose on their entry and the Ardrigh and Ardrighan at once took their seats on the golden, emerald-encrusted thrones with their crimson satin coverings, canopies, curtains, and steps, elevated on a platform in the centre of the house.

When the Ardrigh and the Ardrighan took their seats on the cathair rioghdha (royal chairs), the "ten" stationed themselves about in their respective places; the chief herald held the Sleagh, or Spear of State.

The royal princes were honoured with special seats beside the throne, and were "the observed of all observers."

The ceremony was then proceeded with, and numerous presentations took place. Everything went off well, and everybody seemed pleased, including the rivals themselves.

The aois ciuil, or musicians, discoursed ciuil binn (sweet music); the arsendtec, or songsters, sang go binn (melodiously). The assembly interchanged civilities, or friendships, as the case might be, through all the formal ceremony; and not even once during the whole time had the Ardrigh occasion to touch the craoibh ciuil—musical branch.

When the ceremony was over, the whole party were entertained at a grand banquet in the great banquetting-hall of Teach Miodchuarta, a much more pleasing affair by far; and what with feasting and music, conversation and singing, dancing and chess playing, it was far advanced into the night when the chariots were taken out and drawn up before the entrance of Teach Miodchuarta, to bring from thence their respective owners by various routes through the city to their several homes.

•

ᴀn cuιʒeᴀὺ ċᴀιbιᴏιl.

CHAPTER V.

ꞁꞁeulᴄᴀ ᴀιʒ Cιúʒuʒᴀὺ.

CLOUDS THICKENING.

THE next morning Diarmaid and Maelmordha were introduced to the scene and companions of their future studies in the Mur Ollamhain of Tara.

In pagan times such religion as was then known, together with law, science, art, literature, and military tactics, were all combined in the curriculum of all the great schools of the country, of which Mur Ollamhain was the chief. But with the introduction of Christianity there had sprung up colleges and monasteries where the youth of the country, as well as of foreign nations, were grounded in every kind of science and art, sanctified and ennobled by the greatest of all sciences—the science of the saints ; however, as these seats of learning were not calculated to train youth to martial exercises beyond a certain attention to gymnastics, and as all were obliged to spend some time in acquiring the military art, without a knowledge of which they could not fulfil their duties, or maintain their position in a country long famous for the bravery and valour of its military orders, so they were obliged to spend a certain portion of their time at one or other of the military schools attached to every court.

Our hero and his brother had already, besides their sacred and profane studies at the college of Cluain-Irared, undergone a preliminary course of military training here previously ; but all were expected, if possible, to perfect themselves at the high military court of the nation—in the Mur Ollamhain at Teamhair. Here, accordingly, it was necessary that they should remain for a time to perfect themselves in the science of war, as well as in all the various courses of literature and art.

At seven years they were entered, and a slender lance was put into their hands and a sword by their sides. From this to fourteen they were instructed in letters and discipline, when they took their first vows. They were now exercised every day in casting a javelin at a mark, in which they became so expert as to be certain of transfixing an enemy with it when within range. The cran-tubal, or sling, was very much used in ancient times, from which they darted balls with great force and direction. At the use of the sword and target they were uncommonly skilful, and they fought on foot, on horseback, or in chariots, according to their situation and circumstances. At eighteen they took their last vows.

As already noticed, the martial training of children commenced at the age of seven years, and the more important training of their minds at the earliest dawn of reason. None were ever permitted to be idle ; all were usefully employed from the highest to the lowest ; education was free to all : the highest perfection of human knowledge was attainable by all, 'free of cost ; all were expected to avail themselves of this wise provision of Irish rulers ; the highest offices of the State, ranking next to royalty, were the prizes for industry and application to literary pursuits ; while, on the other hand, the man who, however noble, or even royal his birth, or however vast his riches, who neglected to cultivate his mind, was incapacitated from holding even the lowest office in the State, and could never enjoy any honour, emolument, or dignity ; on the contrary, he was branded with disgrace, and scorned by even the humblest of the people.

As a consequence, it should not be wondered at that in ancient Eire an ignorant person was as rare a curiosity as a white blackbird, especially when it is well known that the Irish in all ages were famed for their love of learning, and if they have since been reduced to ignorance, it is because their jealous enemies have razed to the ground their schools and colleges and have burned and destroyed mountains of Irish writings; set a price on the head of the schoolmaster as well as of the priest, each of whom they put on a level with the wolf; made it a crime, punishable with fine and imprisonment, to be caught teaching the Irish to read ; and all this that it might be in their power to defame and calumniate their victims, by enforced ignorance of all literature, ensure their degradation ; and by the destruction of their national annals, as well as by the above-named system of making the acquisition of any kind of knowledge impossible, rendering the Irish people totally ignorant of the past glorious history of their country, that thus they might be reduced to the condition of grovelling, degraded, slaves to their oppressors, just as by the plunder and robbery of their broad lands and immense wealth they were reduced to be the poorest country in the world—the hewers of wood and the drawers of water to the foreign horde, who have grown fat on the land and the wealth which is the rightful inheritance of the children of the soil. Little dreamed the Irish of that and succeeding centuries of the return which still, later on, was to be made to their posterity by the very country which they were then raising from barbarism and ignorance.

Although the monasteries had supplemented in a great degree, and, in some measure, superseded the ancient houses of learning, yet the latter did not sink into mere military schools, but continued to fulfil all the purposes of their institution.

As education of the very highest class was not confined to a few, as it is now-a-days, but embraced the entire population of all ranks and degrees, as well as multitudes of foreigners, those who had the direction of those matters, so far from dispensing with old educational establishments, rather found it necessary to be continually increasing the number of schools and colleges.

Thus while training them in all manly exercises, they were also instructed in all the subtler sciences ; otherwise they would be liable to forget much of what they had already learned in the monasteries.

Diarmaid and Maelmordha now proceeded to finish the twelve years of hard study in all the various branches of education, and as Diarmaid considered himself destined for a position on which a " fierce light " is said " to beat," he felt it all the more incumbent on him to take good care that he should be second to none in the acquisition and cultivation of all those branches of knowledge which, necessary to the humblest, was absolutely indispensable to the heir of the monarchy. This great college had educated his ancestors for centuries, and they had reflected credit on their " alma mater."

For five years our hero and his brother applied themselves closely to all their studies—literary, legal, philosophical, poetical, musical, and military—going daily through all the evolutions and feats of the Fianna Éirionn, or Fenians of Ireland, and fulfilled, or were sworn to all the conditions imposed by law upon that celebrated order.

During this time they had prudence enough to refrain from all exhibitions of disaffection or discontent, though they had many private conversations among themselves and many comments on passing events. They saw the hollowness of the royal favours bestowed upon them and easily understood the motives. They also learned during this period a great deal concerning

8

the sentiments and hopes of their own party, which was much stronger than even they had supposed.

In Mur Ollamhain itself they had many friends among the various branches of the Ollamhain, as well as a large part of the students, amongst the principal and most devoted of whom was a young man named Amherghin Mac Amhlaghaidh,* on whom was very shortly to be conferred the highest degree within the power of the college to bestow. Then it came to their knowledge that a strong feeling in Diarmaid's favour pervaded a great portion of the Fenian ranks in the seven duns of Teamhair. Still they durst not, at least as yet, take advantage of all these signs of a divided people, for the loyal portion of the community, including, as such communities always do, the cowardly, the selfish, the paid servants of public departments of State, the private place-hunters, the palace tradespeople and merchants, and the motley throng which in every country have ever worshipped success, whether right or wrong.

All these prionsa Diarmaid despised, for he knew that the moment he ascended the throne, could he succeed in doing so, all these would fall at his feet with protestations of fidelity and life-long allegiance, and be as extravagant in their demonstrations of loyalty to him as they now were to the reigning prince.

But, besides these, there was another party honestly and conscientiously devoted to King Tuathal—honestly, because they were incapable of deceit, or pretending to anything they did not feel, even for the sake of court favours; and conscientiously, because they really believed that Tuathal was the lawful monarch, and Diarmaid but a seditious pretender.

These, and they were not a few, Diarmaid dreaded, even while he respected and admired them; and would have preferred one convert from their ranks to a hundred of the half-hearted, time-serving flunkeys, who would scarcely deign him a gracious look, but whom his possible good fortune would bring in thousand around his chariot wheels.

It is, however, but fair to say that this latter class, though many, were but a minority of the inhabitants—the good and true, on both sides, making the bulk of the population. Still, whether from having Diarmaid in their midst, or from whatever cause it arose, his partisans increased considerably from the time of his arrival at Teamhair, and though great caution was used, and great pains taken to conceal the growing disaffection, still the authorities were not deceived.

* Avereen Mac Auley.

Many a long conference had Tuathal with his Airlighe ar da Cleth; many a longer one with his Ardrighan, and becoming more frequent as dangers began to thicken, until at length it was resolved to give Diarmaid an opportunity of doing or saying something that would compromise him and give the Ardrigh an excuse for ridding himself of so formidable a rival.

Accordingly it was arranged that the out-door sports should be more frequent, and that Diarmaid should always be of the party, which had not always been the case hitherto. In pursuance of this arrangement, public and private entertainments, hurling and other games, hunting, shooting, horse-racing and boat-racing, &c., followed each other, without anything occurring out of the usual course, until at last, one morning early, when the Ardrigh, his "ten," and a few other attendants were taking a constitutional ride, they, on their homeward way, came upon a party of the students of Mur Ollamhain, who, under the direction of a military commander, were practising their feats. On coming closer, Tuathal observed that Diarmaid, Maelmordha, Amergin Mac Amhlaghaidh, and a few others whom he had begun to suspect of partiality towards the prince, were of the party.

As the Ardrigh and his party came upon the scene, Prince Diarmaid was in the act of performing the "fod-bheim," or sod-blow feat. This feat, when performed in battle, was always done in contempt. Now, however, they were only practising, and no ill-will existed between the prionsa and his antagonist The latter, however, as was his duty, sought to parry the blow, and kept moving in such a manner as to render the feat as difficult as possible. The prince raised his jewelled sword for the purpose of cutting the sod from under the feet of his antagonist, whose agility was such that he appeared to be everywhere at once. Their commander and his companions, as well as the Ardrigh and his suite, were in breathless suspense for a moment, as Diarmaid elevated his arm. Like a flash of lightning the green-dyed blade shot past the dazed eyes of the spectators, penetrated the green sod precisely under the spot where, at the moment, the lively youth had landed; but the hearty cheers which were formed in an instant in the throats of the beholders were stifled in their birth—for lo! the sword of the young prince was still in the ground, while his antagonist was exulting at the distance of the "cast of the dart" from the sword-blade of the discomfited prionsa. Astonishment was depicted on every face; but the Ardrigh, unable to control his delight, cried out:

"Ha, Diarmaid Mac Cearbhall, thou art a promising Fenian.

Why, the humblest of the Fenian ranks would have performed that "fod-bheim" successfully, with half the trouble which thou hast had in failing."

Diarmaid—"Beware, O Tuathal, of what thou sayest. If thou dost insult me again, I will show thee with whom thou hast to deal. And now do not look so furious, but draw near to the spot where my sword yet remains in the sod and see if thy sarcasms be just."

The Ardrigh dismounted, as did also those in his company, and drew near to the spot indicated. The other students and their officer already surrounded it, while three of their number were endeavouring to unearth a huge stone which had lain beneath the sod, and had just been the cause of the ill-success which had attended the prince's fod-bheim. At length the stone was removed, and of course explained to the satisfaction of all the prince's mishap; though everyone wondered how it came there. Prince Diarmaid taking his sword and half-sheathing it, turned to the Ardrigh, and haughtily exclaimed:

"Now, O Tuathal, it is time thou shouldest apologise for thine insulting expressions. I have yet to learn that I or any Fenian is expected to pierce with his sword a stone, and such a stone, too."

Tuathal, angrily—"I did not know, O Diarmaid, that such stone was there, nor could I ever suspect it. But as for apology, it is thy duty first to apologise for thy threats to thy sovereign."

Maelmordha—"Thou forgettest, O Thuathail Maelgairbh, that it is Diarmaid who is thy sovereign, and thou usurpest unjustly his lawful inheritance."

Tuathal—"Ha, Maelmordha MacArgatain, so thou hast come to the use of thy tongue at last, hast thou? but I will teach thee how to address thy sovereign. Take that, until the brehons have awarded thee the punishment due to thy seditious language."

As the Ardrigh uttered these words, he struck Maelmordha with his horse-switch, but as he did so, Prince Diarmaid, incensed beyond measure at this outrage upon his brother, unsheathed his sword, and before anyone knew what he was about, cut the sod from beneath the feet of the Ardrigh, who, unprepared for this crowning indignity, was in the act of laying his hand on his sword lest Maelmordha should resent the insult offered to him; and ere he could grasp the hilt, he felt the ground give way under his feet, and himself in the act of falling, until he, with a sudden bound, cleared the spot which had been separated from the surrounding earth.

All this was the work of a moment. Maelmordha saw, and

for the present, at least, felt himself sufficiently avenged, and realising the situation, whispered something to some of his companions, who immediately left the place. The outraged monarch, as soon as he recovered himself, turned fiercely upon Diarmaid, who was engaged parrying with his sword the approach of the Ardrigh's attendants to arrest him, and at every step backing further from them. But Tuathal now seeing the position of affairs, shouted to his following :

" Ho, there, what are ye all about ? Why do ye not stop the rebel ? Are ye too mixed up in his conspiracy against me ? Stop him, I say. Stop him, or your lives shall pay the forfeit."

But it was too late. Diarmaid had the advantage from his very position ; for the moment his sword came from under the feet of Tuathal ; he, without delay, backed from the scene, brandishing his good sword in defence of his person.

Amherghin Mac Amhlaigh and others of his friends urged him to escape without a moment's delay, and he had already placed a good distance between himself and the king's party before they had time to recover from the astonishment and bewilderment of so unexpected a climax.

The whole thing took place in less time than it takes to relate it ; and it was only as the Ardrigh recovered his self-possession that some amongst his party, including new arrivals, recovered theirs, and dashed in pursuit of the young fugitive. The others were only roused by the angry words of Tuathal, and they, too, were starting after their companions, when the Ardrigh re-called them, and bade some of them mount their horses and not fail to bring the delinquents back to justice, while he ordered the remainder, including the "ten," to accompany himself home to the royal palace.

Arrived in the city, they found it in a state of great excitement, for the students had flown with the first news, and others who saw the after-transaction from a distance had arrived with more particulars. It soon reached the palace and the ears of the Ardrighan, who at once sent a detachment of Fenians, under her most trusty officers, to meet the Ardrigh, and act as he should direct them, according to whatever turn affairs had taken.

They met their royal master and his retinue on the Bealach Milés.* He directed them on the roads they were to take in pursuing the brothers and their adherents who had fled with them, and told them then when they came to a certain point to separate into different parties, taking different directions, that some of them might be sure to overtake the fugitives.

* The road of Miles, between Rath Miles and Druim Aoibhin.

Then the Ardrigh and his attendants resumed their ride home, passing through the city, which was commencing another day's business, and he was received with cheers as he passed along from crowds of people who had gone out to meet him, or waited to see him pass along.   He cordially returned their salutations, and felt reassured of their loyalty.

As he neared Tulach Aoibhin he descried the Ardrighan and several of her ladies through the windows of the grianan, and at once rode up to the entrance of that palace, and bounding up the staircase, was in an instant locked in the arms of his loving and beloved spouse.

In truth, from the first rumour that reached her ears, much as she had desired a pretext for getting rid of Diarmaid, she became a prey to the keenest anxiety ; and after despatching assistance to her husband, she, with her ladies, kept a look-out from those windows of the grianan, which looked in the direction whence she knew he would come.

After having discussed the matter in all its bearings, the Ardrigh left the grianan for the Council Chamber, where he was soon surrounded by his Airlighe ar da Cleth.   The result of their conference did not transpire until the return of all the pursuers who had been despatched after Diarmaid, but who, after scouring all the surrounding country in vain, returned to Teamhair with the disheartening news.

The anxious citizens received the intelligence with diverse feelings, according as their sympathies were with the monarch or his rival ; but the most intense excitement and curiosity was manifested as to what would be the next step taken.

Not long were they left in suspense.   Hundreds of busy hands were employed in writing out as many copies of the proclamation which king and queen and council had resolved on in case the pursuers should not be successful.   It was carefully written in large straight letters, which could be easily read at a considerable distance, and ran as follows :—

" PROCLAMATION.

" Tuathal Maelgarbh, Righ Meidhe* and Ardrigh Eireann.†
To all our faithful subjects and trusty lieges.

" We hereby offer a reward of one thousand milch kine to any person whomsoever who shall bring to us the heart of Prince Diarmaid Mac Fergus Mac Cearbhall, who is in rebellion against our person and throne, and has grossly outraged our royal person. Given this 8th day of August, 544."

* King of Meath.   † Supreme Monarch of Ireland.

An t-séṁaḋ Caibioil.

CHAPTER VI.

Aiṟ an Seaċṟán.*

ON THE SHAUGHRAUN.

WHEN Prionsa Diarmaid fled from the angry monarch, he bent his steps in the direction of the nearest shrubbery. This, it is true, was the private property of a flaith, but that circumstance did not trouble the prionsa much under existing state of affairs. He would not harm the shrubbery, and his life or his liberty were at stake. Having penetrated the copse, he stood for an instant to listen to any sound that might indicate the whereabouts of his brother or other companions. Directly he heard what he thought was a low soft whistle, but lest it should only the wind breathing through the brushwood, he waited for an instant longer, when the sound was repeated, this time unmistakable. Diarmaid at once moved towards the point whence it proceeded, and after some little difficulty, owing to the thickness of the shrubbery, he reached the spot where he thought his brother was, and as he looked about in search of Maelmordha, the latter laid his hand on his shoulder, as he said:

"Ah, Diarmaid, mo dhear bhrathair,† I pray thee be silent, and rest for a little in this brake, here it is thickest of all around. They are upon thy track."

Diarmaid—"They are indeed, O Maelmordha, gradh mo croidhe,‡ and they—but hark, there they are. Are we safe here?"

Maelmordha, in a whisper—"We are; but let us lie close together, and as flat as we can, this loose brushwood will cover us completely. This is the best place I could discover. Did they see thee enter this brake?"

Diarmaid—"I am sure they must have seen me, and that they will follow. Here they come!"

For the next five minutes the brothers lay at full length on the ground, their arms round each other's necks; their hearts throbbing against each other's bosom, while their pursuers ran

* Air an Seacrán: On the shaughraun; Wandering; the state of having nowhere to rest one's head.
† (Pr. Mù yar-raw-hir.) O my brother. ‡ Grá ma chree, love of my heart.

through and through the shrubbery on every side, and so close did some of them come to the spot where they lay, that hope well-nigh forsook the brothers. However, the pursuers either did not see the place, or if they did, they did not seem to think it in any way suspicious-looking, for presently two or three of the pursuers, after having searched to no purpose, stood together to consult at a little distance from where the two young men lay concealed, and came to the conclusion that unless their comrades discovered the fugitives, they were not in the shrubbery; and those comrades now coming up empty handed, it was agreed that those whom they sought had found refuge in the dwelling-house or other premises of the flaith, and that there accordingly they should seek. In pursuance of this design, they left the shrubbery on the opposite side from that on which they had entered, when immediately the brothers sprang up, Diarmaid exclaiming :

"Quick, Maelmordha, quick; to the forest, to the forest!"

Keeping close together, they made their way as quickly as possible through the thick shrubbery until reaching the furthest end; with some difficulty, they crossed the mearn which divided the property of the flaith from the adjoining forest. Once here they breathed more freely, though they still felt that they must not unnecessarily lose time. They, therefore, sped through the forest as fast as they could, but after a considerable time, found themselves worn out with fatigue. Still they pull on bravely for some time longer, until at length Diarmaid exlaimed :

"*Mo dhear-bhrathair,** I can proceed no further; I must give up at last."

"I, too, am worn out, mo gràdh,† and have been this long time past; but the hope that we might reach yonder *biadtach*, before being overtaken by our pursuers has kept me up."

"Are we near the biadtach ?"

"I think I can discern it even now through the trees."

"Then I will try to hold out a little longer, if thou art able."

"Take mine arm, *mo mhuirnin.*‡"

"Nay, Maelmordha, thou must be as fatigued as myself."

"Well, here is the end of the forest, and here to the right a little is one of the four roads that leads to the biadtach."

"What if we should be overtaken there before we shall have time to rest, which is most probable ?"

"While thou art taking refreshments, I will keep watch, and warn thee of the approach of our foes."

---

* My brother.   † My love.   ‡ My passionately beloved.

"And what wilt thou do for refreshments, O Mael-mordha?"

"Oh, I will manage to take something, any way at all, if our pursuers give me time, and if not I shall wait for a better opportunity, further on."

"*A dhear-bhrathair mo chleibh,** that shall not he; thou shalt take thy needed refreshment, and rest too, just so long as I am permitted to take mine."

"But, *a chuisle mo chroidhe,* that may not be long, and thine is all the risk and all the danger; thou alone art the rival of Tuathal Maelgarbh; thou alone true Ardrigh na Erionn."

"Agus is tu mo dhearbhrathair, agus mac mo mhatair.†"

Saying these words, Diarmaid put his arms round Maelmordha's neck, and kissed him passionately; another instant and they were at the door of the biadtach, which they were about entering, when they were met on the threshold by Amherghin Mac Amhlaighaidh.

"Ha, Amherghin, thou here?" cried Diarmaid.

"Yes, most illustrious prince," replied Amherghin, saluting, "by direction of thy noble brother I sent some of our friends, as yet unsuspected, back to Druim Aoibhin for our horses. I did not think it prudent to go myself under the circumstances, as my fidelity to thee, O Prince, is but too well known."

"Well, that is right," said Diarmaid; "but I fear we shall not get our horses."

"Well, Prince, let us hope that we shall. In any case our friends are to rejoin us."

"Is this to be the meeting-place?"

"Nay, prince, my coming here was an afterthought. We did not decide on any place in particular, as we did not know what steps thou wouldst be obliged to take, oh, most noble prince."

"Well, how are they to know where to find us, for we shall be obliged to leave this as speedily as possible?"

"I suggested to Amherghin," said Maelmordha, "that, in the event of our having to fly, it would be in the direction of thine own patrimony, O my brother."

"That is all the information I could give them," affirmed Amherghin.

"Then," said Diarmaid, "it may be a considerable time before we meet them, especially if they are obliged to come on foot, so we had better take the shortest route to the Sionnain."‡

* O brother of my bosom.
† And thou art my brother, and the son of my mother.　　‡ Shannon.

"We might take *an Ardsgoil Chluain Irared*,* on our way, where we might safely rest and meet with many friends," suggested Maelmordha.

"Truly, we have many friends there, my brother, but we have also many foes. I would for the present avoid all public places."

"It would be the wisest thing just now; also all highroads, cities, and towns," said Amherghin.

"Then," said Maelmordha, "suppose we avoid the river, and make our way to Deas Teabhtha.† Once there we can see our way more clearly."

"That, my brother, is the best course we can take."

While they thus talked, they partook of a plentiful meal, which the brugh-fer and his waiters had set before them, after having first presented them with tubs of water to bathe their feet. Though they were not quite sure of the politics of those by whom they were surrounded, they tried to appear as indifferent as possible, and Maelmordha contrived to slip a few silver coins into the hand of one of the servants, and directed him to keep watch, without seeming to do so. Half an hour elapsed and no sign of their pursuers, caused much surprise to the trio; they began to think that none of them thought the princes would risk stopping at a public biadtach, which, in fact, they would not have done had the news of the quarrel with the Ardrigh had time to reach it. But as this news was liable to come at any moment, our wanderers thought it prudent to pursue their journey without further delay. They therefore set out from the opposite door of the biadtach to that by which they had entered; and as agreed upon, travelled through the country, having the Greek town of Truim on the right or north, and Magh n-Ailbhe on the left or south side. By this means they avoided meeting many persons, especially as they also kept clear of the river, which was always full of boats and people gliding backwards and forwards. They had not proceeded far into the wood beyond Trim, when they heard horses galloping at some distance behind them. They instinctively turned round, but could see nothing, owing to the obstruction caused by the trees.

"Hurrah!" cried out Maelmordha.

"Why didst thou cry out?" asked Diarmaid.

"Why, to let our friends know where we are."

"How knowest thou whether they are friends or foes?"

"I have no doubt they are the friends for whose coming we are so anxious."

---

* The College of Clonard.   ‡ South Teffia, in west of Westmeath.

"It may be so," said Amherghin," but I have misgivings about it. Still if they are not those whom we expect, they may be other friends or sympathisers ; at all events they need not necessarily be foes."

"I think our foes have missed our path," said Diarmaid.

"Hark !" said Maelmordha, "they approach nearer every moment."

"Stay ye here," said Amherghin, "while I try to obtain a glimpse of them without being seen."

The two brothers remained motionless beside a large tree, while Amherghin was away, but in a few moments he ran back breathless with terror and excitement, exclaiming !

"*Faraoir! faraoir!** they are the Fenians of King Tuathal. They are on our track. · We must conceal ourselves at once."

"What shall we do ?" said Diarmaid, "they have horses and we have none."

"Their horses have brought them quickly upon us, but they are of no avail in such a forest as this. They are dismounting already," replied Amherghin.

"If we remain on the ground they may capture one or all of us; our only course is to climb the trees," said Maelmordha.

"Thou art right my brother," said Diarmaid, and here are some very close ones. Let us mount."

In another minute the three *fir oga* were perched on as many trees, at a great height above the ground, waiting with keen anxiety to see what would happen next. They were not kept long in suspense. The Fenians, for such they were, now came very close to the spot where the fugitives were standing a few minutes before. They darted about in all directions, though never very far from the vicinity of the friends.

"Where can they have gone to ?" exclaimed one of them at last.

"Art thou sure that they were here at all ?" asked another.

"I am certain I heard a voice cry out ' hurrah !' and I am equally certain that it was from somewhere hereabouts the voice proceeded."

"But," asked a third, "what reason hast thou for thinking that the voice was that of Prince Diarmaid?"

"I do not think it was Prince Diarmaid's voice, but it struck me as being very like the voice of his brother, and where Prince Maelmordha is, his brother is not very far off."

"That is true ; but thou wert not near enough to distinguish

* (Pronounced for-reer) alas !

the voice of Lord Maelmordha, even though thou wert well acquainted with it, which I doubt."

" Well, well, whoever it was, there is no trace of him now; I feel there is no use in losing any more time here ; we had better proceed further ; they may have fled on hearing our approach."

The trio in the trees, on hearing this, breathed more freely, for they had heard every word of what passed. They were already relaxing their hold on the branches, as a preparation for freedom, when all at once their hearts stood still, as they listened.

" Would it not be well to examine those great trees before we quit so suspicious-looking a place as this ?"

"Dost thou mean to climb all these trees ?   Why we would require a reinforcement."

" No, I fear that would be hopeless, and perhaps after spending the day thus uselessly, we might miss one or two, which would perhaps contain the object of our search."

" Well," said another, " lest we should be questioned about the matter, we will give some of these trees a good shaking, and if they contain any forbidden fruit, it shall be deposited at our feet."

" Ha ! ha ! ha ! We shall see."

This was very unwelcome news to the "forbidden fruit;" so they clung for dear life to the branches and upper part of the trunk, while their pursuers shook vigorously several of the other trees round about them, until it appeared as if they were going to miss the right ones. At last, however, one of them came under the very tree on top of which Maelmordha sat. His position was now a very critical one. Well he knew the immense physical strength of these men, and he had no reason to suppose that the particular individual, who now stood beneath, was in any way inferior to the rest of his comrades ; consequently he put forth all his strength and energy for the final struggle; and he had need of both, for while he clung with desperation to the thorny branches, the great tree swayed to and fro, with such violence and rapidity, that it seemed every moment as if torn up by the very roots. For an instant it stopped, and a gleaming hope shot through the heart of its occupant; but it was only for an instant, for the Herculus beneath, letting go his hold, ran backward a few paces, when with one giant-spring he plunged in among the branches, only a very little distance below the unhappy Maelmordha, who now nearly lost all hope, expecting every moment a hand-to-hand encounter with his antagonist. He grasped his lance, point downwards, even while the same hand assisted the other to enable him to keep his desperate hold on the tree, which rocked and heaved as furiously as ever. Maelmordha's every sense and every nerve was stretched to the utmost tension, for the desperate encounter he felt was coming, as his enemy every instant ascended higher and higher, when suddenly, a voice from below called out in a commanding tone:

"Hallo, there, come down out of that, there is no use in losing any more time here; it is evident that the princes have escaped so far; but we must follow them, or answer for it to the Ardrigh."

Before this address was half finished the object of it stood beside his leader, to whom he said:

"I was in hopes that I could succeed in capturing one, if not all of the fugitives. I had a suspicion of that tree."

"Why, didst thou see anything in it?"

"No; I saw nothing; but the unusual size and closeness of it induced me to think that it might be preferred as a hiding place to many others which grow around it."

"Oh, if that is all, we had better seek elsewhere. They have had too long a start of us already. Call thy comrades."

The comrades having been all brought together, two or three of them were ordered to bring the horses of all round by the northern side of the wood, which was much thinner of trees, while their companions explored the denser part of the forest in hopes of coming upon the fugitives. When they had all fairly gone on their way, the three friends descended from their respective trees, and shook hands all round, congratulating each other on their escape. Maelmordha was specially sympathized with for the perilous position in which he had found himself. His bleeding hands were kissed by Diarmaid, and after his example by Amherghin. They sat down on the grass to rest, and to give their pursuers time to go a sufficient distance out of their intended path. They wondered what had become of those who had originally pursued them on foot, and how it came to pass that these horsemen could have been so quickly put upon their track. Thus they speculated and conversed about what had occurred, and what they would now do, until they felt sufficiently rested, and deemed it safe to pursue their journey. On and on they went through the forest, and ere they left it, the monastery bells from the Round Tower of Cluain-Irared, which was behind them a few miles to the south-east, struck upon their ears; they fervently joined in spirit with their former companions and tutors in worship of

the Most High, and as they now felt no fear of being overheard
by any whose interest or duty it was to capture them, they
commenced to raise their voices in chanting the psalms, which
they knew were being then chanted in the church of the
monastery, and which this time they offered in thanksgiving for
their deliverance, and in supplication for their future safety.
Soon after their voices died away they emerged into the open
country; and their first act was to take a longing look at the
dear old cloigteach of Cluain-Irared, which reared its immense
height in the distance. Never before, perhaps, did they regard
it with so much affection. Never before did the world seem
so empty, so deceptive, so inadequate to supply the inward
cravings of man's heart. Mur Ollamhain was a glorious institution; an institution which, for antiquity, learning, and refinement every Irishman must feel proud; and our young princes
did feel proud of it; but, for all that, as they stood there, they
questioned if they did not feel happier, far happier at Cluain-
Irared, the sanctuary of saints as well as scholars. But they
had no time then for idle reminiscenses of the past; the
present, and the immediate future was before them in all their
stern reality. They knew not what to-morrow would bring.
Hope in Providence, and a secondary though innate reliance
on their own brave, manly hearts, together with their fraternal
affection, and the devotion of their faithful follower and friend,
were the treasures of their exile. Their way now lay through a
smiling country. Nothing but fields of corn, or flax, or hay-
ricks, and the other evidences of farming, met their gaze, or
else pastures of kine, or sheep, dotted the landscape. Espying
a comfortable farm-house a little way off, they concluded to visit
it, Amherghin proposing that he should precede them a little distance to see that all was safe. This was agreed to, so Amherghin,
after a little, disappeared inside the farm-house. He soon
emerged again, and beckoned to his companions, who quickened
their pace. A little dog which happened to be outside, barked
at them, but was speedily quieted by a little golden-haired girl
of about four years of age, who took him up in her arms.
Diarmaid and Maelmordha shook hands with her and patted
her on the head; they then entered the house, where they were
hospitably entertained, and had their wounds, especially Maelmordha's, dressed. Having rested for a little, they took leave
of their entertainers, but did not offer them any compensation,
as it would be a great insult to even the humblest householder.
However, Diarmaid satisfied his conscience by presenting to the
little girl several bright gold coins, which gave great pleasure

to the child. Again resuming their journey, they traversed a highly cultivated country, and though they met with many inviting-looking homesteads, they did not think it prudent to stop oftener than was absolutely necessary. Thus they travelled for many days, without any sign of their expected friends, though so far they had succeeded in baffling their foes. The nights were passed either in a public biadteach, or in a cottier's, or farmer's house ; though sometimes, when no habitation of any description was in view, they were obliged to lay themselves down on the grass. This was especially the case when their way led through a wood. Those inconveniences would not occur but for their outlawed condition, for they felt constrained above all things to avoid all cities, towns, and other populous places. At last they entered the country of Deas Teabhtha, in which part of the private patrimony of Prince Diarmaid was situated. This fact raised their spirits not a little, and with renewed courage they proceeded on their weary journey. At last they came to the boundary which divided Diarmaid's property from that of his neighbour. This they joyfully crossed, and had no sooner done so than they sent up a loud huzza! Still, the fact of being on his own ground, was as yet but of little avail to Diarmaid, or his companions, for the outward boundary on their side was skirted by a forest. Into this forest they accordingly entered, and plodded along while ever they were able. At last when their strength failed, they sat themselves down to rest, in as sad a plight as any they had been in since their flight. Still they were not without consolation. Diarmaid could call the ground on which he lay, and the trees which surrounded him, his own. Then they were nearer to safety, and, so far, at least, they had escaped their pursuers. Here they lay for some time, listlessly conversing with each other, and expressing surprise at the delay of their friends, assigning several reasons for it, that they feared the risk, lest they should be caught; that they were unable to get the horses, and come on, on foot, in which case they might not meet for long enough ; that they had got off with the horses, but had been overtaken by the officers of the Ardrigh, and that they were now suffering for their temerity. Many other causes they assigned, but were unable to come to any conclusion. Then they commenced to talk about their pursuers, wondered what had become of the first batch, on foot, who entered the residence of the Flaith. Were they delayed there ? Or did they leave the house by an opposite way ? Where went the horsemen who had so nearly captured them ?

What route did they take after leaving the forest, &c. By degrees the conversation died out, and their eyelids were beginning to close from the effects of the over fatigue they had gone through, when—

"Hist ! what is that ?" exclaimed Amherghin.

"Horses galloping," said Maelmordha, "to the trees ! to the trees !"

"Ho !" said Diarmaid, "they have dared to pursue me into my own territory; but Tuathal cares nought for that. He would as soon have me captured here as elsewhere; perhaps sooner."

By this time they had climbed the trees, and waited anxiously for the result. They heard the galloping approaching nearer every moment until at length it ceased, and now they heard voices and footsteps approaching. It appeared as if horses were being led through the forest. On and on they came, the three friends peered through the trees to try to get a glimpse of the newcomers. The latter led their horses right under where the friends were ensconced. They were chatting as they came along. Right in front of where Amherghin was mounted came the foremost of the band. He was talking to those beside, and immediately behind him. The listeners in the trees heard him say :

"It is very singular that we have found no trace of them so far. I am quite at fault."

"After all," said a second, "it is not very surprising, considering the caution they must have observed, and, the great extent of ground over which they must have travelled by this time. It is just possible that we are not on the right track at all."

"We must be on the right track," said a third, "for this is Prionsa Diarmaid's own territory, and there is nothing more likely than that he shall try to reach it by the nearest possible route."

"Yes," said a fourth ; "and, besides, this is the way we were directed to come by Amherghin Mac Amlaghaidh who told us ——"

"That it was the route Prince Diarmaid would most likely take should he be obliged to fly," exclaimed Amherghin himself, appearing suddenly before the speakers.

The latter stood stock-still with astonishment at the unexpected apparition.

"Didst thou fall from the skies, or whence ?" asked four or five in one breath.

"No," replied Amherghin, "I fell from a tree, on recognising ye. And the princes are here, too, all safe."

On this the two brothers jumped from their hiding-places, and appeared before their astonished friends, who sent up a cheer of wild delight, and waved their *barreads* with exultation.

After a general hand-shaking all round, they all sat down on the grass together to relate their adventures; and while the horses grazed at a little distance, one of the new comers produced a tiaga, or large leather-satchel, which was stuffed with provisions. This was welcome to the weary fugitives; and while the meal was being prepared, another went towards one of the horses and carried back a cruit, or harp, which he presented to the delighted Amherghin.

"So, Amherghin," said Diarmaid, "our friends did not forget thy harp."

"I told them, prince, not on any account to forget it, if they could by any chance secure it. How much shorter our past journey would have appeared had it been in our company."

"That is quite true," said Maelmordha; "and when we have partaken of our much needed meal, and related our respective adventures, thy sweet harp and sweeter voice shall make us, for awhile, forget our forlorn condition."

"Thou art complimentary, *mo thiarna*,* and it shall always be the proudest object of my life to earn the good opinion of thy royal brother and thyself."

They then proceeded to discuss the ready-cooked meal, which was set before them, and which the whole company declared they enjoyed better than any they had ever before partaken of. When the new arrivals had heard the story of their royal friends, and the doubt and surprise they and Amherghin expressed regarding their pursuers, they were able to clear up these difficulties. They assured them that from what they could learn, they were convinced that the flaith, into whose house their pursuers had entered in search of them, was secretly attached to Prince Diarmaid, for the pursuers were detained there a considerable time, and the flaith would not hear of the officers of King Tuathal leaving his house without been hospitably entertained. The officers were nothing loath, so that by the time that they left the loyal flaith they were a long way behind the objects of their pursuit. As for the horsemen, who followed in their wake, it was explained that they had been sent by the Ardrighan on the first rumour of what had taken place; they met the Ardrigh long before he entered the city, and consequently were enabled to come up with the fugitives

* My lord.

sooner than would otherwise have been possible; they had scoured the whole country, and they had had the pleasure of meeting them at their journey hither, "though they little guessed the nature of our ride," continued the narrator. "Indeed, once fairly out of Teamhair by stratagem, we soon discovered that many persons mistook us for volunteers of King Tuathal, in the pursuit of his enemy."

This last observation caused great amusement to the hearers, who were now in better spirits than they had been since their flight. Diarmaid now called on Amherghin for a song, before they resumed their journey. Amherghin, after tuning his harp, proceeded to comply, and burst forth into the following song of Ossian :—

[TRANSLATION.]

" From Boisgne first host-leading Gorrie sprung ;
From Gorrie, Conn, in lays of victory sung ;
The generous Farlagh boasts a sire in Conn,
And in Treanmor a brave and gallant son.
Next from Treanmor the festive Cumhal came ;
From Cumhal, Finn, of great prophetic fame ;
The last of all the illustrious line behold
In Ossian, son of Finn, now poor and old.
Oh ! did the Fenians breathe this vital air,
Thou son of Calfruin, ne'er would I repair
Thus to thy cell, nor pass the weary time
In listening to the dull, eternal chime
Of thy church notes—when in Maynoothe's sweet bowers
My Caoilte passed with me the happy hours,
No want we knew—but now behold me, sage,
With generous pity, worn by care and age,
The sole survivor of a numerous line,
Thus left in want and solitude to pine."

This concluded, the harpist was loudly cheered, and they would have insisted on another song, but that the princes thought it better to be moving ; they could stop again farther on. Diarmaid, however, complimented Amherghin, and expressed his concern that one like him, who had taken out the highest degrees at Mur Ollamhain, should lose himself in following an outlawed prince, who might never be in a position to adequately repay his services.

"Oh, prince, thou knowest me not, when thou speakest so. I have resolved to devote my life to thee, and, whether in prosperity or adversity, I will remain faithful to thee till death."

Diarmaid held out his hand to Amherghin, exclaiming: "Thanks, a thousand thanks, my friend, and I trust Providence will give me the power to reward such devotion."

" My best reward, oh, prince, is the consciousness of having done my duty to him whom I believe to be my lawful sovereign."

"Nay, O Amherghin, if I am ever Ardrigh, thou shalt be Ard Fileadh."*

The approving cheer which went up from their companions completely drowned the grateful reply of Amherghin ; but once more the prince and the poet clasped hands.

All then got into moving order, but as yet they could not mount their horses, they had to lead them through the thicker part of the forest. After a little, however, the trees became more scattered. The company then prepared to mount. The horses belonging to Diarmaid, Maelmordha, and Amherghin showed evident demonstrations of delight at the near prospect of again carrying their respective masters, whose journey now became much easier than it was before. After awhile they were able to gallop, as the obstructions to their progress became fewer. Soon they came again upon a smiling, cultivated country, inhabited by some of the thriving, prosperous clansmen of Prince Diarmaid. Though taking the less frequented ways, they were soon recognised. By degrees the news spread, when nearly every inhabitant within a reasonable distance poured out of their homes to greet their beloved flaith. Though Diarmaid appreciated this evidence of devotion in his own people, it made him anxious and uneasy lest the tumult of the demonstrations should attract strangers, and possibly enemies, to the scene. He consequently explained his position to them, and begged of them to forego their intention of acquainting the rest of his tribe-men of his arrival, as a crowd of even the most attached friends would only expose him and his faithful followers to the risk of capture. This representation had the desired effect ; but the prince and his company were obliged to partake of the hospitalities of the people, who also took the opportunity to give him part of his rents and dues, in money and in kind. They were soon all loaded with provisions and with various useful articles, until the prince declared that any more would only impede their progress, and he absolutely refused to take kine, sheep, or other animals. It would be impossible for the present. It was then arranged that these animals, as well as other commodities, should be sent from time to time to the country about the confluence of the Sionnain and the Brosna. Diarmaid did not as yet know the exact spot where he would take up his precarious abode. All being arranged, the travellers took a warm

---

* Chief Bard, or Poet Laureate.

farewell of Prince Diarmaid's devoted people, whose prayers and benedictions followed them on their way. On they galloped through Teabhtha, always observing the utmost secrecy. The swiftness of their horses soon brought them to an earthen wall, when Maelmordha exclaimed :

"Lo ! Diarmaid, my brother, we are now at the boundaries of Artibra, which, as thou rememberest, thou didst bestow on our old school-fellow, Ciaran Mac an t-Saoir."

"Well, my brother," replied Diarmaid, "dost thou think that Ciaran would refuse us permission, now that we are *air an seacràn*,* to travel over lands, that, as prince and heir, I bestowed upon him in trust for the church and her children at home and abroad."

"Nay, Diarmaid, I meant not that, but I am not without hope that we may now meet with an old friend, whose sanctuary will shield us from danger."

"I would much wish to meet with Ciaran once more; I have not heard that he has, so far, made any use of Artibra —let us cross the wall—but we know that he has erected a monastery in the Inis Aingin. We may perhaps some day sail up the Sionnain to visit him."

"I fear," said Maelmordha, "that my horse is breaking down."

"That is unfortunate just yet. If we were once at the Brosna——"

"Ah, but I am sorry for my poor horse."

Here Maelmordha began patting it.

"I am sorry, too, Maelmordha," said Diarmaid, "especially as it is the brother of my own fine animal. What could have happened to it? I had thought they were the two best animals in all Midhe. Let us dismount for awhile to rest him."

All accordingly dismounted, and while the horses rested and fed, Maelmordha's horse being particularly petted and attended to, their respective owners sat down and partook of some of the provisions at their disposal, after which Amherghin, the most perfect musician of the party, sung several songs of chivalry and war, accompanying himself on his *cruit*. Several others of the party also amused themselves in this manner, with Amherghin's harp. When they had spent a little time thus they remounted their steeds ; after travelling for some time, dismounting, to lead their horses wherever the trees became too numerous, they in the end reached the banks of the Brosna, without, so far as they

* On the Shaughraun.

could see, meeting with any sign that their old companion had as yet inhabited Artibra. This latter ride was somewhat prolonged by Maelmordha's steed having become weaker and more exhausted at every step. At length, when within a short distance of the river, it broke down completely, and refused to proceed any further. The poor animal lay down, surrounded by sympathising bipeds and quadrupeds. Diarmaid's horse made the most affectionate demonstrations of love and sorrow, which the invalid seemed to acknowledge as well as it could. The bystanders were very much affected by this natural love displayed by two beasts."

"This affecting spectacle," said Diarmaid, "ought to be a lesson to men, who are bound together by human ties."

"We, at least," said Maelmordha, "have nothing to reproach ourselves with in that respect."

"No," said Diarmaid, "we never had; but there are many who appear utterly dead to all natural feelings, even while they easily coalesce with foreign elements. But I fear the poor animal is going fast."

"He is dead," said Amherghin, a minute later.

"And I have lost a true friend," said Maelmordha.

"And my steed is stricken with sorrow," said Diarmaid.

"They were two superb animals," said Amherghin. "What raven blackness!"

"Shall we bury the dead animal?" asked one of the attendants.

"Yea," said Maelmordha, "we cannot remain here."

Many hands set about preparing a grave with such implements as were at their disposal, and soon Maelmorhda's black steed was lovingly laid in earth, with a covering of green sods placed over him.

Diarmaid patted his own horse and led him away; the rest followed his example. When they got a few paces away each offered his horse to Maelmordha, but he declined, on the ground that he could not bear to ride any other horse just yet, and that it was scarcely worth while, as they were very near the river Brosna.

"Then," said Diarmaid, "we shall all walk to the river."

This they accordingly did, some of the attendants going a little before, to guard against surprise from a possible enemy. The royal brothers and the rest of their party continued their course, as the scouting party gave no signs of danger. One of the last-named party had, in fact, called one of the *bad-feara* (boatmen), and having questioned him, discovered that he was

the son of one of Prince Diarmaid's tribe-men. This welcome intelligence induced him to let the young man into his confidence.
The result was that in a few minutes several other boats lay in
readiness to receive the prince and his party. Nothing could
have been so fortunate as this accidental rencontre with Seamus,*
for such was the boatman's name. He was ardently attached
to Prince Diarmaid, and was, besides, very popular with his
fellow-boatmen. He soon had several whom he could trust
about him ; others he sent for to take charge of the horses.
When everything was ready, he called aside the chief of the
scouting party, and conversed with him for a few minutes in
low tones. The intelligence conveyed by the boatman appeared
to be rather alarming, for his new acquaintance ran back to
meet the approaching royal party, who, seeing his alarming
attitude, suddenly stopped in the course. When he was within
speaking distance, the prince called out :

"What is it, Peader ?†   Is there any danger ?"

"Nay, oh, illustrious prince, there is no immediate danger ;
but yonder boatman, who is none other than thy trusty adherent,
Seamus Mac Aodh, has informed me that the usurper, Tuathal
Maelgarbh, has banished thee out of the kingdom of Midhe, and
set a price of one thousand milch kine upon thy heart."

"A *Chineamhuin*,"‡ exclaimed Diarmaid : "then is my life
in even more danger than my liberty."

"But how came Seamus Mac Aodh to learn that, while we
have heard naught concerning it before ?" asked Maelmordha.

"Thou forgettest, *mo thiarna*, that we have travelled by the
most unfrequented ways, while Seamus has been plying up and
down the public river, and has, moreover, been meeting with
people from several of the cities and towns of Midhe."

"Is then the sentence of the Ardrigh proclaimed throughout
all the kingdom of Midhe ?" asked Amherghin.

"Throughout every city and town of Midhe, and all along
both banks of every Midhian§ river, the proclamation of Tuathal
Maelgarbh sets forth that Prince Diarmaid Mac Feargus Mac
Cearbhall is, by his royal fiat, banished from the kingdom of
Midhe ; and further, that one thousand milch kine shall be the
reward of him who shall lay the prince's heart at the feet of the
Ardrigh."

"Though now surrounded by loyal friends," exclaimed Prince
Diarmaid, "I know not how soon I may meet the foe whose
interest it will be to tear the heart out of my body."

* (Pronounced Shemus) James.   † Peter.
‡ (Pronounced hyinn-a-winn) oh ! fate.   § Meathian.

" Before that foe can reach thy heart," exclaimed Maelmordha, fervently, and throwing his arms around his brother's
neck, " he must first pierce mine."

Diarmaid returned the embrace but was too full to speak.
All then knelt before Prince Diarmaid and pledged themselves
solemnly to be faithful to him unto death. Seamus, who was in
sight, now joined them, and united his vows to theirs. Diarmaid
received him warmly, and confided himself and his friends to his
keeping. All then proceeded to the river bank, where their
horses were taken in charge to be brought to the stables of a
neighbouring friendly flaith, the father of Amherghin, and they
themselves entered the boats there ready to receive them. A
favourable moment, when none of the other passenger boats,
which were plying up and down the river, were attracted to the
royal party, was taken advantage of for Diarmaid's descent into
Seamus's own boat. Maelmordha, Amherghin, and a few others
sailed with him in this boat, the rest of the party occupying the
other boats. When all was in readiness, the corachs were put
in motion, and sped swiftly along the river Brosna, without attracting any particular notice from the river or the banks.
They did not go far, however, until they had an opportunity of
reading the "Proclamation." When Diarmaid had read his
" sentence," he turned calmly to Seamus, and said :

" The first part, O Seamus, of this fiat of Tuathal Maelgarbh,
it is my intention, at least for the present, to obey; and in
furtherance thereof, I beg of thee to take us as quickly as possible outside the kingdom of Midhe ;* for the rest we must trust
to Providence alone."

" We shall do our best, oh prince, and shall take thee and thy
friends out of Midhe as quickly as our corachs will carry us ; but
thou knowest, oh prince, that excessive speed would attract undue attention, besides endangering collision with other passengers on this crowded river."

" Well, thou art the best judge of that. I leave all in thine
hands."

The voyage down the Brosna was not marked by any parti-
ticular incident, save that now and again some individual or
other in some passing corach, recognised and saluted the prince
and his brother. These encounters, though friendly, sometimes caused no little concern to Diarmaid and his friends,
especially as the "Proclamation" was posted at intervals all along

---

* The ancient kingdom of Meath extended to the Shannon, which river
divided it from the kingdom of Connacht.

the Brosna, on both banks, and as the passengers whom they were constantly meeting were bound, many of them at least, for the capital. Still they sailed along, though the repeated meetings with the "Proclamations" seemed to unhinge Mael-mordha even more than they did his brother, especially those posted on the right bank of the Brosna. At last he exclaimed :

"Is it not extraordinary, O Diarmaid, that Tuathal, or his servants, have had the temerity to post those outrageous pro-clamations, even on thine own property; or at least what was thine own before thou didst grant it to Ciaran Mac an t-Saoir ?"

"It is certainly rather humiliating; but I am convinced that Ciaran knows nothing about it, else he would never per-mit it."

"Would he dare to remove them ?"

"I am certain he would, but it is evident he is not in Artibra at all."

"Where then can he be? We know he has long ago left Cluain-Irared."

"Oh, yes; he has founded a monastery in Inis Ainghin, where, no doubt, he may be found. We must seek him."

"I suppose it would be imprudent to remove the postings ourselves ?"

"It would be very dangerous in such a crowded place as this. It must not be thought of."

"Now, Diarmaid, my brother, I have something to say to thee."

"And what is it. *mo gradh* ?"

"We are now very near the river Sionnain, where thou wilt be much safer than within the territory of Midhe. Well, thou and Tuathal Maelgarbh are rivals; he has usurped thy throne, and from that throne has pronounced sentence of exile and death upon thee. Is that just ?"

"Just! no; but what of that ? Tuathal Maelgarbh is Ardrigh n-Erind, *de facto*——"

"And thou art Ardrigh n-Erind *de jure*."

"Ah! well, suppose so. Still I cannot make out what thou art driving at."

"Well, look, O Diarmaid, here now is another copy of the 'Proclamation' which Tuathal has issued against thee. Now, hast not thou just as good a right to issue such another 'Pro-clamation' against Tuathal himself ?"

"It is absurd. I am not at Teamhair."

"What of that ? Thou art Ardrigh ; is not that enough ? Wherever thou art, there is the 'court,' and the seat of thy power. The golden throne, and the state chambers of Rath na Righ, and Teach Miodchuarta are not the source of royalty, they are but its emblems. Tuathal has usurped these; but all lawful power vests in thee alone. This corach here, or,—if thou landest first—a stone, or the stump of a tree, will serve for thy throne until the dawn of a better day."

"And when I am enthroned in state on the stump of a tree, what am I to do?"

"Issue such another 'Proclamation' as that," pointing to another, "against the traitor, Tuathal Maelgarbh. We shall not be short of parchment or of scriveners."

"Good! and what then?"

"Why, then, some one will proceed at once to carry thy sentence into execution."

"Oh!"

"That will not be murder or assassination."

"Oh! no."

"But I am serious, O Diarmaid; it will be but carrying out a legal sentence."

"I wonder what would our old master, Finian of Cluain-Irared, say to thy legal sentence?"

"What would he say to Tuathal's sentence."

"I do not think he would approve of either."

"Well, Tuathal is the aggressor, and he deserves banishment, if not death, for his crime."

"Lo!" exclaimed Diarmaid, "we are at the confluence of the Brosna with the Sionnain."

"And thou art safe."

"I am not so sure of that just yet."

Having entered the river Sionnain they encountered numerous other corachs plying between the cities and seaports of Mumhain* and Connacht, also vessels of a larger build, which carried Irish and foreign merchandise along that noble river. Here they crossed over to the Connacht side of the river, where was situated a public biadhtach. Having rested and refreshed themselves here, they again entered their boats, and continued to sail down the Sionnain for about five miles, until they reached the confluence of that river with the Suck. Here they were invited to sup at the great rath of a noble flaith, who had known Diarmaid and Maelmordha from infancy. They remained here all night, and the next morning resumed their voyage. Care was always taken that no stranger should, under any pretence

* Munster.

whatever, be allowed to enter the corach in which Diarmaid
sailed. Still, as they went northward, Diarmaid and Maelmordha often expressed surprise that no trace of anything approaching to any kind of building was observable in any part of
Artibra, either during their ride, through a portion of it, or on
its boundaries (southern) along the Brosna and the Sionnain,
or its Sionnain-skirted western mearn. However, when they
arrived at the extreme northern boundary of Artibra, they disembarked, and entered a great rath belonging to Mac
Amhlaigh, Lord of Calraidh (Calry), Amherghin's father.
Here they were hospitably entertained ; they were shown all over
the rich grazing and tillage lands, as well as the gardens and
orchards of the flaith. Before they left this (for they dare not remain even here), the flaith exacted a promise that they would often
again call at his house. This was agreed to, and they once
more entered their boats to continue their sail further down the
river, stopping on their way now at an humble cottage, again
at a lordly mansion ; at one time at the Midhian, at another at
the Connacht side of the river; sometimes they would stop a
night at the house of a brughfer, sometimes at that of an artificer. In answer to all inquiries as to why they would not take
up their abode at each of these different kinds of houses, they
invariably replied that the prince was obliged, for greater safety,
to remain as much as possible on the rivers. In this manner
many weeks passed by, the royal party sailing up and down the
Sionnain ; sometimes northward to Loch Ri, sometimes southward to Loch Dearg, now taking a ride down the Suck again,
even daring the Midhian river Brosna. Diarmaid's clansmen had
kept their word. Every other day brought cattle, sheep, pigs,
poultry, honey, fruit, wines, suitable articles of dress, &c.
These tributes Diarmaid did not exactly need, owing to the
hospitality of all his friends along both banks of the river, still
they enabled him to make presents to his friends and followers,
and to give alms to the poor and sick, and to all who might
stand in need. It was, besides, a proof of the integrity and
devotion of his people, who sent him even more than his due,
at a time when, being on the shaughraun and outlawed, he could
not recover his tributes, were his followers unwilling to pay.
Many friendly greetings and messages of loyalty usually accompanied the tributes. Among the rest, he was assured that
hundreds of brave and manly hearts and hands were at his service whenever he should require them. All this was very consoling to the prince, who returned his hearty thanks, and
frequently suitable presents as well.

ᴀn τ-seᴀctᵯᴀᵬ ċᴀiᵬᴉᴅiL.

CHAPTER VII.

ᴀn ᵱᴀᴉᵬeᴀ́ct.

THE PROPHECY.

ONE day, as they were sailing along the Sionnain, they perceived among the crowds of boats and other small vessels, one
in which were several men, apparently in the garb of monks ;
they were at too great a distance for our wanderers to distinguish
more. Soon they stopped, and were observed to disembark on
the banks of Artibra. On perceiving this a strange hope took
possession of Diarmaid and Maelmorda. In compliance with
their wishes, Seamus increased the speed of their corach.
When they arrived at the spot where they saw the monks disembark, they did in like manner—Diarmaid, Maelmorda, and all
their followers. They penetrated into the interior of Artibra,
in hopes of coming up with the monks. Very soon they saw
them at a little distance. Following in the same direction, they
came up with them at the place called Druim Tibrait, or the
Hill of the Well. Some of the brethren were in the act of
cutting down trees with biaila, or axes, which they had brought
with them ; others were clearing the hill. On hearing the footsteps behind, one of them turned round, and in another
moment Diarmaid and his old school-fellow, Ciaran Mac an t-Saoir
were clasped in each other's arms. Ciaran next embraced Maelmordha, and in turn greeted all the rest. When they had each
related all their adventures since they had parted in Clonard
College, Ciaran inquired why they had not visited him at Inis
Ainghin, where he had founded his first monastery, thanks to the
generosity of Diarmaid. Diarmaid replied that he and Maelmordha had gone to his monastery, but they were told that he
was away on a mission ; they were prevented calling again by
the numerous invitations which they were obliged to accept
from their numerous kind friends along the river.

"We did not make ourselves known to thy monks," said
Maelmordha.

" Surely ye were not afraid of *them*," said Ciaran.

"Oh, no ; but we had determined to visit Inis Ainghin again."

"Ye shall always be at home at Inis Ainghin and at Artibra," said Ciaran.

"What work is about being done here?" said Diarmaid.

"The erecting of a small church," said Ciaran.

"Well, may that indeed be its name," said Diarmaid, 'Eglais Beg' (or the Little Church)."

"Plant the pole with me," said Ciaran; "and let mine hand be above thine hand on it, and thine hand and thy sovereign sway shall be over the men of Eire before long."

"How can this be?" said Diarmaid, "since Tuathal is Monarch of Eire, and I am exiled by him."

"God is powerful for that," said Ciaran.

They then set up the pole, and Diarmaid made a new and solemn offering of the place to God and the Abbot Ciaran. All then set to work, both Ciaran and his monks, and Diarmaid, Maelmordha, and their attendants, and very soon a good temporary building was erected, sufficient for present needs, to be enlarged, improved, and extended by Ciaran, his monks, and their respective successors. This was the humble origin of the famous monastic school, which was afterwards known as Clonmacnoise, and which soon bid fair to eclipse the glory of Clonard itself. The ruins of Clonmacnoise are all that English vandalism has left of this ancient seat of religion and learning. When will freedom again dawn on the posterity of the founders and patrons of this and myriads of similar institutions, which in these early ages dotted all over the land of the Gael?

An t-octṁaḋ caibroil.

CHAPTER VIII.

Rún Maelmopḋa.

THE PROJECT OF MAELMORDHA.

The Abbot Ciaran invited the brothers and their party to stay with him for a few days; this they cordially agreed to, and they all rather enjoyed the novelty of the situation. Maelmordha seemed rather restless, and towards evening disappeared; but, owing to the frequent moving up and down through Artibra of the other young men, his longer absence was not noticed. Seamus, the boatman, was therefore a little surprised to see him coming towards him all alone. He saluted respectfully, the young lord returned the courtesy, and coming nearer, exclaimed :

" Seamus, my good fellow, couldst thou bring me back to Teamhair, all alone ?"

" Back to Teamhair ! and alone ! Is my lord serious ?"

" Perfectly serious, Seamus. Canst thou do it at once, without letting my brother or any of our friends know aught about the matter ?"

" But remember the risk, *mo thiarna*, even though the Ardrigh is absent."

"The Ardrigh absent! What meanest thou, O Seamus ?"

" That King Tuathal has left Teamhair for Greallach Eilti,* where he is to hold an assembly on to-morrow."

" Ha, then he has come half way; but how knowest thou that Tuathal has come to Greallach Eilti ?"

" I heard it about two hours ago from an old neighbour who passed me on the river."

"Good; then thou canst row me along the Brosna and through the three lakes† to Greallach Eilti."

" Hast thou considered the matter well, *mo thiarna ?*" asked the astonished Seamus.

"Well, Seamus," replied Maelmordha, after a few minutes' reflection, "after all, I think I will not go this evening."

" I am very glad to hear it. Thou wouldst lose either thy liberty or thy life; or wouldst, perhaps, be held as a hostage for thy brother."

" Well, I will sleep over it. We are now stopping with the Abbot Ciaran at Druim Tibrait, in here, and most probably I will seek thee here in the morning; as yet I know not the hour; but if thou art not here I suppose any of thy comrades will find thee in yonder biadhtach ?"

Seamus signified assent, but said :—" I hope thou wilt change thy mind."

" Well, Seamus, should I do so I will send one of our followers to tell thee so. *Slán leat mo chara.*"‡

Maelmordha returned to the new building, and felt gratified that no one asked him any questions : in fact it was supposed that he had merely taken a walk through Artibra.

The Abbot Ciaran invited all his guests to join himself and his brethren in chanting the canonical hours in the new Eglais Beg, and the sound of the divine praises were for the first time

---

* In northern part of present county of Westmeath.
† Lakes Ennel, Owhel, and Iron.
‡ Health with thee; farewell, my friend.

borne on the evening breeze from the wilds of Artibra. The passengers on the Sionnain at first thought it proceeded from Inis Ainghin, until from that island also proceeded the familiar sounds. Many were the questions asked concerning what was evidently a new foundation, but as yet no one was able to give a satisfactory answer. Meanwhile, Maelmordha had been considering what course he would take. At last he concluded he would go to Greallach Eilti, but not by river, if he could help it. Early in the morning, when no one was within hearing, he thus addressed Diarmaid :

"Thou knowest, *mo dhearbhrathair*, that I have lost my black steed."

"Yea, Maelmordha, I know, and am glad thou hast not forgotten the poor animal."

"I shall never forget him ; but I am without a horse."

"Well, none of us had any occasion for a horse since we came here. All our other horses are safe with Mac Amhlaigh ; and when the time comes that we may use them thou wilt have more horses than thou canst make use of. I can get plenty of them in rents, and besides, there is scarcely a family on both banks of the Sionnain and elsewhere who would not be delighted to present thee with the best animals in their possession, both for my sake and thine own."

"I know all that, O Diarmaid, *mo ghradh*, but I want one immediately, and I would ask thee for the temporary use of the best animal belonging to our company—thine own black steed, the fellow of my dead one."

"And where art thou going, *mo dhearbhrathair* ?" asked Diarmaid.

"Thou hast a right to ask that question; but, Diarmaid, thou wilt not press it ?"

"No, if it is a secret; but it is the first time I knew thee to refuse me thy confidence."

"Now, that is hard; when thine interest is dearer to me than mine own life."

"I know that," said Diarmaid, embracing and kissing his brother ; "but thy life is as dear to me as mine own, and far dearer than mine interests."

"Then why refuse me thy steed for awhile ?"

"I have not refused thee ; thou knowest it is at thy service at any moment thou dost want it, and it is thine for good if thou dost prefer it to any other. But I fear, by thy manner, that thou art going in the way of danger that I am unable to comprehend."

"Thou, a Fenian! and thou talkest to another Fenian of danger!"

"But thou art but one, while there may be multitudes of Fenians against thee if thou dost rashly beard King Tuathal in Teamhair."

"But," said Maelmordha, starting, "what makest thou think, Oh, *mo dhearbhrathair*, that I have any thought of returning to Teamhair?"

"I know not, but something in thine eye tells me that thou art bent on something desperate. Tell me that I am mistaken."

"Well, I am *not* going to Teamhair, of that I can assure thee."

"Then where art thou going to?"

"Well, since thou dost insist upon knowing, I must tell thee; but thou wilt at least promise that thou wilt not forbid or try to foil me in any way."

"Thou placest me in a predicament—thou must have some serious business in contemplation."

"But thou wilt promise. It is not much."

"I will promise, on condition that it involves nothing dangerous to thee."

"Ha! ha! ha! danger again. Oh! shade of Fionn Mac Cumhal!"

"But thou forgettest, O Maelmordha, that with all our Fenianism we had to fly before the superior numbers, as well as the established authority, of our fellow Fenians."

"No; that was a different matter. Fionn Mac Cumhal himself would have had to fly before such odds. But I intend to perform a feat that is not often heard of in Eire, and certainly not elsewhere. I may as well tell thee all. Thou mighest have noticed my absence on yester-eve; well, I went down to the Sionnain banks where we landed to come here; I saw and spoke to Seamus; I wanted him to bring me to Teamhair without telling him why I wanted to go there; he tried to persuade me to forego my intention, on account of the risk, 'even though,' as he said, 'the Ardrigh was not there'——"

"Not there!" exclaimed Diarmaid.

"Not there," continued Maelmordha; "and when I expressed my surprise, as thou didst now, he told me that he had been informed that Tuathal was already at Greallach Eilti, where he is to hold an assembly on to-morrow."

"In the Rath?" asked Diarmaid.

"At the Rath, in the open air, as it is an assembly of the people."

"And is it there thou wantest to go ?"

"Nowhere else, O Diarmaid."

"And why dost thou wish to go there ?"

"Look here, Diarmaid, Tuathal has now reigned eleven years ; that is, he has, during that period, usurped a throne which by right belonged to thee. Not satisfied with that, he has even dared to issue a proclamation condemning thee, his true sovereign, to exile and death. Now, does not the man, guilty of such crimes, deserve to die the death of a traitor ?"

"True ; but, after all, he *is* Ardrigh."

"I think we have settled the question of title already. It now remains to be seen how long he is to be permitted to retain a title to which he has no just claim."

"We have a strong party which is ready at any moment to take up arms against Tuathal Maelgarbh ; but as yet we have not been able to bring matters to a crisis."

"But, Diarmaid, I am going to bring matters to a crisis, and that, too, before to-morrow's sun has set."

"Thou art not going to kill Tuathal ?"

"No, no ; I am only going to execute him."

"That is a distinction without a d:fference."

"Nay, thou knowest that I have never harmed a living thing; that I would not hurt my greatest enemy, or thine ; not even Tuathal Maelgarbh, were his injuries to thee other than the usurpation of thy crown, and a rebellion against thy authority."

"But how dost thou intend to carry out thy mad project ?"

"It is not mad ; he has set a price upon thy heart; well, I will slay a whelp, take out its heart, and carry it on the point of my lance to Greallach Eilti ; he and the people with him will think it is a courier with thy heart, and I shall have no difficulty in gaining instant access to his presence——"

"And then ?"

"And then I will pierce his own heart with my lance, and thou shalt then be, *de facto,* as well as *de jure,* Ardrigh n-Erind."

"And how thinkest thou to escape the vengeance of his court and servants after the commission of such a deed ?"

"The suddenness of the movement will so take the people by surprise, that before they have time to recover their self-possession, thy black steed will have borne me with safety from the place. Now thou understandest why I am so desirous to ride thy horse in preference to all others."

"Yea, but I do not quite approve of it."

"Why so, O Diarmaid ?"

"For many reasons. First : I like not the murder of——"

" It is *not* murder, O Diarmaid."

" No, only killing——"

" It is *not* killing; it is the execution of a rebel and a criminal."

" Before a rebel or a criminal can be lawfully executed it is first necessary that he should be judged and condemned by lawfully-constituted tribunals."

" I grant all that; but as Tuathal's sentence is passed, I may lawfully execute him."

" And, pray, when and where has his sentence been passed ?"

" Hast thou forgotten what I said to thee ere we had left the Brosna for the Sionnain, concerning the proclamation of Tuathal Maelgarbh, and what course I wanted thee to take in the matter ?"

" Ah ! I remember how, as Ardrigh *de jure*, I was to enthrone myself on a stone or on the stump of a tree, and thence issue a proclamation, condemning the rebel and usurper, Tuathal Maelgarbh, to exile and death. But I do not remember that I have done it."

" No, *thou* didst not do it; but the Ardrigh of heaven hast done so for thee by the mouth of his servant and representative, Ciaran Mac an t-Saoir, Abbot of Inis Aingin and of Artibra."

" Dost thou suppose, then, from the words he made use of on yesterday that he would sanction thee taking my adversary's life ?"

" I know not whether he would sanction the particular manner in which I have resolved to ensure as speedily as possible the fulfilment of his prophecy; but such implicit faith and confidence do I place in the words he has spoken, that I am as certain of the success of my plan as I am that its result will be thine elevation to the throne of thine ancestors."

" And thou dost not believe that thou wouldst not be doing wrong in taking the life of Tuathal ?"

" No, Diarmaid, I do not believe it; I tell thee again that I would not hurt, much less kill, Tuathal or anyone else, under any other circumstances whatever. I am merely doing what I should be obliged to do at thy command, wert thou on the throne, and Tuathal conspiring against thee. I would that he spared me the necessity of removing him from the throne in such a manner, for I have no desire or liking for the business; but as matters stand I look upon it as a sacred duty, and if thou hast any doubt upon the matter thou canst question the Abbot Ciaran himself."

" Then let us question him now."

" He is now at meditation, and must not be disturbed; besides, my brother, it is now nearly time that I should be starting. So thou needest not fear, unless thou hast some other reason."

"Well, as I said before, I have many reasons; but that and another are the principal."

"And what is the other, O Diarmaid?"

"It is the danger of losing thee, mo dearbhrathair. Of what avail would the throne be to me if it were the cause of my losing the companion and playmate of my childhood?"

"Nay, mo dearbhrathair, thou wilt not lose me; and if thou dost, why, I shall think it but a small return for all thy love and kindness to lose my life in thy service."

"O Maelmordha, mo dhearbhrathair, that is extravagant; thou must not go."

"Why not, mo ghrádh; though I spoke thus there is really no fear whatever if I am to have thy steed; he will carry me far out of the reach of those who would revenge him whom they call their king. And I shall myself be the first to carry to thee the account of my exploit, and to greet thee as Ardrigh n-Erind."

"But lest it should miscarry, at least instruct someone else what to do, and let him take thy place."

"It will not miscarry; and to no other person in the world would I entrust the performance of the project I have marked out for myself."

"But if, after all, thou shouldst not be able to carry it through, and lose thy life in an abortive attempt on Tuathal's life?"

"Nay, Diarmaid, I see thou doubtest my courage or my bravery, or else thou thinkest that I am incapable of any feat I have undertaken to perform."

"Now, mo mhuirnin, thou must not take on so; thou knowest I did not mean to offend thee. So come down from thy high horse and mount mine, and go with him whithersoever thou wilt."

An naonmað caibioil.

CHAPTER IX.

Cleaf maelmorða.

THE FEAT OF MAELMORDHA.

A LOVING kiss and affectionate embrace was all the answer the delighted Maelmordha could give, and exulting in the success of his last stratagem, he hurried off to send one of the attendants to Amherghin's father for the steed of which he had the temporary custody. He himself having blackened his face and hair, giving an appearance of hair where there was none, next arrayed himself in the plain woollen garb of one of the boatmen, which articles Seamus procured for him, and had conveyed through the messenger whom Maelmordha had sent to him for the purpose. When at length he presented himself before the astonished Diarmaid, the latter declared that, had the former not spoken he never would have recognised him. They then took a most affectionate farewell; Diarmaid, though full of misgivings, feared to give any further opposition, lest he should again hurt the feelings of his brave and loving, though obstinate brother. Maelmordha then dashed off to meet the horse, in order to avoid being seen by either their own followers or the monks, for he thought it best to lead as few as possible into the secret. He soon met his brother's steed, on which the attendant was riding towards him; the latter dismounted, and in another instant Maelmordha was riding at full speed in a northerly direction. After about twelve miles' journey, he reached Athluain,* where he stopped at a biadhtach to refresh himself and the horse. He shunned observation as much as possible. He then continued his journey, and towards evening reached another biadhtach, where he put up for the night; he was now about a mile from the river Ethnea,† and concluded to rest the horse there all night that he might be fresh for the morrow's work. When he had seen his steed well fed and groomed and put up, and had himself partaken of the rich and abundant meal that was spread before him, he rambled out to look about the country. He found that there were plenty of animals of the kind he sought, and satisfied with the result, he returned to the biadhtach. It was nearly overcrowded with people who were on their way to Greallach Eilti to take part in the assembly of the succeeding day. It is hard to say how he might have fared had his identity been suspected; but so complete was his disguise, and so full were the people of the morrow's doings, that he escaped all recognition. The next morning, after breakfast, all the strangers took their departure, with the exception of Maelmordha, who remained behind, partly to ensure a proper moment for the attack—it would not do to be there before the time—and partly to give the horse as much rest as possible, for the animal would need all its strength at the critical moment. Accordingly, about noon, he was mounted on the black steed; he started from the biadhtach; but before he took the destined road, he turned a little to the right, where he had

* Athlone.   † Inny.

been exploring the evening before; and scarcely had he proceeded a few steps, when the bark of a whelp fell upon his ear; with a bound he rushed on the animal and killed it with one stroke of his lance; he then cut out the heart, and fixing it upon the point of his lance, he remounted, and turning his horse's head, rode at full speed for his destination.   On coming to the Ethnea river, he crossed Ath Maighne, or the ford which led from southern to northern Teabhtha.   Galloping about a mile and a-half further, he soon heard the indistinct murmurs of the multitude.   Stray stragglers whom he passed on his way looked their astonishment; others, more bold, cried out: "Lo, he beareth Diarmaid's heart!" Maelmordha heard, and rode on.   Once or twice he narrowly escaped death at the hands of some of his brother's sympathisers, who not knowing him, and still less suspecting his *ruse*, thought he was bearing their favourite's heart to the usurping monarch.   Now, he could see the rath, and could even distinguish the Ardrigh seated on an eminence, with a great concourse of people around him.   As those who formed the outer ring saw the horseman approach at full speed, and bearing a heart at the point of his lance, they cried out:

"Lo! here cometh a courier bearing the heart of the traitor to the Ardrigh.   Make way.   Let him pass."

And the words ran through the assembly, and the people opened a passage for the courier up to the very spot where Ardrigh Tuathal was seated, and as the strange horseman tore through the path so cheerfully made for him, a ringing cheer of loyalty arose from the throats of the assembly.   All made way, officers and nobles, for the now far more important though humble looking courier, who would not condescend to look at anyone but King Tuathal himself.   And still the cheers went up from the people as the horseman galloped up the eminence where was seated the smiling, haughty, triumphant-looking Ardrigh, who, now at last, was rid of a powerful, dangerous rival.   Now, at least, his throne was secure; now he could reign in peace over Eire.   Of what reward was not this loyal courier worthy?   He was evidently a very humble man; oh, he was in the garb of a boatman! well, he would be a boatman no longer.   He should have his thousand milch kine, he should have much more, he should have——

At this moment the strange horseman was face to face with the Ardrigh; but instead of dismounting and on his knees presenting the long-desired heart, as Tuathal expected, he rushed madly forward, and before anyone knew what he was about, he plunged the heart-laden spear deep into the heart of the Ardrigh himself. Death was instantaneous, and before anyone knew what had happened, Maelmordha, without waiting to extricate his spear, wheeled round to the left, and had well-nigh escaped, when a dreadful shout arose behind; he was pursued by many horsemen, and in another instant he lay weltering in his own blood, pierced by a hundred spears. The multitude, on finding that their monarch had been slain by stratagem before their very eyes in the noon-day, were frantic with grief and rage. Thousands of voices sent up their wailing caoine,* and the assembly which had a little while before met in joy broke up now in sorrow, as the remains of the late Ardrigh were borne from the place in melancholy procession to Teamhair. As for Maelmordha, the cause of all this, he lay there a mangled corpse, as yet uncared for, with no one as yet to chant his caoine. Were there none among all that throng to sympathise with the cause for which that unknown dead young man had dared and suffered and sacrificed his life ? None ! At least, none while the dead king and the crowds of his faithful subjects who had met there to do him homage, remained upon the scene. But when they had departed out of the place, two men stole cautiously towards where the corpse lay stretched upon the ground. They bent over him and touched him gently, when one of them exclaimed :

"Ah ! there is no hope, he is already cold and stiff; we can do nothing for him."

"Poor fellow !" exclaimed the other man ; "he has put a period to the distractions in which the rivalry of the princes has so long plunged the country."

"And has paid for it with his life. Come, we had better remove him to my house, it is the nearest."

"Ay, we can at least pay him the last sad offices. We shall have to wash this black off him. I wonder why did he thus disguise himself ?"

"I heard some of the people say that he must have been in the confidence, or at least in the service of Prince Diarmaid, and that having turned traitor and slain him, he was obliged to thus disguise himself, lest he should never reach here alive."

"Yea, but we now know that such surmise cannot be correct. Yonder heart, which with the lance was taken from the body of the Ardrigh, was found on examination to be the heart of a whelp. Besides, the man who would kill Tuathal would not kill Diarmaid. He must have been one of the close intimates of Prince Diarmaid, and thus disguised himself, lest he should be identified too soon for the success of his plan."

* Küeen.

"We must examine him closely here, we are at the house."

They then bore the corpse into the house; it was one of those oblong buildings with flat roof, which was supported in the interior by oaken pillars at regular intervals. The fireplace and candelabrum were in the central hall; between the pillars were the *imdai*, on one of which they laid the corpse. They then commenced to wash it, and great was their surprise when, on removing the black from the face and hair, they beheld, instead of the rough-looking boatman, a youth of extreme beauty and delicacy of complexion, and adorned with beautiful nut-brown hair; greater still was their astonishment when they recognised in the noble-looking features a strong resemblance to their beloved prince.

"Great heavens!" exclaimed one of the men, "can it be that it is Prince Diarmaid himself?"

"Nay," replied the other, "it is not he; but I am now certain it is none other than his stepbrother, Maelmordha Mac Agatan."

"What ought we to do?"

"Thou and thy family can guard the corpse, and invite the *mná caointe** to chant his praises and lament his untimely end, while I bear the news to Prince Diarmaid."

"And dost thou know where to find him?"

"I know nought, save that he is on the Sionnain; but I doubt not I shall be able to find him."

"I wonder does he know aught of the feat of Maelmordha?"

"Well, it is hard to say; but one thing is certain, Maelmordha came not by the Sionnain."

"No, he came on horseback. Was the horse also killed?"

"No, it was slightly injured, but my son led it off here before we dared approach the dead body of its master."

"Then it is on the premises?"

"Yea, and well-cared for. I doubt not it would be able to carry thee; it is not much injured, and I am sure there would be no objection to thy riding it into the possession of the prince."

"I am sure not, but I would rather go by the boat along the Sionnain; it would be the surest place to meet Diarmaid."

He then set off, running down to the banks of the river Ethnea, where he got into a corach, and sailed along that river into Loch Ri, and thence into the Sionnain, keeping a sharp look out all the way to Artibra, when, seeing no sign, he inquired,

---

* Kűeening women.

and was told where the prince was. Following the directions given him, he disembarked, and landing, penetrated into Artibra. He perceived several young men moving about, and going up to one of them, asked if he had lately seen Prince Diarmaid, that he desired to see him.

" Prince Diarmaid cannot be seen now," replied the party addressed, " he is overwhelmed with grief for the loss of his brother."

" Then he is aware of his brother's death ?"

" The rumour first and then the whole account of the affair reached us both from the Sionnain and the Brosna. Whence camest thou ?"

" I came direct from Greallach Eilti and from the house where lieth Maelmordha Mac Argatan."

" Then I know that Diarmaid will see thee. We were preparing to go thither. Follow me."

The two men then walked towards the Eglais Beg, at the door of which they met the Abbot Ciaran, who informed them that Diarmaid was within, and did not like to be disturbed. However, on hearing an explanation, he volunteered to inform the prince. The latter was prostrate before the altar, and it was some time before Ciaran could prevail on him to move. At length, however, he appeared in the wicker hut into which Ciaran had previously ushered the stranger. Their interview was long, and when at last they emerged, Diarmaid conducted the stranger into the proinnteach, which the industry of the monks, aided by Diarmaid's attendants, had already in a fair way of completion. Consigning him to the care of the guestmaster, the prince returned to the church, never quitting it until the abbot himself, late at night, took him forcibly in his arms, and deposited him on his bed in the cell assigned to his use.

An veicmav caibivil.

CHAPTER X.

An c-Avlacav.

THE FUNERAL.

The next morning, after Mass, the Abbot Ciaran and Prince Diarmaid, with all the followers of both, including the stranger, left the new monastery, and going down to the banks of the Sionnain, entered the numerous boats, which, according to previous arrangement, were there to meet them. The royal boat, in which Diarmaid, Ciaran, Amherghin, and a few others sailed, was a roomy, well-finished vessel of polished oak, with the royal Sun Burst flying half-mast high. When all was ready the procession of boats sailed along the river, attracting universal observation. They were soon joined by others, until nearly all the boats on the Sionnain were following in the wake of the royal banner When they had sailed about a mile, they stopped to take in a coffin, which had been ordered from a stone cutter, who resided and worked at this spot. It was of white marble, sculptured in crosses, *seamhrógs*,* sunbursts, the Fenian harp, and sacred inscriptions. It was placed carefully in the royal boat, and the miniature fleet resumed its sad voyage. When they arrived at Loch Ri, they found it full of loyal sympathisers, who had come from various parts of the surrounding territory to await their arrival. The greatest number of these were obliged to remain there until their return, as the Ethnea river could not accommodate them all. When at last the voyagers landed, they were met by a great throng of people, for the news had now spread far and wide. Universal sympathy was expressed on the faces of the multitude. Some few thoughtless persons who were for congratulating Prince Diarmaid on his new position, and greeting him as Ardrigh n-Erind, were speedily brought to their senses by the sight of the object of their worship, for in truth, Diarmaid, notwithstanding his handsome presence, noble bearing, and royal attire, looked anything but a new-made king. His woe-begone expression of heart-rending anguish went straight to the hearts of the beholders, utterly crushing out all thought of politics or rivalries, and welling forth in sympathetic union with his own dèep sorrow. Several carbads were in waiting to receive the principal members of the party. The prince and the abbot having been, by the stranger who brought the news, introduced to the men in whose house the brother's remains lay, they all set out for the house; they were not long in reaching it. The whole way was lined with sympathisers, besides those who followed on foot. There was no cheering or anything like an attempt at it, though, some at least, thought the present state of affairs was at variance with their experience of what the first public reception of a new sovereign was wont to be. When the chariots stopped at the door of the house, their occupants alighted amidst the crowds who surrounded it. They entered; Diarmaid advanced to the couch on which his brother lay; the *mná caointe*, who

* Shamrocks.

were chanting the history and praises of the deceased, looked at the prince as if to gather from his actions and manner inspiration for fresh outpourings of extempore lamentations. But the stricken expression which had already been so contagious, now had its effect on the *mná caointe.* These hired, and even at best but political sympathisers, stood speechless in the presence of such genuine domestic affliction, they forgot suddenly all their eloquence and rhetoric, and as if by common consent, backed out of the presence of death, and joined the crowd without the house. Meantime, Diarmaid, without uttering a word, had fallen on the dead body of his brother. The master of the house, with the Abbot Ciaran, Amherghin, his father, and a few of the principal personages, stood at a respectful distance for some time, until Ciaran thought the thing had gone on too long; he then went over and gently tried to remove the prince, but the prince refused to stir; the abbot reminded him that time was passing, that the remains of his brother should be coffined, as they had a long journey before them. But the prince replied he would not allow the body to be coffined that day at all, nor perhaps the next, and that the journey could be performed on one day as well as on another. Ciaran represented that any such departure from their original arrangements would seriously inconvenience the multitudes of their friends who had come to assist at the funeral, who were even then impatiently awaiting them on the roads and on the rivers, and who would be disappointed at its non-arrival, and would be obliged in great part to return to their homes, if there were any undue delay. Ciaran finally remonstrated with Diarmaid on the sinfulness of his excessive grief, representing to him that it was flying in the face of the Sovereign Lord of All, who in his inscrutable designs had deprived him of a beloved brother, in the same moment that he granted himself a crown, thus making use of Maelmordha as an instrument——.

"What is that thou wouldst say, my son?" suddenly exclaimed Ciaran, as Diarmaid fixed upon him a look of questioning astonishment.

"Nay," replied Diarmaid, "nothing just now; this is neither the time nor the place. I am ready now to do as thou wilt."

Diarmaid then took one long embrace of his dead brother, impressing upon the beloved, though now unconscious features, a parting kiss, and wearily raised himself from the couch. Many hands then set about making all necessary preparations. The corpse of Maelmordha was fully arrayed in his own splendid attire, which he had left behind him at Artibra, but which Diarmaid had taken care to bring with him.   Then the Abbot Ciaran placed a silver crucifix upon his breast, and commenced to read over him the prayers for the dead, until the *fenn*, or funeral car, arrived at the door, when he ceased, and the body, which had been placed in the beautiful white marble coffin, was removed into it, not, however, until Diarmaid had taken another fond embrace and another parting kiss.   The fenn was covered with black satin, which hung down all round, and was bordered with silver fringe.   High up on top was placed the white coffin, over which was laid the Gal Greine, yet so as not to hide the coffin.   At the corners and sides were placed other flags, as that of the Red Branch, with its golden lion, the green banner of the Fenians, with its harp and crown, and others of minor import-ance.   Wreath of sheamrógs and of ivy were placed on the coffin, and the whole conveyance was drawn by eight magni-ficent black horses, including Diarmaid's own, which had now recovered from its slight wound.   Great numbers of carbads of various classes were there with their occupants, ready to form into procession; some of them were drawn by four horses, others by three, two, and one, according to the means or position of their owners.   All their gay colours were, however, concealed with black or white coverings.   Others rode on horses, always using black ones whenever procurable.   Multitudes followed on foot, the mná caointe set up the caoine; others lined the roads on either side all the way to the banks of the Ethnea.   Arrived here there was a general dismounting from horses and chariots. The coffin was taken down from the fenn and placed in an ele-vated position in the royal boat, where it could be seen by all on river and on land.   It was placed immediately under the Gal Greine, which floated half-mast high.   When Diarmaid, Ciaran, Amherghin, and several of the nobility had entered this boat it commenced to move on, the other boats, being fast filled with people, followed in regular succession.   The boats of private persons which followed the funeral generally displayed their own particular banner and device.   The voices of the *mná caointe* rose above the waters of the Shannon, the chorus being taken up by thousands of people on the river, and lining its brink on each side, the whole way :—

"Och! och! mo bhron,
    Oh, why did our brave prince die ?
    Oh! woe! woe! woe!
    O Maelmordha, of the sharp spear !
    Why didst thou die ?

Why leave a brother's arms
To face the King of Terrors—
  Grim Death?
Who closed within his icy embrace
King Tuathal and thee.
Och! orro! orro! ollalu!
To die in thy youth and beauty,
In the fair budding morn of thy manhood;
While yet the roses were fresh upon thy cheeks,
The sunshine in thy bright brown eyes.
O Maelmordha, thou wert fair as brave,
Smooth and white were thy hands,
And long thy fingers;
Thick and in ringlets was thy nut-brown hair.
Sweet was the music of thy mouth,
And melodious the tones of thy voice;
Thou wert tall and stately, brave and true,
A hero among heroes,
A Fenian among the Fians!
  O Maelmordha!
And thou didst die so soon—so young,
So beloved of thy brother,
And so regretted by all!
Oh! pitiable is the tale!
Oh, grief! oh, woe!
Och! ollalu!
Pierced by a hundred spears
  Is our beloved!
Mo bhron! mo bhron!
But yester morn, thou wentest
From thy brother's arms—
  Thy Diarmaid!
Wentest forth from fair Artibra!
Riding gaily on a black steed,
Wentest to thy destruction
  At Greallach Eilti!
Holding at the point of thy lance
  A whelp's heart!
Thy beauty disguised under sordid forms,
That thou mightest rid Green Eire
Of the usurper—thy brother's rival!
Who is now being carried to his tomb,
As thou art, O, Maelmordha!
  Oh, grief! oh, grief!
O, Maelmordha Mac Argeadan!
Fair skinned Teamhair
Shall never more behold thee,
Nor shall gallant Midhe,
Nor far-stretched Magh Breagh.
Inisfail mourns her lost son,
Diarmaid our Ardrigh, a loving brother,
The Fenian host, a worthy comrade,
All mankind, a perfect man!
Oh! Sionnain! Sionnain! Sionnain!

Woe is the day that thou bearest on thy breast
The noble form of the gallant Maelmordha;
Fair Artibra, receive once more
In thy Cluain-mac-nois—
In thy calm retreat, the son of the noble!
Holy monks! holy abbot!
In prayers and psalms and sacred office,
Consign the remains of our beloved
To the holy earth which ye have sanctified!
Let Prince Diarmaid's gift—
    The Eglais Beg—
Be the place of Maelmordha's resurrection!
Saints and angels, receive his soul!
Mother of Jesus, take him by the hand!
Son of Mary, grant him rest!"

Slowly and sadly died away the solemn strains of the caoine, to rise again in loud, piercing wails from the many thousand throats that glided along on the Shannon's waters, or surged and swayed on either bank.

When the long procession entered Loch Ri, they found it, as before, full of ships and boats, which were so stationed as to leave a passage through the lake for the royal funeral. When it passed through, they immediately fell in behind, and followed it through the Sionnain; the banks on both sides were thronged with people as before, who had long been waiting patiently for its approach. When they arrived at Artibra, they found it very difficult to get through, owing to the multitude of vessels that were awaiting their arrival. Partly, indeed owing to this fact, but much more out of respect for the prince and his dead brother, the ordinary everyday traffic was for the time suspended. After some difficulty, the royal vessel succeeded in drawing up at the nearest point to the new monastery. The other boats followed as close upon it as they could, and soon all the boats were emptied, and the multitudes followed the coffin into the monastic grounds. The coffin was brought into the Eglais Beg, and there placed in state before the new temporary altar. Then all who could be accommodated were admitted, and after a slight refection to all who chose to partake of it, the caoine having ceased, a procession formed of the monks entered the little church, and under the direction of the Abbot Ciaran, commenced the office for the dead. Their voices could be heard by the multitudes without, who united their intentions with those of the monks. When this was over, a few of the monks were left to continue the chant, who were to be relieved in turn by all the rest, that the prayers might not cease day or night. Thus, those who had obtained admittance left, to give room to others, and in this manner all the people were enabled to enter the church in batches at a time. This continued for eight days, during which time crowds of strangers came from all parts, including visitors from the monastery of Cluain-Irared. The old school-fellows and teachers of Maelmordha and Diarmaid, headed by the holy Finian himself, and many of our old acquaintances, native and foreign, including Aristophanes and Bec Mac De. Many came also from Teamhair, brimful of information, as well as of sympathy, but they found little opportunity of conveying the former. Every morning the holy sacrifice was offered for the departed Maelmordha by Ciaran and such of his monks as had arrived at the dignity of the priesthood, also by the Bishop Finian and some of his priests who accompanied him, as well as clergymen from different other parts of the country. One morning after the Abbots Finian and Ciaran had celebrated Mass, they and Prince Diarmaid were closeted together, conversing over many things connected with the memory of Maelmordha, and going over all the events that had occurred. At length, Diarmaid said :

" I cannot express the gratitude I feel that ye have not refused to offer up the holy sacrifice and other prayers for Maelmordha, as I fear many would have done. The possibility of such a result to the daring feat of my brother was the most poignant source of my first grief."

" Was it anything concerning that subject that thou didst refer to at the house in Greallach Eilti, where thy brother lay ?" asked Ciaran.

" Yea," replied Diarmaid, " I felt at once relieved and surprised at thy words to me there ; thou didst say something about him being an instrument; at all events, thy words told me that thou didst not believe him to be a ——."

Diarmaid's tongue refused to utter the word, but Ciaran came to his relief.

" My son, I know what thou wouldst say. Believe me, I have thought the matter over long and anxiously, aye, even before we reached Greallach Eilti, and before that time I had concluded to pray for Maelmordha. Since the arrival of our holy father here"—saluting Finian—" we have talked the matter over, we have prayed for light; we have taken into account Maelmordha's previous great virtue, and tender, generous disposition ; his great love for thyself, the peculiarity of his character and idiosyncracies ; the strength and evident conscientiousness of his moral and political views, which he so curiously intermixed ; the unhappy divisions of the kingdom into two rival parties; the justness of thy claims, O Diarmaid, and Tuathal's usurpation—all these forces acting on a temperament like Maelmordha's, makes a very different case to that of a man who would take a fellow-creature's life to gratify, without any of those considerations I have mentioned, a sordid ambition or wicked revenge."

"Then it is the same as if he had killed Tuathal in war, or by decree of the law in peace?"

"My son," said the Abbot Finian, "on account of a heavy cold, I am not able to say much to thee; but let me tell thee that it is only the peculiarities of Maelmordha's special case that relieves his memory from the stain of murder. No other person could plead Maelmordha's example in extenuation of a similar act. Our friend Ciaran here has told me all the conversations which passed between them, as well as those which thou hast related from time to time. I know myself of old much of the inherent peculiarities of Maelmordha's character; and taking everything into consideration I am convinced that where others would be condemned, thy brother has found mercy."

"Whether he was right or wrong, Maelmordha was most certainly convinced that Tuathal was an usurper and a criminal, whom he was lawfully justified in putting to death," replied Diarmaid.

"And, there can be no doubt," said Ciaran, "that the prophetic words with which God inspired me in thy regard, and which I uttered in his hearing, precipitated the climax which we now deplore, and for this reason I now take on myself the entire responsibility of Maelmordha's act."

Diarmaid warmly pressed the hand of Ciaran, and in his presence and that of Finian made renewed voluntary offerings to the monastery in behalf of Maelmordha, which he promised to carry into effect as soon as he was established at Teamhair.

On the day appointed for the interment, the people commenced to assemble from an early hour, the river was black with boats full of people destined for Artibra. They poured in in thousands from almost every part of the country. At the appointed hour the Solemn Office and Mass for the Dead was chanted by hundreds of priests and monks, including several abbots and bishops. This over, the coffin was removed from its position before the altar and carried outside the Eglais Beg. It was then carried around the exterior of the church three times, the long procession of religious and of the laity following, as well as the crowds would permit. After the third time, they

stopped at the spot where the grave was dug, just outside the
church at the altar side, and into this grave was the coffin
lowered, amidst the universal wailing of the people. The grave
was filled in, and at the head was placed a marble tombstone,
from the same establishment which had supplied the coffin, sculptured with sacred emblems and the name of the deceased. Then
the last absolution was given, and the people prepared to depart,
having witnessed the first interment that had ever taken place in
Artibra, but which was destined to become the favourite burial
place of countless thousands. Just, however, as the people
were preparing to depart, a deputation of the principal inhabitants of Teamhair approached Prince Diarmaid, and first having
expressed their condolence with him in his bereavement, one of
their number—the chief herald—presented him with the spear
of state, and saluted him as Ard Righ n-Erind. At these words
all present knelt also, though the circumstances of the time and
place precluded any joyous demonstrations. Diarmaid accepted
the spear of state, which was tendered to him as a badge of his
new office, and thanked the deputation, and then inquired
whether the late king was yet buried:

"He was buried, O King," replied the spokesman, "on
yesterday morning; and I conceal not the fact, O King, that all
classes of people, thine own party, no less than his, turned out
to do honour to his memory."

"And I honour them for it," replied King Diarmaid, "for
death is a terrible thing, and in its presence we should sink all
party feuds and jealousies. I would now that Tuathal had lived
and sat longer on my throne, so as my brother were left to me. I
hope ye did not leave Teamhair until after the obsequies of the
late Ardrigh?"

"Nay, we took part in all the ceremonies of King Tuathal's
burial, e'en to the very last; but when it was over, thou wert
proclaimed Ard Righ n-Erind, and we lost not a moment in setting ·
out for Artibra, and coming at full speed, that we might be in
time for the other funeral ceremony of to-day, ere we formally
tendered our allegiance with the spear of state."

"And what of the Ardrighan?" asked Diarmaid.

"The Ardrighan of Tuathal Maelgarbh has fled almost distracted to the Convent of Cill Daire. There is nothing to
prevent thee, O Ardrigh, from taking immediate possession of
Teamhair."

"I will not take possession just yet. It is enough that I
have been proclaimed."

"But Teamhair awaits thee, O King. Even the late King's

most ardent adherents will now receive thee with loyalty as their sovereign."

"Ah! I always thought so. Accomplished facts, then, are the right things after all. A few days ago I was the anarchist and the rebel whom it was the duty of all who claimed any respectability to shun. In another few days when I arrive at Teamhair, these same people will be more extravagant in their demonstrations of loyalty than the faithful people who have either outwardly or in secret taken my side where there seemed the least possibility of hope. O Maelmordha, what a change thou hast made by the sacrifice of thy life; and thou wert worth them all put together. Now, my friends, I know ye all, either personally or by sight, and I know that all of ye have been ever faithful to me, else I would not speak as I have done. I am very glad that ye have paid honour to the remains of the late king; it is the least ye could do; and I once more return ye all my most hearty thanks for your loyalty and devotion."

"But wilt thou not, O King, come at once to Teamhair? Thou art proclaimed, 'tis true, all over the country by this time, but thou hast yet to be legally inaugurated on Lia Fail."

"I must stay here for a little while to recover myself. Ye must be aware that so soon after my bereavement I could not think of taking a principal part in such a ceremony. It would be utterly at variance with my feelings."

"Pardon me, O King," said the Abbot Ciaran, who stood near, "I have been speaking with our old master, the Abbot of Cluain-Irared, and we are of opinion that thou oughtest to lose no time about thine inauguration. Thou hast already given way to too much grief, which is very injurious to both soul and body, and the very excitement of the ceremony of inauguration will positively have a good effect on thee; and if thou wilt not take it amiss we would urge thee to accede to the solicitations of thy people by the mouths of their delegates."

"Then I will yield to thine and the Abbot Finian's advice, and will set out with ye all on to-morrow."

All who would were then entertained in the proinnteach, including the deputation, and most of the visitors remained there over night, that all might set off together the next day. Then people departed, some to their homes, others made directly for the capital to be there beforehand. But all remembered to their latest breath, and their posterity after them for many ages related in turn to *their* children the story of the "Feat of Maelmordha," *Cleas Maelmordha!*

END OF PART II.

an cReas cuid
Part III.

se bliaoana oeuz 'n oéiz.
SIXTEEN YEARS AFTER.

an ceuo caibioil.
CHAPTER I.

finian azur Columcille.
FINIAN AND COLUMKILLE.

SIXTEEN years had passed away, and now, towards the close of the month of October, in the year 560, we find ourselves once more at the great monastery of Cluain-Irared. It has undergone some changes since we saw it last: new streets have been added, cells built, the town without much improved; several new buildings have been found necessary to the monastery and school, among the principal of which was a *tech aeïdhedh*, an "enclosure" or "house" of guests. This was erected for reception and lodging of newly-arrived travellers and strangers. The institution has extended in every way; it is also changed in its living element. Some of the youths who, twenty-two years ago, were engaged in hard study are now professors of the various branches; and this is true not only of natives, but also of foreigners, for our old friend, Aristophanes, is now one of the professors of Greek in the college. His predecessor in thé post had, with many others of the monastery and school, passed to his reward; others on completing their education had left to pursue their various walks in life. Many had settled down to worldly pursuits; others had entered the Church, and were priests, or monks, or abbots either here or in other parts of the country. Ciaran, as we know, had founded the monasteries of Inis Ainghin and Artibra, already beginning to be called Clonmacnois, and enticing multitudes to its now famous schools. He also founded

11

other schools, and fulfilled the prophecy of Finian in his regard,
that he would give a rule to half the monasteries of Eire. But
he himself had long since passed to a better world. Seven
months after we saw him last—seven months after his friend had
ascended the throne—Ciaran Mac an t-Saoir, abbot and founder
of Clonmacnois, went to his reward. The two Brendans quitted
to found the monasteries of Clonfert, Ardfert and of Birr respec-
tively. Ruadhan was now abbot of Lothra;* Columcille was abbot
of many foundations, the principal of which were at Doire Cail-
cach,† Dairmhagh,‡ and Ceananus.§ The latter place was one of
the royal residences of his old school-fellow, Prince Diarmaid, who
was now reigning king, and had bestowed it upon him for the
honour of God and the Church. We already know the fate of
Diarmaid's half-brother, Maelmordha. Ninnidh is now bishop
of Achaid Conaire (Achonry), a see founded by Finian himself.
Others were already famous in their various walks in Church and
State. Bec Mac De had some six years before died at the palace
of Teamhair, "the poet, philosopher, and friend of Ardrigh
Diarmaid Mac Cearbhall;" he was also famous throughout
Eire and Europe for his deep learning, many works, and prophetic wisdom. Other foreigners besides our Greek friend also
remained in Eire, to serve in various ways the country from
which they received so many advantages. Others returned to their
own countries with the patriotic intention of fashioning their
own countrymen as much as possible after the model of the
Gaedhilic race. The ragged, boorish-looking young Saxons
whom we saw landing at Cluain-Irared long ago, had for the most
part returned to their native Britain, to astonish the inhabitants
of that country, so far as even to ask themselves, could such
superior individuals be indeed their own countrymen? But the
said countrymen themselves felt not a little pained when they
contrasted their own people with the noble race they had left
behind in the Emerald Isle. But, like good men that they were,
they still loved their own country best, even with all its shortcomings, its ignorance, its barbarism, and its crimes; and so,
instead of despising it, railing and sneering at it, scorning it,
trampling on it, and disowning it; instead of renouncing their
own names and taking Irish ones, in order to make themselves appear better than their fellows; instead of affecting
Irish fashions and wearing Irish colours, in order to insult the
feelings and prejudices of their own countrymen, and as an indi-

---

* Lorha, in north of present county Tipperary.
† Derry, it is called *cailceach* from *cailc*, a cinder, because *Doire* (oak forest)
was burnt to cinders.—*Canon Burke.*   ‡ Durrow.   § Kells.

cation that they have transferred their allegiance from their own to the neighbouring isle, and tell their less fortunate country-men in effect, if not in words, that they despise them, that they look down upon them, and are ashamed to own them for com-patriots ; and that they themselves, having the advantage of an Irish education, know how to appreciate the history and the glories of that country, and that, in short, they would be Irish-men if they could. No ; those good Saxons were not guilty of such meanness or baseness ; it was not thus their Irish masters taught them ; on the contrary, they returned home, animated with the spirit of their holy teachers, and burning with a desire to elevate the moral and intellectual tone of their own countrymen from their present deplorable condition. To this end they meant to de-vote their lives, and they were encouraged by assurances and pro-mises of assistance from the Green Isle they had left. They knew that Irish monasteries were about to send learned and talented men to found similar institutions in Britain, that thus they might more effectually educate the British nation than they could by receiving them at home. The present students of Cluain-Irared were unborn at the opening of our tale, but they now filled the vacant places of our old acquaintances ; they studied the same sciences, languages, and literature ; they played the same games ; they quarrelled over politics like their predecessors, save that the political events about which they quarrelled were somewhat different. New monks, and many of the old, continued to ply their several handicrafts in the various workshops, while their brethren taught in the schools ; the agricultural department was more flourishing than ever ; the canonical hours were as strictly observed as ever ; the. perpetual choir in the church was perpe-tual still ; the cloige-na-mainistire (monastery bells) chimed as delightfully as when our Greek traveller first heard them ; the light still burned at night. The Abbot Finian, now venerable in years, continued to be the presiding spirit that governed the whole.

But just now the whole establishment is in a state of the greatest excitement. Our hero, the reigning Ardrigh, Diar-maid Mac Feargus Mac Cearbhall, who has now been six-teen years on the throne, is about to hold his sixth triennial convention of the States of Eire at Tara, called *Feis Teamh-rach.** The illustrious abbot and bishop of Cluain-Irared, by virtue of his office and position, held a seat in that august assembly. His establishment, in common with all the other colleges throughout the country, always broke up on such occa-

* The Convention or Parliament of Tara.

sions to enable all who would, especially the students, to take part in the games, sports, feastings, and general diversions which always accompanied it.   Many of the students had already taken their departure for Teamhair, in company with their parents and friends, who had called for them, making Cluain-Irared their way for that purpose.   Others had of themselves gone off in groups.   But, as yet, the greater number remained, and the friends of many of them kept pouring in for the purpose of having their company to the capital; accordingly there was constant commotion, some coming while others were going away; they came and went by road and by river.   People from foreign lands, who had sons or relations in the college of Cluain-Irared, also came.   Some of these had been to Eire before on such occasions, others now came for the first time. They would see their young friends, and they would see the Grand Convention of the States General of the most polished people on earth : it was quite an event in their lives.   They were most courteously received by Finian and his brethren, and were shown all over every department of the whole concern, just as was our friend Aristophanes after his arrival.   It is un-necessary to dwell on their astonishment ; they had simply never seen anything approaching it before.   They were, among the rest, shown the *Leabharagan* (library).   Conan was leabhar coimhedach still, but he was sinking into the vale of years, and he was now assisted by a younger and more vigorous man, who took upon him the heaviest parts of the duty, though the learn-ing and experience of Conan was always at his service, and that of the students and visitors.   They now received the foreigners, and spared no pains to convey to them a general idea of the contents of the library, which, by the way, had been conside-rably enlarged, receiving additions to its stock of literature both from within and without that institution.   Some of the number of the visitors appreciated all they saw and heard, while others, no doubt, thought that the workshops without, or the pasture lands and what was on them, much more worthy of attention. However, when the illuminated MSS., which had also increased, were shown, all present expressed their admiration.   After showing the various varieties of this beautiful art, the assistant of Conan looked about him as if for something he could not find, and then asked the latter a question; the reply of Conan brought an expression of recollection to the face of his assistant; however, the latter merely intimated to the strangers that as they had completed the inspection of the library, he would now escort them to the church, which they had not yet seen.

On their way to the church, Sean* stopped at the Abbot
Finian's house, knocked at the door, and being invited to enter
did so; the holy abbot was reading at a small table, but as the
assistant entered he raised his head, and addressed him:

"Well, my son, what is it that makes thee look so troubled?"

"Venerable Abbot, I have shown *na daoine uaisle so*† through
the library, but I have not shown them the Book of Psalms."

"Well, I presume they know what a Book of Psalms is,"
smiling.

"Oh, but, my father, I have shown the principal illuminated
works; but I would fain show that, as it is somewhat different.
Knowest thou, O father, where it is?"

"Didst not thou thyself, my son, hand it to the Abbot
Columb, who requested me to lend it to him on his visit here a
few days ago on his way to Teamhair?"

"Yes, my father, and the Abbot Columb is somewhere about
here still, though we see little of him. Perhaps he spends all
his time somewhere *aig léigheadh an leabhair*."‡

"Well, I have been informed how and where he is spending
the short time that remains, but I have concluded not to notice
it until he returns the book. However, if thou wantest to show
it to our noble visitors thou must seek the Abbot Columb on thy
own account."

"Then, holy father, I shall do so."

And Sean, making his obeisance, left the sanctum of his
abbot, and overtaking the visitors, who had wandered in the
direction of the church, he led them to the sacred building.
As they entered the church they found there several of the
native visitors, who came from distant parts of the country.
They were speaking in whispers; the choir chanted the
psalms as usual, but were not disturbed. The librarian looked,
but seemed disappointed; those who accompanied him, after a
short prayer, commenced to examine the sacred edifice; some
of the others, after a little, entered behind the linen veil which
cut off the sacristy; the librarian, after listening a little, followed
them. When he lifted the veil, there before him stood the
Abbot Columcille, who had just risen from before a table on
which were writing materials. He was now speaking to the
visitors, many of whom were well known to him. Sean now
came up to him and introduced the foreigners; all conversed
together a short time, they then passed the screen into the

* Shaun (John).
† *Pr.* naw dheenna ooishlya so, these noble people, gentlemen.
‡ *Pr.* auigleoo an lyowarh, at reading of the book.

church again, Columcille in the excitement forgetting his previous employment. No sooner had Columb left than Sean went
to the table and examined the manuscript which lay upon it;
he found beside it the Book of Psalms for which he sought;
but, observing that the MSS. which was a copy of this was just
finished, he left both untouched, and returned by the outer door
to the Abbot Finian's house.

Meantime the Abbot Columb, with the party of visitors and
many belonging to the establishment, wandered through the
grounds, inspecting everything and returning in time for supper;
as they again entered the building, the attention of the visitors
was directed to a little cell at the very door, which one of the
monks told them once belonged to the Abbot Columb when he
was a pupil of the Abbot Finian's. On this the Abbot Columb
disappeared, and the monk continued to inform the party that
this monastery was originally very small, and each pupil had to
build his own cell and occupy it. Columb being directed by
the Abbot Finian to build his cell at the door, the young scholar
built it, instead, on this very spot, which at that time was a considerable distance from the door. The Abbot, on finding that
his order had not been obeyed, called Columb and asked
him why he had not followed his directions, observing,
at the same time, that the spot on which he built his cell
was not at the door but a long way from it. But Columb replied :—" True, it is not, but the door will be at this place hereafter." And this prediction was accomplished, this monastery
extending its boundaries on all sides, and becoming the nursing
mother of several other famous universities. The visitors were
much moved at the recital, though some of them were too much
accustomed to hear wonderful things concerning Columb to
be greatly surprised. They now entered the monastery, and
repaired once more to the refectory, and took their seats at the
ample board.

Meanwhile when Columb left the party at the door to avoid
hearing his own praise, he went straight to the sacristy, where
he found all exactly as he had left it. He put away his writing
materials, and laying his completed copy of the Abbot Finian's
Book of Psalms, which he had been transcribing in secret, in a
place where he could be sure that none would observe it, he then
took the original book to return it to his old master, and meeting that gentleman in the hall leading to the refectory, he
handed him his psalm book; but, to Columb's inexpressible surprise the old abbot also demanded the copy. Columb, perceiving that he had been discovered, at once refused, but Finian in-

sisted, and their raised tones soon brought out some of the strangers; hereupon Finian and Columb, by mutual consent, referred their difference to the assembled strangers, and for this purpose entered the refectory. The Abbot Finian explained that Abbot Columb had borrowed his Book of Psalms which he held in his hand, and that without his permission he had transcribed a copy for himself; he (Finian) therefore claimed the copy. Columb, on the other hand, as stoutly maintained that the copy was his, it having cost him great pains and labour, even staying up the greater part of many nights in order to have it finished before the breaking up of the school. Several of the party expressed great concern that there should be any misunderstanding between two such old friends, and recommended various means of an amicable settlement, but all to no purpose; Finian should have the copy, and Columb determined to keep it, and even refused to produce it. Each insisted that he had justice on his side; each appealed to those present, to the staff of the college and the strangers; but perceiving that everyone looked perplexed and embarrassed, they mutually agreed to leave the matter to the arbitration of the Ardrigh Diarmaid. This decision was received with applause by the gentlemen present, who were not sorry to be thus relieved from so embarrassing a position. They then proceeded to examine the original book and admire the rare beauty of its illumination. After partaking of supper, and spending some time in agreeable conversation, the chimes pealed forth, and the whole party repaired to the church, where they joined the monks and students in singing the divine office, after which they were shown to the simple but clean and commodious cells, and soon the busy sounds of life, both within and without the monastery, were hushed in profound repose.

The next morning, when the travellers awoke, they found all about them life and bustle as on the previous day. The monks —who had risen several times during the night, as was their custom and rule, to sing the divine praises at the prescribed hours—had now been some hours at their several occupations, though some of the brethren were put about somewhat by the general excitement and hilarity of the numerous students, who for the past few days were continually setting off for Teamhair, either in companies or with parents or friends. Such as had not yet departed now joined the monks and our travellers in the church, in order to assist at the holy sacrifice before setting out. All again formed into procession and returned to the monastery; and having partaken of breakfast in the refectory, those whose

duty did not detain them prepared to take their departure for
Teamhair, in company with their numerous visitors ; and while
the elders of the party conversed about the politics of the
period, their more youthful companions enjoyed themselves
pretty much as boys ever do under such circumstances, and
although they were well-behaved in such company, still the
graver travellers were not permitted to reach Teamhair without
being subjected to some harmless tricks. And now, while they
are prosaically plodding along, we shall use our privilege of
flying on the wings of imagination and arrive before them at
the chief seat of Eire's power and glory.

ᚪn ᴅᴀᚱᴀ ċᴀıᴃıᴅıᴌ.

CHAPTER II.

ꝼeıꞅ Ceᴀṁᚱᴀċ.

THE CONVENTION OF TARA.

FROM the four provincial States of Eire, and all their sub-
divisions ; from Alba, or Scotland, which, as well as the Isles,
was then tributary to the Irish monarch, came thousands of persons of all classes, in the train of their respective delegates, to
the capital of the royal kingdom of Midhe, and of the Irish
Empire—Teamhair na Riogh—where, following the example of
his predecessor for twelve hundred years, from the time of
Ollamh Fodhla, 700 years before Christ, down to his own time,
the Ardrigh, Diarmaid Mac Fergus Mac Cearbhall, was about
to hold the triennial Fes of the nation, to attend which the
members of that august assembly, together with their families
and retainers, had for some days previously been leaving their
homes in various parts of the country, and travelling along the
five great roads to Temor's royal seat, the colonial deputies
arriving at the nearest seaports, and travelling by road or river
to the metropolis, where the great house of assembly, as we have
already seen, was situated. Already a numerous throng filled the
biadtachs, or houses of hospitality, as well as the private residences and also the newly-erected pavilions, which many of
the people had brought with them ; and as fresh streams of
people poured in in their thousands every succeeding moment,
those temporary habitations sprung up as if by magic in every

direction, presenting a very varied and picturesque appearance, some being pure white, and others of every hue, and of all sizes to suit the convenience of their owners. But as the last half-hour is always the busiest, so the day preceding that on which the Fes was to open far surpassed its predecessors in the countless multitudes which it witnessed pouring into Tara from the five great roads aforesaid. The "magnificent plain" it-self appeared too small to contain the immense masses of people, of animals, and of vehicles which now covered it. From the Slighe Cualann, by Bray and Dublin and Ratoath, came the King and Queen of Laighin, the princes and chiefs, ollamhs, and people; from the Slighe Dala, the great south-western road from East Munster and Ossory to the southern side of the hill came the King and Queen of Tuath Mumhain,* their princes and retainers, &c. (its track at Tara still); by this road also came the King of Deas Mumhain,† with his Banrighan (Queen), his son, and followers; from the Slighe Miodhluachra, the northern road‡ (in the direction of Duleek and Drogheda) came the King and Queen of Uladh, and the Kings of Ailech and Oirghialla, and the other princes, and lords spiritual and temporal; by the western road, Slighe Asal (a continuation of Fan na g-carbad) came the King and Queen of Olnegmacht, or Connaught, and the Princes of Breffni, Ui Fiachrach, &c., and all the nobles, bards, and other followers of the princes. An immense number jour-neyed by the Slighe Mor (which struck off from the Fan na g-carbad) the great western road, defined by the Eiscir Riadha. All these great roads were also fed from the bealachs *bothers*, and other minor roads as well as from the ship and boat-laden rivers.

As we have here already observed, it was decreed by law that the roads should be always kept clean and in per-fect repair. No mud or dirt of any kind was allowed to accumulate at any time. But now as the multitudes poured in to Teamhair, they found all the approaches to it as clean as roads could be; this was all the easier, as the roads over which the chariots rolled were constructed of great large, square stones, fitted together as nice as possible, so that there were few crevices in which dirt could long remain; besides which there were men constantly employed at such times as these in removing any dirt that might be made by the continual streams

---

* North Munster.   † South Munster.
‡ The present road in that direction is supposed to be identical with the ancient one, i.e., Northern.

of horses and chariots and waggons. . Indeed, it would be well
if the legislators of the nineteenth century took a leaf from the
book of their predecessors of the sixth. How those worthy
ancients would stare aghast could they see the mud-immersed
streets of Ath-Cliath Duibhlinn, and the effects on every person
and thing that touched them. But their lives were cast in
pleasanter places and times than ours. It would never do in
those days of unrivalled prosperity, of gorgeous habilaments,
gilded chariots, and prancing, well-kept steeds, to have every
thing ruined by dirty streets and roads. The law then was
strictly enforced; and as at such times as for any cause,
whether fair, synod, games, or Fes, as at the present, particular care was taken beforehand to have all approaches to the
place of meeting well cleaned and repaired if necessary (those
were very frequent, for in ancient Eire there was always something which brought the people from their homes to some
particular point of the country); so it is not surprising that notwithstanding the immense multitude which assembled at Teamhair from all parts, near and far, the people and all about them
looked clean and bright; it must be remembered there were
no railways; those even from the most distant parts had to
travel in carbads, or chariots, or on horseback.

What a sight presented itself from the Druim Aoibhin, or
the beautiful or delightful hill, on this, the last day of preparation. It was surrounded, as far as the eye could reach, on every
side, all over the magnificent plain, by continually increasing
crowds of all ages and conditions; some were on horseback,
mounted with more or less magnificence; some were seated in
one, two, three, or four-horse carbads, or chariots (many of
which were highly ornamented), but by far the greater number
on foot, presenting an ever varying spectacle. There kings,
queens, princes, and princesses, chieftains and chieftainesses,
lords and ladies, flaiths* of the seven different grades; there
were knights of the golden garter, chain knights; and there
were the Curraidhe na Craoibhe Ruadh, or Knights of the Red
Branch; there were bishops, priests, and abbots, ollamhs, filés,
seanachies, bards, musicians, brughaidh; there were also the
officers and men of the renowned Fenian army, warriors,
soldiers, merchants, traders, and navigators, ridires and daltins,
kerns and galloglasses, besides an immense concourse of the
general people of all age and condition, and of both sexes.
The men were attired in triuibis (tru-is) or hose of woollen stuff,

* Nobles.

generally striped, or plaided, and which united in a single piece pantaloons and stockings; ionar, a surcout, or doublet of any colour; and flowing cloaks of crimson, green, gray, or brown; some wearing a kind of coat buttoned down to the knees; they wore the hair long and flowing, and terminating in the glibbe, or coulin, so much in vogue with the ancient Irish, and so cele-brated by her bards; they also wore the crommeil, or mustache; their heads were surmounted by a barread, or cap, correspond-ing to the rest of their attire; their feet and those of the women were encased in boots or shoes of tanned leather. The women wore a piece of snow-white linen, curiously transformed into a headdress, and combs; they wore loose dresses, striped, or plaided, and confined at the waist by ornamental belts; they wore mantles of every colour in the rainbow, besides some of neutral tints; ornaments of gold and silver were extensively worn by the mass of the people of both sexes, as rings, earrings, brooches, chains, bodkins, &c.; ornamental brass and bronze pins fastened the mantles: they were of various forms and sizes, covered with a beautiful green patina, and of tasteful and neat workmanship; spring brooches, of Celtic trumpet pattern, the acus fixed by a loop, some having the pin formed by a spire of two or more coils attached to one end, and, passing along the back, is looped in a catch behind; triangular brooches with trumpet ornaments; buckle brooches, trumpet pattern; spring brooches, decorated down the centre and along the edge; five-coiled brooches, &c.; rings of gold, silver, bronze, copper, stone, jet, amber, &c., varying in diameter from $\frac{7}{8}$ of an inch to $3\frac{1}{2}$ inches, worn on thumb, or finger, or attached by ligatures to the ear, or appended with other ornaments to neck-laces. Some of the thumb-rings had projecting knobs. Neck-laces of beads, of stone, glass, bone, jet, and particularly amber, with pendants or amulets, &c.; star-shaped beads were used as buttons, some even made of a whitish, polished flint. Some of the poorer, and many even of the more affluent, wore beautiful shells as necklets, bracelets, &c.; and yet, notwithstanding all this variety, the law of colours was strictly observed; for though there was a great variety of hues taken as a whole, yet the majority wore but two colours, which was the usual number for the general people; slaves wore only one, soldiers three, brughaidhs and others four, flaiths five, ollamhs six, and kings and queens seven, the highest number. And as it was entering the winter season, cochal criochinn, or skin dress, was exten-sively worn in a variety of ways, and being ornamental as well as warm, had a very elegant effect. At that time, when the

country was half covered with wood, the mountain passes and
rocky fastnesses afforded secure retreats to the cu-allaidh
(wolf), the sinnach (fox), the broc (badger), the madradh
crainn (martin), and the squirrel; and the river's banks swarmed
with dobhar-chu (otters), their warm furs afforded the people
in great plenty a means of clothing and decoration, not now
procurable except by importation.   Indeed at that time, and
long after the forests were cut down, or submerged in bog, pel-
try formed a considerable article of traffic and exportation.
Accordingly, all the furs above-named were worn by both
sexes; and as at that time also róna (seals) abounded on the
coasts of Ireland, that highly-prized article of modern attire—
seal skin—formed a pleasing contrast to the furs of the land
animals.   The furs of the smaller animals also, as the gearr-
fiadh (hare), the coinin (rabbit), the madadh (dog), &c., being
ornamental and warm, were used for head gear and other ornamental purposes.   Buck skin pantaloons, ornamental leggings,
coisbheirt, i.e., buskins, or half boots.   The *ara* (charioteers)
wore pointed caps, green tunics, woollen vests, and gold gibne.
The dress of the higher classes, besides being of a greater
variety of colours, was of finer and more costly texture, but in
form similar; thus a great number of princes, nobles, and ladies,
who mixed through the throng, presented a most gorgeous
and brilliant spectacle: gold, silver, and jewels abounded.   The
artificers of Teamhair, previous to the opening day, drove a
roaring trade in all their various callings, and the ordinary
traffic was greater and more difficult than ever.   Now, however, the ' *cios*' or tribute of King Diarmaid were added to the every
day traffic.   Thus from every direction were constantly arriving
cars laden with ·swords, shields, and coats of mail; others with
drinking-horns, chess-boards, backgammon-boards, &c., others
again with green, scarlet, crimson, or purple cloaks.   Following
those were droves of oxen, cows, sheep, hogs, &c., in thousands, all these coming from the provincial kingdoms, as
tributes to the Ardrigh.   In all directions might be seen the
banners of the kings, princes, and various clans; they were of
every hue—green, blue, crimson, yellow, but red predominated:
hence Ireland got the name of Banba-na-m-Bratach-Ruadh, i.e.,
Ireland of the Red Banners.   The devices of those banners were
even more varied than their colours; some represented trees,
as the yew, the mountain ash, the oak, &c.; some of animals,
as the wolf-dog, greyhound, lion, leopard, deer, &c.; others
of weapons, as shields, swords, battle axes; some of musical
instruments, as the cruit (harp), pipes, corns, &c.; but the

banners of the Curraidh na Craoibhe Ruaidhe, or Knights of the
Red Branch were remarkably beautiful ; it represented a golden
lion on a green satin flag ; it waved and glittered in every direction ; and here it may be observed that this lion, which was the
emblem of Irish chivalry hundreds of years before England
emerged from barbarism, was the original of the rampant
animal that now rears his head wherever British Empire holds
sway; but like many other things they borrowed, or usurped,
they will not even acknowledge whence they obtained their
heraldry. But the banner which waved pre-eminent from the
towers of the royal palace was the celebrated Gal Greine. Add
to all this the constantly increasing number of many-coloured
tents; the palaces, monasteries, biadtachs, and private residences being insufficient to accommodate the numerous throng
that kept pouring into Magh Breagh, the constant hum of the
voices of the multitude, mingled with the bleating and lowing
of the tributary sheep and oxen, the neighing of the horses, the
gay laughter of youth, and the music of the cruthire, dispersed
through the crowd in all directions.

It was some time before this enormous and varied crowd
could be got into anything like order, the great difficulty being
to get the immense number of carbads, or chariots into their
proper places, which was the locality at Teamhair, leading from
the hill to Brugh na Boinne, and which was called Fan na
g-Carbad, or the Slope of the Chariots. From this struck off the
Slighe Mor, at the northern head of the hill, and joined the
Eiscir Riadha, or Great Connaught Road from Ath Cliath
(Dublin) *via* Trim ; and when it is remembered that all persons
of every rank, had to travel either on horseback, or in chariots,
together with the fact that a great number of those vehicles
were brought as tributes to the Ardrigh, it may be conjectured
what an immense space they occupied on the Fan an g-carbad.
Then the thousands of horses, oxen, sheep, and swine were to
be got into their places. At last all this was accomplished, and
the late comers made their way through the crowd, returning
salutes from old acquaintances, many of whom they had not
seen since the previous Fes. They, for the most part, sought
out the places where they were to take up their abode during
their stay. This, to the late comers, was no easy matter, for
many, to make sure of a good place, had arrived a month before
the time, especially such as resided at great distances, or
whose affairs would permit them. Every day, down to the very
last, had brought its reinforcements of delegates or of pleasure
seekers. The fourteen great public biadtachs were now over-

crowded; so were all the various classes of houses, rich and poor, of the seven bailes of Teamhair. The farmers and the artificers, the traders and the merchants, the *literati* and all others, had their dwellings full of their friends from all parts of the country, and also frequently of strangers. Wise people brought their own pavilions with them, which they erected anywhere and everywhere they could, and shared them with others who had none and could not procure a lodging. When towards the close of the eve of the opening day they had all been put up they presented a very curious spectacle: they were planted on every available spot of ground; the private lands of the inhabitants became, for the time, public property; every field was thick with these many coloured habitations, so were the courtyards of the houses. It was with the greatest difficulty that the officers who had charge of the ceremonies could prevent pavilions being erected on those fields set apart for the public games and sports. The provincial kings on their arrival were conducted to the palaces set apart specially for their use on the royal hill—the Righ Laigean (King of Leinster), to the Long Laighnech (Long Loynagh), or Leinster House; the Righ Connacht (King of Connaught), to the Coisir Connactach (Coshir-Connaughtagh), Connaught Banquet House; the Righ Mumhain (King of Munster), to the Long Muimnach (Long Mueenagh), or Munster House; the Righ Ulladh (King of Ulster), to the Ecrais Ulladh (Aghrish-Ulla), or Ulster House. The queens and princesses were sumptuously accommodated in the Grianan n-inghin, each in her own private apartments. Other illustrious personages were crowded into every spare space, in the various royal buildings, or into the houses of the aires, or of the officers of state. The provincial literati were accommodated, as far as possible, in the Mur Ollamhain. When all these tired travellers had partaken of refreshment they retired to rest as early as possible, in order to be up betimes to take part in the morrow's festivities.

Early on the morning of the first day of the national Fes the Hill of Teamhair and all the surrounding Plain presented a most sublime spectacle. As Ireland was at that time an Island of Saints, her people, of all grades, never thought of undertaking anything, whether of business or pleasure, without first invoking the aid of the Most High, and consequently the first thing to be done was to assist at the Holy Sacrifice. All the bishops and priests who came to the Fes, celebrated not only in the churches, monasteries, and convents, but in the royal palaces, in the biatachs, in private houses, in pavilions, and out in the open air; temporary altars were erected everywhere by eager hands, and the kneeling multitudes that covered the magnificent Plain, offered up, by the consecrated hands of thousands of priests, the great Eucharistic Sacrifice of the New Law. This grand act of sublime worship over, the enormous throng proceeded to inaugurate the various amusements for which they were assembled; and the immense Plain, which but now resembled one vast temple crowded with an enormous congregation, its many thousand altars, and as many priests, with their hands raised to heaven, or extended over the heads of the countless worshipers, is now transformed into a scene of the most intense excitement, until the din is suddenly hushed by the blowing of trumpets. In answer to this blast of the trumpets all the shieldbearers of the territorial chieftains were seen working their way through the crowd from every direction, until they were all assembled around the doors of the Teach Miodchuarta, where the bolsgari, or marshall of the household, received from them the shields (*sciata*) of their lords, which he then, according to the directions of the genealogist, hung up, each in its assigned place. This over, the shieldbearers departed, and intermixed again with the crowd. Then the trumpeters appeared again at the doors of the Teach, and blew the trumpets a second time; and now the shieldbearers of the chieftains of the military bands assembled round the door in like manner, where the bolsgari received their lord's shields from them also, and hung them up at the other side of the hall, according to the orders of the seanchaidhe, and over the seats of the warriors. And now again, for the third time, the trumpets were sounded, and as it fell upon the ears of the multitude every eye was turned upon the door of Teach Miodchuarta, and every tongue was hushed, and every ear was attentive, and the herald proclaimed, amidst universal silence:

"Let the kings, princes, and nobles of Eire, and the pastors of the Church, and the chiefs of the ollamhs, and the heads of the people, salute the Ardrigh in the High Chamber of Teamhair."

And now, amidst a buzz of general excitement, the nobles and the warrior chiefs, the bishops and abbots, and such of those important personages named by the heralds as had during the morning hours been mixed up with the general throng, now made their way, as quickly as they could, to the royal presence. And as soon as they were into order, a procession was formed, and commenced to move towards the Teach Miodchuarta, and into the Convention Hall, preceded by the heralds and announced by a flourish of trumpets. . They proceeded up either side of the great hall, falling into their respective places, each under his own shield, all remaining standing until, last of all, the Ardrigh entered, accompanied by the ten who always attend him, and took his place on the throne. And now let the reader conceive the magnificence of the scene thus presented. The shields of the delegates decorated the oaken pannelling to its full extent of 300 feet on either side, as well as its breadth of 80 feet at either end. These shields were for the greater part of silver, many beautifully embossed with gold, some were altogether of gold, and highly wrought. Above, or below, there were the helmets, of great variety of workmanship, and having the necks and forepieces all of gold. Over those waved the banners, of various colours and devices as described before, the banners of the Fiana and of the Red Branch Knights being conspicuous, and the Gal Greina, or Sun Burst, in its place of honour directly over the throne, also the Craobh Cuinl. The throne itself was erected in the centre: it was of gold, studded with emeralds.

The Ardrigh, elevated in the centre, on his golden throne, under the national banners, and facing the west, shone resplendent in his seven-coloured robes of state, golden aison, or crown, *Roth Croi*,* immense golden torque, five feet seven inches in length and about twenty-seven ounces in weight.† The rest of his attire and ornaments resembled more or less that of the other delegates, which we may describe in general terms, making allowance for the number of colours which were more or less restricted according to their various grades, and also allowing for the different tastes, Their *triuibis* (tru-is) combining pantaloons and hose, were generally plaid,‡ thus combining in the one article as many colours as they were allowed to wear; shirts (leanna) of white, kingly linen, embroidered with gold; embroidered tunics (imar) of blue, green, or saffron colour; cloaks of crimson, blue, or purple, or any colour, with golden borders or deep fringe of golden thread, and fastened at the throat with clasps of gold, these were of great variety and

* The *Roth Croi*, Royal Brooch, was worn as the distinctive emblem of the Monarch of Erin; it descended from monarch to monarch from the remotest times.
† To be seen in the Royal Irish Academy.
‡ This was the origin of the Scotch plaid. It was invented in Ireland ages previously, in consequence of the law of colours, instituted by Achy Edgathach. The invention of plaid obviated the necessity of having as many articles of dress visible as would enable the wearer to display all the colours to which he was entitled.

beauty of form. The general names for pins, fibula, brooches, &c., were dealg, birian, daillenn, bro-lagha (spearlike), escasen, cartait, roith, croir, and breathnas. Some were what is known as the Tara brooch; some were plain, some richly studded with gems. The Fenian officers present wore the eo* (*pr.* yo) pattern; brooches of Keltic trumpet pattern, its acus fixed by a loop; some have the pins formed by a spire of two or more coils attached to one end, and passing along the back, are looped in a catch behind; also curiously decorated gold finger and thumb rings, bracelets, armlets and anklets. The girdles they wore were of divers patterns, some of the richer with golden buckles, and studded with precious stones; sandals of more or less magnificence, some of golden network, and with buckles of gold. There were golden collars, golden gorgets, and bracelets (fleasg), crescents, large hollow golden balls, fibula, &c. The Chain Knights and the Knights of the Golden Garter were distinguished by the golden garter, decorated and worn conspicuously. The Knights of the Red Branch, the famed Craoibhe Ruadh, were identified by a golden lion, and so of the other Gradh Gaisgaidh, or orders of chivalry. The swords, too, of all those various ranks were very beautiful and of great variety, ornamented with gold and silver; ivory-hilted, jewel-hilted, studded with brilliants and emeralds. The kings and sovereign princes wore crowns; the ollamhs, bards, sean-achies, brehons, and learned professions generally, wore laurel wreaths; their robes were long and flowing, called the canabhas, of the very finest texture, and of the six colours; they wore golden ornaments also, all regulated according to law. But the most beautiful of all the garments worn in that illus-trious assembly was that of the Ollamh Fileadh, or Chief Bard's; it was called the taeidhean, or ornamented mantle, made of the skins and feathers of various coloured birds. The effect, in conjunction with the robes of silk and wool, and the ornaments of gold may be imagined. The fileadh were also crowned with laurels. Then there were the prelates of the Church, to whom, of course, the laws of colours and ornaments did not apply, they following only the law of the Church. But their appear-ance was not the less magnificent; their richly embroidered vestments of silk and gold, studded with precious stones; their mitres ablaze with brilliants; their croziers of gold and silver, set with gems; their rings and pectoral crosses, all gems of art—as indeed, was everything manufactured in Eire at that time —combined with their exceptionally sanctified and majestic

Eo, lit : salmon.

12

appearance, rendered those Christian supplanters of the Pagan
Druids the brightest ornaments of that renowned assembly—
an assembly which has never been equalled, much less surpassed, either previously or since that time, by any other nation
upon earth, and which had existed for upwards of 1,200 years.

Before the Ardrigh's cathair rioghda (royal chair, or throne)
extended a table, at which sat his chief secretary ; on the right
sat the King of Uladh ; on the left the Kings of Tuath Mumhain, and of Deas Mumhan ; the King of Gaelan, (or Laeghan)
took his seat opposite the table, his face towards the throne,
the King of Olnegmacht, or Connacht, sat behind the throne,
as also the Kings and Princes of Alba (or Scotland) and the
Isles, and the chief secretaries of those kings sat between
them and the table. And on the right and left of the King of
Uladh sat the Princes of Dal Araidhe (Newry, and part of Down
and Antrim), of Dal Riada (different, the country east of Antrim),
Oir-thir (i.e., east-land, not exactly known), Ui Earca Chein
(Antrim), Dal m-Buinne (Upper Massarene), Ui Blathmaic
(Newtownards and Bangor, Co. Down), Duibhthrian (Dufferin,
Co. Down), Arda (the Ards, east of Down), Leith Chathail
(Lecale), Boirche (between Dundalk and Dun Sobairce), Cobha
(in Down) and Muirtheimhne (Louth), and the King of
Oirghiall sat on the left, and on the right of the Ardrigh, the
distance from him being such that his sword should reach the
hand of the King of Eire, and near him sat the chiefs of the
nine Triocha Ceads, or Cantreds ; and the King of Ailech sat
with the Kings of Uladh and of Oirghiall ; and right and left of
him sat the Princes of Lurg (in Fermanagh), of Cuileantraidhe,
of Tuath Ratha (in Fermanagh) (Tooreah), Ui Tiachrach (in
Tyrone), Ui mic Caerthainn (in Derry), Cianachta (from Munster), Li (in Coleraine), Tuathas of Tort (in Artrim), Magh
Itha (in Donegal), Tulach Og (in Tyrone), Craebh (in Derry),
Inis Eoghain (in Donegal). And right and left of the Kings
of Mumhan were seated the Princes of Muscraidhe (Muskerry, in Thomond), of Uaithne (Owney, in Limerick and
Tipperary), Ara (north-west of Tipperary and west of Limerick),
Corca Luighe (Cork), Dairbhre O Duibhne (in Kerry), Boir-
inn (Burren, in Clare), Ciarraidhe (Kerry), Baiscinn (in
Clare), Corcomruadh (Corcomroe), Seachtmhadh (in Tip-
perary), Deise (Deese, in Waterford), Osraidhe (Ossory), Loch
Leine (Killarney), Raithleann (in Cork), Orbhraidhe (Orrery)
Ui Fidhgheinte (in Limerick), Aine (in Limerick), Dal Chai,
(in Clare), Ui Liathain (in Cork), Irrluachair (Duhallow)s
Ui Ghabhra (in Limerick), Brughrigh (Bruree), Eile (King's,
County). On right and left of the King of Laghain sat the

Kings and Princes of Ui Failain (north of Kildare), Cualann (north of Wicklow), Forthuatha (in Wicklow), Inbhear (Arklow), Ui Feilmeadha (in Carlow and Wexford), Ui Ceinnsealaigh (in Carlow and Wexford), Racilinn (in Kildare), Fothart Osnadhaigh (in Carlow), Ui Drona (Idrone), Ui Bairrche (Queen's County), Ui Buidhe (in Carlow), Laeighis (in Queen's County), Ui Criomhthannan (in Queen's County), Failghe (in Kildare), and Ath Cliath (Dublin). And right and left of the King of Olnagmacht, or Connacht, sat the Princes of Cruachan (Rathcroghan, in Roscommon), Umhall (in Mayo), Greagraidhe (in Sligo), Conmaicne (in Galway and Mayo), Ciarraidhe (in Roscommon and Mayo), Luighne (in Sligo), Dealbhna (in Galway), Ui Maine (between Suck and Shannon), Ui Briuin (Breffny), Siol Muireadhaigh (i.e., the seed or race of Muireadhach, Muilleathan, King of Connaught), Ui Fiachrach (in Mayo and Sligo), and Partraidhe (in Mayo). And right and left of the King of Teamhor sat the Princes of Breagh (in Meath), of Magh Logha (in Meath), Laeghaire (in Meath), Ardghal (in Meath), Caille Eachach (King's County), Feara Tulach (in Westmeath) (the men of the hills), Teabhtha (in Westmeath), Cuircne of the Caladh (in Westmeath) (i.e., of the marshy district), Ui Beccon (in East Meath), Cailla Fhallamhain (in Westmeath), Deise (in East Meath), Dal Iarthair (in Westmeath), Luighne (in East Meath), Fear Arda (south of Louth) (men of the heights), Saithne (north of Dublin), Gaileanga (in East Meath), and Claen Rath (in East Meath). And the chief secretaries of all these princes sat at the table. The *tanaiste* (heirs apparent) signify second in command, or according to some, from Tan, a territory; and the *rioghdamhna*, from righ, king, and damhna, material, hence Roydamna, a person eligible to be a king (in case of the failure of the tanist). Those important adjuncts of the nation were ranged behind their respective kings or princes. The bishops numbered about three hundred, and the abbots about the same. The *Ollamhain* were ranged behind the throne. The *Ard Ollamhs* (High Poets, or Poet Laureates) of the several kings; the *ollamhs re dan* (professors of poetry); the *ollamhs re seanchas*, or chroniclers and historians; the *seanchuidhe*, or antiquarians and genealogists; the *filidhe*, or poets and bards; the *saoithe*, or sages; the *breitheamh*,* or judges and lawgivers. Next to these were the second class of the Irish aristocracy; they were termed *tighearna*,† or *tiarna* (lord); there were of

---

* From Breithe, judgment.
† From Tir, territory; or from tigh, house; arna, top-man; root, àr, high, noble.

these lords about two hundred, each possessing a territory equivalent to a barony, or sometimes two baronies, and holding rank as such. Ranged behind them were the third class of the Milesian peerage, called *taoiseach** (chiefs); of these there were more than six hundred, all heads of clans, and each possessing a district, equal in extent to about a parish, or sometimes two parishes, or more, and varying, on an average from ten thousand to thirty thousand acres; and these chiefs held a rank similar to that of the principal landed gentry of modern times. There were also present the *aire tuisi*, the *aire ard*, the *aire forgill*, *aire dessu*, *atre echtai*. The Gradh Gaisgaidh, or orders of chivalry, were most numerously represented, especially the Red Branch Knights, the Chain Knights, and the Knights of the Golden Garter. There were also the higher officers of the renowned *Fianna Eirionn*, or Fenians of Ireland; the Clanna Deagha, and the Clanna Morna; the *triaths*, or military lords, or chiefs, and a great array of warriors; after these, the *flaiths*, another class of gentry, of the seven different grades; then the ceana,† or heads of clans, they were very numerous; and though last not least, the *brughaidhe*,‡ head farmers, who held large farms under the chiefs, and were very numerous and wealthy, possessing great flocks, much cattle, corn, &c., and were entitled to a place in the assembly of the nation, as were also the biadtachs,§ or keepers of those immense establishments of the same name.

When all these various orders of delegates had taken their places, according to their several ranks—amidst universal silence, the whole assembly standing, the Archbishop of Ard Macha,‖ *comharba* of St. Patrick, arose, arrayed in full pontificals, and holding in his hand the *Bachell Isu*, or Staff of Jesus—offered, to the Most High, the deliberation of the asembly, and then proceeded to read the

"BEANNACHT PHADRUIG.¶

THE BLESSING OF GOD upon you all,
Men of Eire, sons, women,
And daughters; prince blessing,
Good blessing, perpetual blessing,
Full blessing, superlative blessing,
Eternal blessing, the blessing of heaven,
Cloud-blessing, sea-blessing,

---

* From Tus, first, or foremost.   † *Pr.* kan.
‡ From Bruighe, a farm.
§ From Biadh, food, and Teach, a house.   ‖ Armagh.
¶ Blessing of St. Patrick.

Fruit-blessing, land-blessing,
Produce-blessing, dew-blessing,
Blessing of the elements, blessing of prowess,
Blessing of chivalry, blessing of voice,
Blessing of deeds, blessing of magnificence,
Blessing of happiness be upon you all,
Laics, clerics, while I command
The blessing of the men of heaven,
It is my bequest, as it is a perpetual blessing, THE BLESSING.'

Then the Ard Ollamh stepped forward and read as follows :—

"TEAMHAIR, THE HOUSE, in which resided the son of Conn,
   The seat of the heros on Liath-druim,*
   I have in memory
   Their stipend to the chieftains.

Every king who occupies strong Teamhair,
   And possesses the land of Eire,
   He is the noblest among all
   The hosts of Banbha† the fertile.

If he be a rightful King of Teamhair,
   It is right for the chiefs,
   To make each of them submission even at his house,
   To the just and justly judging king.

It is due of him to acknowledge the hosts
   When they come into his assembly,
   It is due of them to give hostages each man,
   When they come to Teamhair . . . . TEAMHAIR.

TEAMHAIR is not due to him,
   Unless he be a very intelligent historian
   So that he may tell his chieftains,
   The stipend of every person.

That he may not give beyond right to anyone,
   That he himself may not pass a false sentence ;
   That no quarrel take place in his house,
   For that is the great restriction of his restrictions.

That he may not wage fierce war
   With the host of the province of Conchobhar,‡
   That Teamhair be never wasted
   By war with the sons of Rudhraidhe.§

It is his right to be at mighty Teamhair,
   And all to him obedient ;
   If he himself break not his faith,
   His provincialists to him are obedient."

* One of the names of the Hill of Teamhair (Tara).
† A bardic name for Ireland.
‡ i.e., of Uladh, or Ulster, from Conchobhar Mac Nessa, king about time
of Christ.
   § The ancient inhabitants of Uladh, or Ulster, from King Rudhraidhe
A.M. 3845.

Then the provincial kings, princes, chiefs, &c., each in the order of precedence, did homage to the Ardrigh, and at the same time made to him a formal tender of their respective tributes,* which on their arrival had been delivered to the officers appointed to receive them, the Ardrigh in his turn formally granting to them the stipends† to which they were entitled, but which were only to be delivered to them on the eve of their departure for their several homes. When all this had been gone through with the strictest regard to the rights of each, and to the laws and usages of the country, and all were seated in their exact places, the ollamhs, filés, brehons, and seanachies unfolded the ponderous tomes, which contained the writings of the Ollamhain and breithmne the rolls of the laws, and the chronicles of the Gael; and these were on the table, and the secretaries of the provincial kings and princes, as well as of the King of Eire, spread their parchments before them, and prepared to take down the speeches of the delegates and laws and regulations which should be enacted by the Convention. And the Ardrigh having announced that all the various ranks there assembled were equal, and free for their words, and that the first to rise should be allowed to speak unto the end, and that when all who had a mind had spoken, their right hands should be counted, and that they should avail. And everything being now ready, the business of the assembly commenced. But being of the wrong sex, we had better not intrude on their deliberations, lest we should spoil all; so while the delegates are settling the affairs of the nation, we shall see how the time passes with the non-delegates.

---

* Eineachlann.   † Tuarastol.

NOTE.—A short time ago the *Freeman's Journal* described the English Parliament as follows :—" In this country (Ireland), and in other lands, all lovers of liberty have regarded it (the British Parliament) with sincere admiration, as the *oldest* and purest of all forms of popular representation, and as the august mother of all existing free assemblies. All others are mushrooms. High above all of them towers the *grand old form* of the Parliament of Britain, the secret of whose longevity and strength, its triumph over every foe, and its survival through every danger, is its *freedom*."

A correspondent of the *Irish World* (New York), has drawn the attention of the Irish and other people across the Atlantic to this gross and fulsome falsehood. But perhaps these words are too strong; it may be pure ignorance which dictated the above wonderful assertion; but in any case it is a most lamentable misfortune, that the *only* daily instructor of the Irish people—supposed too, to represent them—should dare to make such an assertion in a city abounding with historical evidences and descriptions of what was *really* the "*oldest* and *purest* of all forms of popular representation, and the august mother of all existing free assemblies "—to wit, the "*grand old form* of the

Δn τReΔs cΔιbι'οιL.

CHAPTER III.

neΔṁ—τeΔċoΔιṗιο.

THE NON-DELEGATES.

WHILE the Teach Miodchuarta was being filled with the delegates from every part of the kingdom, their several families were thronging the other apartments of the building and of the other royal palaces and the adjoining buildings. A constant stream of gaily-attired ladies and officers, youths and maidens, foreign ambassadors and their families, kept moving here and there through the various apartments, engaged either in earnest conversation or giving way to careless mirth : some discussing politics, the various important questions which occupied the attention of the delegates at that moment ; some of military tactics, some of their relations with foreign countries, or of foreign commerce, &c. ; others, again, discussing the respective merits of the different colleges and schools; spoke of new foundations; of the rising stars which issued therefrom; of various questions, ecclesiastical or civil ; of the time of keeping Easter ; of the relations with Rome ; of the ignorance and idolatry in which the sur-

---

Triennial Parliament, or *Fés* of Tara—'which towers high above' all other assemblies, including the much-lauded Parliament of Britain. Lovers of liberty in this country (Ireland), and in other lands, may regard the English Parliament—(which, by the way, ordered a day of public thanksgiving to *God* for the Cromwelliam massacres of the Irish people)—with sincere admiration and wonder at its longevity of 1,100 years, and its triumph over every foe (including the Irish), but the historical fact is that the Parliament of Tara was instituted by Ollamh Fodhla 700 years B.C., and continued down to the English Invasion—a period of nearly 1,900 years ; that it was in the eighth century of the Christian era that the Parliament of Britain was founded, on the model of that of Tara, by Alfred the Great, who was educated in Ireland, and who also introduced into England the judicial and legislative institutions on the model of those of Ireland ; and that the present division of England into shires with their governing bodies were also copied from Ireland. As Alfred lived in the eighth century, when the Irish Parliament was 1,500 years old, how can the British Parliament, which was only then born, be the 'august mother,' of all others ?"

But it is another instance of the truth of the remark of 'Trans-Atlantic,' that "It is stereotyped lies that have shielded the British system from popular resentment and overthrow these hundreds of years past."

rounding nations were immersed, and the probable result of the
intended evangelisation of those countries by Irish missioners ;
some discussed various questions of national interest, as the
several merits of the ollamhs and filés, and the lately published
works of many young students in the numerous colleges. Young
people discussed questions interesting to themselves, their
schools, their studies, their kind teachers, that numerous body
of holy men and women who abandoned all that the world holds
dear to devote themselves to the instruction of the youth of both
sexes ; and   numerous good-humoured little disputes arose
as to the respective merits of their various alma maters, each, of
course, claiming their own to be the best ; some laid out schemes
for the future, built castles in the air, would be great kings or
queens, or would astonish the world by some remarkable feat or
prowess ; would gain renown as a Knight of the Red Branch, or
of some of the other orders of chivalry ; or they would do deeds
of bravery and heroism as Fenian warriors ; some, on the contrary, would go preach the Gospel to the barbarous nations of
Germany or Helvetia, or spread the faith in Gaul or Britain, and
devote their lives to instruct the ignorant Saxons ; others would
stay at home and follow in the footsteps of their saintly teachers ;
they too, would take the tonsure or the veil, and found convents
and monasteries, and keep alive the flame of piety and learning in
the land of their birth ; but among all this, love was not forgotten, and the old, old story was told again and again, from
hundreds of young lips, in that vast assemblage.

The numerous suites of apartments of all the buildings were
fully occupied.   Some chatting in groups ; some listening to the
different musicians and singers ; others playing at chess or back-
gammon; some, again, where they had room, dancing, and all
enjoying themselves according to their taste. The Ardrighan gave
receptions in Rath na Riogh to all the distinguished personages,
native and foreign, who were not among the delegates.

And now the reader follows a group that are just entering the
gorgeous Grianan n-ingean (Sunny Palace of the Ladies),
furnished in gold and silk, and filled with a very brilliant
assemblage. On a magnificent imda, where we formerly saw the
Ardrighan of Tuathal Maelgarbh, is now seated Mughain,* the
partner of the secret thoughts of Diarmaid Mac Cearbhall. She
is his second wife, and first saw the light in the palace fortress
on the Rock of Caiseal (Cashel). Her father is amongst the
delegates as King of Deas Mumhan, or South Munster. She
is arrayed in a robe of purple, bordered with gold, and having a

* Pr. Mooan.

scarf of plaid, which contained the seven colours, a golden torque round her neck, and earrings; her wrists encircled by magnificent bracelets, and her beautiful dark hair surmounted by an asion, or golden crown, from the plaits of which depended the mella. Though still handsome, she has a sickly appearance, having considered herself, though ailing, obliged to conform as far as she was able to the exigencies of the occasion. She was surrounded by her ladies-of-honour, and provincial queens, princesses, and ladies, all arrayed in the greatest magnificence. The ladies had previously been engaged in conversation on the various topics which then engaged the attention of the country; and as the young damsels were full of projects interesting to themselves, and did not much trouble themselves about politics, so the queens and elder ladies had all those subjects to themselves; and though that jealousy of their sex, which seems to be so natural to man, had shut them out from all participation in the making of the laws, yet as those laws, when made, affected them as deeply as they did men, and as they were sure to be the greatest sufferers from the mistakes, not to say prejudices and selfishness of men in the making of those laws, so they discussed them in all their bearings, religious, civil, and social; then passing from those to a variety of other subjects, viz., literature, match-making, &c., after which they amused themselves by chess-playing, listening to the tales of the times of old; again to the music of the cruit (harp) or the ceis (charmer), anon to the songs of the maidens; sometimes they would walk through the various apartments of the grianan; sometimes they would go out for a better sight of the various amusements of the people than could be obtained from the windows, or would drive in their chariots through the surrounding country, visit some church or convent, and would stop now and again to watch the progress of some game, or feat, or race, or hurling match. And as the occupants of those four-horse gilded chariots were recognised by the people, deafening Irish cheers rent the air. Notwithstanding the great numbers who had followed the deer or the wild boar into the neighbouring forests, or others who had set out to explore the country in other directions, determining to see all they could while the feast lasted, one would almost imagine all Eire to be collected on the magnificent plain where all was life and animation. Bards and fileas, cruitire and clairseoir, and other oirfidech, kept up a continued concert of vocal and instrumental music; the harps, charmers, violins, pipes, horns, &c., played sometimes separately, sometimes all together, sometimes in slow and

solemn strains, sometimes as accompaniments to the voices of
the bards as they detailed in measured strain the past history of
the country, and deeds of heroism, or sung of love or war;
again they would play merry tunes; and immediately the rinceadh, or Irish dance, would be performed by the young men
and maidens; others engaged in running, hurling, racing, &c.;
other groups were collected here and there playing at fitcheal
(chess); others engaged in the old Irish games resembling
the Olympic games of Ancient Greece; while the more aged sat
by looking on, and conversing with each other on the various
scenes that were passing before their eyes, as well as on the more
important topics which engaged the attention of the country, or
a passing carbad of royal or noble ladies or gentlemen (wives,
sons, and daughters of the delegates) would excite their attention
for a moment. The Tuath da Danaan goldsmiths and artificers,
dyers, builders, &c.; Firbolg dealers in skins, furs, feathers,
and stuffs; farmers and graziers; merchants of all kinds, native
and continental; students from all the colleges and convents
throughout the country: those were the most numerous class,
and represented every nationality as well as Eire—Clonard
College as a type of the rest, but some had a larger number of
students. The College of Ardmacha (Armagh) at the time of
which we write had no less than 7,000 students, and fully a third
of these were Saxons. There were hundreds of other colleges
throughout Eire which it would be impossible to name here; but
it may be guessed what a throng of students mingled on those
occasions with the numerous other classes which composed the
country. All these various classes, and many more, such as
daltins (attendants on knights), kernes and galloglasses, Saxon
slaves, &c., all enjoyed themselves thoroughly at one or other
of the various amusements named, or in chatting in groups. All
through the city and for miles around, the whole scene resembled
an immense parterre: the variety of colours of the various
dresses of the people, of the banners, and the pavilions mingled
with the innumerable vehicles, gilt and ornamented in various
degrees of magnificence; the gold and silver mountings of the
horses and chariots, and the swords and helmets of the warriors
glittering in the sun. In the midst of all—the din of the immense multitude, the music of the oirfidech, the animated
conversation of the merchants and others, the merry peals of
laughter elicited by the jugglers and fools and the noise of the
mills—a sudden commotion on the Druim Aoibhin (Beautiful
Hill) caused a wild cheer to go up from multitudes of
throats; and as others looked to see the cause, they perceived

issuing from the portals of "Tara's Halls" great numbers of
the delegates. The business of the day was over, and while
some repaired to their apartments or dispersed themselves
through the throngs of knights and ladies who promenaded the
halls and chambers of the palaces, others preferred to take the
air and mix with the people without, and amuse themselves thus
for the time that remained before assembling for the evening
banquet.

ᚪn ċeᚪꞇꞃᚪmᚪᚖ ċᚪᛁᛒꞃᛟᛁᏝ.

CHAPTER IV.

ᚪn ꝼᏝeᚪᚖ.

THE BANQUET.

As the Ardrigh of the aerial world had all day shed his benignant
beams on the august assembly which had but a century before
renounced his claim to its worship, and had from that time
merely admired in him the beauty and majesty of the Creator of
all things, and been contented to share the glory of the Ardrigh
of Eire during the debate of the princes, bishops, and ollamhs
of the nation, and, no doubt, highly interested in all that passed;
for having travelled over all the earth and penetrated into every
corner and crevice thereof, and seen how much the nations of
the world needed the vivifying, civilising care of Eire—what
her schools had done for the sons of other lands, and how
idolatry, barbarism, ignorance, and sin vanished before the
learning and sanctity of the missionaries of the Island of Saints
and Scholars, as does darkness at the approach of the first rays
of his own refulgent light—and now as the assembly breaks up,
he, too, not envious that he is no longer worshipped as a god,
but pleased that so noble and learned a nation should, as one
man, and without the shedding of a drop of blood, have embraced the religion of the one God, to whom alone he owes all
his glory; and bestowing a kind look on all around, his last
bright ray kissing the golden crown of the chief of the august
assembly, he good-naturedly takes his departure through bound-
less space on his carbad of golden glory to take another look at the
vast countries which were destined as the future inheritance of
the exiled children of this "most noble island," that for the entertainment of the evening the Ardrigh of Eire should have no
rival save the partner of his secret thoughts.

The preparations having been completed by hundreds of willing hands, the delegates, who had during the interval been amusing themselves within or without the palace, began to re-assemble, this time accompanied by their families, the ladies and such of the princes and nobles as were disqualified by youth or other causes from taking any part in their deliberations, but who now left their sports and pastimes for the enjoyment of the evening banquet.   The great hall was brilliantly lighted up with thousands of wax candles in the seven grand chandeliers which . were reflected again a thousand-fold in the innumerable gold and silver shields which ornamented the oaken walls, and re-sembled so many mirrors; most of the silver ones were embossed with gold, and had a gorgeous glittering effect underneath the many-coloured banners with their various devices which sur-rounded the vast banqueting hall; but conspicuous among the rest waved the magnificent banners of the Fenians, and of the Curaidhe na Craoibhe Ruaidhe (Knights of the Red Branch); and heading all, immediately over the throne, reared the national banner, the Sun-burst of Eire.   The immense apartment was scented with a pro-fusion of the rarest flowers, which also enhanced the beauty of the scene; they were set in vases of gold and silver in every available spot of the great table, and also round about the walls under the shields on small tables of porphyry, jasper, and serpentine.   It being the end of Foghmhar (October), and approaching Geimh-raidh (the winter period), the blazing fireplaces were not the least grateful objects in the hall.   The tables were laid with every variety of viands, served in gold and silver plate.   The iasc (fish) was of every kind the sea or the rivers of the land produced; salmon was the special prerogative of the Fenians, and was here served to their officers on plata d'or (plates of gold); milrad (venison), mairt-fheoil (beef, *pr.* mortyóil) caoir-fheoil (mutton, *pr.* ceer òil), laoig-fheoil (veal, *pr.* lee óil), róst, (roast meat, *pr.* rósth), all kinds of serccol (fowl meat), serccol tarsain or tinnes (salt fowl), foreign wines; and as there were so many thousands to partake of all those good things, we may be sure that the " 150 stout cuthgaire, or cooks, of the 27 royal kitchens (coisteannac, *pr.* cuish tyan ac), had all a busy time of it; then there was fion fionn (white wine) and fion dearg (red wine) served in golden goblets, handed round by 300 cup-bearers (dailemh, i.e., fer dailemh dighe, dividing drink), besides beoir (beer), and lionn (ale), and midh and other liquors served in horns mounted in gold or silver, and in a boige, a small vessel with a handle weighing five ounces of pure gold, given as a reward to filés and ollamhs; arán (bread) and cais (cheese) and mil (honey), and every variety of meas (fruit) in season.

The regulations concerning the privileges of the different orders were as strictly observed in this vast assemblage as if it were an ordinary family gathering. The kings, queens, and the saoi of literature shared alike their portions of primchrachiat or prime steak; the Fenian officers were served with salmon; to the various other grades were assigned their just right. The ranaire,* or butlers, dailemh,† or cup-bearers, and fosedh, or waiters, were so numerous that every individual of the multitude of illustrious guests was attended to with precision and promptitude. As the royal and noble guests filéd into the banqueting-hall, amid streams of music, they presented a most brilliant spectacle in their gorgeous attire of every hue, and their ornaments of gold, silver, and precious stones. Immediately under the Sun-burst, on the throne of gold, studded with emeralds, were seated the Ardrigh of Eire and the partner of his secret thoughts, as well as of his crown and dignity; they were attired in robes of state, with torques and crowns of gold. On either side of the great table on regal couches were seated the numerous guests in much the same order as was observed at the Fes, save that now they were joined by their families. The kings, queens, princes, princesses, ollamhs, filés, brehons, bards, seanachies, chieftians, knights, tiarnas, flaiths, and all the other representatives of the various departments of state, with their wives and children; the foreign delegates and ambassadors and their families. The bishops also and the abbots and some of the clergy felt constrained on such occasions to depart from the strict observance of almost perpetual abstinence and mortification, and to condescend to the innocent entertainments of their flocks. Grace having been said, and the Blessing of St. Patrick been repeated as before, the entertainment commenced. The whole was enlivened with strains of delicious music, and in the intervals were snatches of conversation, which soon became general. The various topics of the day were discussed—liberty and patriotism, peace and war, science and law, the foundations of new colleges and convents, literature of the great authors of the past, contemporary authors and their works, criticisms thereon; in short, every subject of their Fileacht. The Ardrigh pledged his guests first, as was his duty, the privileges observed as before, the King of Oirghialla being entitled to every third horn of goodly ale from the King of Eire, which is accordingly pre-

---

* Ranairi, i.e., fer roinn bidh.　　† Dailemh, i.e., fer dailamh dighe.

sented to him in a splendid carved drinking-horn, beautifully
ornamented, the rims being wreaths of gold. His queen re-
ceives the same as her right, from the Queen of Eire. The
fruit also is regulated by privilege. The ladies drink *methgath-
lin*, or mead.

The bards and musicians played and sang of the glorious
actions of their ancestors, the genius of their ollamhs, and the
exploits of their heroes, ancient and modern, which excited
the applause of their illustrious company, and inspired the youth
with enthusiasm and intrepidity of mind, as well as desire to
excel, if possible, the prowess and genius of those of whom their
poets sang, oblivious of all around, save the almost inspired
singing of the bards, and hanging on their lips with rapture, so
that it was some time before the thanist Colman Mor himself,
so famous in court and field, could arouse him to a sense of his
surroundings in time to hear the unanimous call of the guests
for the new poem composed by our old friend, Amherghin Mac
Amhlagh the chief bard of King Diarmaid (for the king had kept
his promise), concerning the history of the name of the very
place in which they were assembled. Amherghin, now approaching maturity, and who had from the commencement led the
concert, now stepped forward majestically, in his taeidhean, or
ornamented mantle, made of the skins and feathers of various
coloured birds, and his rings, torque, circlet, and other ornaments of gold, and having acknowledged the compliments of the
assembly, modestly prefaced his poem by a declaration that he
was indebted for the particulars of it to the old sage and historian, Fintan, who had departed to a still more glorious land.
Then taking his cruit (harp) he swept the chords with a master
hand, producing a prelude of such exquisite sweetness and finish
as charmed the audience and surprised even those who had the
pleasure of hearing him every day; but they concluded that he
had bestowed more than ordinary pains on the composition,
which was to accompany the praises of his beloved Teamhair;
and now, amidst the universal silence of the vast assembly, the
glorious voice breaks forth in solitary grandeur, and in unison
with his harp swelled forth to "lords and ladies bright," and in
addition to the united charms of the poetry and music, giving
the information to those who knew it not, of the origin of the
name of the hill on which stood the magnificent pile in which
they were assembled. And now every sense of the body and
every power of the mind of every individual then present were
concentrated on the chief bard, as he burst forth into the following song :—

" Temor of Bregia, whence so called,
　Relate to me, O learned sages,
　When was it distinguished from the Brugh ?
　When was the place called Temor ?

" Was it in the time of Partholan of battles ?
　Or at the first arrival of Cæsar ?
　Or in the time of Nemid, famed for valour ?
　Or with Ciocal of the bent knees ?

" Was it with the Firbolg of great achievements ?
　Or with the race of fairy elves ?
　Tell me in which of those invasions
　Did the place obtain the name of Temor ?

'O Tuan ! O generous Finnchadh !
　O Bran ! O active Cu-alladh !
　O Dubhan ! ye venerable five,
　Whence was acquired the name of Temor ?

" Once it was a beauteous hazel wood,
　In the time of the famed son of Olcan,
　Until that dense wood was felled
　By Liath, the son of Laighne, the large and blooming.

" From thence it was called the Hill of Liath,
　And it was fertile in crops of corn,
　Until the coming of Cain the prosperous,
　The son of Fiacha Ceannfionan.

" From thenceforth it was called Druim Cain,
　This hill, where the great assembled,
　Until the coming of Crofinn the fair,
　Daughter of the far-famed Alloid.

" The fortress of Crofinn, well applied,
　Was its name among the Tuath da Danaan,
　Until the coming of the agreeable Tea,
　The wife of Heremon of noble aspect.

" A rampart was raised around her house
　For Tea the daughter of Lughaidh,
　She was buried outside in her mound,
　And from her it was named Temor.

" The seat of the kings it was called,
　The princes, descendants of the Milesians,
　Five names it had ere that time—
　That is from Fordruim to Temor.

> " I am Fintan, the Bard,
>   The historian of many tribes;
>   In latter times I have passed my days
>   At the earthen fort above Temor."*

The applause which followed was reward highly appreciated by the Ard Filé, coming, as it did, from the highest representatives of a nation, of whose people poetry formed a great part of their education ; nor would they be satisfied till it was again repeated, which desire having been complied with, Amherghin was permitted to rest, while a chorus of bards, accompanied by their harps, charmers, and violins, entertained the assembly with another effusion in praise of the chief seat of Eire's glory, and of one of the most famous of her kings and lawgivers.   The audience wound up to the highest pitch of enthusiasm, listened, while the bard sang :—

> " Temor, the most beautiful of hills,
>   Under which Erin was warlike,
>   The chief city of Cormac, the son of Art,
>   Son of valiant Conn of the Hundred Battles.

> " Cormac, in worth excelled,
>   Was a warrior, poet, and sage ;
>   A true brehon of the Fenian men,
>   He was a good friend and companion.

> " Cormac conquered in fifty battles,
>   And compiled the Psalter of Tara,
>   In that Psalter is contained
>   The full substance of history."

Various other songs were sung of love and war.

Next followed, by desire, one of the compositions, or rather extempore productions, of Fergus Fionbell, or the sweet-voiced, who was chief bard to the Fenii in the third century, and whose poems were held in high estimation in the sixth.   It was sung in parts by the bards, and it was entitled :—

---

* This translation being literal, and, of course, not in rhyme, loses much of its poetic beauty, as well as its force of language, it should be heard and understood in the original to be appreciated ; besides, a knowledge of the history of the country previous to the sixth century, in which it was composed and sung, and of the various remarkable personages mentioned in it, is necessary to make it clear.

"ODE TO GOLL, THE SON OF MORNI.*

" High-minded Goll, whose daring soul
  Stoops not to one chief's† control !
  Champion of the navy's pride !
  Mighty ruler of the tide !
  Rider of the stormy wave,
  Hostile nations to enslave ! ‡

" Shield of freedom's glorious boast
  Head of her unconquered host !
  Ardent son of Morni's might !
  Terror of the fields of fight !
  Long renowned and dreadful name !
  Hero of auspicious fame !
  Champion in our cause to arm !
  Tongue with eloquence to charm !
  With depth of sense and reach of manly thought ;
  With every grace and every beauty fraught !

  " Girt with heroic might,
  When glory and thy country call to arms,
  Thou goest to mingle in the loud alarms,
    And lead the rage of fight !
  Thine, hero !—thine the princely sway
    Of each conflicting hour ;
  Thine every bright endowment to display,
    The smile of beauty and the arm of pow'r !
  Science beneath our hero's shade,
  Exults in all her patriot's gifts array'd ;
  Her chief the soul of every fighting field !
  The arm, the heart, alike unknown to yield !

  " Hear, O Finn, thy people's voice !
  Trembling on our hills, we plead—
    Oh, let our fears to peace incline thy choice !
  Divide the spoil, and give the hero's meed ;
  For bright and various is his high renown,
  And war and science weaves his glorious crown !

  " Did all the hosts of all the earth unite,
  From pole to pole, from wave to wave,
    Exulting in their might ;
  His is that monarchy of soul
  To fit him for the wide control—
    The empire of the brave !

* Translated by Miss Brooke. It was composed by Fergus to allay the embittered feelings of the rival septs of Morni and Boishna, of which Goll or Gaul, and Finn were the respective leaders. Time—Middle of Third Century. Place—Palace of Finn, at Almhain (Allwinn) county Kildare.
  † Finn Mac Cumhall, then General of the Irish Militia.
  ‡ "Besides standing armies, the Irish kept a considerable naval force, by which they laid other countries under contribution."

"Friend of learning! mighty name!
Havoc of hosts, and pride of fame!
Fierce as the foaming strength of ocean's rage,
When nature's powers in strife engage,
So does his dreadful progress roll,
And such the force that lifts his soul!

* * * * *

"Finn of the flowing locks, oh, hear my voice!
No more with Goll contend!
Be peace henceforth thy happy choice,
And gain a valiant friend!
Secure of victory to the field
His conquering standard goes;
'Tis his the power of fight to wield,
And woe awaits his foes.

"Not to mean, insidious art
Does the great name of Goll its terrors owe;
But from a brave, undaunted heart
His glories flow!

* * * * *

"Finn of the dark-brown hair! oh, hear my voice!
No more with Goll contend!
Be peace sincere, henceforth thy choice,
And gain a valiant friend!
In peace, though inexhausted from his breast
Each gentle virtue flows;
In war no force his fury can arrest,
And hopeless are his foes.

* * * * *

"Spirit resolute to dare!
Aspect sweet beyond compare,
Bright with inspiring soul! with blooming beauty fair!
Warrior of majestic charms!
High in fame and great in arms!
Well thy daring soul may tow'r—
Nothing is above thy pow'r!

"Hear, O Finn, my ardent zeal,
While his glories I reveal!
Fierce as ocean's angry wave,
When conflicting tempests wave;
As still with the increasing storm,
Increasing ruin clothes its dreadful form;
Such is the chief, o'erwhelming in his force,
Unconquered in his swift, resistless course!

"Though in smiles of blooming grace array'd,
And bright in beauty's every charm;
Yet think not, therefore, that his soul will bend;
Nor with the chief contend,
For well he knows to wield the glittering blade,
And fatal is his arm!
Bounty in his bosom dwells,
High his soul of courage swells!

Fierce the dreadful war to wage,
Mix in the whirl of fight, and guide the battle's rage!
Wide, wide around triumphant ruin wield,
Roar through the ranks of death, and thunder o'er the field

" Many a chief of mighty sway,
    Fights beneath his high command;
Marshals his troops in bright array,
    And spreads his banner o'er the land.

" Champion of unerring aim!
    Chosen of kings, triumphant name !
        Bounty's hand and wisdom's head,
Valiant arm and lion soul,
        O'er red heaps of slaughtered dead,
Thundering on to glory's goal!

" Pride of Fenian fame and arms !
    Mildness of majestic charms!
    Swiftness of the battle rage!
    Theme of the heroic page!
    Firm in purpose, fierce in fight !
    Arm of slaughter, soul of might !

" Glory's light ! illustrious name !
    Splendour of the paths of fame !
    Born bright precedent to yield,
    And sweep with death the hostile field !

" Leader of sylvan sports; the hounds, the horn,
    The early melodies of morn !
    Love of the fair, and favourite of the muse !
    In peace, each peaceful science to diffuse :
    Prince of the noble deeds ! accomplished name !
    Increasing beauty, comprehensive fame !

>   *   *   *   *   *

" Hear, O Goll, the poet's voice !
    Oh, be peace thy gen'rous choice !
    Yield thee to the bard's desire !
    Calm the terrors of thine ire !
    Cease then here our mutual strife,
    And peaceful be our future life !"

GOLL—"I yield, O Fergus, to thy mild desire :
    Thy words, O bard ! are sweet ;
    Thy wish, I freely meet,
    And bid my wrath expire.
    No more to discontent a prey,
    I give to peace the future day :
        To thee my soul I bend,
        O guileless friend !
The accents of whose glowing lips well know that soul
        to sway."

BARD—"O swift in Honour's course ! the generous name !
    Illustrious chief, of never-dying fame !"

The applause which greeted these and other songs having subsided, there followed some instrumental music, either from one or from many instruments together ; now charming the ears of the audience by the exquisite sweetness of the ceis ; again firing their souls with enthusiasm by the martial strains of the stoc (stuck), and the cruit, and the tiompan, the fidiol, the cuishla ciuil (cushla ciool) and the clairseach.

After this the seanachies commenced to amuse the company with stories of deeds of valour, and tales of adventure, of love and war, as follows :—

"THE TALE OF LIA FAIL.

" Now, it happened upon a day, as Eochaid Ollamh Fodhla* did commune with Nearton the Ollamh,

" That Ionar, Ard Cruimtear of Gaelan did come into the tent of Eochaid, and he did say:

" ' As I did rise, three mornings now are passed, from the arms of the image of death, and had purified my head, my feet, my hands, and my heart,

" And forth had walked to refresh my spirit ; lo ! three young men drew nigh unto me, and one said :

" ' If I see Ard Cruimtear, 'twere good he knew we have tidings for the ear of the chief of Eri, fit to be told and heard.'

" And I did return unto Asti, nigh unto the Mount of Gaelen,† with the young men, and I did inquire of them what manner of thing it was the chief should know.

" And Saor, one of the youths, did stand up before me, and he did tell :

" ' We be of the Gaal of Sciot, of Iber, and have hither come with words for the ear of the chief, a son of Cier, as we hear, whose heap is raised on the rocks of the terrible sea, behind the utmost limits of our land ; and hither have we come to tell :

" ' Our fathers of old time did leave the land of Iber with Cathac, one of the race, and his mind was to be chief. And when the chiefs of Iber would not have it so, Cathac did call unto him a company of young men, and they did provide a ship upon the gathering together of all the waters behind the land.'

" ' And before the day that he, who was to be chosen king, was named, Cathac and the young men were together.

" ' Now, long and long before this time, one whose name we never heard was to be called chief; and the night before the day he was to come forth into the presence of the Gael,

" ' A mighty stone, white as snow, round as the head of man,

---

* King of Ireland 700 years B.C.   † Mount Leinster.

smooth as the arrows for the warrior's bow, was borne in a chest drawn by many beasts, the priests surrounding the way they moved.

" ' And the priests said, how Baal had sent the blessed stone, even from the bosom of the mountains, that rear their mighty heads above the plains, they formed by his own hands, white and round, and smooth, to show unto the chief, e'en what he ought to be.

" ' And mighty Baal forth did send his terrible voice, saying, " Let all the race for evermore, receive the name of Chief on Liafail (for so they called the stone) from the mouth of the high priest, the servant of Baal on earth."

" ' And thus were four chiefs named.

" ' Now before the day, the chief who crossed the way Cathac desired to move, was to come forth and take his seat on Liafail, lo, Cathac and the young men did bear away the blessed stone to the ship that floated on the waters behind the land of Iber, and thereon they had much store ;

" ' For being but few to journey on the land, they would move on the face of the waters in search of their brethren, led by two of the race to the extremity of the world of land to the sun's going, as they had heard.

" ' And they were driven from their course.

" ' These words have we heard ; it is but a tale of other times long passed, told from mouth to ear; it was but breath ; what hath been said fit for the chief to bear, remains :

" ' We are of Ion, companion of Cathac ; our fathers told the vessel was borne to this land, and here was broken, but all the men came safe with Liafail ; and Firgneat did lead our fathers to their caves, and when they came to understand the words concerning Liafail,

" ' Chiefs of Iber, Gaal of Sciot, look on this stone,

> " ' So smooth, so fair, so round, and so compact,
> Be thus ; guard well this blessed gift,
> And in what land this messenger shall stay
> A chief of Iber shall still bear the sway.'

" ' Firgneat would not suffer him to abide with us; and when the Danaan came to hear the words, they did bear away our Liafail from them,

" ' And Liafail is now in Oldanmacht,* and called Stanclidden; the Danaan cast their lots beneath him, as we hear :

" ' Thither send, O King! and have the name of Chief on

* Connaught

Liafail from the priests' mouth ; so will the land remain to a son of Iber and the Gaal of Sciot evermore.'

"And Eochaid said, ' Let me see the youths.'

"And Saor repeated his tale ; and Eocaid inquired of the young men if they did ever hear what time these things did hap ?   But they had no note, only that the Danaan then were not upon this land.

"And the youth did speak most part in the tongue of the Gaal of Sciot, though not throughout.

"And they do dwell upon the hills and in the vales that touch the waves of the world of waters, and of the sea of Iber unto the waters that do spread themselves upon the land as thou goest towards the south.

"And Eocaid did send Saor and a company of gallant youths to Meirt, Chief of Oldanmact, with a present of four horses and a piece of fine cloth, and a request to give Stanclidden unto Saor ; Stanclidden which is Liafail.

"And Meirt did commune with those about him, and they were of a mind to consent unto the desire of the son of Er.

"And Eocaid had sent a car for Liafail, and he was placed thereon, and Saor and the young men returned with him to Eocaid.

"And when the day came for seating Eochaid, and all the assembly were on the Mount, and a mighty congregation of the children of the land were round about, what time Baal had touched Iarsgith.

"And the heralds proclaimed aloud :

"' Let Eochaid, the son of Fiaca, the son of Seadna, the son of Ardfear, the son of Eolas, of the race of Er, son of the hero, sit Erimionn.' "

"When the air had ceased to tremble for shouts of joy,

"Eocaid said, ' Let Saor of the Gaal of Sciot of Iber be called.'

"And he was raised upon the shields of the tallest of the warriors, and Saor did repeat the tale of Liafail, and when he had made end,

"Eochaid did speak unto the heralds, and they did say aloud :

"' The desire of Eocaid is towards Liafail.'

"Thus spake the heralds, but the Cruimtear and the Carneac held their peace ; they remembered of Luban and of Cromcruad, as the days of Tighernmas.

"But when it did seem good in the eyes of the people, and all the chiefs were consenting unto it, Ionar stood up, and he did say :

" ' Is it the will of the congregation that Erimionn receive the asion and mantle on Liafail ?'

" And all shouted, ' Yea.'

" And Eochaid was seated on Liafail, and the Ard Cruimtear of Gaelen placed the asion on the head, and the mantle laid he on the shoulders of Eochaid.

" And the Ard Cruimtear and all the priests turned their eyes towards Baal, and bowed their head.

" And all the assembly turned their faces towards Eochaid, and clapped their hands and shouted.

" And when silence abided, Erimionn did speak again unto the heralds,

" And they did say aloud:

" ' From this day forth for evermore, what if this Mount be called ' the Hill of Tobrad,'*

" And all said, ' Yea.'

" And the tale of Liafail, and all the acts of the day whereon Eochaid Ollamh Fodhla was proclaimed Erimionn are taken down as Eochaid did bid unto me, Neartan, the son of Beirt, Ard Ollamh of Ullad, to remain with the words of the chronicles for ever."

After these came other tales, as "The Tain Bo Cuailgne," (cattle prey of Cooley) ; " Oidhbeadh-na-g-Curraidhe " (or Death of the Heroes) ; " Brisleach-Muighe Muirthemne ;" "Tochmare Mocmern ;" "Destruction of the Court of Da Darge," &c.

All the various ranks of the seanchaidhe, the ollamh, anroth, cli, fochlog, and driseg, contributed their respective shares to the general entertainment.

After this, the tricks and witticisms of the cainte (satirists), cleasaige (jugglers), amadana (fools), and fuirscoire (buffoons), kept the assembly in continual merriment until dancing (the Irish rinceadh) commenced and occupied the remainder of the night ; the chiefs and princes having deposited in their drinking seats their red gold rings to pay for their seats at Uisneach, another palace of the King of Eire, where assemblies and sports were held in the month of May, which had been called in pagan times Beltine.

And now having endeavoured to describe what passed within the royal palace, we will next see how it fared with the less fortunate multitude outside.

* Hill of Tara.

An cuigṁaḋ caibḋiol.

CHAPTER V.

na biaḋċaċa.

THE HOUSES OF HOSPITALITY.

As the sun sank to rest behind Ara-na-Naomh (Aran of the Saints), and the fabulous Hy Brasil, the Isle of the Blest, the legend of which has been so beautifully rendered by Gerald Griffin, the vast multitude began to disperse: those who lived in the neighbourhood, to their homes; the retainers and servants of the provincial kings, princes, bishops, ollamhs, and nobles, to their several tents, and all strangers to the houses, tents, and the fourteen biadtachs, or houses of hospitality so called, generally at cross roads, and, as we have seen, always well supplied with provisions and meat, boiled in large cauldrons, and in which supplies of various kinds were always kept ready cooked for all comers.

On occasions like the present, however, when people poured into Tara from all parts of the country, and even from other countries, the biadtachs round about the scene of the festivities were always more than equal to the demands made upon them. According as the very diverse multitudes, wearied with the sports of the day, poured into the hospitable roofs for rest and refreshment, all their wants were amply supplied. And, although their surroundings were simplicity itself when compared with the magnificence of the royal palaces, yet their actual entertainment, mental, social, and physical, was in no way inferior to that enjoyed by the higher ranks of their nation. The walls were, indeed, nearly invisible from the number of shields with which they were dotted, but instead of gold and silver they were made of leather, wood, or brass, or some other simple material, though very many of them were embossed with silver, or ornamented in various ways, and seen as they were between a great array of banners, of divers colours and of many devices, had a very striking effect. Instead of the gorgeous, highly-wrought brass chandeliers, and their myriads of wax candles of the royal banqueting hall, these humble places of entertainment were lit up with immense candles formed of rushes, twisted

many times, until they were of great thickness; great numbers of them were placed at intervals at either side. Instead
of the golden thrones and royal couches of "Tara's Hall,"
there were long, plain forms, ranged at either side of the
equally plain substantial tables. The fireplaces, in which
great logs blazed and crackled, were laden with large *coiri umha*,
or copper cauldrons, in which joints of meat of various kinds
were being cooked. At other fireplaces were various kinds of machines, each of which turned no less than thirty spits, all in working
order, which had been so contrived by ancient artificers. It
will be seen there were ample convenience for cooking for the
large number of people who were swarming in, filling the
benches, and ready to do justice to all the good things prepared for them. Many of the military, not being able to find
accommodation at the numerous large tables, were obliged to
use their shields for that purpose, on which to eat their dinner;
the numerous cauldrons and spits were now relieved of their
burdens, and fresh joints put in their places to supply the ever
increasing demands. And now as they take their seats round
the hospitable board, every individual of the vast throng is
served with a plentiful supply of the best viands of every kind,
and they were none the less palatable, that, instead of being
served in silver and gold, they were handed round to each in
vessels of less pretensions. Immense tureens of polished stone
and pottery held the soups, which was served in stone bowls and
cups ; on dishes and plates of stone and wood, were piled all the
edibles—fish of every variety, fat beeves, dainty venison, pork, fresh
and salted ; goats and sheep's flesh ; but beef predominated, for
Eire was unrivalled for the multitude and excellence of her cattle:
they formed, *par excellence*, the riches of the nation. Smaller
game also—turkeys, geese, ducks, fowl of every kind, rabbits
and hares ; bread and butter, and cheese, milk and honey ;
apples and nuts also, and every kind of fruit, were there in
profusion. Various kinds of drink also—wine,* at least
foreign ; ale, beer, mead, spring water from the wells, &c.,
were drank out of vessels of horn, wood, stone, and pottery,
and methers of which there were various kinds—carved drinking-
horns, variegated drinking-horns, drinking-horns of various
colours, drinking-horns with handsome handles, curved drinking-horns ; they were of various shapes, some even were ornamented with silver. And while the gay throng chatted, and
talked, and laughed, they did not forget the privileges which

. * The Vine was cultivated in ancient Erin.

they were entitled to according to law. The bards and musicians, who were there in great numbers, had their primchrochait (prime steak) ; the Fenian men, their salmon ; the historians a crooked bone ; the hunter, a pig's shoulder ; the cooks (cuthgaire) and trumpeters (cornaire) "cheering mead." No man could presume to assume the title of biadhtach who had not seven townlands, each townland comprehending seven plowlands ; he was also to have seven cows going, and be master of seven herds of cattle, each herd containing 120 cows ; his house was to be accessible by four different roads ; and a hog, a beef, and a mutton were always to be ready for the entertainment of the traveller ; of such houses there were no less than 1800 in the two Munsters only. The attendants, with an eye to business, took care not to delay unnecessarily the sons of music, so that they were enabled before long to tune their several instruments, and entertained the rest with strains, gay or solemn, paying special compliment to the Fenian heroes of bygone times, animating those of their listeners whe belonged to that glorious band to enthusiasm and a thirst for military glory. The following Fenian song was sung alternately and in chorus by a numerous band of musicians :—

" THE CHASE.*

OISIN.

" ' Oh, son of Calphruin ! thou, whose ear
Sweet chant of psalms delights to hear,
Hast thou e'er heard the tale,
How Fionn urged the lonely chase
Apart from all the Fenian race,
Brave sons of Inisfail ?'

PATRICK.

" ' Oh, royal born, whom none exceeds
In moving song, or hardy deeds,
That tale to me as yet untold,
Though far renown'd, do thou unfold.
In truth severely wise.
From fancy's wanderings far apart ;
For what is fancy's glorying art
But falsehood in disguise ?'

OISIN.

" ' Oh, ne'er on gallant Fenian race
Fell falsehood's accusation base ;
By faith of deeds, by strength of hand,
By trusty might of battle-brand.

* Translated by the Rev. W. H. Drummond D.D.

We spread afar our glorious fame,
And safely from each conflict came,
Ne'er sat a monk in holy chair,
Devote to chanting hymn and prayer,
  More true than the Fenians bold ;
No chief like Fionn, world around,
Was e'er to bards so generous found,
  With gifts of ruddy gold.

" 'If lived the son of Morné fleet,
  Who ne'er for treasure burned ;
Or Duiné's son, to woman sweet,
  Who ne'er from battle turned ;
But fearless with his single glaive,
A hundred foemen dare to brave ;
If lived Macgaree, stern and wild,
  That hero of the trenchant brand ;
Or Caoilte, Ronan's witty child,
  Of liberal heart and open hand ;
Or Oscar, once my darling boy,
Thy psalms would bring me little joy ;
If lived the Fenian deeds to sing,
  Sweet Fergus with his voice of glee,
Or Daire, who trilled a faultless string,
  Small pleasure were thy bells to me ;
If lived the dauntless little Hugh,
  Or Fillan, courteous, kind, and meek,
Or Conan bold, for whom the dew
  Of sorrow yet is on my cheek ;
Or that small dwarf whose power could steep
The Fenian host in death-like sleep—
More sweet one breath of theirs would be
Than all thy clerks' sad psalmody.'

PATRICK.

" ' Thy chiefs renowned, extol no more ;
Oh, son of kings, nor number o'er,
But low on bended knee record,
The power and glory of the Lord.
And beat the breast and shed the tear,
And still his holy name revere—
Almighty, by whose potent breath
Thy vanquished Fenians sleep in death.'

OISIN.

" ' Alas ! for Oisin—dire the tale !
 * * * * *

Where now are the royal gifts of gold,
The flowing robe with its satin fold,
  And the heart-delighting bowl ?
Where now the feast and the revel high,
And the jocund dance and sweet minstrelsy,

And the steed, loud neighing in the morn,
With the music sweet of hound and horn,
And well-armed guards of coast and bay ?
All, all, like a dream have passed away ;
And now we have clerks with their holy qualms,
And books, and bells, and eternal psalms ;
And fasting, that waster, gaunt and grim,
That strips of all beauty, both body and limb.'

PATRICK.

" 'Oh ! cease this strain, nor longer dare
Thy Fionn, or his chiefs compare
With Him who reigns in matchless might,
The King of kings, enthroned in light.
'Tis He who frames the heaven and earth ;
    'Tis He who nerves the hero's hand ;
'Tis He who calls fair fields to birth,
    And bids each blooming branch expand :
He gives the fishy streams to run,
And lights the moon and radiant sun.
What deeds like these, though great his fame,
Canst thou ascribe to Fionn's name ?'

OISIN.

" ' To weeds and grass his princely eye
    My sire ne'er fondly turned ;
But he raised his country's glory high,
    When the strife of warriors burned.
To shine in games of strength and skill,
To burst the torrent from the hill,
To lead the van of the bannered host,
These were his deeds, and these his boast.'

*   *   *   *   *

PATRICK.

" 'Here let this vain contention rest,
For frenzy, bard, inspires thy breast.'

*   *   *   *   *

OISIN.

" 'This arm, did frenzy touch my brain,
    Their heads from thy clerks would sever,
Nor thy crozier here, nor white book remain,
    Nor thy bells be heard for ever.'

PATRICK.

" Oh, son of kings, adorned with grace,
    'Twere music to mine ear,
Of Fionn, and his wond'rous chase
    The promised tale to hear.

OISIN.

" ' Well, though afresh my bosom bleeds,
    Remembering days of old,   :
When I think of my sire and his mighty deeds,
    Yet shall the tale be told.'

OISIN'S TALE.

" ' While the Fenian bands at Almhain's* towers,
In the hall of spears passed the festive hours,
The goblet crowned, with chessmen played,
Or gifts for gifts of love repaid.
From the reckless throng Fionn stole unseen,
When he saw a young doe on the heath-clad green,
    With agile spring draw near ;
On Sceolan and Bran, his nimble hounds,
He whistles aloud, and away he bounds,
    In chase of the hornless deer.

" ' With his hounds alone and his trusty blade,
    The son of Luno's skill,
On the track of the flying doe he strayed,
    To Guillion's pathless hill.
But when he came to its hard-won height,
    No deer appeared in view ;
If east or west she had sped her flight,
    Nor hounds, nor huntsman knew.

    *   *   *   *   *

" ' There, while he gazes anxious round,
Sudden he hears a doleful sound,
And by a lake of crystal sheen,
Spies a nymph of lovelist form and mien ;
Her cheeks as the rose were crimson bright,
    Her lips the red berry's glow ;
Her neck, as the polished marble white,
    Her breast, the pure blossom's full blow ;
Downy gold were her locks, and her sparkling eyes
Like freezing stars in the ebon skies,
Such beauty, O sage ! all cold as thou art,
Would kindle warm raptures of love in thy heart.

" ' Nigh to the nymph of golden hair,
    With courteous grace he drew—
" O hast thou seen, enchantrees fair,
    My hounds, their game pursue ?"

NYMPH.

" ' Thy hounds I saw not in the chase,
Oh, noble prince of the Fenian race ;
But I have cause of woe more deep,
For which I linger here and weep.'

* Almhain (pronounced Alwin), the Palace of Finn Mac Cumhall, on the hill of Allen, county Kildare.

FIONN.

"'Oh, has thou lost a husband dear?
Falls for a darling son thy tear,
    Or daughter of thy heart?
Sweet, soft-palmed nymph, the cause reveal
To one who can thy sorrow feel—
    Perchance can ease thy smart.'

"The maid of tresses fair replied:—
    'A precious ring I wore,
Dropped from my finger in the tide,
    Its loss I now deplore;
But by the sacred bounds that bind
    Each brave and loyal knight,
I now adjure thee, chief, to find
    My peerless jewel bright.'

"He feels her adjuration's ties,
    Disrobes each manly limb,
And for the smooth-palmed princess hies,
    The gulphy lake to swim.
Five times deep diving down the wave,
Through every cranny, nook, and cave,
With care he searches round and round,
Till the golden ring at length he found;
But scarce to the shore the prize could bring,
    When by some blasting ban—
Ah! piteous tale—the Fenian king
    Grew a withered, gray old man!

"Meanwhile the Fenians passed the hours
In the hall of spears, at Almhain's towers;
The goblet crowned, with chessmen played,
Or gifts for gifts of love repaid.
When Caolite rose and asked in grief,
'Ye spearmen, where is our gallant chief?
Oh! lost, I dread, is the Fenian boast—
Then who shall lead our bannered host?'

*   *   *   *   *

"'To urge the quest, we then decree,
Of Finn and his hounds, the joyous three,
    That still to triumph led.

"'And soon from Almhain's hall away,
With Caoilte, I, and our dark array,
    North to Slew Guillin sped.
Then as with searching glance the eye
    O'er all the prospect rolled,
Beside the lake a wretch we spy,
    Poor, withered, gray and old.
Disgust and horror touch the heart,
To see the bones all fleshless start,
    In a frame so lank and wan;

We thought him some starved fisher torn
From the whelming stream, by famine worn,
  And left but the wreck of man.

" ' We asked if he had chanced to see
  A swift chased chieftain go,
With two fleet hounds across the lea,
  Behind a fair young doe.
He gave us back no answer clear,
But in the nimble Caoilte's ear
He breathed his tale—O tale of grief!—
That in him we saw the Fenian chief !

" Three sudden shouts, to hear the tale,
  Our host raised loud and shrill—
The badgers started in the vale,
  The wild deer on the hill.

    *   *   *   *   *

" Of Cumhall's son then Caoilte sought,
What wizard Danaan foe had wrought,
Such piteous change, and Finn replied,
   ' 'Twas Guillin's daughter—me she bound
By a sacred spell to search the tide
  Till the ring she lost was found.'

" Then Conan spoke in altered mood—
  ' Safe may we ne'er depart,
Till we see restored our chieftain good,
  Or Guillin rue his art !'
Then close around our chief we throng,
And bear him on our shields along.

" Eight days and nights the caverned seat,
Where Guillin made his dark retreat,
  We dig with sleepless care ;
Pour through the windings close the light,
Till we see, in all her radiance bright,
  Spring forth the enchantress fair.

" A chalice she bore of angled mould,
And sparkling rich with gems and gold ;
Its brimming fount in the hand she placed,
Of Finn, whose looks small beauty graced.

" Feeble he drinks—the potion speeds
  Through every joint and pore ;
To palsied age, fresh youth succeeds—
Finn of the swift and slender steeds
  Becomes himself once more,
His shape, his strength, his bloom returns,
And in manly glory bright he burns !

" We gave three cheers that rent the air,
  The badgers fled the vale,
And now, O sage, of frugal care,
  Hast thou not heard the tale ?"

When the deafening cheers which rewarded the musical genius of the bards who had treated the audience to this beautiful Fenian poem had subsided, several of the other bards and musicians present were called upon for the "Battle of Gamhra," which request they complied with.   Several others followed, as "The Lamentation of Cuchillin," love songs, &c.

Then came the turn of the seanachies with tales of other times, as "Imteachta an Ghiolla Decair,"* or "The Adventures of the Dissatisfied Clown.

Interesting stories of Queen Meadhbh, of Conn of the Hundred Battles, of Cormac Mac Art, the Courtship of Finn Mac Cumhaill with the Princess Ailbha, and several other tales on every conceivable subject.

"THE DEATH OF CAOILTE AND DUTAMA.

"Eochaid Ollamh Fodhla abideth on Tobrad.

" Peace and contentment are throughout the nation of Eire.

"The king hath gone towards Dun Sobairce (Dunseverick), ring after ring, what time Baal entereth the threshold of his house Iarsgith."

" Now, when he had ruled in Ulladh two score rings,

"And the messengers have gone forth to call the assembly of Eire to Tobrad, he sent to Fionn his son to come unto him.

"And when Fionn was about to return to Dun Sobairce, Eochaid said unto him, 'Tarry here with me till Iarsgith, then return to Ulladh, and I will go with thee.'

"And as Baal was entering Iarsgith, the king took his departure from his tents on Tobrad with Fionn his son, and Neartan the ollamh.

"And Eochaid would go by the way of Mur Ollamhain to see the youths, and to give a charge concerning them.

"And when it was known that the king purposed to take that way, a great multitude accompanied him, and a train of damsels came forth to do honour to the king.

"And Eochaid went unto Mur Ollamhain and he tarried there for awhile ; and as he moved towards the river, one came unto the king, and said :

"' Youth of Gaelen (Leinster) have desired to race on their horses before the king.'

"And Eochaid was conducted to a little hill, whence he could look over the way the horses were to run, and all the damsels came about him.

* Pronounced Imhaght an yilla dacker.

"And as the horses were changing their course to go by the waters of the Buadaman, the horse of one of the young men ran headlong into the river, and the youth was flung, and he sunk to the ground, and he lay there.

"And a great uproar and loud lamentation were raised; and when one of the damsels nigh unto the king heard what had happened, and that the youth covered over by the waters was Caoilte, the son of Deag, chief minstrel of the king,

"She ran violently towards the river, and threw herself into the waters.

"And what time the boats came and the ropes were brought the young man and the damsel were in the arms of death.

"And a loud cry was raised, and Eocaid lamented, and the company bore the weight of the lad and of the damsel to a chamber of Mur Ollamhain.

"And the king did not go on his way, he lodged in the chamber of the Ard Ollamh, till the little heap was raised. The cloth of death that covered the young man did also cover the damsel; they were laid side by side; the heap of one is the heap of the other, and the name of the damsel was Dutama.

"Is not the mournful song of the bards for the death of Caoilte and Dutama amongst the writings of the bards in Mur Ollamhain?"

Other tales followed of Catha, or Battles; of Longasa, or Voyages; of Toghla, or Destructions; of the Tana, or Cattle Spoils; of Tochmarca, or Courtships; of Fenian tales, and tales of slaughters, sieges, and tragedies.

Although the jugglers* and fools† had not all this time been idle, having, on every opportunity, during the evening, been tickling the assembly, now commenced in good earnest their congenial calling, and for the next hour, the immense gathering were kept in a continual fit of laughter and general merriment. After which, the musicians struck up lively tunes, and tables and forms, and other impediments being removed, a general dance commenced, and continued with spirit during the remainder of the evening. And thus ended the first day's celebration of the Fes of Teamhair—the five succeeding days being repetitions of the first with more or less variation—thus, while the delegates were engaged, as on the first day, in the business of the nation, their relatives, friends, retainers, and the rest of the people enjoyed themselves in music, dancing, hunting in the neighbouring forests, parties of pleasure to places of note within

* Cleasaige.   † Amadhana.

14

convenient distances, hurling, playing at chess and back-
gammon, and other games, &c.; the day's proceedings or sports
winding up as before with the grand banquet in the palace, as well
as the great entertainments in the biadtachs, in all of which the
music, songs, and stories were each evening different, and the poets,
besides reciting well-known poems of others, and compositions
of their own, were also expected to call forth their powers
in that particular branch of poetry called *Dichedal*, or improvi-
sation; some person present would suggest the subject, and the
bard would forthwith burst forth into an unpremeditated lay.

————

An c-seṁaḋ caibroil.

CHAPTER VI.

Cabairc breiċe air an m-breiċeaṁain.

JUDGING THE JUDGE.

ON the sixth day of the Fes, while the delegates were engaged
in winding up the various matters which had occupied them
since the opening day, and which were to be inscribed on the
Rolls of Mur Ollamhain, and the non-delegates were amusing
themselves pretty much as we have described above, two young
men walked arm-in-arm through the various throngs, engaged
in animated conversation, though now and then stopping to look
at some amusing tricks of the jugglers, or to watch the progress of some game, or to join a group of persons who would be
discussing some interesting question, but they would invariably
resume their walk and their interrupted dialogue. They were
our old friend, Aristophanes and Ainmire, nephew of Muircheartach MacEarca, a former monarch of Ireland. As they
were in the middle of a heated discussion, each suddenly felt
a hand laid on his shoulder, and turning round they beheld
Fearghus (son of the above-named monarch and cousin of
Ainmire), who exclaimed:

"Why, boys, you had better not quarrel; leave that to lords
abbots."

Aristophanes and Ainmire, laughing: "Oh! we are not
quarrelling, but we are just discussing the abbots and the
Ardrigh."

Ainmire—"Where is do dhearbhrathair?"*

Fearghus—"When the business of the Fes closed, the Abbot Columb called him aside. There is considerable anxiety as to the result of the Ardrigh's arbitration between him and the Abbot Finian; each party has his partisans."

Aristophanes—"We were discussing that point when thou camest up; but I fear thy cousin Ainmire is rather hard on King Diarmaid."

Fearghus—"How is that, Ainmire; dost thou think he will not do justice by the Abbot Columb?"

Ainmire—"I fear he will not; I fancy he has a prejudice against him."

Fearghus—"Let us be moving towards the palace, that we may be in time to hear the judgment."

Animire—"Perhaps it has already commenced."

Fearghus—"Oh, no, impossible; we shall be in time. But what makest thou think that Diarmaid is prejudiced against the Abbot Columb?"

Ainmire—"Well, I cannot say that I can give any particular reason, it may be only imagination; but we shall see. In fact, I cannot conceive how he is permitted to reign at all in a Christian country, with his druids, and his magic, and other remnants of pagan superstition."

Fearghus—"Well, those matters give great offence to the nation; but, then, he is the lawful monarch."

Aristophanes—"And then, on the other hand, he has built and endowed many great churches and monasteries."

Ainmire—"Ay, he would compromise matters and serve two masters,"

Fearghus—"How is that?"

Ainmire—"Why, on the one hand he would serve our Lord and the Twelve Apostles, and on the other, Crom Cruach and the twelve signs of the Zodiac."†

---

* Dhu yar-ra-hir, thy brother.

† Before the introduction of Christianity all the pagan kings and chiefs had a cromcruagh, or idol, representing fire or the sun, and twelve inferior deities around him composed of pillar stones, with heads of gold, representing the signs of the Zodiac. Tigearnmas was the first Irish king who introduced Druidism and the worship of idols into Ireland, B.C. 900, and while worshipping Crom, along with a vast number of his subjects at Magh Sleacht in Breifne on the feast of Samhuin (1st Nov.), he, with three-fourths of his people, were struck dead by lightning, as a punishment for having introduced idolatry into the kingdom. It was the same great idol, together with the famous temple, which was afterwards destroyed by St. Patrick, who built a church on its site under the name of Fenagh; it was long celebrated as a seat of learning and religion. Cromleach, Crom's stone.

Aristophanes—" Why, surely, thou dost not mean that he worships idols."

Ainmire—" Well, not directly. He worships the true God and honours his saints; but is not druidical superstition an indirect worship of Satan ?"

Aristophanes—" There can be no doubt of that; still, I do not think he views it in that light. It is time, however, that the druids were relegated to their oak groves."

Ainmire—" It is time they were relegated out of the country altogether."

Aristophanes—" Where were they on All Hallows, or on what they call Samhain ?"

Ainmire—" Oh, they would not dare celebrate Samhain while the multitude around celebrated the Church's feast of All Saints."

Aristophanes—" Perhaps it is that King Diarmaid encourages them through a mistaken love for the traditions of the country."

Fearghus—" It were well, then, that he displayed equal love for other traditions of the country, less sinful and more important."

Aristophanes—" To what dost thou refer, O Fearghus ?"

Fearghus—" I refer to his repeated attempts to dictate to the provincial delegates. In truth he has tried our patience sadly within the past six days. I have heard complaints of his conduct at former conventions, but I never quite understood it until now; this being the first at which I had the honour of being present as a delegate."

Aristophanes—" Oh, ye delegates are very tenacious of your privileges; I do not wonder he tries to show you he is a high king in deed as well as in name."

Fearghus—" But it is a despotic and unconstitutional proceeding, utterly at variance with the laws and customs of the country, and so says thy friend Ruadhan, the Abbot of Lothra."

Aristophanes—" Ah ! my old friend and the king's old foe."

Ainmire—" And I do not see why it should be tolerated."

Aristophanes—" Well, I certainly would not approve of the Ardrigh taking advantage of his exalted position, to infringe the rights and liberties of the provincial kings, or of the people at large; but what is the use of an Ardrigh at all, if his position is merely one of honour, without a vestige of power beyond that of those who are his tributaries ?"

Fearghus—" Why I wouldst thou have the provincial kings mere deputies in their own dominions ?"

Aristophanes—" No, certainly not; they have as good a right

to their respective kingdoms as King Diarmaid has to his own kingdom of Midhe ;* but we must remember that besides being king (righ) of Midhe, Diarmaid is also high king (Ardrigh) of all Eire ; and that pre-eminence in dignity ought also to carry with it pre-eminence in power."

Fearghus—"Thine argument is plausible, and it appears that Diarmaid is so convinced of its truth that he is determined to carry it into execution, if he can ; but that is exactly the point on which the delegates differ from him, and which, during the course of the Fes, had well nigh threatened to disturb the good understanding which it is desirable to maintain."

Ainmire—"And, besides, that would leave the whole nation at the mercy of one man."

Aristophanes—"Not more than each particular kingdom is at the mercy of its particular sovereign ; and you know that that is impossible under such a constitution as yours. All the various classes have their weight in the government of the whole."

Ainmire—" That is true, but as Fearghus says, it is not likely to succeed, as Diarmaid has too many against him ; so we may flatter ourselves that the liberties of the country are safe."

Aristophanes—" I do not know that. One part of the country is often fighting against the other, and if union is strength, division is weakness. Your country can never be safe from the possibility of foreign invasion until all its forces are united under one strong supreme monarch, who, while banding all firmly together for the common good, will yet leave the provincial kings the undisputed sovereigns of their respective territories."

Fearghus—" Yes, thou art right ; that would certainly be a most desirable state of affairs, if it could only be accomplished ; but I fear Diarmaid is not the man."

Ainmire—" No, Diarmaid is not the man ; but stay ——"

This conversation was carried on as they moved through the motley crowd of various classes and nationalities, and as Ainmire uttered the last word, they stopped and formed part of a crowd of persons who were watching a hurling match which was being played with great ardour and skill by a number of youths, several of whom were recognised by the three friends as Eochaidh Forghiall ; Curnan, son of Aodh, son of Eochy Tiormcarna, King of Connaught ; Lorcan, son of Conall MacTadhg (Teige), one of Diarmaid's chief officers, and several other youths. Having watched the game with much interest for a few minutes, the three companions moved away. Ainmire remarking that

† Meath.

Curnan and Lorcan appeared as if they were inclined to quarrel, but Fearghus and Aristophanes thought there was no fear, that their apparent difference was the result of excitement incident to hurling. They then ascended the Hill of Temhair, making their way through the crowd, who were anxiously awaiting and commenting upon the expected judgment of the Ardrigh.

ᴀn ᴄ-ѕеᴀᴄᴛṁᴀᴅ́ ᴄᴀıbıᴅıl.

CHAPTER VII.

· Ꞑeıᴄ́é Cꞃoꞃoᴅ.

UNTOWARD EVENTS.

WHEN the three friends entered the judgment-hall they found it crowded to its utmost capacity, though the Ardrigh had not yet made his appearance. Perceiving Domhnald, Fearghus's brother, in close conversation with the Abbot Columb, they endeavoured to join them, but had scarcely succeeded, when a flourish of trumpets was heard, and almost immediately the heralds ushered in the Ardrigh, who was attended by the *ten**, who never leave his royal presence, viz., a grandee, a bishop, a brehon, a physician, a poet, an historian, a musician, and three stewards. All rose as he entered, and having seated himself on the cathair rioghda (royal chair), and the heralds having proclaimed silence, he opened his royal lips and electrified the audience by his judgment:

"*Le gach boin a boinin*, to every cow belongeth her little cow (or calf), and in the same way to every book belongs its son-book (copy); accordingly the book that thou didst write, *O Columcille*, belongs by right to Finian!"

This decision was received by cheers from the party that sided with the Abbot Finian, and with frowns and exclamations

---

* The law which required the perpetual attendance of these "ten" on the king was enacted by King Cormac Ulfhada, in the third century, for himself and his successors, with this difference, that in pagan times a druid made one of the number, but after the introduction of Christianity, a bishop was substituted. Diarmaid, however, had both, though he did not always deem it prudent to bring them in juxtaposition, especially when a great number of people were assembled, or before the Church representatives. Lands were assigned to certain families, each of which was to be employed in one of the above-mentioned offices to the sovereigns of the various principalities.

of dissent and dissatisfaction by the friends of the Abbot Columb, who, rising from his seat, hotly exclaimed:

"This is an unjust decision, O Diarmaid! and I will avenge it on thee."

On this the Abbot Finian also rose and said:

"The decision of the Ardrigh is most just, for to me belongs the son-book, which was written from my Psalter."

Confused murmurs ran through the assembly, the partisans of Columcille and those of Finian waging a war of words; the latter entreating the Ardrigh to order the son-book to be restored to the possession of its parent; while the former as eagerly pleaded the cause of filial independence. Some tried to read the opinion of the brehon—one of the "*ten*"—but the face of that functionary was impenetrable. The case had not been brought before the judges, whose particular business it was to hear and decide on all such cases, but it had been left to the arbitration of the Ardrigh, and now the litigants must abide by the result.

While King Diarmaid (whose continued striking of the craobh ciuil, or musical branch, failed to produce silence) was surveying the vast assembly, at least the half of whom had dared to call in question the justice of his decision to his very face, and meditating how to bring them to a sense of their duty while in his presence, their murmurs, exclamations, and mutual recriminations became every moment louder and more loud, until, penetrating beyond the walls of the palace, it was taken up by the multitude outside, and in a few minutes assumed such proportions as to rouse the Ardrigh to an effort to suppress such dangerous symptoms; but every attempt to make himself heard now proved unavailing, even the heralds failing to produce silence, so great was the noise occasioned by the numberless voices, from which he could distinguish nothing save the demand on the one side for the restoration of the son-book, and the energetic opposition to that demand on the other. Perfectly bewildered and enraged by the din, both from within and without, which resembled the rushing torrent of many waters, he rose from his royal seat and waving his sceptre authoritatively, he commanded the Abbot Columcille to restore the son-book to the Abbot Finian. The expressions of anger to which Columcille's partisans now gave vent were drowned in the ringing cheers of Finian's friends, but mingled with it there came from without shouts and cries, and an indescribable hubbub which struck the hearts of those within with an unaccountable awe, and each party forgot their differences, as an officer, followed by several others, rushed in, and breathless from excitement and horror, thus addressed the monarch :

"Pardon, O King, our unceremonious intrusion; but woe, alas ! has come upon the land; the Feast of Teamhair is violated; Lorchan, the son of thy best beloved officer, Conall Mac Tadhg, lies a bleeding corpse on yonder faitche,* struck down by the hand of thy royal hostage, Curnan Mac Aodh, Mac Eochy Tiormcarna."

Ere the officer had concluded his account, the whole assembly had made for the door amidst expressions of grief and horror; the Ardrigh throwing up his hands in a perfect frenzy of grief and rage, precipitately left his royal chair, calling alternately on Christian and pagan powers, and giving orders to everyone he met to visit the offender with summary justice; but though everyone was looking for Curnan, and some had seen him, yet no one could find him, until at length word was brought to Diarmaid that Curnan was safe in the arms of Columcille. This news incensed the Ardrigh more, and in a tone not to be gainsayed, ordered the culprit to be torn from the abbot's arms and consigned to instant death. And now was enacted a most heartrending scene. The officers of justice, followed by the Ardrigh and great numbers of people, directed their steps towards the spot where they were informed the Abbot Columb was endeavouring to protect his client, and informing the abbot of the orders they had received requested him to give the offender into their custody. But Columb refused to give up Curnan, alleging as his reason that the youth had sought his protection, which he had extended in virtue of the right of sanctuary with which he was invested.

King Diarmaid, angrily—"But I say to thee, O Columb, that thou must deliver up to the officers of justice that young culprit; *he* has violated the sanctuary of the Feast of Teamhair, when it is more than ever unlawful to engage in strife; *he* has shed the blood of the son of my dearest friend ; *he* has ignited a spark which, if not quenched in his blood, may lay the whole country in a vast conflagration; *he* has committed the worst of crimes, and I say to thee, O Columb, that *he* must die !"

By this time the parents of Curnan, his grandfather, the King of Connaught, and several other relations and followers, having been apprised of what was coming on, arrived on the spot just in time to hear Diarmaid's last words. The crowd made way; the distracted mother threw herself on her son, who was still held

* Lawn.

fast by Columcille. The scene that followed is beyond description ; even Diarmaid himself appeared for a moment melted and irresolute, the other relations of Curnan, including his father and grandfather, with great numbers of the people, had sank on their knees before the monarch ; the three friends, Fearghus, Aristophanes, and Ainmire, who had seen the youths playing together, gave it as their opinion that the quarrel resulted from the heat and excitement of the game, and that no ill-feeling existed between them. Unfortunately though, there appeared to be no doubt whatever as to whose hand struck the blow that deprived Lorcan of life ; even Curnan's best friends did not attempt to suggest the possibility of the deed having been done by some other hand ; it had been witnessed by too many persons ; those, however, and especially the young companions of the unfortunate youth, declared emphatically that the unfortunate occurrence was partly accidental and wholly unpremeditated, and that no one was more shocked and horror-stricken than Curnan himself, when he had seen what he had done. Amid prayers for mercy and cries for justice, expressions of commiseration for the dead youth and his parents, on the one hand, and on the other for the distracted mother and afflicted father of Curnan, and of sympathy with himself, the crowd again opened, this time to admit the stricken father of the unfortunate boy, the spark of whose young life was thus suddenly extinguished. His appearance diverted attention from the hapless Curnan and his unfortunate relations. Throwing himself before the Ardrigh, he cried out :

"O King, I have served thee long and faithfully ; thou hast been pleased to honour me with thy particular friendship ; my beloved son, my darling child, the pride of my life, the hope and comfort of my old age, his mother's joy, has been struck down by an assassin's hand ——" (Cries of no, no, no). "Will it be said that my lord king refuses to see justice done to his faithful servant ; shall my gray hairs go down in sorrow to the grave ; is all thy sympathy with the murderer, and none with his hapless victim ; is this thy high sense of justice, O Diarmaid ; is this the reward of my long and faithful services ; is this —— O King, I demand of thee the instant execution of the murderer of my child."

Columcille—"Cruel man! Would the blood of Curnan bring back to thee thy son ? Dost thou think to appease his spirit by the oblation of a holocaust ? Were he permitted to return for one moment, he would plead more earnestly than any of us for the pardon of Curnan. Hast thou never offended thy

God ? and if thou hast, has he meeted out to thee, measure for measure ? Hadst thou ever had a mother ? Didst thou not see how thou didst wring this woman's heart (pointing to Curnan's mother) when thou didst call her son a murderer ? And I bid thee, O Conall, never attempt to do so again. Well thou knowest he is no murderer. All who witnessed the unfortunate occurrence unite in asserting that it was an unpremeditated act, and, that it resulted from some differences at hurling ; and moreover, that even when striking the blow, Curnan had no idea of taking life, but on the next instant was more horrified than anyone else on his discovering how the affair had culminated. And now I tell thee, once for all, that I will never yield him up to the. civil power, and I warn thee and all others to respect my privilege of sanctuary."

Conall—" O Columcille, thine arguments are as new, I have no doubt, to all these people as they are to me. He must not be called a murderer ; well, it is all the same to me by what name he is called ; he has deprived me of my child. Thou speakest, and indeed truly, of the mercy of God to those who have offended Him ; thereby implying that as He 'forgives us our trespasses, so ought we to forgive those that trespass against us.' Truly, if everyone would adhere to the maxims of the Gospel, it would be a happy world. From my heart I would wish to forgive that unhappy youth. But for what purpose has God ordained kings and princes and brehons, if not to do justice between those over whom they reign. What would become of society were everyone permitted to strike down their neighbour for some petty difference, and then shield themselves from public justice behind this merciful injunction of our Redeemer, which was only meant to regulate the conduct of private individuals."

" Columcille—" The distinction which thou drawest between public justice and private vengeance would be most true and just were Curnan really the murderer of thy son ; but as thou knowest, it was a pure accident, the execution of Curnan would be a real murder, and on the heads of his executioners and their abettors would be the blood, not only of this unfortunate youth, but of his sorely afflicted mother. Look, O Conall, look on that mother's grief, and if thou hast a heart, see if thou canst demand the murder of her child !"

As he spoke the abbot pointed to the grief-struck mother of the unhappy Curnan, and all the people by word and look expressed their sympathy, but Conall said :

" O Columb, thou hast struck a chord, and in a manner too, that thou little dreamest ——"

Then suddenly flinging his arms aloft, every attitude and expression betokening the intense grief which had taken possesion of his soul, he cried out:

"Come! O lord High King! Come, O Abbot Columb! Come, all ye nobles and people, come! and I will show ye a mother's grief! Come! come!"

As Conall uttered these last words he turned to leave the spot, waving his hand with such an air of mingled command and entreaty that not only the deeply-impressed multitude, but even the haughty Diarmaid himself, mechanically prepared to follow. Reaching in a few minutes the lawn where the dead youth lay, surrounded by another crowd, which opened on their approach, a spectacle presented itself which caused the hearts of the beholders to stand still. There lay the youth who, a short while previously, had been full of life and health and vigour, with high expectation of a glorious and brilliant career in court or field. There he lay in all the stony rigidity of death, his young life shortened, all his hopes, at least for this world, frustrated; and bending over him, the scarcely less corpse-like figure of a matronly lady; her stony eyes rivetted on his, her hands clasped in agony; no hysterical sobs or cries escape from her, no tear is shed, not even a muscle moves to show that her soul is the tenant of her body. Conall, by gesture alone, directs the attention of the people to the spectacle; he dares not trust himself to speak. The people look and are horrified, and from the hearts of that vast multitude an unspoken prayer ascends to heaven that God would vouchsafe to this sorely-afflcted mother the relief of abundant and heart-wringing tears. The relations of Curnan look, and a dread foreboding takes possession of them. The Abbot Columcille looks and fears for his client, but clasps him all the more closely to his privileged person. But Diarmaid looks, and that look seals the fate of Curnan. Turning fiercely to the officers of justice, he cries out:

" Ho! there, officers, seize the slayer of Conall's son, seize him! seize him, ye—— What! will not the Abbot Columb deliver him up?"

"Columcille—" Never, O Diarmaid! I have granted my protection, and I shall never now withdraw it. And I call upon thee, O King, to respect the privilege of sanctuary which appertains to all persons or things connected with the Church."

"Diarmaid—"Have I not told thee before, O Columcille, that I will not, cannot, in this case, regard thy sanctuary, and that thou must deliver up that youth to the justice of the law?"

Aedh (Curnan's father)—" But, O King, I beseech thee,

hear me ; this death which thou wouldst inflict upon my son is not according to the laws of the country. Let him be tried before the brehons, and I will abide by the result."

Diarmaid—"Never shall that be ; the brehons would but inflict an eric,* which thou knowest could never compensate for the life of the youth or the woe and bereavement of his parents. Besides, thou knowest that it is the law, and moreover, thou also knowest that I have no power to pardon thy son. The power I seek is denied me by the country. Let my brehon read the law."

The brehon (one of the "ten") then drew from a fold of his mantle a parchment, which related to the laws regulating the Fes of Tara ; he read the following extract from the roll :

"Without theft, without wounding a man
        Among them during all this time ;
    Without feats of arms, without deceit,
    Without exercising horses.
    Whoever did any of those things
    Was a wretched enemy with heavy venom.
    Gold was not received as a retribution from him,
    But his soul in one hour."

Eochy Tirmacharna (King of Connaught)—"But this was no "heavy venom," but an accident ; and we shall pay the highest eric the judges shall award, and we shall make every other compensation in our power, if thou wilt but spare our child."

Here the confusion caused by the swaying and tumult of the people, the efforts of the officers of Diarmaid to seize on Curnan, assisted as they were by numbers of the people who sympathised with the afflicted parents of the dead youth, and opposed by Columcille and those who felt for the unfortunate position of Curnan and the grief of his relatives, and especially of his mother, who had swooned away on hearing the Ardrigh's fresh orders, and who was being tended by some of the people. As the King of Connaught prayed for the life of his grandson to the impatient Diarmaid, the latter was exasperated by the opposition of Columcille, against whom he had already entertained feelings of intense hostility ; and now seeing that his

* A money fine.
    At the Feis Teamhrach it was a sacred and established usage that the man who committed a rape or robbery, or who struck, or attempted to strike another with any hostile weapon at it, should inevitably suffer death, and neither the king himself nor any other person had the power of pardoning his crime.

officers were reluctant to force away the youth from the sanctuary of the abbot's arms, he strode forward, and goaded on as he was by the party that sided with what they considered the side of justice, he excitedly and in a voice that almost parlysed the more timid of the mutitude, thundered forth :—

"Officers, I command you, on pain of instant death, to seize, bind, and forthwith execute the slayer of Conall's son ; pay no regard to the sanctuary of Columcille ; Curnan paid none to that of the Feast of Teamhair ; and hark ye, be quick about it, lest others be got to do your work, and ye be sent to bear Curnan company to the other world."

A short and terrific struggle ensued, in which a large number of the people attempted a rescue from the officers of justice, as soon as they succeeded in wrenching their prisoner from the powerful arms of Columcille, who denounced themselves and their master in no measured terms. The relations of Curnan now harangued the multitude, and heading their party, were about to make a desperate onslaught on the opposing party for the rescue of their young relation, when suddenly silence and horror took possession of the assembled multitude ; some threw up their hands into the air, many fell on their knees in the attitude of prayer, but by far the greater number turned away their heads, or covered their eyes with their hands, while many others stopped their ears, as ominous sounds fell upon them—the sounds of the executioners' work, followed by the groan and stifled prayer of a departing soul. The silence of the grave followed, so deep, so awful, that as each one of all that immense multitude slowly opened his eyes, he almost expected to find himself the sole living inhabitant of the beautiful hill or the magnificent plain. Soon, however, as they sufficiently realised the dreadful tragedy which had taken place, the many and conflicting feelings and passions of the vast assemblage found vent in tears, groans, lamentations, denunciations, threats of vengeance, mingled with prayers and supplications to heaven for both victims, together with the expressive and touching *caoine*,* which was sung by many voices over the dead youths as they were removed—the one to the royal palace of Diarmaid, and the other to the Coisir Conacthacth (Connaught House, on Tara Hill)—for though Diarmaid, in a softened mood, induced by awe, when the deed was done, had offered another part of the palace as a sort of peace-offering, his offer was declined.

The unfortunate mother of the hapless youth, whose murder

* Pronounced kueené, the funeral song.

was called an execution, had never, up to this, recovered from the swoon into which she had fallen, on hearing the sentence on her son, and thus was saved the sight of his death struggle, was borne carefully to the house of a flaith, lest she should recover, only to learn the fate of her child. The tumult which would inevitably have followed the tragedy, was speedily suppressed by the orders of the family of Curnan, who were not disposed to have any disturbance just then, but were anxious to return home quietly to inter their young relative, and afterwards settle accounts with Diarmaid by recognised means.

The Abbot Columcille, immediately on the execution of Curnan, had sought out King Diarmaid in the crowd, and the Ardrigh, already somewhat uneasy as to the probable consequence of his two-fold quarrel with such a powerful and influential personage as Columcille, connected as he was with a powerful royal family, and tenacious of his rights and privileges, sought to avoid another encounter; but as he turned to give orders, concerning the abbot, to one of his guards, the now irate ecclesiastic came down on him with denunciations of his tyrannical conduct, and then and there threatened him with the vengeance of God, and of the Clanna Nials of the North. But Diarmaid insisting on the justice of his decision, both with regard to the book and the youth, and fearful of trusting himself further in a dispute with the injured abbot, contrived to penetrate through the crowd, and thus escape to the interior of the palace, not, however, without first giving orders for guards to be set to watch the abbot, and others to guard the frontiers of Midhe to prevent his escape.

An τ-oċτmaḋ ċabroil.

CHAPTER VIII.

An Ceiċeaḋ.

THE ESCAPE.

THE Abbot Columcille, finding himself virtually a prisoner, and perceiving that notwithstanding the incessant moving to and fro of the motley crowd, there was a constant watch upon his movements by the guards of the Ardrigh, came to the conclusion that it was necessary to elude the vigilance of those functionaries with as ltttle delay as possible. Contriving to speak to one of his attendants without attracting suspicion from the guards, he ordered him to collect his fellow-servants, and at once proceed by the Slighe Midhluachra, or the Great Northern Road, to Tirconnell, the abbot's native place. This order was immediately put into execution, the attendants meeting with no opposition from the guards. Columb's next step was to make good his own escape, and for this purpose, having first sent up a prayer to heaven for assistance, he proceeded to move from the immediate precincts of the royal palace, down the "Delightful Hill," through the City of Teamhair, across the magnificent plain to the frontiers of Midhe, having passed not only the multitudes of all kinds of people, but before the very eyes of the guards told off to watch him, for, as the old chronicle says, "the justice of God threw a veil of unrecognition around him." Once beyond the immediate dominions of Diarmaid, he breathed more freely; but lest he should be pursued if he travelled by the high road, he determined to take the longer route across the mountains. He passed the night at the monastery of St. Buite (Monasterboice).* The first thing he heard the next morning was that he was pursued by the guards of the Ardrigh; so partaking of a hasty breakfast, he left Monasterboice and made for the mountains. Owing to the lateness of the season, and the unfrequentedness of the path he had chosen across the hills which lay between him and Oirghialla, it required all his native cheerfulness and piety to bear up against the hardships of his lonely journey, rendered more wearisome and perilous by the reflection on the many trials he had so lately passed through, and the fear of being pursued and overtaken by the soldiers of the Ardrigh. One day, when these sad reflections more than usually oppressed him, he all at once, rising from a stone on which he had seated himself to take a short rest, and at the same time to meditate on his sad condition, and proceeding on his journey, burst forth into the following hymn, which has been preserved from the wreck of the nation's literature, and is illustrative of the man and the times :—

"ALONE I AM UPON THE MOUNTAIN.

"Alone I am upon the mountain ;
  O God of Heaven ! prosper my way ;
So shall I pass more free and fearless
  Than if six thousand were my stay,

* In present county Louth. The ruins are still to be seen.

My flesh, indeed, might be defended,
But when the time comes life is ended.
If by six thousand I was guarded,
Or placed in islet in a lake,
Or in a fortress strong protected,
Or in a church my refuge take,
Still God will guard his own with care,
And even in battle safe they fare ;
No man can slay me till the day
When God shall take my life away ;
And when my earthly time is ended,
I die, no matter how defended—
  My life !
Without His will no less can it be made,
As God shall please so let it be,
Nor can they add to it without his leave,
The lot which He has given that I shall see,
Nor prince upon his throne one hour can get
Of life beyond what God for him has set—
  A guard !
A guard, indeed, may guide a man full safe,
But never guard can keep a man from death,
For One alone has rule of every fate—
Alone can give or take our mortal breath.
Nor shall I fear though poverty may come,
The Son of Mary still shall give my share ;
For all the Master portions out some dole of food,
And under his protection all shall safely fare.
What is well spent, to bounteous hand returns,
What is denied the niggard keeper spurns.
O Living God, alas ! for evil-working men,
That which they think not, comes to mar their life,
That which they hope for vanishes away,
And leaves them lonely in a world of strife.
No augur's word can tell our future fate—
No bird, no omen, say how long our death shall wait,
I trust not in a bird, or twig, or dream,
But in the Lord of heaven's eternal might ;
He who has made us all will help me now,
Nor leave me in this mountain lone to-night.
I have no love of earthly kin or kind,
The love of Christ, the Son of God, fills my mind.
The great King's Son, my Lord and Abbot, rules :
All that I have is in the great King's hands.
The houses of my order are at Kells and Moone —
He will protect my people and my lands,
Praise be for evermore, and endless merit,
Unto the Father, Son, and Holy Spirit."

Refreshed and strengthened by his trust in Providence,
Columb proceeded on his journey, and soon leaving the
mountains behind him, his road was thenceforth easier; he
stopped at the various monasteries and biadtachs on his

route to refresh himself, but made no delay beyond what was absolutely necessary. Having in this manner passed through Oirghialla and the country of the Feara Manach,* he at length reached his old home in Tirconnaill in perfect safety. Here, owing to the previous arrival of his attendants, he found his relatives in possession of the principal facts relating to his quarrel with Diarmaid, and now he was besieged on all sides with questions as to details, Columcille stating truly every-thing as it occurred. The hot blood of the Clanna Nials could ill brook such an insult ; and taking council with the men of Tir-Eoghain,† they determined to take part in the war which they felt must inevitably take place between Midhe and Connaught. They only awaited the arrival from the Fes of Teamhair, of their friends and countrymen, and especially of Domhnald and Fearghus, the sons of the former monarch of Eire, Muircheartach Mac Earca, and their cousin, Ainmire, son of Sedna. When at last they did come pouring into the countries of Cinel Chonail, and Cinel Eoghan, by the Slighe Midhluachra, or great Northern Road, and all the bealachs and bothars, and all the other roads from Tara, they brought such news as tended rather to increase than diminish the ire of their countrymen.

an naomaú caibroil.

CHAPTER IX.

Leigeaú na React.

THE READING OF THE LAWS.

An Domnac.

THE SABBATH.

MEANWHILE, the multitude on Druim Aoibhin and Magh Breagh had slackened considerably. The royal family of Olnegmacht, or Connaught, had taken their departure for their own homes, taking with them all that remained of their murdered boy, and followed by all their retinue and people. Those of other parts of the kingdom, who sympathised with them, and whose business

---

* Fermanagh.　　　　　　　† Tyrone.

or duty did not oblige them to remain at Tara, also repaired to their various homes. Still, great as was the number of departures, they could scarcely be missed out of the numerous throng who found it no easy matter to get away, even so short a time before they intended ; so, as the next day was Sunday, they elected to remain till the following Monday. It was, however, in no gracious mood that they all at once beheld the chief brehon mount the Lia Fail, and heard the heralds proclaim :

"Let the chief judge read aloud the words on the roll of the laws of Eire, and let all the people attend thereunto."

And the people lapsed into silence ; the chief brehon commenced :

"Sixteen years have been completed since Diarmaid Mac Fearghus Mac Cearbhall hath been chosen to sit on the throne of Eire, since which time the kings and princes of the land, the pastors of the Church, and the chiefs of the Gaal have placed him even here, the tie and the knot of the cincture that is to bind together the affections of all the children of the land.

"That he may do somewhat to justify their thoughts of him, he hath laboured without ceasing to give the laws a form and strength, moreover to protect the children of Eire from violence and oppression.

"Eire is the birthright of all the children of the land : the king hath his portion, the princes, the nobles, each hath his portion thereof ; the priests, the ollamhain, the bards, and the minstrels have their portions.

"And the Gael by their clans have their portion thereof.

"From the earth man derived sustenance, whereby to live. Hath any increased his store of cattle, or of stuff, or of arms ? Let his words as to these, and these like stand : '*Of his portion of the land none can have dominion longer than he doth abide thereon.* His children and the mother of his children shall dwell thereon till portion be made ; then let not the woman who bore, nor the damsels who are to bring forth, be forgotten ; are not all the race born of woman ?'

"Sons of Eire, honour and respect thy father.

"Love, honour, and respect, and tenderly cherish all the days of thy life the mother who bore and suckled and reared thee up.

"Let thy hands minster unto her in all her necessities ; let thy eye never look upon thy mother but in thanks and gentleness.

"Sons of Eire.

"Let the strength of thy arms protect the weakness of the daughters of the land ;

" Let none enter into the office of another.

" The minstrel to his harp—

" The bard to his measures—

" The ollamh to philosophy, to nourish the young mind with lessons of truth and wisdom, thereby to teach man to subdue his passions.

" The sage to wait on the moon, and mark the seasons, and note times, and watch the motion of Tarsnasc.*

" The people to make laws—

" The judges to declare the words thereof—

" The king to see them observed—

" Ardrigh to watch over Eire."

Here a large number of persons who had come to the spot while the chief brehon was reading, made such a commotion at the mention of the Ardrigh, that the judge's voice was entirely drowned, and those who had been attentively listening in hopes of hearing the laws that had just been made at the present Fes, remonstrated with the disturbers, and hereupon a discussion ensued between these two parties; the one refusing to let the brehon proceed any further, as he was the representative of Diarmaid, who made himself so obnoxious in many ways since the commencement of the Fes; the other party maintaining that the laws which were about to be read were not made by Diarmaid, but by the assembled delegates of the whole nation, of whom Diarmaid was only the president; and protested against the conduct of the disturbers, which, they said was showing disrespect, not to the Ardrigh, but to the laws of their country. This was emphatically denied by the others, who affirmed that they had the highest respect for the laws of their native land, which they never transgressed; but that it was King Diarmaid and his abettors who had violated them, and that too, at a most solemn time, and in a most outrageous manner, and finally declared their conviction that Diarmaid would find to his cost whether the Son of Mary, or Crom Cruach, was the most powerful; and whether the Christian Abbot Columcille would not eventually prove more than a match for the pagan druid Traechan. All this time the chief brehon, having made several abortive attempts to make himself heard, was at length advised by the inferior justices who surrounded him, as well as by several other notable personages present, to defer the reading of the laws to a more opportune moment, especially as all parties would sooner or later learn all about them through the brehons of their

* Tarsnasc, the constellation of Orion

respective kingdoms. The chief brehon having assented to this, descended from his elevated position, and was soon lost to sight. This having pacified the disturbers, all was again quiet, many returning to the particular amusement at which they were before engaged, while the greater number stood in groups discussing the scene they had just witnessed, the probable consequences of the late unfortunate fiasco, and speculating as to the nature of the laws which they had been prevented from hearing read. A little later the banquet in the royal palace took place, which the readers may judge was a much quieter affair than on the five preceding evenings. However, the entertainments in the biadtachs, though somewhat diminished in numbers, owing to the premature departure of many who sympathised with the bereaved families, was yet freer, and the guests less restrained in conversing on the subject, than those who were in the presence of, and actually the guests of, the Ardrigh.

The next day being Sunday, Masses were celebrated from early morning by the thousands of bishops and priests present, both within doors and without; and a thrilling spectacle it was; the sad, double tragedy of the preceding day giving a greater impulse to the devotion of the people, who, now that the excitement was over, were able dispassionately to review it in all its details; those who had been led away by party, now deploring its results; and many a heartful prayer went up to heaven for both the unfortunate youths; every Mass which was celebrated on that day being offered specially for them—and perhaps never before were such immense congregations assembled, joined together heart and soul as one man in earnest, heartful supplications to the Father of Mercies; many choking sobs mingled with their prayers, and if any distractions came, it was the thought, perhaps, that few, very few, as were the pagans remaining in the country after the death of St. Patrick, yet in this land, almost entirely Christian as it was, the very highest person in the realm, if not entirely a pagan, had yet such sympathy for its doctrines and practices as to retain in his services some druids, with all their incantations and superstitions, all the while professing submission to the laws of the Church. And yet this bitter reflection had its consoling point, inasmuch as those half-hearted Christians were more rare than the pagans themselves: the vast majority of the people being so ardent, sincere, and enthusiastic in their practice of the maxims of the Gospel, and holding in such horror everything opposed to it, as already to have earned for themselves that glorious title which following centuries confirmed, that of Island of Saints. According to the

custom of the time, the people joined with the religious in reciting at the proper hours during the day and evening, the
Divine Office of the Church.   In the intervals during meals or
recreation, the minstrels played sacred music, and the bards
sang hymns in honour of God, of his Mother, and of the saints.
Still, they did not consider the due observance of the Sabbath a
bar to innocent amusement—that was not an age of puritanical
hypocrisy;—so accordingly they now and again played and sang
secular airs and songs for the amusement of the people, which
while they had nothing in them to which the most soberminded
could take exception, yet had the effect, by taking the mind of
the people for awhile from graver subjects, of causing them
by this temporary relaxation to return with greater ardour to
their devotional exercises.   Still, things were less lively than
they generally were, even on Sunday, at any previous Fes, owing
to the sad events of the day before; and it was with less regret than
was usual on such occasions that the multitude prepared to take
their departure to their several homes on the following morning.

Having heard Mass and breakfasted, they began from an
early hour to move along the five great roads and all the minor
ones, either on horseback, in carbads of various kinds, according
to their rank or means, or on foot.   The whole of Monday was
spent departing or preparing to do so; for though great numbers
went after breakfast at various hours; many lingered on till later
in the day, some even until evening, in order to take all the amusement they could before leaving, or to witness the granting of *an
tuarastal* (the stipends) to the grandees, and their departure
alterwards.   This ceremony was shorter than usual, owing to
the abrupt departure of the royal family of Connaught and the
minor princes of that kingdom, as well as the northern chieftains
of Tir Eoghan and Tir Chonail, and others, who became the
enemies of the Ardrigh on account of his harsh conduct to
Curnan, for what they believed to be an accident purely unpremeditated and unintentional.

ᴀn ᴅeıᴄᴍᴀᴅ ᴄᴀıbıᴅıl.
CHAPTER X.

ᴀn Tuᴀpᴀpᴄᴀl.

THE STIPENDS.

GREAT was the crowd that assembled on Druim Aoibhin to
witness the granting of the stipends to the provincial kings and
princes.   At the appointed hour, the Ardrigh announced by the

heralds and a flourish of trumpets, and accompanied by a long retinue of the officers of the court, not forgetting the inevitable ' *Ten*,' who took their places close to him, emerged from the royal palace, and took his seat on the Lia Fail. The provincial notabilities who were entitled to stipends had already assembled. The officers who had charge of the articles about to be delivered to the princes took their places in proper order, according to the rank of the provincials, so that each king or prince was served in his own turn, according to the order of precedence. The immense piles of various articles which were now about to be granted away, were a dazzling spectacle. It is needless to again describe the appearance presented by the grandees themselves; this we have endeavoured to do already in a former chapter. They now appeared in all their glory, in the open air, before the Ardrigh, in front of the palace of Rath na Righ; and everything being now ready the business commenced. Then in obedience to the command of the Ardrigh, the King of Ulladh* steps forward to receive his stipend, which consisted of 50 swords, 50 steeds, 50 cloaks, 50 cowls, 50 scings,† and 50 coats of mail, 30 rings, and 10 greyhounds, 10 matals, 10 drinking-horns, with handsome handles, 10 ships (these latter were not on the spot, but at Inbhior Colpa, now Drogheda Bay), 20 handfuls of leeks, 20 seagull's eggs, and 20 bridles, adorned with cruan‡ and carbuncle. All these were granted to the King of Ulladh every three years, and so of the rest.

To the King of Laighin (Leinster), of Green Waters: 10 bondmen, 10 fleet quick-eyed hounds, 10 scings, 10 ships, 10 coats of mail, 30 rings, 50 swords, 100 bay steeds, 10 sheltering cloaks, 50 cowls, 10 choice drinking-horns, and 10 royal matals.

To the King of Caiseal (Cashel), or Deas Mumhan :§ 160 cloaks, 8 bright shields, 7 plough yokes, 140 short-horned cows, 8 steeds, 8 chariots (fully yoked), 8 rings, and 8 drinking-horns.

The King of Oirghialla received for stipend, free hostage-ships for his hostages—9 hostages, one for every cantred, to the King of Eire, without incarceration or fettering, a befitting attire for them, a steed, a sword with studs of gold, elegant apartments, and their custody to be in the hand of the King of Teamhair, and they are to be clothed and fed by him, and they are to be in the secrets of the King, and withering (a curse) is upon

---

* Ulster.   † Scings, part of the trappings of a horse.
‡ Cruan, a precious stone of a red and yellow colour.
§ Desmond—Munster.

them if they escape from their hostageships, and worse to the king if he put on fetters.

The King of Ui Dortan received 3 purple cloaks with borders, 3 shields, 3 swords, and 3 coats of mail.

To the King of Ui Tuirtre: 8 fine purple cloaks, 8 bay steeds, 8 shields, 8 swords, 8 drinking-horns, 8 hard-working, good-handed bondmen.

To the King of Dartraidhe: 4 bondmen of great valour, 4 swords, 8 steeds, 4 golden shields.

The King of Fearn-mhagh received for stipend: 6 beautiful drinking-horns for ale, 6 shields, 6 curved swords, 6 fair women, and 6 chess-boards.

To the King of Liathruim: 3 beautiful steeds, 3 shields, 3 swords of battle, 3 mantles, and 3 coats of mail.

To the King of Ui Maith: 4 drinking-horns, 4 swords, 4 shields, 4 cloaks, and 4 iron-gray steeds.

To the King of Ui Eachach: 6 purple cloaks of four points, 6 shields, 6 swords, 6 drinking-horns, 6 dark-gray forked steeds.

To the King of Araidhe: 20 drinking-horns, 20 swords, 20 greyhounds, 20 bondmen, 20 horses fit for expedition, 20 speckled cloaks, 20 matals (soft in texture), 20 drinking-horns, 20 quern-women.

To the King of Dal Riada: 3 well-trained black steeds, 3 women, 3 huge bondmen, and 3 ships (right gallant).

To the King of Oirthir: 4 bondmen who will not kill, 4 handsome bay steeds, and 4 very beautiful ships.

To the King of Ui Dearca Chein: 5 horses, bright (as the sun), 6 war swords, 6 drinking-horns, and 6 bondmen of great merriment.

To the King of Dal Buinne: 8 drinking-horns and 8 cups, 8 bondmen, 8 handsome women, and 8 horses of fine action.

To the King of Blathmaic: 8 handsome, expensive bondmen, and 8 steeds, with bridles of old silver.

To the King of Duibhthrian: 2 rings, 10 steeds, 10 shields, 10 scings, and 10 ships on Loch Cuan.*

To the King of Boirche: 6 great spirited horses, 3 matals, 3 inclining drinking-horns, and 3 beautiful hounds.

To the King of Cobha: 10 drinking horns, 10 swords, 10 ships, and 10 cloaks with their borders of gold.

To the King of Muirthemhne: 6 tall drinking-horns full of ale, 10 ships, 10 steeds, and 10 red tunics

* Strangford Lough.

To the King of Breagh : 20 steeds, 20 greyhounds, and 20 swords.

To the King of Saithne : 40 cows, and a steed.

To the King of Deise : 20 beeves and 20 wethers.

To the King of Luighne : 20 steeds with saddles.

To the King of Gailanga : a javelin with its mounting of wrought gold, and 20 splendid bridles, ornamented with cruan and carbuncle.

To the King of Drung : 3 curved, narrow swords, and 3 very beautiful steeds.

To the King of Loch Lein : 10 bay horses, 10 ships, 10 coats of mail.

To the King of Brugh-righ : 10 tunics, brown and red, and 10 foreigners without Gaedhealga (Irish). (That is, not knowing Irish or Gaelic).

To the King of Ara : 6 swords, 6 shields, and 6 mantles of deep purple.

To the King of Magh Locha : 5 swords, 5 shields, 5 short cloaks, 5 steeds, and 5 white hounds.

To the King of Laeghaire : 10 strong steeds, 10 bondmen, 10 women, 10 horns and 10 hounds.

To the King of Ardghil : 7 shields, 7 steeds out of Alba (Scotland), 7 large women, 7 bondmen, and 7 hounds.

To the King of Cailla Eachach : 7 strong steeds, 7 swords, 7 drinking-horns, and 7 well-coloured cloaks.

To the King of Feara Tulach : 6 steeds, 6 swords, 6 red shields, and 6 foreigners without Gaedhealga.

To the King of Teabhtha : 8 shields, 8 swords, 8 drinking-horns, 8 mantles, and 8 bondwomen.

To the King of Cuirene : 6 shields, 6 horses, 6 cloaks, 6 bondmen, and 6 drinking-horns.

To the King of Ui Beccon : 5 steeds, 5 chequered (plaid) cloaks, and 5 swords.

To the King of Caille Fhallamhain : 5 shields, 5 horns, 5 steeds, and 5 bondwomen.

To the King of Dealbhna : 8 swords, 8 shields brought across the brine, 8 steeds with slender legs, 8 bondmen and 8 bond-women.

To the King of Arda : 8 foreigners, 8 fierce horses, 8 drinking-horns, 8 cloaks with ring-clasps, and 8 exquisitely beauteous ships.

To the Sons of Chieftains : 12 ships of war, 12 lances, on which there is poison, 12 swords with razor edges, 12 suits of clothes of every colour.

All those present having received their stipends according to their rank and order of precedence, the stipends of the kings and princes who had departed so abruptly were delivered into the care of officers deputed to take charge of them, and thus sent to their various destinations ; they were as follows :—·

To the King of Cruachan :* or Connaught, 200 steeds, 60 cows, 4 rings, 4 drinking-horns adorned with gold, 4 shields of red colour, 4 helmets of equal colour, 4 coats of mail after them and 4 lances.

To the King of Ultonian Eamhain : varigated drinking-horns with their peaks, and sets of chessmen with the chess-boards. The full breadth of his face of gold, 200 cows, and 200 steeds, 20 beehives and 200 chariots.

To the King of Leath Chathail : 8 bondmen (tillers), 8 bay steeds, and 8 curved drinking-horns.

To the King of Aileach : 50 swords and 50 shields, 50 bond-men, 50 dresses, and 50 steeds.

To the King of Ui Niallain : 3 shields, 3 swords, 3 drinking-horns, and 3 steeds.

To the King of Ui Breasail : 5 purple cloaks of fine brilliance, 5 scarlet cloaks, 5 swords, and 5 steeds, swift and of goodly colour.

To the King of Ui Briuin Archoill : 3 tunics with golden hems, 6 steeds, 6 bondmen, and 6 women.

To the King of Feara Manach, 5 cloaks with golden borders, 5 shields, 5 swords, 5 ships, and 5 coats of mail.

To the King of Mughdhorn and Ros : 6 bondmen of great energy, 6 swords, 6 shields, 6 drinking-horns, 6 purple cloaks, and 6 blue cloaks.

All the stipends having been thus distributed, both to those who were present and in the names of such as were not, they were deposited in the cars (except the cattle and the ships) by those whose business it was to see them arrive carefully at their several destinations, and all arrangements having been completed, the hundreds of vehicles containing them began to move towards the five great roads · which led to the different places for which they were bound, the cattle accompanying them, and the bondmen and bondwomen, either mounted thereon, or when available seated on the cars, or sometimes walking, or else sailing in the ships along the coast to their new homes, whenever ships formed part of the stipends of the chiefs. The retainers, followers, soldiers, students, merchants, traders,

* *Pr.* Croghan.

professional men, musicians, knights, and all the various classes
also now took their departure in earnest, as well as the royal and
noble families, the bishops, abbots, ollamhs, &c., having taken
leave of the Ardrigh and his Ardrighan and family, and of the
other kings and princes, and commenced their homeward
journey. The abbots, monks, and students returned to their
respective schools and colleges, or else, as was customary,
change to some other than that which they had previously attended ; all the other classes returned to their respective
homes and duties. The foreigners embarked for their own
countries, having bid farewell to their young relatives, whose
studies were not yet finished, or taking with them those whose
education was completed. By degrees Magh Breagh was resuming its wonted appearance ; there were comparatively few
besides the immediate subjects and retainers of the Ardrigh and
the general citizens. Some of the young people, however, were
putting every moment to account before separating ; games of
various kinds were still being played by such as were not engaged in anything more important, or were too young to take
much to heart the sad scenes which had occurred. Some such
groups, having at length tired, stood conversing eagerly together with some young friends ; pledges of mutual friendship
passed between them, and plans for future meetings ; and by
degrees, began to move away to make their final preparations
after a hearty leave-taking.

---

an aonṁaó caibioil veuᵹ.

CHAPTER XI.

Aṗoṁᵹ a ᵹ-Coṁaiṗle.

THE ARDRIGH IN COUNCIL.

THE court of "the brown-haired Diarmaid" had now resumed
its wonted appearance, the Fes being over, and the delegates,
their families, and all their following departed to their several
homes. None were now to be seen in the vicinity of the Tulach
Aoibhin (Delightful Hill), save the royal family, the officers of
the court, the ladies of honour, the everlasting " *Ten*," hovering
for ever about the person of the Ardrigh ; all the servants, male
and female, of the royal household ; the councillors of state, who

every morning attended the Ardrigh for the transaction of business; the ollamhs, filés, orators, and men of science; the engravers of gold and silver, carvers, modellers, knights, &c.; all these and many more, every day flitted in and out through the palace of Teamhair. One thousand guests were daily entertained there in the most hospitable manner; and now that it was relieved from the crush of overpowering numbers, which necessitated the removal of many articles, those articles were once more arranged in their proper places. Besides, there were daily to be seen various classes of persons at the other buildings of Teamhair. The thousand soldiers, some of whom always kept guard at the Tur-Trean-Teamhrach (Strong Tower of Tara); there were also the lucht-tighe (household troops); the lucht-curmcate-righ (the body guard) of the king. Then at the Mur Ollamhain, the constant stream of authors who daily besieged it to learn the fate of their compositions from the learned sages of the Rialta na Fileadh; the pupils, also, during the hours of recreation, might be seen basking in the sun, or amusing themselves as they thought fit; in short, many and various were the classes of the people who daily, all the year round, either for business or amusement, might be seen in the vicinity of "Tara's Halls," where the "harp," unceasingly, "the soul of music shed," perhaps softening the asperities of the lawyers, whose duties to their clients brought them to the "legal" division of the " Riaghalta of the Mur Ollamhain." The city was as busy as ever, trade and commerce flourishing, and all the manufactures in full working order.

Nodlaigh (Christmas) came with its hallowed associations and its family gatherings; it must, however, be observed, that the Anniversary of the Babe of Bethlehem was observed in this Island of Saints at that time as a religious rather than as a social festival—greater fervour and devotion, more bountiful supplies to poor families, midnight Masses, heralded by the joyful ringing of many bells, in a country in which bells abounded, all these were the principal features of the observance of the great Christmas festival; and though festive gatherings were not neglected, yet they did not, as they do now-a-days, supersede its religious observance, making the "glad tidings of great joy" an excuse for indulgence in sin and excess.

The new year came in much the same way as its predecessors, but it was destined to witness the culmination of the sad catastrophe which had marred the last days of the Fes of Teamhair, since which time couriers had been flying between the courts, most deeply interested, to wit, Teamhair, Cruachan, Tir Eoghan, and Tir Chonaill, each official message only making war more and more imminent, and causing the lovers of peace to despair of any chance of an arrangement or compromise between the parties. While matters stood thus, the Ardrigh, one morning, while surrounded by his arligh ar da cleth (councillors of state), who attended him every morning for the transaction of routine business, notified to them his good pleasure that they should have a special meeting to discuss the situation, and then, having ascertained how long it would take them to consider their resolution, appointed a day for the meeting.

On the appointed day there was a full attendance of the council, together with as many ollamhs, brehons, seancheadhea, filés, clergy, doctors, and professors, warriors, knights, and ladies, as could gain admittance; all being seated in their places long before the appointed hour, they were engaged in discussing the *pros* and *cons* of the situation in all its bearings, until they heard the flourish of trumpets and the voices of the heralds, and all rose in time to greet the Ardrigh, who entered and seated himself on the *cathair rioghda* (royal chair); he was attended as usual by the " *Ten*," who stationed themselves about him. Silence having been obtained, and all being again seated, King Diarmaid opened the meeting, and though he addressed only his council, his words, and the words of all who followed him, could be distinctly heard by the entire assemblage.

Ardrigh—" Let the ollamhain of our high chamber of Teamhair hearken to our words : the disastrous events of the late Fes have destroyed the good understanding which had previously existed between ourselves and the provincial kingdoms. The son of one of our most esteemed officers was most foully murdered——"

Expressions of dissent and head-shakings greeted these last words.

Ardrigh—" Well, he was struck down with a brazen hurley while playing at coman* with Curnan, the son of Aodh, and grandson of the King of Connaught; and as no one called in question the identity of the perpetrator of the deed, we deemed it due to the parents of the slain, to ourselves, to justice, and to the law, to order the execution of Curnan. You all know the opposition we met with, and the conduct of the Abbot Columcille on the occasion, how by extending his sanctuary to Curnan, he obliged us to violate it; his threats, and his subsequent escape from the vigilance of our guards : you are acquainted

* Hurling.

with all these incidents. Well, we have not heard much from him since, save indirectly. His kinsmen, the Clanna Nialls of the North, have chosen to take to themselves the supposed insults to the abbot, and neither is their wrath confined to the affair of Curnan, but embraces also that of the Abbot Finian's Psalm Book. Domhnald and Fearghus Mac Earca, who were here during the Fes, are the mouthpieces of the Northerns. Had We known the turn affairs would take, We would not have allowed either them or their cousin Ainmire to escape. However, as it is, they are making common cause with the court of Cruachan in demanding satisfaction of Us for Our manifold transgressions. Now, We would fain know the opinion of Our Council, which we have convened for the purpose, whether it is just or dignified to permit the provincial kings, princes, and people to sit in judgment on Our acts, and attempt to punish Us for exercising Our supreme prerogative."

Ardollamh—"O high King and sages of Eire, truly the occasion which calls us together is a sad one. We have all witnessed the unfortunate occurrences of the late Fes, and we shall have reason for congratulation if matters proceed no further. The past cannot be recalled, but it is in our power at least to stay further complications. Even though, as I firmly believe, the killing of Conal's son was a pure accident, yet, it was no less true that compensation was due to his afflicted family. Had it been before the breatheamhain*, they would have inflicted a heavy sent *eric*, which would have been sufficient to meet the case, it being accidental; but as the Ardrigh adjudged that nothing but blood could atone for blood, and in pursuance thereof, ordered the execution of Curnan, it is but natural that his parents and his family, powerful as they are, should look upon themselves as the aggrieved parties, and resent the indignity, and, if possible, demand satisfaction. We must bear in mind that the King of Connaught is an independent sovereign, as absolute in his dominions as is the Ardrigh in the kingdom of Midhe. Still it is incumbent on us all to provide that Teamhair, which has ever been pre-eminent in honour and dignity, if not in power, shall continue to maintain its position in the sight of the children of the land. This laudable desire, however, is not to be accomplished by ignoring the rights and trampling on the feelings of the provincial royal families. I trust my Lord King will forgive this plainness of speech, but we have been assembled here for the discussion of this subject, and we have been invited to speak

* Judges

our minds freely. I have no other object in view than the honour and happiness of my king and country. I deplore the disunion and discord which is so rife among my countrymen, and which is the only stain on an otherwise brilliant national character. Shall we ever learn mutual forbearance and brotherly love ? Would it not be better for Midhe, as well as for Connaught, Tir-Eoghan, and Tir Chonail to seek a reconciliation, and make some sacrifices for the common good, instead of being perpetually engaged in wasting our strength and lavishing our resources in weakening and humbling our own countrymen, who like ourselves are ever engaged in that dissemination of learning, and in the pursuit of science, manufacture, and commerce, sharing with ourselves, as the common children of a common land, the admiration and wonder of all European states."

The Taoiseach Buidhne*—"Let not my Lord King and council be led from the path of duty by the words of the Ardollamh. No one can regret more than I do the untoward events which have led to these complications ; but now that they have occurred, and have served to illustrate the spirit which pervades certain provincial families, including some of their members, who, from their vocations, one would suppose to be free from the resentments and factious spirit of more worldly beings—now that the Ardrigh has been threatened by Tir-Chonail, Tir-Eoghan, and Conacht, it is the duty of all loyal men to support the dignity and supremacy of Teamhair. It is too much the fashion for the tributary states to declare war against Midhe for every slight cause, often originating with themselves, as in the present instance ; for was it not Curnan, by his illegal slaying— even though accidental—of Conal's son, that originated the quarrel with Conacht ? And again, was it not the secret transcription of the Abbot Finian's Psalm Book, that led to the dispute between him and the Abbot Columcille, and the subsequent judgment—just or unjust—of the Ardrigh ? And now that they brought the consequences of their—— well, their mistake or inadvertence, if you will—upon their own heads, they forthwith cry out that they are the victims of the Ardrigh's injustice and cruelty—they demand satisfaction, and incite each other to revenge their fancied wrongs on the Monarch of Eire. It is evidently our duty to meet this case as it should be met. No good will come of any half-hearted, weak-spirited measures ; it will only bring on us the contempt of the nation, and sink the highest regal seat of the realm to a level with its tributaries. Let us not deceive ourselves ; we have to deal with three very power-

* A Military Commander.

ful families, and all their adherents and followers; and their *Curraide Craoibh Ruadh* (Red Branch Knights) are as valiant and as well disciplined as our own Fianna Eirionn (Fenians of Ireland). Let us bear in mind the indubitable fact that, while we are talking, they are arming! Let us give up useless declamation, and turn our attention to the more important work of preparing to meet the threatened danger. Neither let us wait to be attacked, and thus give to our foes the triumph of setting hostile foot upon the paramount kingdom; but rather let us arm at once, and bear down upon our would-be assailants; and then when we have restored order by force of arms, let the Ardrigh, if he is so minded, make terms of friendship with the so-called aggrieved parties. But now let us be up and doing, the moments we are wasting can never be recalled. Let the Ardrigh but give his sanction to the muster of the forces, and let the council loyally support him; the forces of Laghaen (Leinster) will aid us, and, united, we shall bid defiance to North and West, and to all that may be leagued with them against us. To arms! to arms!"

The Ard Epscop.*—"Oh, Ardrigh and Ollamhain of Eire, it is with the deepest pain and grief that I have listened to the words of the Taoiseach Buidhne, who appears to view the case in an entirely wrong light, and from a purely military standpoint. It is scarcely fair to charge the unfortunate Curnan with originating this unhappy quarrel; he was a good youth, and was as incapable as anyone here of deliberately imbruing his hands in the blood of a fellow-creature. That he did actually slay the son of Conal in the heat and excitement of coman; no one can deny; but that it was as unintentional as it was unpremeditated, is equally indisputable. Now that blood has been shed on both sides, it would be very unfortunate if there were any more sacrifice of human life in this most lamentable affair. It would not at all be dishonourable or humiliating to make some compensation to the family of Curnan, and thus heal in some degree their wounded feelings. It would be much better than engage in a disastrous war, especially when the Connaught men will be aided by those of Tir Chonail and Tir Eoghan. As to the observation of the Taoiseach Buidhne, that the Abbot Columcille has been inciting the Clanna Nialls to make war upon the Ardrigh in revenge for that affair of the Psalm Book, and alleges some threats which he used; well, all I can say is, that I am sufficiently acquainted with Columcille to know that he would be

* Archbishop.

utterly incapable of what has been alleged against him. That
he should have felt most keenly on the matter of the Psalm
Book, and even that smarting under the disappointment, the hot
blood of Niall of the Nine Hostages should have given vent
to threats by his mouth, is perhaps only to be expected; but
that, after mature deliberation, and after having undergone a
long and toilsome journey, during which he composed a beautiful
hymn; after all this, I say, it is impossible that he should continue to entertain feelings of resentment. We must also remember that some of his friends were here at the time to see for
themselves; and, moreover, that his attendants preceded him
home, so that on his arrival, instead of detailing his wrongs, he
could only answer the questions of those who already knew the
facts of the case, and whom it would be both unlawful and
useless to attempt to deceive. At the same time, however, as
they have insisted upon making his quarrel their own, and are
determined to wipe out the insult by joining their forces to those
of Conacht, with the royal family of which they have now become
identified—for they consider that the execution of Curnan, in
violation of the sanctuary of Columcille, is an outrage upon
themselves—I am not so sure that he will not bless their united
arms; he will feel that he is in some measure the cause, however unwittingly, of their going to war, and perhaps he will think
that he owes it to the memory of Curnan. If I should be correct
in my surmise that Columcille will bless the arms of our opponents, I tremble for the consequences to ourselves. The
Taoiseach Buidhne has observed that our Fiana Eirionn are at
least equal to the forces of West or North. Now, there can be
no question of that, no one can be prouder than I am of the
glories of our Fenian army; but we must remember that neither
the Fenians nor the Red Branch, nor yet the Clanna Morna, nor
any other military order have been the same since the battle of
Gaura. Besides, it is quite possible that our forces will have to
fight, not so much the forces of Conacht, Tir Chonal, and Tir
Eoghan, as the invisible, but infinitely more powerful force
which the Abbot Columb's prayers may array against us. We
all know what wonderful things he has already done—a man
who can change the fruits of the earth; whose blessing changed
water into wine while a little pupil at the College of Clonard;
raised a dead man to life—a man who could perform these and
many more miracles by invoking a blessing, will not be less
powerful in obtaining a victory for those to whom he imparts his
benediction. All I will say in conclusion is, that I would much
rather he was with us than against us; and that I would strongly

advise the Ardrigh and the council to seek a reconciliation, and thus avoid the useless effusion of Christian blood."

The Ollamh-re-Seanchaidhe—"Alas! my Lord High King, and council, that we should be assembled for the purpose of debating whether or not we should engage in strife unto death with our brothers, the children of our fatherland. Too long has our country been rent and torn by domestic wars, which never did any good, but only served to keep the different tribes and clans of Irishmen at variance with each other, wasting their energies, their military skill, and their very life-blood in destroying their fellow-countrymen, to whom they should be bound by ties of the fastest friendship. Of what avail is all the Irish blood that has been shed by Irishmen? Has it made our country better or happier, or more prosperous? Has it not had rather the contrary effect? Here we are, the most civilised nation on earth, possessing a constitution the most polished in the world, renowned for the learning, arts, science, law, commerce, and manufactures, which render us unique among the nations, and draws to our shores thousands from all the neighbouring islands, and from the islands and the continent of southern Europe, who carry back with them from our national institutions the seeds of the future civilisation of their own countries. And yet, notwithstanding all this, we are a spectacle to the world of a house divided against itself! If union is strength, disunion is weakness. Fancy a houseful of brothers who would be so busy quarrelling amongst themselves as to be incapable of resisting a common enemy who cometh to despoil them all equally of their inheritance? And yet I fear me we shall eventually drift towards that deplorable end, if we do not cease at once and for ever our senseless, foolish, domestic feuds. Perhaps our very hospitality to strangers, and our desire to raise them from ignorance and barbarism, may be the very means of our undoing; for while they carry away with them the knowledge and civilisation which we taught them, they may at the same time carry with them another kind of knowledge which we never intended they should, namely, the knowledge of our weakest points—a knowledge, too, which they or their children may turn to account at some future time, when they may, perhaps, take advantage of some domestic wars to help themselves to a slice of our most fertile and wealthy country; and may heaven grant that the entire of our beloved land may not at some future day become enslaved to some power which will perhaps owe everything they have worth possessing to the generosity of ourselves and our children. But let it be remembered that heaven helps only

16

those who help themselves. It will not help us in spite of ourselves. If we wish to continue a free and independent nation, and to uphold the proud position we now enjoy, we must use all our energies and employ all the means, all the knowledge, and all the experience which we possess, which has come down to us from remote antiquity, and which has been gradually increasing and developing during twelve centuries of civilisation— from the time when Ollamh Fodhla promulgated our constitution 700 years before Christ, down to this year of grace, 561. Let, I say, all these advantages be utilised for the further consolidation and union of the various kingdoms and clans which compose our nation. Let none know any jealousy or rivalry, save that of trying to outvie each other in contributing to the well-being, happiness, and union of our beloved Banba."*

The Gaisgadhach†—" Oh, high King and sages of Fodhla,‡ were our land united in the manner we have just heard, and all her people in perpetual peace and harmony, where, I ask, would be the glory, civil and military, for which she is so renowned? What would be the use of our military schools, in which such wealth is lavished in training our youth in martial exercises and military tactics from the earliest age, if they were never to have an opportunity of earning the rewards of valour and heroism, and of proving themselves worthy of their illustrious and heroic ancestry, for, after all, there is no school like the field of battle ; there alone can the hero prove himself. Why, in every department, as well as the military, it is this very jealousy and rivalry which has made us great among the nations. In literature, in science, art, and manufactures, in commerce, and in the military art, it is our mutual jealousies and contentions which has brought all these to such perfection, by each kingdom, principality, and family endeavouring to surpass all the rest. Besides, any failing or shortcoming of one is sure to bring upon it the criticism or censure of the others. Thus, what we have just now heard condemned, has contributed, perhaps as much as any other cause, to the general good, by creating and fostering that wholesome spirit of emulation, which more than anything else tends to draw out the hidden powers of the mind, and to develop the physical resources of the body. And although we are the only nation which cultivates the more refined arts and sciences, we by no means stand alone in the cultivation and practice of the arts of war. Look at all the surrounding nations ! Look at Britain,

---

* A bardic name for Ireland.   † A military officer.
‡ Another bardic name for Ireland.

look at the fierce domestic wars between the kingdoms of the Saxon Heptarchy! look at the battles fought by the various hordes of Germany and Helvetia. But you will say all these are barbarous states, and we ought to be ashamed to follow their example, and that their mode of warfare is rude and barbarous, while we bring it to scientific perfection. Well, there are France and Spain and other countries more civilised than Britain or Germany, and they also are perpetually engaged in internecine strife, not only those of their inhabitants who are yet sunk in barbarism, but those to whom civilisation and enlightenment have extended their beneficent rays. But civil war is not confined to barbarous and semi-barbarous states. We all know the history of the Roman Empire, its high civilisation and perpetual warfare, and even now Italy is not free from contentions and strife. Look again, this time at refined, cultivated Greece, with its history nearly as glorious as our own, and what do we behold? —the highest civilisation and refinement side by side with continual wars and conflict. Will not her heroes and warriors go down to posterity, together with her philosophers, her statesmen, her legislators, and her poets? There is a peculiar analogy between her institutions and our own, and a proof, if proof were wanting, that the practice of the art of war is quite consistent with the cultivation of literature, art, science, and all the most elegant pursuits in their highest perfection. To arms! then to arms! and let no sentimental weakness deter us from following in the footsteps of those who have gone before us, and whose deeds of heroism and feats of arms have acquired for our country the respect and fear of foreign nations. Without going into the causes which have led to this dispute—and which I deeply deplore—it is enough to say that our dignity and honour demands that we shall not permit any tributary kingdom to beard us in the manner in which we are threatened. Let us prove to North and West, as well as to the nation at large, that we are as pre-eminent in power as in honour—in deed as in name. Again, then, I repeat—to arms! to arms! Faire! faire!!"

The Aire Forghaill—" Oh, Ardrigh and council of the land, seldom have we been called to decide upon so painful a question as that which now engages our attention. I will not go over what has been already said, but there is one remark of the last speaker to which I must take exception—it is that which ascribes the respect and awe in which we are held by foreign nations to our domestic warfare. Now, I cannot at all agree to that. Though it is sometimes necessary—as I believe it is in the present instance—to defend ourselves from even domestic aggression, and to uphold the supremacy of this paramount royal seat, yet I cannot defend the suicidal practice of perpetual internal strife. Other nations have been referred to—Greece especially, as having more resemblance in its laws and institutions to our own country. It is to be hoped that the resemblance shall not be rendered more perfect by being involved in a similar fate, from similar causes, thus presenting to future ages the twin-spectacle of two ancient, highly-polished learned nations reduced by their own insane divisions and mutual discord to the horrors and degradation of slavery to merciless, unscrupulous barbarians. As to the respect and dread with which I admit we are regarded by foreign nations, it is entirely owing, not to our domestic wars, the consequences of which come home to none save ourselves, but rather to the achievements of our countrymen, for many ages, in other lands. To the glorious feats of Ugaine Mór (Hugony the Great), who was Ardrigh of Eire three centuries before the Christian era, and was contemporary with Alexander the Great, who sailed with a fleet into the Muir-Toirrian (Mediterranean Sea), landed his forces in Africa, and attacked Sicily, and having proceeded to Gaul, was married to Cæsair, the daughter of the king of that country. And we know that we are indebted to the grandson of Ugainé, Labradh Loingseach (Labra of the Ships), who, having been exiled from Eire, attained a high military command in the armies of Gaul—for the introduction into this country of laegea (spear), which has given its name to one of our provinces (Leinster), and which he brought with his 2,200 Gaulish soldiers. Again, we have his grandson, Aengus, who became Ardrigh 280 years before Christ, and who, entering into alliance with the Gauls, invaded Greece and Asia Minor with powerful forces. Then, during the Punic Wars, our Irish ancestors sent auxiliary troops to their Keltic brethren, the Gauls, who, in alliance with the Carthagenians, under Hannibal, fought against the Roman armies in Spain and Italy. Conairé Mór (Conairé the Great) and Crimthan Nianiar (the Heroic), both of whom were Monarchs of Eire about the commencement of the Christian era, made expeditions into Britain and Gaul, and assisted the Picts and Britons in their wars with the Romans. Then again, amongst the foreign expeditions of Irish princes of that period, I may mention that of Eogan Mór, or Mogha Nuadhat, the famous King of Mumhan (Munster), in the second century, who went to Spain and married Beara, a Spanish princess, who was daughter of Heber, King of North of Spain (in the country afterwards called Castile), and returned home with a powerful force of Spanish auxiliaries. In the first century, the Curraidhe Craoibh Ruadh (Red Branch Knights), and in the second and third centuries, the Fianna Erionn (Fenians of Ireland) made several expeditions to Britain, and as allies to the Picts, Caledonians, and Britons, fought against the Roman legions; and Cormac Mac Art, the celebrated Monarch of Eire in the third century made descents into Gaul and Britain, and assisted the natives against the Roman power. Soon after Crimthan III., who became Ardrigh, invaded Gaul and Britain, broke through the Roman Wall, and at the head of the Irish, Picts, and Britons, fought against the Roman armies. Then again, our celebrated countryman, Carausius, who was a native of Carman (Wexford), or, as Ptolemy, the Greek geographer, calls it, Menapia, and who was famed for his extraordinary military abilities and bravery, trained from his youth in naval expeditions, having entered the Roman Army in Britain in the reign of the Emperors Diocletian and Maximian, and being appointed commander-in-chief of their fleets in the Northern Seas to bring under subjection the Franks, Saxons, and Scandinavians, who attacked the Roman settlements in Gaul and Britain, and having conquered these pirates, he attained such power and popularity, that in A.D. 288, he assumed the purple, and declared himself Roman Emperor in Britain; and having defeated the forces of the Emperor Maximian in several naval engagements, Maximian was forced to acknowledge him as his associate in the empire. Several Irish expeditions into Alba,* during several centuries, resulted each time in our countrymen obtaining settlements in that country, until Cairbre Riada led his forces there in the third century, and possessed himself of that country. In the latter end of the fifth century, the three brothers, Fergus, Loarn, and Aongus, led colonies to other parts of Alba, and subdued the greater portion of those parts which had not previously submitted to Irish arms, including the Western Isles, and even yet these countries acknowledge our sway. Then we must not forget the renowned Nial Naighiallach, who took hostages from nine different nations, and had many conflicts with the Roman arms, as it was in one of his expeditions to Gaul that he met and carried home with him as captive, among several others, the boy who was destined at a future day to take captive in his turn our entire nation to the

---

* Scotland. Scotia was one of the ancient names of Ireland, and her people, Scots, which names were applied to Alba after its colonisation from Ulster. For a considerable time afterwards Ireland was often called Scotia-Major and Scotland Scotia-Minor, until at length the name of Scotland was eventually transferred to the latter country.

faith of Christ. And when Nial's nephew, the heroic Dathi, led
his forces into Britain, broke through the Wall of Severus, he
made the mighty Roman power again quail before Irish prowess,
and having carried his victorious arms through Gaul to the foot
of the Alps, died there the hero of 150 battles. Little wonder
that the mighty powers of Roman legions, who subdued nearly
the whole world, never dared to set foot on Irish ground, pre-
ferring the evidence of their senses and their experience to the
interested representations of an exiled Irish prince, who would
have their aid in furthering his pretensions to the Irish crown.
Why, our country abounds with trophies brought from almost
every nation by our ancient warriors and modern heroes. All
this is, together with our learning and civilisation, the true cause of
the proud position which we hold among the nations of the
earth, and is a far greater source of pride than the miserable
domestic quarrels which have never been of any advantage, but
are a continual source of weakness and of danger. At the same
time, when Irishmen *will* make war upon their countrymen to
avenge private wrongs, it by no means follows that the threatened party are to tamely submit to forfeit their lives and liberties
without a struggle to defend them, especially when the kingdom
thus threatened is the highest regal seat of the realm—the seat,
too, entitled to the respect and submission of all the provincial
states. However, owing to the peculiar circumstances of this
particular case, and all that has occurred, I would recommend a
peaceful settlement. It would be better for all parties, and
would save the useless effusion of much Irish blood. Besides,
I am not quite sure that it will be a question of the relative
bravery or prowess of the armies of Central and Eastern Eire, on
the one side, or of Western and Northern Eire on the other.
If what we hear is true of the Abbot Columcille blessing the
arms of his friends, I fear we shall' be sending our forces to
encounter—not the discipline and valour of Connaught, Tir
Eoghan, and Tir Chonal—but the very power of the Most
High. We know that the Great Being whose blessing is invoked upon our opponents, created the whole universe by an
act of his will, and that He could, in like manner, annihilate
it. Let us then make peace with our conntrymen, and reserve
our men with their valour, military education, and everything
else which has made our nation, for the defence of our common
country against the possible invasions of foreign foes."

Several others addressed the Council, nearly all of them
looking at the matter in different lights, but being divided into
two parties, the one for peace, and the other for war. By the

time they had all spoken it was found that by holding up their hands they were pretty equally divided. The audience, whose hopes rose and fell with each speaker, according to their own views upon the matter, were now painfully attentive to the wind-up. Whispers ran through the assembly, and ill-suppressed excitement was beginning to buzz upon the ears, when the Ardrigh again spoke :

Ardrigh—" The discussion which has just taken place is but another proof of the utter impossibility of ever getting a number of men to agree upon any one single subject. Still, one would imagine that Our Council, various though their callings be, who profess such loyalty to Our person and throne, and to the honour and glory of their country, would sink their differences and prejudices, and unite, as is their duty, in supporting Us in Our efforts to maintain the honour, integrity, and supremacy of Our royal seat. Of course, We allude to those members of Our Council who were good enough to find fault with Our actions, and to advise Us, in effect, to go down on our knees to every one who chooses to insult Us. Of course they have sugared over their arguments with the usual amount of plausibility, of which We have such long experience. It is needless to go over all the arguments which have been adduced in favour of Our opponents, but We will confine Ourselves to one. We are well aware that Our people, and the nation at large, charge Us with super-stition, because it is Our pleasure to retain the services of Our druids, in opposition to the wishes and feelings of this now almost entirely Christianised land. Well, as We do not interfere in the slightest degree in matters of religion with any, even the humblest of Our subjects, We do not think it too much to ask that We be allowed, at least, the same liberty, especially when it is well known that We have done more for the Roman faith, in various ways, including the foundation of colleges and monasteries, in which Christianity, and it *only*, is taught, than many who are so horrified at what they call Our druidical superstitions. But it strikes Us that there is, at least, an equal amount of super-stition on the side of Our censors. What is it but superstition to maintain, as has just been done, that the Abbot Columcille, by his prayers or blessing, can turn the tide of battle in favour of his own friends, and against Us, without any reference to the bravery, heroism, or military skill of either armies. Well, We have just come to oppose superstition by superstition, and if the Abbot Columb blesses the arms of Our enemies, Our druid Traechan, the son of Teninson, will bless Our arms, and place such a charm be-tween us as shall protect Us from the charm of Columcille, and at the same time prove to the whole nation that druidism has not yet lost all its power. We cannot conclude without sincerely thanking the faithful councillors who have stood by and supported Us in Our necessity; We shall not forget it. After what We have said, it will be understood that it is Our intention to muster Our forces and proceed at once to enter the country of Our foes. Let the chief officers immediately set about marshalling the forces under them into battle array. Faire! faire!! To arms! to arms!! to arms!!!"

an Dara Caibidil Deug.

CHAPTER XII.

Cat Cula Dreirṁne.

THE BATTLE OF COOLA DREVNEY.*

As the Ardrigh Diarmaid uttered the last words, he rose from his *cathair rioghda* (royal chair), which was the signal for the general rising of the whole council and audience. A scene of the wildest excitement followed. Soon the council-chamber was deserted, and the battle cries which had been taken up in the chamber by those who favoured the Ardrigh now spread like wild-fire, far and near, among the throngs who had collected outside, entirely drowning the counter-cries of those who had been all along for peace, as well as others who had decided in favour of war, but who on hearing the last words of Diarmaid regretted their decision and would have recalled it if they could. However, it was now too late, and the multitude who though pretty equally divided, appeared almost unanimous from the fact that those who were in favour of war were by far the most noisy, as is generally the case. By degrees, however, as Diarmaid's exact words had reached the multitude, their wrath knew no bounds, at what they considered his blasphemies, and as a consequence their enthusiasm toned down considerably. They were for the most part deeply imbued with religious feelings, still many there were who loved war for its own sake, quite regardless of all its causes and effects. The soldiers, when called out, had only, of course, to do their duty, and there was many a sad farewell taken of friends whom, perhaps,

* Cooldrevney.

they were never to meet more on this earth ; yet were they encouraged by their mothers, and other female friends, for the
utmost wish of the women was that their children might die in
the field, as it was, next to knighthood, a distinguished honour
to be ranked in the national troops. By the time they were all
mustered, they presented a magnificent spectacle. The Fianna
Erionn was the standing national militia, instituted long before
the Christian era, and brought to the greatest perfection in the
reign of the celebrated Cormac Ulfhada, monarch of Ireland in
the third century. None were admitted into this military body
but select men of the greatest activity, strength, stature, perfect form, and valour ; and when the force was complete it
consisted of seven Catha, that is battalions, or legions, each
battalion containing 3,000 men, making 21,000 for each of the
five provinces, or about 100,000 fighting men in time of war
for the entire kingdom. The Ardrigh had, for the time being,
chief control over these forces, but they often resisted his
authority. A commander was appointed over every thousand of
those troops, and the entire force was completely armed and
admirably disciplined, and each battalion had their bands of
musicians and bards to animate them in battle and celebrate
their feats of arms. A considerable number of the great military force of Midhe now assembled on Magh Breagh, including
the warriors of the seven duns of Teamhair, under the command
of their several officers of divers grades. They were principally
known as Taoiseach, and Taoiseach-Buidhne, Flaith, Ceann-
Feadhna, or head of a force, and Ceann-Sloigh, i.e., the head
or leader of a host. Then there were the Laoch, Curraidh,
Gaisgidheach and Niadh, and Urraidh, or champions, chieftains,
and heroes. The *Ceithearnacha* (Kerne), or lightfoot infantry,
were armed with laigeana (spears), lanna and craoiseagha
(lances, javalins, and halberds), gatha and saigheada (arrows and
darts), bolg-saigheada (a bag or pouch for arrows, or a quiver),
sgians (daggers, or large knives), biaile (hatchets), tuagh-catha
(battle-axes), claidheamha (swords), and the cran-tabhuila
(slings). The handles of these weapons were generally of ash,
to which was fitted the long, sharp-pointed iron or steel head ;
the javelin was tied to the arm or shoulder by a thong or cord
of great length, so that they could hurl it at the enemy at
several yards' distance, and recover the weapon again ; thus, by
whirling it rapidly round the head and then casting with such
force that they penetrated the bodies of men, even through their
armour, and killed their horses at great distances. These
ceithearnacha had no defensive armour save the sciath, or

shield, made either of wood or of wickerwork, covered with leather, or partly of bronze, sometimes being entirely composed of that metal. "They were so nimble and swiftfooted, like stags, that they ran over mountains and valleys." They were divided into bodies of spearmen, dartmen, slingers, and archers. The galloglachs (gallowglasses) were the heavy infantry, a kind of grenadiers, being select men of great strength and stature, armed with claidheamh and tuagh-catha, and also wore the luireacha (armour, coats of mail), which consisted of a net-work of small iron rings, sometimes of strong leather; the sciath, or shield buckler and target, and the cath-barrs, or helmets of bronze, and breast-plates of iron. Their chief weapons were the tuagh-catha and the battle hammer, which was a wooden club studded with short spikes and knobs of iron. These galloglachs were divided into bodies of swordsmen and battleaxe-men, and being the strongest, steadiest, and best disciplined forces generally bore the brunt of battle. The marc-shluagh,* or cavalry, might be considered as mounted ceithern; being chiefly a kind of light horse, they were armed with spears, flint and iron javelins, swords, darts, and scians or daggers; also armour, as helmets, coats of mail, shields, &c. The arms, armour, and equipments of the various officers named above were the same as those of the rank and file, with this difference, that their shields of leather or bronze were embossed with silver and gold, as were also their helmets, and breast-plates, while many helmets, shields, and breast-plates were composed entirely of silver, others of silver embossed with gold, while those of the highest commanders were frequently com-posed altogether of pure ductile gold, highly wrought. Their arms, too, were beautiful specimens of art, and ornamented with gold and silver; their spears and swords especially were of exquisite workmanship, some having beautifully-carved ivory or mother-of-pearl handles, others being gold and jewel hilted, and all highly wrought. They had also another peculiarity, that of having their blades dyed in different colours, as green, blue, yellow, red, purple, &c. This practice was first intro-duced by Eochaidh Faobhar-glas, or of the Green Edge, so called because his own sword blades were green. Then there were the carbads-searrdha (serrated chariots) bristling with scythes, and manned by warriors in armour, and fully equipped; the horses that drew the war charoits were also encased in armour.

---

* A host, army, or troop of cavalry; from Marc, a horse, and Sluagh, a host, Marcach, a horseman.

The chariots of the higher officers were magnificently gilt and ornamented, that of King D:armaid surpassing all the rest.

While all the preparations were making, the people were in a fever of excitement. Groups of persons were everywhere to be seen talking about the events that were taking place. Crowds paraded the streets, unable to lay their minds to anything. As each splendidly equipped regiment appeared before their eyes their cheers and huzzas mingled with the military music that now and again burst upon their ears from every direction. But when one morning the people of Teamhair heard the distant sounds of the *caisneachd* (a species of music to which soldiers march), and soon after descried coming up the Slighe Cualan the Fenian forces of Laeghann (Leinster), and waving over them their emerald green banner, with its golden harp, surmounted by the Irish crown glittering in the sun, and borne by O'Maolmhuaidh (O'Mulloy), the hereditary standard-bearer of Laeghann, as they filed into Teamhair, horse, foot, war chariots and all, they were received with unbounded enthusiasm by the Midhains. Their marshal or commander-in-chief, O'Mordha (O'Moore) of Laoighes (Leix), " of the one-coloured golden shield," rode up to Mac Eochagain (Mac Geoghagan), the marshall of Midhe, and they conversed for some time, looking now and again in the direction of their respective forces. The barracks and biadhtachs were soon filled with the soldiers, who were well entertained there during the day and lodged over the night. The next morning, when all had been got into battle array, great crowds assembled to see them set off, and cheer after cheer went up as they filed past in due order ; the cetherni and galloglacha, the champions and knights, the marc-sluagh and war chariots, their bards and musicians, their standard bearers and banner-bearers carrying the meirge, or standards, and the bratacha, or banners. These were very various, according to the chieftains whom they represented. Some had representations of battle blades, swords, golden crosses, lions, eagles, wolf-dogs, &c.; the colours were equally various—as blue, red, yellow, purple ; bloody eagles on glistening sheet of white satin, oak-trees on various grounds, blue anchors bound with gold cable ; spears with venomous adders entwined, and many others ; the most honoured, however, were the Green Banner of the Leinster Fenians, with its crown and harp of gold, and pre-eminent the famous Gal Greine. This last was borne before Ardrigh Diarmaid, who now amidst enthusiastic applause appeared before the people gorgeously armed from head to foot, and surrounded by the " *Ten*." When the flourish

of *stochs,* or trumpets, which announced him, had died away, and
also the cheers of the people, he ascended his gilded war-
carbad, the " *Ten* " mounted theirs. Then it was perceived that
Frachan the druid was one of the " *Ten*," that is, he was in the
place which of old was the right of the druids, but which, since
the introduction of Christianity, had up to this been filled by a
bishop or priest. The effect of this outrage on the feelings of
the people, was for a time most alarming. The applause which
had greeted Diarmaid was now turned into groans, lamentations
and even threats, and these at length became so menacing, that
it occurred to Diarmaid that he would be obliged to reduce his
own people to submission before he proceeded to settle accounts with the Westerns and Northerns.

But now it became evident that disaffection was not confined to the civilians, but that his Fenian army were beginning
to look most dangerous. They, like other people, were divided
in opinion with regard to the justice of the impending war, but
they had no choice in the matter; it was simply their duty to
fight at the call of their sovereign, but they were, officers and
men alike, most fervent Christians almost to a man, and they
had no sympathy with the druidical superstitions of the
Ardrigh, but felt very much disposed to rebel. All this Diarmaid was very soon made aware of; but he was not yet without hope ; he had the Lagenian Fenians, they would frighten
their Meathian comrades into submission; but as this thought
passed through his mind, O'Mordha (O'Moore), marshall of
Leinster, rode up to him, and an exciting dialogue passed
between them, the end of which was that O'Mordha threatened
to withdraw his forces from Midhe back again to Lagean, and
leave Diarmaid alone to fight his battle against his opponents,
aided by his druid and his druid's master. These last words
were applauded by the bystanders, but they fairly enraged King
Diarmaid. He saw that he would have to compromise the
matter, and then, standing up in his chariot, amidst universal
silence, declared before all that he, and he alone, would be re-
sponsible for the presence of the druid, that he interfered not
with any, either army or people, and that he expected the same
toleration to be shown to himself, that neither soldiers nor
civilians, neither Midians nor Lagenians, had aught to do with
his druid, and that he represented only himself in this particular matter. This speech seemed to pacify them, and so they
relapsed into silence, and permitted the army to go on its way.
The body-guards were in attendance, front, rere, and sidesmen.
Amherghin Mac Amhlaigh, Chief Bard, swept the chords of his

cruit, and forthwith all the bards and musicians of the whole army burst forth into the famous *Rosgh Catha*, or war song. In various parts all the aois-ceoil (musicians) played their several instruments.

The two armies began their march from Teamhair by the Slighe Asal, or North-western Road. This great road brought them straight to the place of battle, crossing on their way the Boinn (Boyne), Amhain Dubh (Blackwater), and finally, the source of the Sionnain (Shannon). As they neared the place of encounter the aois-ceoil and filéadh all joined in a general *cronan*, or chorus, to animate the more the hearts of the united army. Under the exhilarating effects of the military music they marched on towards the Loch Gilleadh (Gilly), and arriving there turned northward, and encamped at a short distance to the north of the lake. Having pitched their tents, they set themselves to prepare for the battle, and many were the comments and surmises of the united armies, as they observed King Diarmaid and Frachan, his druid, walk off towards the direction from which the enemy was expected. They returned immediately and re-entered Diarmaid's tent. Soon, however, the druid reappeared, accompanied by some one, but whose identity was not quite clear, though it was strongly surmised that it was Diarmaid himself disguised, having taken second thoughts and returned for that purpose. They were also accompanied by the " *Ten*," also in disguise, and the bodyguard, and all shortly returned as they went, when the whole force bivouaced for the night. The next morning early they beheld great masses of troops assembled a little to the north-east. Diarmaid and his officers, and the officers of the Laegeni, commenced to marshal their troops in order; the Gal Greine, the royal standard of the Ardrigh, was advanced, and by its side the harp and crown banner of Laegain. Simultaneously they beheld the famous standard of Ulladh (Ulster), borne by O' h-Anluain (O'Hanlon), Prince of Orier, and hereditary standard-bearer of Ulladh. It was of green satin, and on it was emblazoned the Golden Lion, the device of the Curraidhe Craoibhe Ruaidhe (Red Branch Knights). All the minor banners on both sides were unfurled, and fierce battle-cries arose on both sides, mingled with the terrific blasts of the war-trumpets, and the martial strains of the *Rosgh Catha*. The forces of Tirowen (Tyrone) and Tirconnail (Tirconnell) were led by Fergus and Domhnall, the two sons of the late King Muirceartach Mac Earca, aided by their cousin Ainmire Mac Sedna. In the midst of all the confusion King Diarmaid's Druid Frachan Mac Teninson advanced in company with his disciples Tuathan Mac Dimman, Mac Saran, Mac Carmac, Mac Eoghan, and after a few directions from Fraechan, Tuathan advanced to a certain distance, where Diarmaid awaited him, and there in sight of both armies placed the *Erbhe Druad*, or druidical charm over the monarch's head. They then returned, and amidst universal grumbling it was explained to the armies of Midhe and Laegean, that they should not pass beyond that spot. But now their attention was attracted to another object; it was the advance of a single chariot from the ranks of Ulladh. On a nearer approach it was clear that its occupant was attired, not in military uniform, but in the garb of a monk; another glance showed it to be the well-known figure of the abbot Columcille himself, who had seen what had just passed. He approached to within a short distance of the magical circle of the druid, and there, standing up in his chariot, elevated his hands to heaven, and cried out in the hearing of both armies:

"O God, wilt Thou not drive off the fog which envelops our number?

"The host which has deprived us of our livelihood.

"The host which proceeds round the cairns!

"He is a son of storm who betrays us,

"My Druid,—He will not refuse me,—is the Son of God, and may He side with me;

"How grandly he bears his course; the steed of Baedan before the host.

"Power by Baedan of the yellow hair will be borne from Eire on him (the steed)."

Having thus invoked the aid of heaven on the arms of his friends he returned, and now the battle cries, and the shouts, and the trumpet blasts, and the war songs, were all renewed, and the opposing forces rushed to the encounter, and fierce and fast the conflict raged; volleys of stones from the Cran Tuabal whizzed through the ranks of both armies; showers of arrows and darts darkened the atmosphere; spears, and swords, and battleaxes resounded on the shields, helmets, and coats of mail; the scythed chariots worked destruction in the ranks; but suddenly consternation seized the army of King Diarmaid; they now perceived that while their own men went down before the shafts of their opponents, there appeared to be no sign of any gaps in the opposite ranks. This discovery, inexplicable as it was, and unaccountable from natural causes, was on the point of driving them to desperation, when the terrible blasts of brazen war trumpets burst upon their ears from a new direction, and on looking towards the point whence the thundering sounds proceeded, they beheld the standard of the Clanna Morna bearing for its arms Jupiter, a cavalier completely armed and borne by Mac Diarmaid, the standard-bearer of Connacht ; and marching under their banner to the sounds of martial music, the army of Connacht, led by Aedh, the father of the unfortunate Curnan, and son of Eochaidh Tirmacharna, King of Connaught, and Nainnidh Mac Duach, came bearing down upon their left. The army of King Diarmaid, now between two fires, at first fought desperately ; but after a short but furious onslaught on the Ardroyal and Laegenian troops by the united forces of Connacht, Tirowen, and Tirconnell, in which numbers fell on the side of the Ardrigh, while it was observed that they had only succeeded in killing one man, and that was he who had imprudently passed beyond the Erbhe Druadh of King Diarmaid : that monarch ordered the standards to be struck,* and retreating from the scene of battle, after having lost 3,000 men, fled with the remnant of his forces from Cairbre ; and being hotly pursued by the enraged Connacians, with great difficulty saved his life. When they had been a considerable distance on their way home by the Slighe Asal, the soldiers of his own army and those of his Laegean allies, being now at liberty to slacken their speed, commenced to murmur openly against Dairmaid for thus bringing them to wage war upon the Lord of Hosts. They broadly hinted that he was unfit to be on the throne of a Christian nation, that his coronation was a mistake, and that he had brought dishonour on the flags of his country. At another time none would have the hardihood thus to beard Diarmaid ; but now the discomfited monarch bore these taunts in silence, being wholly preoccupied with his own thoughts. When at last himself and his shattered army arrived in his capital, he was received with studied coldness and rigidity. He at once retired to the Grianan of the Ardrighan, he could not just now tolerate the presence of anyone else, while his troops and allies disbanded and scattered through their own friends and consoled those of their fallen comrades. The Lageni remained until next day, when they returned by Slighe Cualan, and Ath Cliath† to their homes in the eastern cuigaidh (province).

* Striking the standard was the signal of retreat. † Dublin.

ᴀn ᴄʀᴇᴀꜱ ᴄᴀᴅʀóiʟ ᴅᴇuᴈ.

CHAPTER XIII.

ᴅiᴀʀᴍᴀiᴅ ᴀᴈuʀ ᴍuᴈᴀin.

DIARMAID AND MOOAN.

WHEN King Diarmaid entered the Sunny Chamber he found the Ardrighan alone, she having dismissed her ladies to the other apartments of that building on perceiving from one of the windows the approach of the Ardrigh; and while he is mounting the staircase we will once more introduce our readers to the royal apartments, where many years before King Tuathal Maelgarbh and his queen so anxiously discussed the coming of Prince Diarmaid to Teamhair. Diarmaid, now monarch of Teamhair, had for second wife Mughain, the daughter of Concraidh, King of Deas Mumhain.* She is thus spoken of by Flann of the monastery :

"Mughain, the daughter of worthy Concraidh,
Son of Duach, King of Deas Mumhain,
Who followed munificence, without guile,
The wife of Diarmaid Mac Cearbhall."

She was now about thirty-five years of age, of medium size, of rather slight figure, her features regular and beautiful, complexion very white, contrasting with the rich pink hue of her cheeks, which told of her now recovered health ; her two rows of white teeth, visible between her cherry lips, resembled strings of pearls in a casket of coral ; her hair was a rich auburn which fell in plaits behind her shoulders, the ends falling into the golden *mella ;* on her head was the Niamh Land ; she was attired in a robe of tartan satin, comprising the seven colours, green predominating ; it was confined at the waist by a *girsat corcra,* or purple waist scarf ; a green *meirge,* or silk veil, hung from the "radiant leaf" down over her shoulders ; it was bordered with gold embroidery ; in her ears were wheel-shaped, golden *au nasg,* or earrings, set with emeralds, matching the *or-nasg,* or finger-rings, the *dornasc,* or bracelets, and the *dealg,* or brooch ; a *fiam,* or gold chain, round her neck suspended a gold cross on her bosom ; and her sandals were of golden net-work, curiously ornamented.

* South Munster.

When Diarmaid entered, Mughain, who already knew the situation, from heralds and from her own observation from the balcony of the Grianan, went towards her husband, as he appeared at the door, and affectionately putting her arms round his neck embraced him without uttering a word; she saw, in fact, that his beloved face wore an expression of dejection and care such as she had never seen there before. Still, without speaking, she led him to one of the luxurious *imdai*, covered with green satin, embroidered with gold, where, yielding to her gentle pressure he sunk nearly invisible in the downy couch. Placing herself beside him, and making for him a *torc* with her alabaster-like arms, she softly said:

"O Diarmaid, mo cheile, mo mhuirnin,* rest thee here yet a little while; I know thou art not, as yet, able to talk to me."

Diarmaid—"A Mughain, chuisle mo chroidhe, blat na finne,† I am never too tired to talk to *thee*; had I taken thine advice, I would have had a different story to-day; but, in truth, I did all for the best."

Mughain—"Thy druid then, O Diarmaid, hast played thee false?"

Diarmaid—"Yea, mo cheile,‡ he has been worsted by the Abbot Columb's druid."

Mughain—"The Abbot Columb's druid! What meanest thou, mo ghrádh?"

Diarmaid—"It was so that Columcille, on the battle-field, designated the Son of God."

Mughain—"Go deimhin!"§

Diarmaid—"Yea, he invoked the blessing of heaven on the army of his kinsmen and their allies of Connacht, and his prayer was heard; for while we lost three thousand men, they lost but one man, and that, he who had passed beyond our Erbhe Druadh: Rag Laim was his name."

Mughain—I am at least glad that thou recognizest in the fortunes of the day the finger of God. And, oh! Diarmaid, mo ghradh, A cheile m'anama !‖ Se Dia tus agus deire, bunn agus barr gach uile nidh.¶ Ta Dia ann gach ait.** Ta Dia maith do

---

* My husband, my passionately beloved one.
† O Mughain! pulse of my heart, flower of all that is fair.
‡ My wife.
§ Indeed.
‖ O Dermot, my love, O partner of my soul!
¶ God is the beginning and the end, the foundation and the top of all thing
** God is in every place.

gach duine ; Ardrigh Neimhe a ta, a bhi, agus a bheidheas go brath."*

Diarmaid—"O a stoir mo cleibh !† dost thou fear that I do not believe in God ?"

Mughain—"Nay, my Diarmaid, but I fear that thou hast sadly forgotten Him ; and thou, O my love, thou too a pupil of Finian of Cluain-Irared."

Diarmaid—"Ah ! those were happy days at Cluain-Irared ; and I knew it not. I longed for the throne, and when it came, it brought nought but bitterness—bitterness in the loss of the brother of my bosom and the friend of my youth, and continued bitterness in the cares, disappointments, and vexations which have added to the weight of my crown and of which thy poor head hast also felt the weight."

Mughain—"Och ! mo bhrón, nach b-fuil sonas ort.‡ Is tu mo bhrón agus mo shogh, m'onoir agus mo naire, mo bheatha agus mo bhas !"§

Diarmaid—" Mo chuisle, agus mo rún gheal,‖ I but sadden thee when I ought only to make thee rejoice."

Mughain—" If thou wouldst make me rejoice, O mo cheile dhilis, thou wouldst turn thy back upon thy druids and their magic, and return to the God of thy youth, who never forsakest those that trust in Him.   Thou hast just seen how He rewarded the faith and trust of the Abbot Columcille ; and rememberest not thou, O Diarmaid, how many years we were married without any sign of children, until with thy consent I besought the prayers of two holy saints, Bishop Aedh of Rath Aedh,¶ and Bishop Finian of Magh Bile,** and the Lord, hearkening to their supplications on my behalf, cured my grief, and took away my reproach by sending us our beloved son, Aedh Slane."

Diarmaid—"Yea, I remember all that, but I have not been as grateful as thou.   But it strikes me as strange that we Gaedhals (Gaels) should, like the Hebrews, reproach a woman with that which is not her fault, especially as we have not the excuse which they had.   We ought rather to feel rejoiced that, without

---

* God is good to every person ; the sovereign King of heaven, who is, who was, and who shall be for ever.

† O treasure of my bosom !

‡ O my sorrow, that thou art not happy.

§ Thou art my sorrow and my joy, my honour and my shame, my life an my death.

‖ My pulse and my fair secret love.

¶ In Meath.

** Moville, in county Down

ourselves interfering with the designs of Providence, those we love are spared the anguish and peril to which the propagation of mankind exposes them."

Mughain—"A mo cheile dhilis, all are not like thee ; many who profess horror of thine unhappy leanings towards paganish mysteries might well take a lesson from thee in social virtue. Thou didst never reproach my early barrenness; but did not I feel humbled before the nation ? Ah! I cannot express what I suffered, though but a passive instrument in the hands of God, who in his own good time yielded to the prayers of his servants, and although with some of the 'anguish and peril' of which thou hast so feelingly spoken, enabled me to present to thee a son, and to the nation a prince, who perhaps may one day reign in Eire."

"Diarmaid—"It will be a long day, even though, from any cause, the throne should become vacant, Aedh Slane could not fill it for many a year to come. It is not long since he entered Mur Ollamhain. No; women have seldom ruled in Eire, but children, never."

Mughain—"Yet I trust that by the time that thou, O my beloved ! hast exchanged an earthly for a heavenly crown, our dear Aedh will be long past the age at which he will be qualified, legally and physically, to take thy place."

Diarmaid—"In any event he cannot at once take my place. The rule of alternate succession forbids that. Is it not strange O mo cheile, that had I been slain at—don't shudder now, thou seest I was not—had I been slain at Cula-Dreimhne, my conquerors, Fergus and Domhnall, the representatives of the Northern Hy Nials, would succeed to our throne to the exclusion of our children Aedh Slane and Colman Beg ; ay, even to the exclusion of Colman Mór himself, who, had he lived, would have been in every way fitted for the high office. But perhaps thou dost not agree with me in that. He was not thy son."

Mughain—"O Diarmaid, how canst thou think so? 'Tis, indeed, but natural that I should love mine own children best, but I am not so unjust as not to see good qualities in the son of my husband, merely because he was not mine, but was the son of my predecessor and rival. No, my Diarmaid, I did grieve more than thou didst credit me with for the untimely death of Colman Mor. He was the pride of the court, and of the field, and the flower of Fenian chivalry,"

Diarmaid—"Thou art my own Mughain. But speaking of Fenian chivalry, dost thou not think that its prestige has suffered from recent events ?"

Mughain—"Nay, Diarmaid, I think not so; we must remember that there were also Fenians in the armies of Connacht, Tirconnell, and Tirowen, besides the Clanna Morna, and the Curraidhe Craoibhe Ruaidhe. Besides, it is absurd to say that these, and these only, defeated the forces of Midhe and Laegean. The truth is, my Diarmaid, both the opposing armies had each their invisible as well as their visible allies. Thy loss of 3,000 men against their one man is a human impossibility. No one ever heard of the like before. Now, thou didst publicly call upon the powers of darkness, that is the simple explanation of druidism, as expounded by thy Fraechan; Columcille, on the other hand, as publicly and solemnly called upon the powers of light on behalf of their opponents; so that while the visible battle raged between Ulladh and Connacht on the one side, and Laegean and Midhe on the other, the more awful, though invisible battle between heaven and hell, was being fought by the invisible allies of both. And what more natural than the result? It was the battle between the Archangel Michael and Lucifer all over again."

Diarmaid—"Then I suppose I am Lucifer, and Columcille is the Archangel Michael?"

Mughain—"Nay, Diarmaid, thou art not Lucifer; thou art much better than some Christians, it is to thy druid that I refer; but in truth, O Diarmaid, I have often grieved much that while with one hand thou didst build and endow monasteries, churches, and schools, with the other thou didst endeavour partially to restore and maintain some relics of pagan superstition."

Diarmaid—"Well, I am really anxious for the good of the Church and the maintenance of the Christian religion, and have spared neither care nor expense for that end; but thou knowest, O Mughain, how much opposition and defiance we meet with from some holy bishops and abbots in matters purely temporal."

Mughain—"If thou dost refer to the affair of Curnan Mac Aedh, and the action of the Abbot Columb in his behalf, I think that, rightly or wrongly, he believed that he was upholding the dignity and prerogatives of the Church."

Diarmaid—"Dignity and prerogatives! What meanest thou, *mo ghradh*?"

Mughain—"The prerogative of the Church in granting sanctuary to whom it listeth, and its dignity in insisting that the sanctuary, once granted, should be respected by the secular power."

Diarmaid—"Ha! the Church claims and insists upon the prerogative of shielding criminals from justice!"

Mughain—" But, Diarmaid, dear, do not, I pray thee, call poor Curnan a criminal. Was it not all a pure accident?"

Diarmaid—" Very well, as thou likest. In fact, now that I have had time to reflect upon the whole matter, I am satisfied that it *was* an accident. But Lorcan was killed, the Fes of Teamhair was violated, and I had no power to pardon the slayer of Conal's son, whether it was accidental or malicious. Why then should the Church, as represented by the Abbot Columb, insist upon the Ardrigh of Eire, setting the example before the whole nation of being first to break the laws and infringe the constitution of Eire?"

Mughain—" That is true; Curnan could not be pardoned."

Diarmaid—" No; Ollamh Fodhla, and the wise legislators who instituted the Fes of Teamhair, took stringent measures for the protection of those who should attend it. Why, if it were otherwise, what would become of us all? Neither life nor property would be safe. All who wanted to plunder might do so with impunity, and those who had a grudge against others might wound or even kill them, and then fly to some church, or to the arms of an abbot, or other ecclesiastic, and there defy the officers of justice and the laws of the land. What a terrible state of affairs that would be! What a contrast to the past it would be! Why even St. Patrick himself, when revising the ancient laws of the country to make them accord with Christianity, left the law relative to the Fes of Teamhair untouched. He, a foreigner, could recognise its wisdom and necessity, while a native, trained up from his youth, and thoroughly instructed in the laws of his country, cooly, before an assembled multitude, demands of his sovereign the abrogation and violation of one of the most necessary of those laws, knowing that that sovereign had no power to do so; and all because he chose to use the name and the authority of the Church, to shield a youth who had come into collision with that law. Why, the very Church itself repudiates the action of Columcille in the matter!"

Mughain—" Go deimhin!* How is that?"

Diarmaid—" Already rumours are afloat that many bishops and abbots, including some of Columcille's old friends, are meditating holding a synod to inquire into the conduct of one of their body, in being the cause of so much bloodshed. Now, such an inquiry can have but one result :—he and he alone is answerable for the battle of Cul Dreimhne. He was not

* Indeed.

bound to give the sanctuary of the Church to Curnan Mac Aedh, but I was bound to see the law of Ollamh Fodhla carried into execution."

Mughain—"The synod must consider that. Thou didst not make that law, and thou couldst not break it. Nevertheless, I trust that the Abbot Columcille shall come reproachless out of the matter. O Diarmaid mo ghradh, the abbot has a loving and tender heart, large enough too, to embrace all the lower creation, and even inanimate objects, His soft, gray eyes have been known to well out great large tears at the sufferings of the birds and beasts, and such is his love for his oak-groves that he would not allow his dear trees to be cut down even for the building of his church, but had it built on a less convenient site to avoid touching them, and when a tree happened to fall in his beloved wood he would allow no one to touch it for nine days, and at the end of that period he would set aside a tenth part for the use of the poor, and a third for the use of strangers, and the rest he would distribute amongst all the people of Doire Calcach."*

Diarmaid—"Yea, Mughain, dilis, I know all that, and it was but natural that he should try to protect a fellow-creature in trouble. But when he could not succeed in doing so, why should he needlessly sacrifice the lives of three thousand more human beings, which could have been avoided by submission to his sovereign and to the laws of his country ?"

Mughain—"Well, surely, he could not know the number he was sacrificing ?"

Diarmaid—"No ; he could not know ; the number might be less and it might be more ; but when he stirred up his relatives to give us battle he knew he was about to sacrifice many lives. And suppose that, instead of three thousand there were killed but three men, or even one, what needless shedding of blood it would be for the sake of one who had forfeited his life to the law, and whom we could not save were he our own son ?"

Mughain—"Thou art quite right, O Diarmaid, mo mhuirnin; but I do not think he reflected in time upon all the consequences, else he would not have pursued the matter so far. And then, Dhiarmaid, dhilis, although he threatened on thee the vengeance of his Northern Hy Nials in the heat of his resentment, we are not so sure that he really instigated his people to take up arms against us."

Diarmaid—"Nevertheless they have done so."

* Derry.

Mughain—" Yea, but they knew of the matter quite independent of him. Fergus, Domhnall, and Ainmire were here at
the time, as well as the family of Curnan ; then the attendants of
Columcille preceded him home to Tirconnell, and no doubt,
on his own arrival there he found it impossible to allay the
irritation and indignation of the northerns at the fancied insult
to their relative."

Diarmaid—" Well, I suppose we Gaedhals are doomed to
perpetual strife and discord. We have been always so, and
most probably always will be. If the Church would only dis-
countenance instead of encouraging our unhappy failing,
Christianity would be a temporal as well as a spiritual benefit."

Mughain—" Ah ! Diarmaid, dear, 'tis not the Church ; 'tis
ourselves still. Eirenacs* are fond of injuring and humbling
each other ; the Church is but a new weapon in their hands. It
is because Columcille was an Eirenac, and not because he was
a Christian abbot that these things have happened. They would
not be possible in any other country."

Diarmaid—" Well, well ; now that they have happened,
what is to be done ?"

Mughain—"Become reconciled by all means. Send for him
at once, and even though he is to blame in the matter, do not
reproach him with it. Neither defend thyself further than to
remind him that in the matter of Curnan, thou wert bound by
the law, over which thou hadst no control. As for the affair of
the Psalm Book, or Cathach† as it is now called, I think there
is a possibility of soothing his wounded feelings. Mocolmoc
of Cluain-Irared, the Abbot Finian's nephew, passed through
this city while thou wert at the Battle of Cul-Dreimhne, and informed us that his holy uncle grieved intensely over all the
untoward events that have occurred during the late Fes, and all
they have led to. He further informed us that Finian would
gladly restore the Psalm Book to Columcille, if by doing so he
could restore charity and good-will amongst ye all."

* Irishmen.
† The *Cathach*.—" The fragment of the original " Book of Battles," contained in the shrine, is of small quarto form, consisting of 58 leaves of fine
vellum, written in a small, uniform, but rather a hurried hand, with some
slight attempts at illumination ; and when we recollect that this fragment was
written about 1,300 years ago, by one whose name, next to that of our great
apostle St. Patrick, has held the highest place in the memory of his own as
well as of foreign countries, we have reason indeed, to admire, and reason to
be proud of the intense and tenacious devotion which could, under most un-
favourable circumstances, preserve even so much of so ancient and fragile a
monument."—*O Curry.* It is now in the Museum of the Royal Irish Academy.

Diarmaid—" Maiseadh !* did he say that ?"

.Mughain—" He did ; and now I think thou canst very easily arrange matters on good footing.   Then for thine own part thou canst bestow upon Columb a piece of ground, or one of our country seats, which will enable him to found another monastery, and by the good which will follow from it repair some of the injuries which have been done."

Diarmaid—" Yea, that pleases me, though Columcille showed little respect for his old master and mine, the Bishop and Abbot of Cluain-Irared ; but thou sayest Finian is ready to be reconciled.   Then so shall I.   Now which of our country seats shall we bestow upon Columcille ?"

Mughain—" Oh, I do not mind ; whichsoever thou thinkest best thyself."

Diarmaid—" We have already given him Dunchiule-Sibrinne Ceananus,† and Scryne."‡

Mughain—" Suirde§ will be very suitable for the purpose ; and I pray thee, O Diarmaid, lose no time in bringing about this reconciliation."

Diarmaid, rising up—" I go at once to direct *mo Rúnaidh* (secretary) to write to Finian and to Columcille.   So farewell until seire (supper)."

Mughain—" Slán leat, mo ghrádh."

* Musha.   Well then, indeed.
† Kells, county Meath, where the Round Tower, Columcille's house, and many other interesting relics still remain.
‡ Skreen, where is also a Round Tower.
§ Swords, near Dublin.

END OF PART THIRD.

an ceatarmaò cuiò.

Part IV.

Doiċaoaɼ an ȝal ȝɼeine.

ECLIPSE OF THE SUN-(BURST).

an ċeuò ċaibɼóil.

CHAPTER I.

Cul-ḟeiċɼineaċ.*

RETROSPECTIVE.

OWARDS the close of a summer's evening, in the year 563, a number of travellers, including aires (lords), anflaiths (rich farmers), brughfers (farmers), ceann-uides (merchants), saors (traders), araidhe (charioteers), and stray travellers of every description, sought refreshment and shelter for the night at the public biadtach at Ratoath, on the Slighe Cualann. Some were pedestrians, many of whom carried their wares on their backs; others came on horseback, others in carbads. These, as well as other kinds of vehicles laden with various species of merchandise, were carefully stowed away for the night in the out-offices, and the horses well attended to. The travellers themselves gathered around the tables to partake of the plentiful supper which was spread before them. They conversed freely on various matters, as the part whence they came, the nature of their business to the capital, the politics of the day, and other topics. While they spoke, fresh travellers continued to pour in, among whom were some foreigners. Places were made for the new comers at the various tables. A French merchant, who

* *Pr.* Cool-heck-shin-yach.

appeared travel-stained and weary, after having bathed his feet in a tub, presented to him for the purpose—an agreeable process, and one, by the way, of which all were obliged to avail themselves—sat down at one of the tables, between a Temorian goldsmith and a shipbuilder from Ath Cliath (Dublin). The latter being engrossed in conversation, relating to merchant and war vessels, with his next neighbour on the other side, and the extent of the order he expected to receive from the Ardrigh, and on other subjects interesting to himself, the French merchant turned to the goldsmith, who was engaged in discussing in silence the dishes laid before him, and consisting of fresh pork, fowl, cheese, new milk, honey, and ale ; the French merchant followed his example ; but as soon as he removed the keen edge of his appetite, he turned to the worthy goldsmith, and said :

" Well, friend, how fares it with Church and State in the dominions of King Diarmaid Mac Cearbhall ?"

" Hást thou, then, my friend, but lately arrived in Midhe ?"

" I arrived but two nights since in Eire itself, after an absence of two years ?"

" Didst thou then hear of the battle of Cul-Dreimhne ?"

" Oh, yes ; it was commencing just as I left, and in Armorica I heard of its termination ; but I was unable to learn more, from being constantly travelling about through many countries, until I at length arrived at Ath Cliath the night before last, where I passed the night. The next day I had enough to do to transact some business in that town, when I at once set out on my way hither. I hope to reach the capital early to-morrow."

" Then, perhaps, thou didst not hear of the reconciliation of the Abbot Columcille with King Diarmaid ?"

" No ; have they been reconciled ? I am very glad to hear that."

" Yea ; immediately after the battle of Cul-Dreimhne, which proved so disastrous to King Diarmaid, he sent for the Abbot Columcille and for the Abbot Finian, and——

" Pardon, pray, how fares it with Bishop Finian ?"

" Oh, Finian is departed to glory."

" Finian dead ! indeed ! Finian the Wise, the Bishop and Abbot of Cluain Irared, the Tutor of the Saints of Eire ! I am very sorry to hear it. He must be a great loss ;"

" Yea, a loss that will not easily be repaired ; but it is a glorious change for himself. However, though he was in no wise to blame for what occurred, he grieved much on account of all the lives that were lost, and in order to smooth animosities between all parties, he restored the Psalm Book to the Abbot Columcille."

" I fancy that Columcille was to blame for all."

" He was indeed."

" But what did King Diarmaid do after he sent for him ?"

" He became reconciled to him, and bestowed upon him one of his royal seats at Suirde (Swords), which Columcille lost no time in converting into a monastery ?"

" And does he now reside at the new monastery ?"

" Oh, by no means ; he has left the country altogether."

" Left the country! Dost thou mean that he has left Eire ?"

" Yea; he is now Abbot of Hy (or Iona) an island of Alba (Scotland). I will tell thee how it came about. Columcille was the cause of two other battles, one that of Cuil Feadha, against Colman Mac Diarmada, in revenge for his having been outraged in the case of Baodan, son of King Ninnidh, who was killed by Cuimin Mac Colman at Leim-en-eich, in violation of the sanctuary of Columb. Then, again, he caused another battle to be fought at Cuil Rathan (Coleraine) against the Dal-n-Araidhe and against the Ulladi, in consequence of a controversy that took place between Columb and Comgall contending for a church at Ross Toratair, because they took part against Columcille in that controversy. In consequence of all these events, a synod of the clergy was held at Tailtain,* the result of which was that Columcille was excommunicated for being the cause of so much bloodshed. Columcille himself was summoned to attend, which he accordingly did, only arriving, however, after sentence had been passed upon him. As soon as he came near the synod house, he was perceived by Brendan, Abbot of Birr, who immediately arose to salute him and embrace him affectionately. The other members of the synod expostulated with him for this, and inquired how he could thus receive and salute a person who was excommunicated ; but the Abbot Brendan replied : " If ye could see what the Lord has been pleased to manifest to me regarding his chosen one, ye would never have excommunicated one whom God so honours." Then they inquired how Brendan knew this, and how God had honoured this man whom they had condemned. Brendan replied that he saw a pillar of light preceding this man of God, and that the holy angels had accompanied him on his journey along the plain. This was sufficient for them, and Columcille was received with due honour. Nevertheless, he felt the need of some

---

* Teltown, county Meath.

special reparation for the bloodshed which he had caused, whether the side which he took was one of justice or not. Accordingly, he informed the synod of his desire, and promised to abide by its decision. Therefore it was that Molaisi, Abbot of Deirnie, or Innis Mairaidhe, decreed that he should leave his beloved Eire, never to see it again, and should, in company with twelve companions, take his departure for some land that had not yet received the light of faith. This he at once submitted to, and then it was settled in accordance with his own desire that he should go to that part of Alba inhabited by the barbarous pagan Picts. His exile, however, voluntary though it was, cost him many a pang, and in the bitterness of his soul, he cried out:

"'Death is better in reproachless Eire
Than perpetual life in Alba.'

"Having obtained from his cousin Conall, the King of the Albanian Scots, the small island of Hy, or Iona, which was an appendáge of the new Scottish kingdom—which in its turn, as thou knowest, is tributary to our own monarch—Columcille, together with twelve of his disciples, set sail for that sequestered spot, where we hear he is expelling the druids, and otherwise making the place fit for the erection of his monastery, before proceeding to explore the region beyond the Grampion Hills."

" And how long is he gone ?" asked the French merchant.

" Scarcely three months."

"I must visit him there some day that my business will permit. I suppose he placed an abbot over his Irish monasteries before leaving ?"

" Oh, yes; and I forgot to tell thee, he founded many more."

"Did he, indeed. How many ?"

" One hundred, including those founded when thou wert in Eire before."

"What a number! And all, I suppose, in full working order."

" All without exception."

" Where are they situated ?"

" Well, I will name the principal. Besides Doire Calcaich,* Dair Magh,† and Ceannanus,‡ where is his beautiful new book; there is the one at Suirde (Swords),§ it is about seven miles from Ath Cliath, over which he placed (St.) Finian Lobhar, Mac Cean as abbot. He founded another on Tor Inis (Tory Island); ‖ another on the site of the battle of Cul-Dreimhne, at Druim-

* Derry.   † Durrow, King's County.
‡ Kells.   § The Round Tower is still at Swords.
‖ Off the coast of Donegal. It has a Round Tower also.

cliffe;* another at Rath Both (Raphoe);† one at Mughain (Moone),‡ given him by Queen Mughain ; one at Doire Eithne (or Kilmacreenan) ; and he founded one at Scryne (Skreen), at which there is a well: thou canst see that establishment on thy way to Teamhair to-morrow."

"Yea, I shall like it. But there is no use in going over them all. Thou sayest he founded a hundred, including those thou hast named ?"

"Yea, friend, and all bid fair to rival the already existing institutions. It is said that the late Ardrighan by her munificence enabled him to found many of them."

"The *late* Ardrighan dost thou say. Is then the fair Mughain dead ?"

"Alas! yes, friend. But how comes it that thou didst not hear that. I never doubted but that thou didst know it."

"I know not how it was, except that it was while I was on the stormy sea, with my mind made up for a watery grave. We had a terrible time of it, and heard nothing from any country for a long period."

"But on thy landing at Ath Cliath, didst thou not hear the sad news ?"

"Nay, though perhaps it was mine own fault; for owing to the great delays I had met with, I hurried from the vessel to a biadtach, where I heeded nobody, but ate my supper and went to bed, having to rise early on the following morning, which I accordingly did, and then ran about Ath Cliath until I had finished my business in that town, when I returned to the biadtach to refresh myself in order to take immediate departure for the city of Teamhair, and here thou findest me on my way thither. And so thou sayest the Ardrighan is no more ?"

"No more for this life ; but she was good as she was beautiful, and has only exchanged an earthly for a heavenly kingdom. She was buried at Cluain Mac Nois, which, no doubt, thou art aware was bestowed under the name of Artibra upon St. Ciaran Mac an t-Saoir by King Diarmaid before he came to the throne."

"Yea, yea, I have heard of that. Artibra, or Cluain Mac Nois is now a celebrated university, resorted to by myriads of the nobles of many lands, including my own."

"Well, Mughain was buried near the church beside Diarmaid's first wife and his brother Maelmordha Mac Argatan. Oh ! it was a sight to see. Thou shouldst have been there."

* County Sligo, also remains of a Round Tower.
† Round Tower destroyed.
‡ County Kildare, where is St. Columcille's Cross.

"Ah! I would have given much to be present. But how doth Diarmaid take the death of his truly beloved wife?"

"Oh, he is distracted. Nothing but the threats of his physicians could induce him either to eat or drink, for he worshipped the fair secret love of his heart even to adoration."

"Ah! and his idol is taken from him. Well, perhaps now he will turn from his superstitions to the service of his God."

"What is that thou sayest friend? Oh, I had forgotten to tell thee that after the battle of Cul-Dreimhne, Diarmaid renounced for ever his druidism and magic. The foundation of the monastery of Suirds was the first act of reparation. He dismissed his druids for ever, and it is consoling to think that when these men die, or are converted, there are none to succeed them, and druidism will be totally extinguished. Well, on their dismissal, Diarmaid, to the great joy of his queen, substituted an anam-chara.* Then he went to visit the blessed Lomman of Loch Uair, who was going on a mission; and after an interview with Diarmaid, he went to converse with Maighnean. Bishop Maighnean and Lomman of Loch Uair † then took leave, embraced, and blessed each other. Maighnean on this occasion preached sermons before Diarmaid. When Lomman of Loch Uair heard the terrors of the Day of Judgment, and the severe judgments of the Holy Trinity, he shouted in loud lamentation in presence of the king and his people. When the king's people heard the admonitions, severe judgments, and hard sayings of the holy cleric, nine-and-twenty of them departed this false world in presence of the king; and Diarmaid Mac Fergus also made his own peace with God from that day forth; and he gave his *Coibsena* (Confessions) and great *Almsona* (Alms) to Maighnean, i.e., a *screapall* from every nose, and a *uinge* (an ounce) of gold from every virgin daughter on her first espousal to a man, or if she should prefer it rather than (to pay) the king's stewards, she may give the garments and clothes which she wore (at her marriage). The king also gave to him the materials of a *trosdan* and a *bachall* (a pastoral staff) of the gold which he got in ransom of the foreigners. Maghnean's sermon at Loch Uair at that time was noble and his covenant with the King of Eire. He gave his blessing to Diarmaid and to his descendants after him. And everything went on well since then. Diarmaid is a good Christian, and when I say that he worshipped his wife, I meant not that worship which belongs to God alone, but that inferior "worship" which every husband owes his wife,

---

* Soul's friend—Confessor.   † Lough Owel, in Westmeath.

but which many are remiss in paying, while Diarmaid, although Monarch of Eire, rendered with such fidelity and even extravagance."

"Well, I am both glad and sorry for King Diarmaid—glad of his conversion, and sorry for his bereavement. Still I think, as the case now stands, that he ought to be more resigned to the will of Providence."

"He is becoming more resigned now, and takes more interest in the duties of his position, which engages his mind, and prevents his dwelling on his loss."

"That is as it should be."

"Didst thou hear of the death of the queen of the late King Tuathal ?"

"Oh, yes, before I went away I heard of her death. She died in St. Brigid's Convent of Cill Daire, where she had resided since her husband's death. And now it is time to retire ; nearly everyone but ourselves are in bed. I thank thee very much for all the information thou hast given me, and I hope thou wilt bear me company to the city in the morning ?"

"I shall be delighted to do so."

"Well, good-night."

"Good-night."

The next morning, after ceadphroinn (breakfast), all the travellers prepared to resume their journey, including the two new friends, who travelled together, chatting merrily on the way, and stopping at Scryne to visit the monastery of Columcille, after which they continued their journey until they arrived at the Cathair Teamhrach (City of Tara), where to their surprise they beheld a crowd near the precincts of the royal palace. Asking what it was, they were informed that it was the Ardrigh was sending his heralds on a tour of inspection all over the country to see that everything was in proper condition. The affair was causing much surmise among the citizens, some of whom shook their heads, for they had heard that some of the notabilities, who were about being honoured by a visit from the royal heralds, would not feel flattered by the compliment, for some of them preferred to have their own way in everything that concerned them, while others took pride in having everything in exact accordance with law.

an Oara Caibroil.

CHAPTER II.

Aeo Suaine.

HUGH GUAIRE.

ARDRIGH Diarmaid Mac Cearbhall was seated on his breas-
fhora (throne) in the Teach Cormaic, in Rath na Riogh. He
was surrounded by his courtiers, the "*Ten,*" and some of the
officers of the Fianna Erionn. They had been discussing the
improved condition of the country, throughout which Diarmaid
had established peace by enforcing respect for the laws, for
the strict administration of which he kept up a constant visitation by his great stewards and Fenians throughout the country.
For some such purpose as this, was he now about to despatch
his representatives. He held the Spear of State—the distinctive
ensign of royalty—in his hand, as he exclaimed :

"Let our chief herald, Bacclomm, appear before us."

That functionary having presented himself and done
homage, the monarch then said :

"We entrust to thy care our Spear of Honour, that, carrying
it before the face of our trusty and well-beloved 'Mac Conraidhe,* ceann-fedhna† (kenn faana), and his company of
Fianna Erionn, all Our loyal subjects, throughout the kingdom
of Eire may receive ye with the same honour and render ye the
same assistance in the discharge of your duties, as if We ourselves were present."

Diarmaid then handed the Spear of State to the herald, who
received it kneeling, and then the ceann-fedhna, and his assistant officers, and the great stewards did homage likewise, and
then rising, backed out of the presence of the Ardrigh. On their
appearance without, they were received with vociferous cheers
by the assembled crowd who had collected to witness their
departure. Soon the company of Fenians were in order for the
journey. They were all superbly mounted, and the French merchant could not help observing to his companion that the
physique and outfit of the Fenians of Eire, well represented the
magnificence of their monarch. Off they started and were soon

* Mac Conray.   † Commander of 100 men]

clattering along the solid pavements of the streets of Teamhair, amidst the enthusiastic cheers of the patriotic and justly-proud citizens of all ranks. They loved their country and its laws, and the great majority almost worshipped Diarmaid for his consistent and devoted loyalty to the institutions of his country; and although over-zeal in those matters had previously led him into errors, and brought him into collision with the strong religious feelings and prejudices of his subjects, all was now forgotten in his change of life, especially as that change in no wise altered his policy or cooled his ardour and devotion to institutions and laws that had for 1,200 years made his country the most polished, civilized, and valiant nation on earth.

The royal detachment made the tour of Midhe, then penetrated into Ulladh (Ulster), always preceded by the Chief Herald, who bore, as his insignia of office and authority, the monarch's royal spear, and who was accompanied by other heralds carrying *stoca*, or trumpets, by which they announced the coming of the Ardrigh's Fianna, on approaching any of the noble residences, at which they intended to claim the free quarterage due to their official dignity while engaged in the examination of the state of the district, and the administration of the laws, by the command of the Ardrigh. They always stopped at the noblest residence in the district in which they happened to be; sometimes it would be that of king, at others that of a prince, or chief, or highest class of *aire*. Their mode of proceedure was this : whenever they came to the house of the principal resident, in which they intended to take up their temporary abode, several blasts of the trumpets of the subordinate heralds notified their approach to the family they intended to honour; then on coming up to the door, the Chief Herald advanced, carrying the Spear of Honour, " horizontally," across his hands.

Now, the construction and size of houses and all their several parts were all regulated by law, according to the rank and position of their occupants. It was one of the requirements of large mansions that the doors should correspond with the rest of the building. This was in order that the dignity of the State should be kept up. Still some of the nobles of those times had their whims, and for one excuse or another preferred narrow doors to wide ones, and would endeavour to evade the law in the matter. But if royalty, or the representatives of royalty, chanced to visit the abodes of these whimsical nobles, royalty was offended, and the nobleman disgraced, for the wall was

18

there and then broken until it would admit the royal spear horizontally; in this manner the deputed royal visitation proceeded. The majority of the houses at which they stopped were in proper condition, and their doors easily admitted the Spear of State, and everything went well; the Fenians were entertained and they inspected the surrounding district, setting in order all that they found that required it. Sometimes, however, they found something to reform in the house at which they stopped : if the door was too narrow, and that the chief herald could not pass the spear in the proper manner, he forthwith ordered the walls to be taken down until the required breadth was obtained. When anything else was wrong they improved it in like manner. Thus they made the tour of Ulladh, passing left-hand wise towards the south-west, in time reaching the boundary of Connacht, which kingdom they entered, travelling south-westwards, and stopping in every district as they did in Midhe and Ulladh. In this manner they at length reached Ui Mainé,* and at once proceeded towards the residence of the chieftain, Aedh Guaire. Loud blew the trumpets, repeated again and again as they neared the castle. At length they drew up before the door, having entered the courtyard within the encircling mound. The Chief Herald going up to the door, at which stood the door-keepers, who had heard the sound of the trumpets, advanced with the Spear of Honour held in a horizontal position, but on coming in contact with the door-jambs, it refused to enter.

"Where is the flaith ?" asked the ceann-fedhna, coming up.

"He is from home," replied the chief steward of Aedh Guaire, who had just appeared on the scene to receive the royal agents in the absence of his master.

"Why is not the door made in accordance with law ?" asked the chief herald.

"I know not," replied the steward, "save that it is the will of my noble master. But we will break the door of either side and make it in such manner as that thou canst bring in the Spear of Honour as thou desirest."

"Well, it is well, for it is the will of the Ardrigh that the walls be taken down until the entrance is wide enough to admit, horizontally, the Spear of State," said the caenn-fedhna.

"Fianns, bring your pickaxes, and remove as much of these walls as I shall mark out," cried the Chief Herald, who there-

---

* A large district situated partly in the present counties of Galway and Roscommon.

upon marked with the spear, at each side of the door, as much of the walls as were necessary to admit the spear.

This work was soon accomplished, for the servants of Aedh Guaire durst not resist, and the Chief Herald entered, holding the Spear short-wise, and was followed by the whole party. They then sat down to a feast that the steward ordered to be prepared for them. Everything went well. The bards, aois-ceoil, amadann and cleasaighe entertained the royal agents during the feast. When it was over it was too late to commence the inspection of the district for that evening, so the Fianns and their officers merely amused themselves, or were shown over the demesne by the servants of the house, until the return of their host. That worthy came home about dusk. Now, it so happened that there were but two persons in the great hall at the time he arrived, to wit, his own chief steward, and the chief herald of King Diarmaid. The rest were about other parts of the premises or in the grounds.

When Aedh Guaire came up to the door, and saw what had been done in his absence, he burst into the house in a storm of rage and indignation, and turning upon the steward, who was the first he encountered, he exclaimed:

"What is this? What has been done? Who has been here? Answer me, sir. Who has been battering down the door? Who has dared to take such liberties in my absence?"

The terrified steward, as soon as he could find utterance, replied:

"During thy absence, O most noble Aedh Guaire, the royal agents of Ardrigh Diarmaid, being on a visitation around Eire, arrived here, and the door being too narrow to admit, horizontally, the Spear of Honour, the Chief Herald was obliged to have the wall at either side broken, until the requisite width was obtained."

"And dost thou tell me that thou and the servants under thee have permitted such an outrage? Is it for that ye are here?"

"What could we do, O most noble master? We dare not resist the officers of the Ardrigh."

"Not resist!" cried Aedh Guaire, now fairly boiling over. "And why not, pray? Were there not enough of ye in it to hurl the intruders from my castle?"

"Nay, be not angry, O noble flaith," said the royal herald, now coming forward, "such a proceeding would but involve thee with our dread sovereign."

"And who art thou, sir, that darest to address me unasked?"

"I am Bacclomm, Chief Herald to the illustrious Ardrigh of Eire."

"Ha! was it thou then that committed the outrage?" said the enraged noble, as he collared the herald.

"We—we—oh! let me go."

"Was it?"

"We but—did our—duty; we—

"Was it thou?" roared the flaith.

"We have done the same at other mansions—and the—owners—oh!—were—not angry."

"Answer my question, sir, was it thou broke down the walls?"

"Thou—insultest the High King whose spear I bear—Oh!—," making an effort to display the spear which he held in one hand, but was cut short by Aedh Guaire.

"What care I for thyself or thy spear, or thy High King. I have my sword, and the man that broke my door shall suffer death."

So saying, the irate flaith plunged his sword into the heart of the unfortunate herald, who sank back gasping into the arms of the steward. The latter, horrified beyond expression, could only cast a look of grief and astonishment on his master, who, interpreting the meaning, brandished his sword threateningly before his shrinking steward, and passing on left the hall by the opposite door, and mounted into the Grianan. Once there he felt secure from intrusion for a time, and he commenced to stride backwards and forwards and round about, apostrophising himself, the herald, his steward, and the Ardrigh. Soon, however, he became calmer, would stop now and again in his march, press his hand to his forehead, and again stride wildly round the room. Numerous ideas appeared to be passing through his mind. At last he stopped again, for perhaps the twentieth time, beat his head wildly with his clenched hand, and exclaimed:

"Good God! what have I done? Have I stained my hands with blood? Am I indeed a murderer? Have I really killed the chief herald of King Diarmaid? But why did he commit an attack on my castle—mine own private property? But what did he do but knock a few stones out of the wall, which could have been replaced? and I have taken his life for the damage. Oh! ma bhròn,* mo gheur chradh.† And he was no burglar, but an officer of state commissioned by the Ardrigh; ha, 'tis all Diarmaid's fault—oh, would that I killed

---

* My sorrow   † My piercing anguish.

him instead of his innocent, hapless herald—but let me see—
Diarmaid—no; 'tis not Diarmaid, 'tis the law. The law requires
a certain width in such houses as this, and Diarmaid had no
choice but to enforce it. But why should the law interfere in
such matters? Why cannot I have what I like? What matters
it to anyone but myself what is the size of my doors, or my
house, or anything else that is mine? If it so pleased me, why
should I not be allowed to have a house like one of my labourers?
But what a fool I am. Everyone should have the same right to
do as he liked as I claim for myself; and then what would become of society : everything else in civil, social and domestic
life should follow my fancy picture in regard to houses, and
then what would become of trade and commerce, much less
science and art. There would no longer be any necessity for
these things ; besides the dignity and grandeur of the country
would be destroyed, and in a few years we should sink into a
condition of barbarism and poverty, unknown even at the
earliest period of our history. Then, from being the foremost
nation on earth, for civilisation and refinement, riches and
glory, the abode of all the polished and elegant arts, the
market of the world, we should in time fall far behind nations
which now envy our prosperity and try to imitate our example.
Oh! I have been a fool, a madman ; I am at war, not with the
chief herald or other officers of the Ardrigh, or with the Ardrigh
himself, but with the laws of my native land—laws, too, which
coming down through centuries, have made her what she is.
I have set myself in opposition to the wise legislators who for
the wisest of purposes have instituted these laws regulating the
dress, houses, furniture, and other belongings of the various
ranks and degrees that go to make up the population of Eire.
Why did I not have my door as it ought to have been ? It would
have added to mine own dignity in the eyes of my servants, and
my tribes-men, and the people in general. But I did not, and now
the law has done it for me ; and I have taken the life of the
officer who carried the law into execution, as if he did it on his
own responsibility, and as if he had not already done the same
at other places with impunity, as I have no doubt he did ; why,
I might as well have quarrelled with the Spear of State itself—
the Spear of State !—but I have quarrelled with it. Precious as
it is, both intrinsically and as a work of art, yet it is nothing in
itself. But it represents the highest authority in the realm!
Great Heavens ! what have I done ? I have committed a double
crime ; I am guilty of murder and treason. I have imbrued
my hands in innocent blood, and I have outraged the

dignity and power of my sovereign and of the constitution and laws of my country. O, mo bhron, I am a lost man ; there is no hope for me; I cannot escape an ignominious death. What shall I do ? How avert the vengeance of the law ? Let me think—how ? Ah—the Church!—the Church alone can save me. And to the Church I fly!"

Here he stopped pacing and went towards one of the windows, and looking out saw, notwithstanding the darkness, a large number of persons in the gardens beneath, coming towards the house from different directions. On seeing them Aedh Guaire exclaimed :

"Ah ! here are the Fianna returning from their rambles. Directly they will be in the house and will discover their murdered companion, and then they will seek out the murderer. They will not in such a case respect even my Grianan. Oh ! I must fly, and at once !"

Saying which Aedh Guaire, grasping his sword, hastily left the Grianan and rapidly descended the staircase, and without daring to trust himself into the chamber of death, turned the other way and left the house just as the foremost of the Fianna were entering at the other side. Looking round on all sides to make sure that no one saw him, he ran into a brake close by, and under cover of the shrubbery and of the darkness combined he pushed through it, and ere he left it he heard the exclamations and lamentations of the comrades of the chief herald over his murdered body. Aedh Guaire, knowing that he had not a moment to lose, as they would soon be in pursuit, on emerging from the thicket cleared the ground rapidly, running with all his might to the house of a friend, about half a mile from his own, where, relating his story, truthfully, he obtained the use of a good horse. His friend asked him where he intended to go, but Aedh Guaire replied that as yet he had not made up his mind, that up to that moment he had only time to think of getting beyond reach of the Fianna, and that the only thing that was clear to him was that he should seek out and put himself under the protection of some powerful ecclesiastic.

"Why, thou needest not go far for that : are there not many here ?"

"Oh yes," replied Aedh Guaire, " there are many who could, if they would ; but they make it part of their duty to insist upon the laws being respected and obeyed, and they will not shield those who violate them. But that is only their own individual opinion. Other churchmen believe that the Church should rule the State and rule it arbitrarily, and that every priest and monk, bishop and abbot should insist upon his right to defy the king and the laws of the land, and protect all scorners of the one and violators of the other who flee to them for refuge from offended majesty. I do not at all approve of what I believe will eventually bring ruin upon the country; but why should I not take advantage of it as well as another?"

"That is quite true, thou hast as good a right to the protection of the Church as anyone else; at all events, it is thy only chance. But wilt thou flee to a sacred building or to the arms of a sacred personage?"

"Oh, it does not signify; either will do; but I will leave this territory, and will, if possible, fly to my cousin Senech, the Bishop of Muscraidhe;* on the whole I think it best. Buide-acas leat agus slan leat."†

"Slan leat."

The two friends parted; Aedh Guaire galloping at full speed towards the Sionnain, where he dismounted, and hailing a boat, he put his horse into it with the aid of the boatmen, and then entered it himself. He was soon on the other bank of the river, where he disembarked and again mounted his horse, and sped to the residence of Bishop Senech, a few miles distant. Arrived in presence of the bishop, he told his story as related before, and finished by imploring the holy man's protection; but the bishop shook his head and looked grave as he replied:

"I fear, my cousin, it will be a task of extreme difficulty."

"But," said Aedh Guaire, "nothing is difficult to the Church of which thou art a bishop, and thou canst save me if thou wilt; King Diarmaid will not dare now to question the rights of the Church. Often has it stayed his avenging arm, and when he refused to submit, terrible has been the penalty."

"Ay," replied the bishop, "bloodshed and death! Ah! the Church's right of sanctuary is a good thing; it has saved many unfortunate people from the oppressions of the great; but I fear me that it is now being fearfully abused. However, thou at least must be saved; but thy crime is one of more than usual gravity, and as I have already said, it will be a task of the utmost difficulty."

"But, father, I cannot see the difficulty. What is there for me to do but simply to remain under thy protection?"

"Were the case of a milder nature," replied Senech, "my sanctuary would, no doubt, be sufficient; but for so serious a case

---

* Muskerry, Lower Ormond.
† Lit., Thanks with thee and health with thee.

as thine, thou must seek more powerful protection than mine. I will bring thee to our common uncle—the brother of our mothers—the Abbot Ruadhan of Lothra."*

When the bishop had hospitably entertained his guest, they both set out for the monastery of the Abbot Ruadhan, which was situated in the same district. On arriving there they found that the abbot was from home, but was expected every moment. While waiting they went over the monastery, and the termoinn lands, admired the fertility of the soil, visited the monastic buildings, and the various offices hard by, as the mill, the kiln, &c. &c. The bishop brought Aedh Guaire under the linden-tree, which grew outside the monastery, which he told him distilled a certain luscious sap into a vessel held beneath it for the purpose. This miraculous liquor, as the bishop told his companion, was furnished by the bounty of God to Ruadhan and his monks, without any labour on their part, but such as proceeded from their prayers and fasting. It had the taste of wine. Each of those who partook of it filled a cup with the liquor, as it flowed from the tree, and it at one time supplied not only the monks and alumni of Lothra, but also their guests. But at length the saints of Eire grew jealous regarding the miracle; they murmured against Ruadhan because their monks and alumni left them and went to him. Accordingly, they formed a deputation and waited on the Abbot Finian, Bishop of Cluain-Irared. Finian then went at their head to visit his old pupil, Ruadhan, and having seen the linden-tree, he entreated the Abbot of Lothra to abandon such an easy way of living, lest it should occasion envy in the other monasteries of Eire. He then blessed the tree, and immediately the sap ceased to flow, so that that night the liquor sufficed only for the monastic family, and not for its guests. Thereupon the guests preferred a complaint to the Abbot Ruadhan, who then said :

" Pour out the spring water for our guests and it shall be changed into wine for them."

The cook went to draw the water from a fountain, when suddenly a fish of wonderful size issued through the rocky bottom of the well. This fish was cooked and set before the guests, together with the water which had been turned into wine. They felt inebriated and fell asleep. Finian and the other abbots who were with him then besought Ruadhan to place his monks on the same footing with their own religious brethren, with which

---

* Lorra, in northern part of present county of Tipperary, about three miles from Lough Dearg.

request he humbly complied. Then Finian said to him and his monks :

"Do ye plough and reap your fields ; these shall produce fruitful crops forever, without further culture or manure."

"Since that time the liquor of this linden-tree has only produced sufficient for the brethren of Ruadhan ; and moreover," continued Senech, "the sap of this tree has this quality— it is bitter to the taste of all others except those persons for whom it is intended. It distilled its sap from the setting sun until the ninth hour of the following day, so that in this manner a refreshment might be provided when fasting time had ended."* Thus did the bishop endeavour to engage the mind of his companion, and prevent him from dwelling on his own sad condition.

As he finished his story of the linden-tree they heard voices behind them, and on turning round they beheld at a little distance coming towards them the Abbot Ruadhan himself, accompanied by his old school-fellow Brendan, now Abbot of Birr, which monastery was situated on the banks of the Sionnain, about three or four miles from Lothra. On coming up they shook hands warmly with Bishop Senech, and Ruadhan embraced his nephew, Aedh Guaire, and introduced him to the Abbot Brendan. Then they all again entered the monastery, where the Abbot Ruadhan entertained them, Senech remarking with forced cheerfulness that there was a time when they would have been treated to some of the luscious sap of the linden-tree without, but that, thanks to the late holy Bishop of Cluain-Irared, was all now at an end. This assumed carelessness of manner did not, however, deceive Ruadhan, for he was not long in discovering that something weighed on the minds of his two new guests, but as they as yet said nothing he did not give expression to his thoughts. Brendan was equally sharp, and so when the meal was ended he rose to go. Senech and Aedh Guaire besought him not to disturb himself on their account, that though they had come hither on a matter of great importance, which, doubtless he had guessed, notwithstanding their efforts to conceal it for a little while ; yet his presence in no wise embarrassed them ; rather the contrary. Ruadhan now united his appeals to theirs, and begged of Brendan to put off his return home till morning, as he must be much fatigued after the day. This being settled, Bishop Senech opened the important business in hand, and Aedh Guaire then related all his adventures over again. Ruadhan and Brendan, as they listened,

* Rev. J. O'Hanlon's Life of St. Ruadhan.

were swayed by conflicting feelings, and were in turn filled with astonishment, horror, fear, and pity. When Aedh Guaire had finished, Senech asked Ruadhan and Brendan what was best to be done, to which Ruadhan replied :

"What can be done in such a case ? The Church is indeed all powerful, but—but——"

Brendan—"But this is an exceptional case. It is really most unfortunate."

Senech—"It is truly unfortunate ; but it is done now, and past recall ; and the question is, what is to be done ?"

Ruadhan—"I know not. If it were anything but what it is, I could shelter Aedh Guaire here."

Brendan—"And canst thou not do so as it is ? Why, thou art now the most powerful abbot in all Eire. Were my influence as great I would have no hesitation in giving sanctuary to Aedh Guaire in my monastery at Birr."

Ruadhan—"There is very little difference ; but in truth, O Brendan, King Diarmaid Mac Cearbhall would not willingly permit thee, or me, or any other abbot in Eire, to interfere with his royal prerogatives, much less his administration of the laws. We know him of old."

Brendan—"Yea, we know him of old. Even in our young days in the College of Cluain-Irared, some of his school-fellows would not acknowledge his claims, and perhaps he remembers it."

Ruadhan—"Ah ! that is my opinion too."

Aedh Guaire—"But, uncle, is there no hope for me ? Art thou really powerless to save me ?"

Ruadhan—"My son, thy unfortunate condition grieves me much. But Diarmaid Mac Cearbhall is, after all, Ardrigh of Eire, and he liketh not the Church's interference in matters of State."

Senech—"No, he does not like the Church to shield—ah ! well—to shield persons who violate the law."

Brendan—"No, he does not like it ; but what of that ; we are more than he ; we represent the Church, he only the State ; we sway the spiritual power, he only the temporal. Let there be a trial of strength between the two powers and see which shall triumph."

Ruadhan—"That is well spoken. In fact thou but gavest expression to mine own thoughts, but——"

Brendan—"But what, O Ruadhan ?"

Ruadhan—"Any quarrel now between the Ardrigh and myself would, perhaps, be ascribed to personal motives."

Senech—" And art thou going to sacrifice our relative here to imaginary fears as to what people shall think ?"

Ruadhan—" Oh, no, Senech ; but a plan just occurs to me, and I would know what ye all think of it."

All—" What is it, O Ruadhan ?"

Ruadhan—" To bring our friend, Aedh Guaire here, across the Scythian Valley* into Britain, and there consign him to the care of the king of that country, who is my warmest friend."

Senech—" Excellent ! It is the safest course to take. There would be danger anywhere in Eire."

Brendan—" There would, indeed ; no matter how sacred the place of sanctuary Diarmaid might invade it. And perhaps it is better to avoid a collision between Church and State."

Ruadhan—" I think so ; and after all, of what avail would be our triumph in humbling the Ardrigh, if it came too late to save the life of our friend here ? What thinkest thou thyself Aedh Guaire ? Wouldst thou like to go to Britain ?"

Aedh Guaire—" Most certainly, O uncle Ruadhan. I am not in a position to choose the place of my habitation. Under other circumstances I would not care to dwell in Britain ; but as I am now situated, any place would afford a safer asylum than Eire. Besides, I have no desire to be the cause of war between Church and State, for notwithstanding my crime, I am loyal to both."

Ruadhan—" Well said, my son ; I am sure thou art heartily sorry for the deed thou hast done in a moment of passion ?"

Aedh Guaire—" I am, indeed, O abbot. I would give a thousand worlds to recall it."

Senech—" Then thou wilt make thy peace with God before thou settest out for Britain."

Aedh Guaire—" With the help of God's grace."

Brendan—" And we shall feel the less conscientious scruples for aiding thy escape."

Senech—" And it would be well if there were no time lost in seeking the protection of the British king."

Brendan—" When, O Ruadhan, will ye start ?"

Ruadhan—" Oh, the first thing in the morning."

The next morning, after seeing Ruadhan and Aedh Guaire set off for Ath Cliath Duibhlinne,† where they were to embark for Britain, Senech and Brendan took leave of the monks of Lothra and of each other and took their departure for their respective homes.

* Irish Sea.　　　　† Dublin.

An treas caibidil.

CHAPTER III.

An Casad.

THE RETURN.

WHEN Mac Conraidhe, the ceann-fedhna and his officers and men who, as we have seen, were entering the house by one door, just as its owner was escaping by the other, were able to realise all that happened in their absence, their grief and horror soon gave place to their official administrative duty. There lay the unfortunate Bacclomm on one of the *imdai*, surrounded by wax candles and by the servants of the house who were trying to discover whether the chief herald were really dead or not. These the ceann-fedhna ordered to be placed under immediate arrest, notwithstanding their loud protestations of innocence. Next he caused the house itself to be surrounded, lest anyone should escape; and as he was about to issue some other orders, dark shadows fell across the entrance, and in another moment the chief steward and a physician stood beside the corpse. The *liagh* (physician), after a very brief examination, declared life to be extinct. A Fenian politely informed the chief steward that he was a prisoner; but the chief steward now, for the first time, perceiving the position of his fellow-servants, without replying to his would-be captive, went up to the ceann-fedhna himself, and handed him a piece of parchment. He then called for more candles, but as none dared to stir, he was obliged to procure them himself. When he returned, Mac Conraidhe was reading the parchment by the light of the wax candles which surrounded the corpse. He looked up, and addressing the steward, said:

"This parchment sets forth the name and title of him who has perpetrated this fearful crime. Though it is tremulously written like the hand of a dying man, I am satisfied that it is in the handwriting of our late comrade, Bacclomm, chief herald of Eire. See, comrades, if ye can recognise the writing."

The officers and some of the men thus appealed to looked at the document, and one and all declared that they believed it to be the genuine handwriting of Bacclomm. Any difference that existed being easily accounted for by the weakened and dying state in which he was when he penned it. Some of them remarked that they did not think that anyone of that *trebhaire* (household) could have any possible means of knowing the handwriting of deceased."

"But did Bacclomm do this of himself, or didst thou suggest it to him? Tell us all about it, thou who wert present; thy fellow-servants declare they were all absent when it occurred. Is that true?"

"Yea, most noble ceann-fedhna," replied the steward, and then he went on to relate the whole occurrence from the arrival home of his master to their own return to the house; all that had passed between his master, himself, and the herald; the flaith's exit from the apartment, the herald recovering from the fainting fit, consequent upon the sword-cut which he had received, and finding himself still in his (the steward's) arms, he thanked him for the friendship he had shown him since his arrival at the house, and asked for parchment, pen, and ink, that he might exonerate himself (the steward) and the servants of the house from all blame in the matter; that he (the steward) then laid him on the *imda*, where he now lay dead; and having procured the writing materials, he supported him, while with difficulty and with many groans and gasps he penned the words which he hoped would clear the innocent from all imputation. He (the steward) then sent one of the servants, who, at this juncture had entered the house for the *sagart* (priest), who came in time, and another for the *liagh* (physician) who, being from home, the servant returned without him. After having given to the suffering herald all the restoratives that the house afforded, the latter at length died in his arms; and then, leaving the corpse to the care of the servant he himself went for the *liagh*, that though he could no longer give him relief, he would examine the body and declare the cause of death, as the law required.

The steward having concluded, Mac Conraidhe asked him where his master was to be found at this hour. But this question, simple though it was, struck a new chord in the heart of the steward, and he burst forth into lamentations and appeals for mercy for his unfortunate master. The other servants, who had been liberated from custody by order of Mac Conraidhe, joined their pleadings to those of the steward; but the ceann-fedhna, intimating that he should perform his duty, ordered a general search to be made. This was accordingly done, the Fianna not leaving a nook or cranny unexplored in all the houses of Aedh Guaire, including the Grianan itself, but all without avail; the flaith was nowhere to be found. The ceann-

fedhna, to assure himself that he could not escape from the
premises, went out and closely questioned all the men who surrounded the houses ; but they one and all declared solemnly
that no human being passed out from any point since they had
been put on guard. Suspicion now reverted again to the servants,
one of the officers affirming his belief that, though innocent of
the crime themselves, they had been guilty of aiding and abbet-
ting the escape of the real criminal, and that they ought to be
re-arrested on that charge. This was at once done by order of
the ceann-fedhna, who paid no heed to their protestations and
declarations of ignorance of the movements and whereabouts of
their master. He next despatched a courier post-haste to
Teamhair to inform King Diarmaid of the tragedy and treason
of that unfortunate day. Detachments of armed horsemen were
also sent hither and thither in search of the escaped flaith, notwithstanding the darkness and the lateness of the hour, the
ceann-fedhna regretting that he had not more men at his disposal. Late as it was, the news soon spread over the neighbourhood, and crowds of men and boys were soon on the scene, and
many remained all night. The next morning nearly the whole
tuath, men, women, and children crowded round the mansion.
One of the first things to be done was to bury the unfortunate
herald. In the early morning the Office of the Church was sung
over his remains ; now the *mna caointe* were wailing forth his
praises and his misfortune until a *fenn*, or funeral car, appeared
at the door. On this he was laid and carried amidst the throngs
of people to the nearest monastery, which was to be his resting-
place, at least for the present, for bringing him home was
entirely out of the question under existing circumstances. The
sad ceremony over, the ceann-fedhna and such of his officers
and men as remained to him, returned to the castle, followed by
the curious and awe-struck crowd. Towards noon, some of the
pursuivants returned without having obtained any trace of the
fugitive. As the day wore on other detachments returned with
as little success, after having scoured the whole country around,
and searched every house, great and small, not omitting the
churches and monasteries, for though they would not themselves
dare to take a criminal from the church's sanctuary, there was
no objection to their making the search when the fugitive was
not there.

Night brought with it the remainder of the scouring party
with the same story, though they had taken a wider range than
their companions had done. Next morning the courier returned from Teamhair with orders from the Ardrigh to the

ceann-fedhna to send off companies of his men to every part of
the kingdom of Connacht, and for himself and a small company
to return to Teamhair—the Spear of State to be borne by Lorcan,
the herald next in rank to the late Bacclomm. The courier likewise informed Mac Conraidhe that King Diarmaid, on hearing
his story, at once sent large companies of the Fianna in search
of Aedh Guaire through every part of the kingdoms of Midhe
(Meath), Laegean (Leinster), Mumhain (Munster), Ulladh (Ulster),
and also fresh contingents to Connacht (Connaught), who would
soon arive. Mac Conraidhe, having disposed of his men according to instructions, took his departure from the castle, which
he closed up, and brought home with him as prisoners the chief
steward and servants of Aedh Guaire ; Lorcan bearing the much-
abused Spear of State preceded the party. They left Ui
Maine, and crossing the Sionnain, passed through Athluain
(Athlone), and soon emerging on the Slighe Mór, or Eiscir
Riadha, rode along the great road until a little beyond Geisil,
they turned into the Slighe Dala, which brought them to Cluain-
Irared, where they were obliged to dismount in order to cross
the Boinn (Boyne). They were not much surprised to find
crowds at this point until they found themselves objects of
curiosity. It was evident they were expected. The news had
by this time been in everybody's mouth. With some difficulty
they got across, and before they were again mounted, the boatman contrived to whisper to Mac Conraidhe that he had something of importance to tell him, but not there. Mac Conraidhe
bade him come to Teamhair as soon as possible, and call upon
him. He then rode off at the head of his men, and arriving in
Teamhair, found the streets full, though it was nearly dark.
They all dismounted at the barracks, and Mac Conraidhe, after
making a hurried toilet, presented himself before King Diarmaid
in one of the sumptuous chambers of Teach Miodchuarta. The
king was seated near a blazing fire, regaling himself with cake
and wine, and having before him the new work of his Ardfileadh,
Amerghin Mac Amlaigh, which he was reading by the light of
wax candles in golden candlesticks, when Mac Conraidhe entered. It was a ponderous tome, entitled " The Dinseanchus,"*

---

* This celebrated work, as well as " The Book of Kells," and many other
works in prose and verse, of eminent Irish authors, were not noticed in the
seventh chapter of Part I., because they had not been written at the time our
story opened, though many, including those above-named, were written before
the date at which we shall conclude. Others during the remainder of the century,
and others again during the five centuries following. But the writer of this
tale endeavours to keep strict chronological order in the relation of everything
contained in it.

and was an etymological, historical, and topographical work, giving an account of the fortresses, raths, cities, plains, mountains, lakes, rivers, &c., of all the kingdoms of Eire! It was destined for the library of Mur Ollamhain for the use of the professors and students; and the colleges of Cluain-Irared, Cluain Mac Nois, Beanachor, Ardmacha, Daire, Ceannanus, Daermaegh, and all the other colleges of Eire, as well as other schools like Mur Ollamhain, were to be permitted to make copies for their own libraries.

"Well, Mac Conraidhe," said King Diarmaid, looking up from "The Dinseanchus," as the ceann-fedhna entered; "what is all this we hear concerning Aedh Guaire, lord of Ui Mainé? Is it true that he has killed our chief herald and insulted our royal Spear of State?"

"Yea, O King, it is, unfortuately, too true; but believe me, I am in no way to blame."

"No; where is Lorcan and the Spear?"

"He is coming, O Ardrigh."

Lorcan here entered, and bending, presented the Spear of Honour to the Ardrigh, who said unto him:

"We appoint thee to the place of thy late chief, Bacclomm, and We entrust Our royal spear to thy charge. Go leave it now in its accustomed place."

The new chief herald kissed the monarch's hand, and taking the spear again into his hands, backed out of the royal presence, after having been presented with a goblet of wine.

After he had left, King Diarmaid again turned to the ceann-fedhna and said:

"Thou wert not to blame, O Mac Conraidhe? Where, then, wert thou when the murder was committed?"

"All of us, save the chief herald, were over part of the demesne. We never even dreamed of such a calamity befalling us, O King."

"Aedh Guaire, we have been informed, was absent from home when ye arrived at his castle?"

"He was, O most High King of Eire; but his chief steward, who with the other servants we have brought prisoners to Teamhair, received us most kindly, and even himself offered to break the narrow door, with the aid of some of the servants, but Bacclomm ordered the Fianna to do so. We were most hospitably entertained, and everything seemed to be as agreeable there as elsewhere. We went for a stroll through the grounds, and knew nought of what had been done till our return, when we found Bacclomm a corpse, and Aedh Guaire fled."

" Then thou didst not see Aedh Guaire at all ?"

" Nay, most illustrious Ardrigh ; none of our party, save Bacclomm himself, saw the lord of Ui Mainé ; he must have escaped before we re-entered the castle."

" Well, we must forgive thee and thy comrades, as it appears ye were not to blame, and, moreover, thou hadst never had such a mishap before ; so let us pledge each other's health, and live in eternal friendship."

The king and the ceann-fedhna then quaffed the rich sparkling wine from the richly-chased golden goblets, after which the king said :

" But if we make allowances for thee and thy comrades, we shall know how to deal with the murderer of our herald. We will not leave a spot in Eire, or in Europe, or in the world, if need be, unexplored, until we find him and make him pay the penalty of his crime."

" But I forgot to tell thee, O King, the boatman who carried us across the river Boinn at Cluain-Irared whispered unto me that he had something of importance to tell me, but not there. I therefore appointed that he should come to my house to-night."

" Well, has he come ?"

" I know not, O High King, I have not yet been at home."

" Ah, we are keeping thee from thy family."

" I love my family much, but I must attend unto my duty. I ought to be satisfied that my sovereign is not angry with me."

" Now, Mac Conraidhe, that question has been settled, so let there be an end of it. What if thou wouldst send to thy house to see if the boatman hath come, and if so, We would like to see him."

Mac Conraidhe left the Ardrigh to fulfil this request, and despatching a messenger to his own house, he returned to his royal master. Soon the messenger returned, bringing with him the boatman, who had been waiting the return home of the ceann-fedhna. When the boatman was ushered into the king's presence, he did homage silently, till the king said :

" How art thou called, friend ?"

" Micheál (Michael), the boatman, they call me, O most illustrious Ardrigh na Erionn."

" The Ardrigh would know what is the information of which thou hast spoken," said the ceann-fedhna.

" Last night," replied Micheál, as I was about to put to my boat for the night, and retire to my humble cottage, a noble-looking horseman gallopped up to me and desired me to assist him in getting his horse into my corach, that I might row himself and the animal across the Sionnain, as there was no drawbridge at that point. Owing to thick heavy clouds which had all the previous part of the night, since darkness had set in, obscured the light of the moon, I could not recognise the noble wayfarer, and I did not know his voice, but just as we landed at the other side of the river, and while we were still getting the horse on land, by a temporary rent in a cloud, the clear silvery light of the full moon lit up for awhile every object, and revealed the features of the traveller."

"And that traveller was——"

"Aedh Guaire, lord of Ui Mainé."

"Ha!" exclaimed in one breath the Ardrigh and the ceann-fedhna. "We thought that was coming. But what didst thou then know of the cause of his flight?"

"I knew nought whatever, O King, nor did I even suspect anything. It is not at all an unusual thing for travellers to cross the rivers at that hour and in similar manner, some of whom we know, and some of whom we do not know. The lord of Ui Mainé was not unknown to me; but it was not till afterwards that I knew the cause of his journey that night, and I considered it my duty to my country and my sovereign to tell what I knew, and thus, as far as I could, put justice upon the right track."

"Thou art a good and loyal man, O Micheál, and thou shalt be well rewarded," said King Diarmaid.

"Ten thousand thanks to thee, O King, and as many blessings on thee and on thy posterity."

"Did Aedh Guaire say aught to thee, O Micheál?" asked Mac Conraidhe.

"Nothing whatever, O noble flaith, save with reference to his passage, nor have I seen or heard aught of him since then."

"Where wilt thou stop for the night?" asked Mac Conraidhe, "Hast thou any friends in the city?"

"None now, oh, excellent flaith, but I will stop in the nearest biadtach."

"Good, and thou needest not go till We tell thee; We may want thee for a witness, but thou shalt not suffer any loss, We will more than repay thee," were the parting words of the Ardrigh before dismissing the faithful and contented Micheál.

After he had left, Diarmaid and Mac Conraidhe exchanged a few more words about the matter in hand, in which it was resolved to send special envoys to Muscraidhe (Muskerry) and the country about; though that territory had been included in the

general search of Mumhain (Munster), and moreover it was by
no means certain that Aedh Guaire was still there or in any other
part of the kingdom of Mumhain. This settled, the ceann-
fedhna took leave of his royal master, and returned to the bosom
of his family, while the Ardrigh soon again became lost in the
pages of "The Dinseachus," which occupied him until his personal
domestics appeared to escort him to the state bedchamber to
rest for the night after the toils and cares of his kingly office
during the day.

***

An ceatramaᵈ caibroil.

CHAPTER IV.

poll Ruaᵈain.

RUADHAN'S PIT.

THE next morning before the monarch arose, he was informed
that a courier had arrived from Muscraidhe.

" From Muscraidhe ?" cried the Ardrigh ; " where is he ?"

" He is below, and beareth important news, O King."

" News from Muscraidhe !" exclaimed the king, springing
up, and more by signs than by words, ordering his attendants to
be expeditious about his toilet. He desired the courier to be
shown up, and when that worthy entered the magnificent apartment, Diarmaid was already dressed and impatient for his
appearance, who at once handed a parchment he held in his
hand, lowly bending before the impatient king.

As Diarmaid read to himself the despatch, he appeared every
moment growing more and more enraged, until he had finished
reading, when he suddenly flung it beneath his feet and stamped
upon it furiously. As soon as he could command his voice, he
cried to his attendants :

" Send for the British Ambassador. Do ye hear ? Let the
British Ambassador be brought hither immediately. Fly now."

The terrified attendants all rushed to fulfil the orders of the
irate king, and in their haste they nearly knocked down the
courier, who stood in their way. This attracted the notice of
the Ardrigh, and he exclaimed :

" Why standest thou there in the way ?"

" I hope my king is not angry with me," said the courier,
deprecatingly.

"No, no, We are not angry with *thee*, but if thou standest there looking at Us in that manner much longer, We shall——"

But the courier was gone.

Diarmaid paced furiously up and down the state bedchamber, thinking every moment an hour until the arrival of the British Ambassador. When at last that foreign delegate appeared, trembling from head to foot, and dreading, he knew not what, the haughty monarch of Eire at once opened fire:

"Thou hast heard of the fate of our chief herald?"

"Oh, yes, most illustrious Ardrigh; all are by this time aware of the facts of that unfortunate occurrence."

"Art thou aware of the fact of the escape of the Chief of Ui Mainé?"

"Yea, O High King."

"Art thou aware of whither he has gone?"

"Nay, how should I know, O King."

"Art thou sure?"

"As sure as of my own existence, O dread Monarch."

"Beware now. Ná ceil an fhirin.*"

"I know not what I am to beware of, and I have nothing to conceal, O King," replied the now thoroughly frightened Briton."

"Then thou knowest nothing whatever of the whereabouts of Aedh Guaire, Lord of Ui Mainé."

"Nothing whatever, believe me, O most royal Monarch."

"Then We will tell thee what this despatch has told Us," said King Diarmaid, indicating with his foot that document: "Aedh Guaire escaped over the Sionnain into Muscradhe in Oir Mumhain,† and sought out his cousin, Senech, who is bishop of that territory. Senech, doubting the sufficiency of his own sanctuary, brought the culprit to their common uncle, who happens to be the Abbot Ruadhan of Lothra, who never bore us any affection, and is the most disloyal and disaffected of our subjects. Well, Ruadhan, in his turn, doubting, and very justly, our recognition of his right to shield public violators of the law, and rebels against our authority, thought proper to bring his nephew over to Britain, and place him under the protection of the British King, and they set out from his monastery in presence of his monks, of Senech, the Bishop of Muscraidhe, and of Brendan, the Abbot of Birr, from whom We expected better. Now, dost thou still insist that thou didst know nothing of all these proceedings, or that thou wert not consulted or appealed to in any way about the matter?"

* Conceal not the truth.   † East Munster, or Ormond (Lower).

" I assure thee, most solemnly, O King, that this is the first I have heard of the occurrence; but I have long been aware that a warm friendship exists between the Abbot of Lothra, and my royal master, the King of Britain."

" Ah! are We to understand then that the friendship of any of our subjects for thy master means rebellion and disaffection towards Ourselves; and that the King of Britain aids and shelters those who violate the laws and institutions of Eire ?"

" Oh, no, no; most excellent Ardrigh of Eire, my beloved master appreciates much the honour of being considered the friend and brother of so mighty and powerful a monarch as thyself; and feels too grateful for the many favours and benefits which this country has bestowed upon Britain, to do aught to injure Eire, or offend her King."

" Well, we would prove thy words. Go now and send word at once to thy master, the King of Britain, to deliver up to Us Aedh Guaire, the Chief of Ui Mainé, without any delay; and thou mayest inform him that should he refuse to do so, We, ourselves, with all our forces, will go over to him, and destroy his kingdom, and remain there until we have found the fugitive from justice. So be quick now, and let us have a speedy answer."

The British Ambassador, glad to escape on any terms, lost no time in leaving the royal presence, and hastened to put into execution the orders he had received; and when, a few days later, he once more appeared in the dreaded presence of the Monarch of Teamhair, it was with a calmer expression and a lighter heart, for he brought to King Diarmaid the news that the British King had yielded up the culprit to save his kingdom from invasion; though not to compromise his friendship with the Abbot of Lothra, it was to him that he had sent back the lord of Ui Mainé, as it was from him he had received the charge. Diarmaid was satisfied with this, knowing that any other course would be treachery, and accordingly he dismissed the ambassador most graciously.

He then called together his bodyguard and his " *Ten*," and ordering the carbads for himself and his suite, prepared to set out for Lothra. Along they dashed on the Slighe Dala, stopping at this biadtach and at that, at one noble rath or another, for rest and refreshment, and resumed their journey until at length they turned from the Slighe Dala into a bealach, which led in a westerly direction to Lothra. Arrived at some little distance from the monastery, King Diarmaid desired his ara (charioteer) to descend and go to the monastery. He thought that that person- age would attract less attention than any of the members of his

suite or his guards. The ara accordingly having received instructions as to how he was to act, walked up to the monastery
and entered. He soon returned, however, and informed the
monarch that he could see none but the Abbot Ruadhan himself, who sat in his own chair. King Diarmaid hearing this,
bade all his attendants to remain where they were, he, himself,
going up to the monastery, and entering saw the abbot in the
place his ara (charioteer) had named, that is, in his own accustomed chair or seat, where he used to say his prayers. He was
in the act of reading when the Ardrigh entered. He rose, and
they cooly saluted each other. Then Diarmaid, conscious that
Ruadhan would not tell a falsehood, asked him where Aedh Guaire
was, to which Ruadhan replied :

"I know not where he is, if he be not where thou standest."

Diarmaid, thinking the abbot spoke in jest, left the monastery
and returned to the guards and the "*Ten;*" he related to them
what had occurred, but added, that as he came along the road,
he had been thinking over the words of the abbot, and on
second consideration he believed that Ruadhan spoke not
in jest, but that there was some meaning in his words. The
"*Ten*" thought so too, and one of them—the brehon—
suggested that a man should be sent to dig under the spot where
the king had stood. At this moment a man with a pickaxe in
his hand passed near to where they were. He was looking
curiously to see who they were, when he was hailed by one of
the guards at the command of Diarmaid. When he came up,
the king asked him his name ; he replied his name was Donnan.
The king then desired him to come with him, and they returned
back towards the monastery. It was now nearly dusk, and as
Diarmaid neared the door he saw a light. On entering, he
found that this light was held by a servant, who was in the act
of visiting Aedh Guaire. This man, in fact, was the only one to
whom Ruadhan confided the secret of his nephew's hiding-
place. He it was who brought him his meals at the hours of
refection, and otherwise attended to him. Ruadhan came in at
this moment, but Diarmaid ordered Donnan to dig a hole with
his pickaxe, at the same time indicating the spot where he
stood. Donnan lifted his pickaxe and struck with all his
might.

"Well," said the king, "what aileth thee, O Donnan ?
Why leanest thou thus on thy pickaxe ? It waxeth late. Hurry
with thy work and let us begone."

Donnan slowly raised himself up, and showed to the astonished monarch his trembling hands, which seemed as if struck

with the palsy. He groaned in anguish, and then for the first time perceiving the Abbot Ruadhan, he fell on his knees before him and cried for mercy, and besought Ruadhan for forgiveness and remission, with his benediction, which Ruadhan accordingly gave him. He next begged permission to remain in the monastery, and to take the habit of a monk. This permission was also granted. And now, Ruadhan perceiving the uncompromising determination of King Diarmaid, called for his bronze bell. A brother having brought it to him, he sounded it, and then the *giolla* (servant) aforesaid, brought Aedh Guaire forth from the cave below. Diarmaid had previously gone to the door, and beckoned to his followers, who by this time were at the house, and now he gave Aedh Guaire into the custody of his guards, and late as it was, ordered the immediate departure of the whole party for Teamhair. Bidding a cold adieu to Ruadhan, the cavalcade set out with Diarmaid at their head. His ara had requested permission to remain with Ruadhan, but the king refused for the present, telling him that when he should have left him at Teamhair he might return if he chose. When they had fairly left what they now called Poll Ruadhain, or Ruadhan's Pit, and were going full speed along the Bealach Muscraidhe, Ruadhan, accompanied by a few of his monks, left the monastery also, and went in the direction of Birr. Arrived there, he informed his friend the Abbot Brendan of what had occurred, and requested of him to go with him to Teamhair to see that no harm befell their friend Aedh Guaire. Brendan complied, and taking also some of his monks, they set off in pursuit of the royal party, whom they overtook at a biadtach, where all remained during the night, and next morning they resumed their journey to Teamhair.

ᚐn cuiᵹeᚐᐁ ċᚐibᚏóiƚ.

CHAPTER V.

mᚐƚƚuᵹᚐᐁ nᚐ Ceᚐṁᚏᚐċ.

THE CURSING OF TARA.

OWING to many stoppages which they made on the way it was near sundown when the royal party arrived in the Cathair Teamhrach. The citizens went out to meet them, gratified that the dignity of their sovereign and the laws of their country were about to be vindicated. King Diarmaid was touched by

the loyalty of his people, and graciously returned their salutations. The prisoner was removed to the Carcair na n-Giall,
or Prison of the Hostages, where his servants already were ; the
guards dismounted and the " *Tin* " descended from their
chariots, and with the Ardrigh entered Teach Miodchuarta. The
people were about to disperse when they found that another
procession was entering the city. This latter party that now
excited the curiosity of the people, proved to be the Abbots
Ruadhan and Brendan, together with some of their monks and
many who had joined them on the way. They rang their bells
which they held in their hands, and with the singing of psalms,
entered the city, and proceeded at once to the Rath-na-Sean-
naidh, which, with the Church, stood between Rath na Righ
and Teach Miodchuarta. After spending some time here the
king sent for them, and accordingly they went to Teach Miodchuarta, and entered the great Banqueting Hall, where the
king was about to sup with his nobles. They thought this a
sign of peace ; so when supper was over they petitioned for
the release of Aedh Guaire ; but their petition was refused,
Diarmaid remaining as inflexible as ever. The party broke up
and all retired to rest.

   Next morning Ruadhan, Brendan, and those who came with
them again craved an interview with the Ardrigh, which being
granted they renewed their petitions for the release of their
friend ; but Diarmaid informed them that his mind was un-
changed, and expressed surprise that their sacred cloth should
have been dishonoured by harbouring one who had committed
such a crime as to murder his (the king's) chief herald, who was
employed in the execution of his instructions, and then coming
here to keep the whole court awake all night by their loud praying and singing.

   " Why speakest thou thus, O King ?" asked Ruadhan; "have
we kept thee awake last night ?"

   " Yea, O Ruadhan, or rather, the noise of your chanting
awoke me from a heavy sleep; but, in truth, although I mention the fact, I can scarcely say that I regret it, for it cut short a
frightful dream."

   " And what was the dream that we so disturbed, O Diarmaid ?"
asked Brendan.

   " I will tell thee, O Brendan. About midnight, being heavily
asleep, I dreamed that I saw a great tree that rooted deeply into
the earth, whose lofty top and branches were so high and broad
that they came near the clouds of heaven, and I saw one
hundred and fifty men about the tree, with one hundred and fifty

broad-mouthed, sharp axes, cutting the tree, and when it was cut, when it fell to the earth, the great noise that it made at the time of the falling thereof, awoke me from sleep and from the dream ; and immediately the notes of thy choir. singing psalms in concert in the church, filled mine ears."

"Wouldst thou, O Diarmaid, know the meaning of thy dream ?" said Ruadhan, "and wouldst thou hear the construction, exposition, and interpretation thereof ?"

"Yea, O Ruadhan, I would know thy reading of it," said the Ardrigh.

"Well, the great tree," said Ruadhan, "strongly rooted in the earth, and branched abroad, so that it reached to the very firmament, is thyself, O Diarmaid, whose power is over all Eire; then the hundred and fifty men, with the hundred and fifty sharp, broad-mouthed axes, cutting the tree, represents ourselves chanting the hundred and fifty psalms of David, that will cut thee from the very roots to thy destruction, that so thou mayest fall for ever if thou dost not grant our petition, and release unto us Aedh Guaire, Chief of Ui Mainé."

During this exposition of his dream, King Diarmaid gradually darkened, becoming every moment more visibly incensed, and struggling to restrain his rising choler ; but the concluding threat fairly upset his equilibrium, and made him forget at once his own dignity and the sacred character of his adversaries and tormentors. In this condition he gave a final refusal. Ruadhan and Brendan then left him, taking their bells with them. He grew livid with rage, stamped his feet, and began to pace up and down the hall ; he was incapable of uttering a word. At last when a few strides enabled him to command his utterance, he threw up his hands and exclaimed, apostrophising himself:

"Great Heavens! was there ever before on earth such a monarch as my unhappy self ? Insulted and threatened in mine own palace by disloyal subjects, and all because I have dared to attempt to fulfil the duties and to discharge the responsibilities of my office. And if I dare to remonstrate, I shall be denounced to my people as a foe to the Church ; for these men consider themselves above me by virtue of their office. Is this Christianity ? No, it is not. Emphatically, no. It is not necessary for the salvation of souls that the time-honoured laws and institutions of the country should be overturned and trampled upon, and the administration of justice defeated and treated with contempt, just because the relatives and friends of a violator of the law happen to be dignitaries of the Church, and as such claim to govern their sovereign, and threaten him with

destruction if he dare to disobey.   No; that is not religion, and
I will treat such conduct as it deserves, and I shall use the
power with which the God of Heaven has invested me, for the
purposes for which He gave it—the protection of my people;
the honour, happiness. and prosperity of my country ; ay, and
the real good of the Church itself.   These men, for the sake of
their own personal feelings, natural though they be, and for an
imaginary and temporary triumph for the Church, would destroy
their country.   But should they succeed, and thus leave the
kingdom a prey to any foreign barbarian who may set a covetous
eye on Eire, and count upon the Church as an ally who will
receive them with open arms, what then becomes of the Church
itself ?   Why, it too will become the prey of the same barbarians, who will first use it and then abuse it.   Ah ! come what
will, the Church stands or falls—temporally of course, and in its
administrative liberty—with Eire.   I shall do my duty."

While the Ardrigh thus communed with himself, Ruadhan
and Brendan were astonishing and striking terror into the
people without.

From the moment they had left the angry monarch, they
commenced ringing their bells and singing psalms, going in
turn through all the buildings on Druim Aoibhin, cursing each
place.   None durst interfere lest they should fall under the displeasure of the abbots.   When they had cursed these places,
they then went without, and walked round the nine ramparts
which surrounded all the royal buildings, ringing their bells and
cursing as they went.   Then they descended the hill, and again
went all round about it, ringing and cursing in like manner, in
the presence of thousands of the terrified people of all classes
who had congregated on hearing the unusual sounds, and who
now stood by, brave, strong men as multitudes of them were, in
mute helplessness and hopeless despair.   They were overwhelmed by the misfortune which had so suddenly come upon
themselves and upon their country.   Oh, how they wished at
that moment that their beloved Teamhair was besieged by all
the countries of Europe at once !   How they would defend it !
How all the chivalrous valour of the great Fenian army would
be brought out on such an occasion !   How they would fight
their myriad enemies against overwhelming odds, until there
was not a man left to acknowledge defeat !   But there they were
with their brave hearts and strong arms, supplemented by the
most approved implements of warfare, utterly powerless against
two men, their own countrymen too, who, wielding the spiritual
power, invoked curses and maledictions upon their renowned

and much-prized Teamhair, the capital, too, and the supreme
seat of the power and the glory of their country. And they
never doubted the efficacy of the prayers, good or bad, of their
spiritual pastors and their temporal foes. They conjured up
before their mind's eye all the consequences of this terrible day.
They looked at the many groups of noble buildings that adorned
the beautiful hill, and fancied they saw them cold and deserted
looking, and then one by one crumbling away and falling into
decay, until at length it looked a desolate, bare hill, with the
indistinct outlines of a strange looking building such as they
had never seen, and which looked like a religious edifice of
some sort they knew not what. Not like a druidical temple, nor
yet like any Christian edifice that they had ever seen. Then
they looked round on the city itself and they imagined that the
houses had all disappeared, as if swallowed up in the earth.
Where were all the warehouses and stores and workshops; all
the magnificent raths and duns of the nobility and gentry; all
the flourishing farms and comfortable cottages? Where were
the chariots and carts and all the traffic and merchandize of
Teamhair? Where the foreign merchants? and where the
native population? Where? where? Oh! what is that?
What strangers are those, now from the north and again from
the east, that carry fire and sword through the land? and those
last bring with them the Church's certificate; and the Church's
children in Eire are commanded to rebel against their native
princes, and to receive on bended knees the masters which the
chief of the church has appointed to rule them. And now, what
is this: rivers of blood deluge the land; the children of the
Gaedhal are] murdered in hundreds of thousands; the heavens
are darkened by the fumes of black smoke, and again lit up by
lurid glare of blazing churches and monasteries; and the groans
of dying abbots, monks, priests, and nuns, pierce the skies, as
their souls are wrenched from their bodies, the hapless victims
of the Church's triumph over Eire. But the hapless citizens of
Teamhair all at once awoke from their frightful day-dream.
Their monarch, their beloved monarch, now in his misfortune,
dearer than ever, emerges from Teach Miodchuarta, and the
sight of him brings them again to a sense of their surroundings.
The unfortunate monarch, who had interrupted his colloquy
with himself, and had witnessed this terrible scene from the windows of the great hall, now tottered rather than walked towards
them; large tears coursed down his pale cheeks, and his whole
expression was so heart-broken that his generous people—ay,
and even those who had up to this been his foes, now forgot

their own sorrows in witnessing the woe of their now idolized monarch. They made an attempt to cheer him, but, ah! what a miserable failure! Instead of the hearty, ringing, Irish cheers, which heretofore had greeted him, his ears were now horrified to hear a weak, faltering, unhuman sound, as if all of his people who were there assembled, were in the agonies of death. At first it startled him as the thought struck him that they too had abandoned him in his hour of need; but a glance all round and he read the truth. They were as broken-hearted as himself, and he knew in that moment that adversity had drawn them more closely together.

Ruadhan and Brendan had by this time come round again to the eastern side of the hill, and towards them the Ardrigh bent his steps. "But they, seeing him, turned towards him, and first ringing their bells* vigorously, they stood before him and cursed himself and his posterity, his city and hill of Teamhair, and prayed God that no king or queen ever again would or could dwell there, and that it should be waste for ever, without court or palace."

As this malediction fell from the lips of the abbots a great cry of anguish went up from the multitude, for they regarded it—and, oh, how justly!—as a curse invoked upon them also, and upon their children and their posterity. But Diarmaid, seeing the utter prostration of the first city of the kingdom at the feet of these foes of the State, and the people's evident belief that all that had been invoked would come to pass, exclaimed:

"Well, God forgive thee, O Ruadhan, and thou O Brendan, for this thing that ye have done, and may He restore Teamhair to her pristine glory ere your successors have cause to curse in their turn your rebellious conduct to-day."

Ruadhan and Brendan—"We are not rebels, O Diarmaid; our power is over all the earth; but thou hast rebelled against us, and thou hast despised the Church's privileges."

Diarmaid then said: "I defend the justice of the nation, that in every place there may be peace; but ye encourage and defend evil; ye shall receive the punishment of blood from the Lord; for in all Eire thy parish shall first fail, and depart from thee."

Ruadhan replied: "Thy kingdom shall first fail, and none of thy race shall hereafter reign."

---

* *St. Ruadhan.*—"In collection of Dr. Petrie there is a bronze bell, which he states to have been found in the holy well of Lothra, in Ormond, and which there is ground for believing, is the bell which St. Ruadhan of Lothra rang as he made the circuit of Tara, when he cursed that ancient residence of its Irish monarch in the sixth century, after which it was deserted."— *O'Curry.*

The king said: "Thy place shall be empty, and swine dwelling in it; with their snouts they shall upturn it."

Ruadhan replied: "The city of Teamhair shall first be un-inhabited many hundred years, and hereafter remain without a dwelling."

The Ardrigh answered: "Thy body shall suffer mutilation, and one of thy members shall perish; for thine eyes being put out thou shalt not see light."

Ruadhan said: "Thy body also shall be butchered by thy enemies, and thy limbs shall be ignominiously dismembered."

The King replied: "A fierce boar with his tooth shall undermine thy buildings."

Ruadhan replied: "Thy thigh shall not be buried in the same place with thy body, but a man shall cast it into mire."

Then King Diarmaid said to them: "Ye defend iniquity, and I virtue, ye disturb my kingdom; however, God favours ye more than He does me. Go, therefore, take away your man, and pay a ransom for him."

Ruadhan said: "It is well; but if thou hadst said so before, thy city, thyself, and thy posterity would have been saved from the curse of the Church."

Diarmaid—"From the curses of thee and thy friend there, thou meanest."

Ruadhan—"Art thou going to release unto us Aedh Guaire?"

Diarmaid—"Yea, when thou hast procured the ransom."

Ruadhan—"Then I shall send for it at once."

The Ardrigh then saluting his people, entered again into the palace, accompanied by his nobles. Ruadhan, Brendan, and the other monks went into the Rath-na-Sennaidh to deliberate on the course to be pursued. The result was that they sent some of their party back to Poll Ruadhain for thirty horses, to present to the Ardrigh as a ransom for Aedh Guaire.

The people returned to their homes with very different feelings and opinions regarding the release of the criminal. Some were glad that he was to be set free, because he was under the protection of the Church, and they were of opinion that the Church and not the State ought to have the regulation of such affairs. Others held a contrary opinion, but still approved of what had been resolved upon, in the hope that the undeserved clemency /of the king would induce the two abbots to relent in their turn, and absolve the king, his children, the royal hill and city from the curses they had invoked upon them, and to substitute in their stead heavenly blessings. Another class thought nothing of all this, but were angry with the

Ardrigh for letting the delinquent off so easily, or for allowing himself to be so easily frightened from the discharge of his duty to his country and his subjects by the curses of angry, proud, interested ecclesiastics, as they termed the two abbots. Others, again, there were who were very much inclined to turn out, and by main force prevent, in spite of the Ardrigh himself, the escape of the murderer. But even some of these, though they would have faced any danger of the flesh, however overwhelming it might be, shrank within themselves when they reflected that their adversary was the spiritual power, and that the more pious of their fellow-citizens and fellow-countrymen, who were by far the most numerous, would sacrifice themselves, their children, and their country in defence of even the temporal power and glory of their Church. For some days the unhappy affair was discussed in all its bearings and probable consequences, by all classes of the people. The aire class, that is the nobility and gentry, discussed it within their manorial halls, or in their as-semblies. They wondered what consequences the destruction of Teamhair would bring to their children and their children's children. Would it reduce them from their high estate to middle or even humble life ? What would be their position in future times ? The merchants, traders, and artificers talked it over with each other, with their customers and with the foreign merchants, with whom they held commerce. They feared it would destroy their trade, manufactures, and commercial enter-prise. The farmers of all classes, rich and poor, trembled for their own fate, for they should share the common doom. The labourers, cottiers, servants, &c., dreaded the misfortune of their employers, which was certain to bring misery and beggary on themselves. The foreign slaves knew that if their masters and mistresses were obliged to sell them they would be carried off to barbarous countries, where they would be cruelly treated, and they felt most of all others incensed against the relentless abbots. The foreign merchants and traders saw the finest market in Europe for their wares, and the mart whence they were in the habit of supplying the rest of the world, with goods of priceless value and unique workmanship, about to be wrested from their grasp and torn from its high pinnacle of unrivalled commercial glory. But of what avail were all these repinings and lamentations ? What care Ruadhan and Brendan for their trade and commerce or any such worldly interests. They were far above such sordid pursuits. Neither cared they for the mere worldly interests of their own countrymen and countrywomen of any rank, degree, or calling. This their victims realized to its fullest extent, and so they talked, and grieved, and brooded over the coming evil, until the arrival in Teamhair of the ransom for Aedh Guaire. When the news spread the people again assembled around Tulach Aoibhin to see the ransom. But when thirty splendid horses of a hyacinth colour, and admirably shaped, met their gaze, none could restrain their admiration. When the Ardrigh, who was a great connoisseur of horses, came out to see them he expressed himself highly pleased with them. The Abbot Brendan suggested that they might be tried; thereupon Diarmaid appointed a day for a horse race. This excitement afforded a temporary distraction to the stricken king and people ; so on the appointed morning they all repaired in their gayest attire to the racecourse, which was about a mile from the Delightful Hill, to the west. Here flocked thousands of people, citizens and country people, on foot. Here came streams of carbads of all descriptions, from the gilt and highly ornamented four-horse carbads of the grandees down to the humblest made, to suit the position or the means of those who could have such a luxury, only at the least possible cost. Others came on horseback. Multitudes on foot. The Ardrigh and all his court came in state, and took up their position on the grand stand, surrounded by the nobility of both sexes. The Abbots Ruadhan and Brendan and their monks did not disdain to be present on this particular occasion. The horses were soon on the ground, those which had come from Poll Ruadhan and those they were to compete with. Their riders had donned their uniform, and were distinguished from each other by the different colours. Everything was in readiness and the race began. All was now excitement and expectation. The magnificent trained horses of Teamhair and the surrounding Tuaths which had before won many a race, were now put into competition with the thirty strange horses from Lothra, and they appeared to know what was expected from them. Many people observed, as they recognised their old favourites that they had never raced so well before. But now the hyacinth coloured horses, one after another attracted attention; their high mettle and remarkable velocity, as they flew round and round, called forth the plaudits of the assembly, and by the time the whole thirty were tried, as well as the other horses which competed with them, the people not only awarded the prize to the beautiful hyacinth horses, but they were heartily tired of their sport. The races had been going on for three days, and at the end of the third day the king expressed to the Abbot Ruadhan his satisfaction at the beautiful colour and forms of the thirty horses, and their spirited mettle,

and extraordinary swiftness, of the ransom he had offered for
Aedh Guaire, and which he (the king) would accept, and would
forthwith enlarge the prisoner. Then he ordered Aedh Guaire
and all his servants to be handed over to the Abbot Ruadhan,
who with Brendan, their monks, and their newly enlarged clients,
prepared at once to take their departure from Teamhair. As
they were setting off, King Diarmaid asked them if they would
not revoke their curse, as he had set free the culprit ; but Ruadhan replied that he (the king) had got a good ransom for him.

"Then," said the king, "Teamhair is cursed for nothing !"

"Nay," said Ruadhan, "not for nothing; Teamhair and thyself are cursed for thy obstinacy and disrespect towards the
Church. We cannot revoke it.

"Rather ye *will* not," said the king bitterly, and he turned away.

But now the people crowded around the unbending abbots,
and they cried for mercy on themselves and on their children ;
but the Abbot Brendan reminded them that they had not been
cursed, only Diarmaid and his posterity, and the palaces and
hill of Teamhair; but they cried out that the destruction of the
royal seat, and of their ancient line of kings, involved their own
ruin, and that whatever fate befell their monarch and his royal
residence would also fall upon them and upon their city. But
the Abbot Ruadhan, looking down upon them from the height of
his seven feet, told the miserable multitude of nobles and people,
that what had been done had been done ; that Teamhair and
the Ardrigh had been cursed, and that cursed they should remain.
He then entered his carbad, his companions entered theirs, and
the unforgiving and unmerciful representatives of the forgiving
and merciful Jesus of Nazareth, drove triumphantly through the
southern side of the city, and by the Slighe Dala, off to Poll
Ruadhan of Lothra. Micheál, the boatman, not being now
needed was well rewarded, and allowed at once to return to his
family, who were made prosperous for life by the bounty of the
Ardrigh.

ᴀn ᴄ-ѕeιѕeᴀᴅ́ ċᴀιbιᴅιᴌ.

CHAPTER VI.

Cuᴀpc Ꮁιᴣᴀṁᴀιᴌ ᴀᴣυp ᴅeιpe.

A ROYAL VISITATION AND A CATASTROPHE.

For two years after the events recorded in the foregoing chapter things went smoothly enough at Teamhair. Immediately after the departure of Ruadhan and his party, Diarmaid's people had petitioned him not to desert Teamhair, but to continue to live amongst them. This being in accord with his own views and will, as well as his sense of duty to his subjects and to the laws of his country, he most emphatically promised to do ; and that promise he was resolved to keep. As yet there was no signs of evil effects from the ecclesiastical curses. Teamhair was still the great emporium of the trade and commerce of Eire and of Europe. Mur Ollamhain, still the prime university of the nation ; the royal groups of buildings, the same as ever ; Teach Miodchuarta was still the great meeting-place of the States General. All the pomp and state of royalty Diarmaid upheld in the very minutest particulars, and his constant passing to and fro through the city ensured the most scrupulous regard amongst his people for the good order, cleanliness, and beauty of all the appliances of private and public life. Nor did he forget to visit occasionally, either personally or by deputation, the more distant parts of his dominions. The affair of Aedh Guaire did not deter him from performing so necessary a part of his duty, though that disastrous occurrence produced very different effects upon different people. The eyes of some were opened to the danger of their country, of disobedience to its laws, and the absurdity of seeking the protection of the Church from the consequences of crime ; thus embroiling Church and State in warfare and enmity for the sake of every individual criminal. Others, however, hailed it as the harbinger of universal liberty, whereby every man would be his own sovereign, with only his own will for law, whereby he could defy and make war upon king and country, kill anyone who dared to execute the laws of the kingdom, and be himself secure from outraged justice.

Diarmaid, however, had his own opinion of his position, his privileges, and his duties, and though weighed down with his

20

misfortunes, he determined, with the help of that God who had ordained the higher powers, to continue to do what he and his predecessors had done for ages. He was now about to go himself on one of these royal visitations, righthand-wise round Eire. The people assembled, as was their wont, to see him off. The guards were mounted and in due order. The carbads were one by one brought into the courtyard before Teach Miodchuarta, and into these each of the " *Ten*," entered. At last the royal carbad appeared. It was drawn by four of the beautiful hyacinth coloured horses, which had been the ransom of Aedh Guaire. Their necks were now adorned with the *mael lann*, or necklace, of gold, having attached to it all round little bells of gold. Their bits were also of gold, also their buckles, rings, and other such things necessary to the harness. The harness itself was of purple-dyed leather, gorgeously gilt. The bridle was richly gilt also, and ornamented with cruan and carbuncle. The ara (charioteer) was arrayed in his yellow vest and triubhis, silver shoes, crimson cochall, confined at the throat by a golden brooch ; a gipne, or golden band, confined the hair and kept it back from the forehead. The hair itself was plaited and hung down behind; and the *tinne*, or quadrangular cap, completed his outfit.

The chariot itself was built of the beautiful arbutus wood of the territory around Loch Leine (Killarney). It was highly polished and inlaid with plates of gold, representing the Sunburst, harps, shamrocks, &c. The upholstery was in keeping. The interior, back, and the cushions of the seat were stuffed with swansdown, and covered with rich tartan satin, comprising the seven hues. The drapery and curtains matched ; the curtains, which hung down on each side, and could be drawn all round at pleasure, being lined with green silk. They were drawn by thick, twisted golden cord, with tassels of same at ends. A plume of peacock's feathers adorned the summit of the canopy. The wheels, poles, and other metal work were of red bronze gilt and ornamented.

The Ardrigh emerged from the palace, and as he did so, was greeted with acclamations by the crowd. But can it be indeed King Diarmaid ? Can that care-worn, emaciated-looking man be indeed the handsome, stately, majestic-looking personage whom we have been endeavouring to follow through all the joys and sorrows, the glories and the humiliations of his chequered career ? What a change ! But two years have passed since one of the greatest misfortunes of his life had come upon him, and he has since then aged twenty years. Though still in the prime of life, his hair—his once beautiful long, glossy, nut-brown hair, is grey from care and sorrow alone. His once plump, rosy cheeks are pale and hollowed. Care sits upon his brow. His once straight and courtly form is bent. His once firm elastic step is now tottering under the weight of his body, as leaning upon the arm of his son, Aedh Slainé, he walks from the palace door to the royal carbad, and mounts into its luxurious seat. He is attired in tartan satin vest, triubhis of very fine textured green lamb's wool ; around one leg the ór-nasg, golden ornamented shoes, a mantle of royal purple, with fringe of gold thread, and fastened with his royal roth croi of gold; a green and gold *barread* covers his head; his golden torc hangs around his neck, a golden jewel-hilted sword hangs by his side. Aedh Slainé places him comfortably, and then takes the rug, which is composed of the wings and feathers of many-coloured birds, lined with green silk, tucks it carefully around his father's knees; then they take a parting embrace, and Aedh Slainé descends, after having performed his self-imposed task of filial devotion, which he would allow no one else to perform; and immediately his brother, Colman Beg, who had run out for the purpose, gets into the carbad for one more parting kiss from his father. Diarmaid blesses him, as he has blessed his brother, and the youth again descends, while the Ardrigh prays fervently to the God of Mercies that a father's blessing may more than counterbalance an abbot's curse. The ara gave rein to the horses, and the royal carbad drove out of the courtyard, and was surrounded by the carbads of the " *Ten*," which, with their occupants, awaited their leader. These chariots resembled in form the royal one, save that they were not quite so magnificent. They were mostly painted, one being black, another yellow, another green, and so on, but all were brilliantly polished, and were more or less gilt ; the wheels and poles of bronze-gilt ; the coverings and hangings were of silk or of satin, but of one colour, as blue, green, crimson, yellow, &c.; the plumes were of black or white ostrich feathers; the horses and their trappings in keeping with the rest. All now got into order, and a portion of the royal Fenian bodyguard led the way, preceded by Lorcan, as chief herald, bearing the Spear of State. The air was rent with the cheers that followed the royal cortege—cheers most consoling to the heart of the poor king, who acknowledged them with the most grateful and friendly salutations.

Taking the southern part of the city, they proceed on their way, first visiting that part of the kingdom of Midhe ; then on through all the kingdom of Lagean, meeting everywhere the most

cordial reception. In time they entered the kingdom of Mumhain, where they were also very well received, save in these
places where the Abbot Ruadhan's influence prevailed. Even
there the people were divided; still nothing of any moment
occurred to mar the visitation. After examining all Mumhain,
they entered Connacht, without molestation from Aeh Guaire or
anyone else, and proceeding in a northerly direction, entering
Ulladh. Here, too, everything appeared to run smoothly, as
they travelled far into that kingdom. At last they entered the
district of Magh Line; and as evening drew near, they hastened
to the residence of a chief, called Banban, the name by which
his castle was known being Rath Beg, or the Little Rath. Rath
Mór,* or the Great Rath, was quite convenient; but as that was
the seat of the lords of Dal Araidhe, who were friends of the
northern Hy-Nials, and also of Ruadhan of Lothra, King Diarmaid
had no desire to put up at their rath. It so happened, however,
that though Banban was loyal to King Diarmaid, he lived on
terms of the closest friendship with his next neighbour, Suibhne,
chief of Dal Araidhe, who was of superior rank to himself. The
blasts of the royal trumpets, borne along the evening air, were
heard by Banban and his family at Rath Beg; and they were also
heard at Rath Mór. When the royal cortege drew up before Rath
Beg, and the chief herald went up first to the chief entrance, he
was received by Banban in person, and invited to enter; this he
did, bringing in the Spear of State, horizontally, without the least
difficulty. Banban then went out to meet the Ardrigh, to whom
he did homage, and invited himself and all his retinue to the
hospitalities of his rath, only too delighted that the Ardrigh had
done him the honour. Soon the whole royal party, king, " *ten,*"
guards, and all, were at home for the night in Rath Beg.

The next morning brought the nobility and gentry of the
surrounding country to pay their duty to the Ardrigh. Diarmaid
received them with his accustomed urbanity; but he noticed that
one family was missing, and that too, the family residing nearest
to Rath Beg. It was also noticed by the assembled *uaisle*
(nobility), and there was much comment thereon. But they
departed to their homes, and as they did so, the family of Rath
Mór heard of what had passed; so during the day, while the
Fianna were absent on their visitation, and Diarmaid was holding conversation with Banban in the principal hall of the rath, a
giolla entered and announced Aedh Dubh (or Black Hugh), the
son of Suibhne, chief of Dal Araidhe. Banban, the lord of

---

* Two miles east of Antrim.

Rath Beg, not perceiving the king's look of reluctance, gladly welcomed the son of his private friend, though political opponent, thinking it a sign of returning allegiance to Diarmaid on the part of Suibhne Araidhe. But the haughty Black Hugh, who had not obtained that cognomen for nothing, merely inclined his head with the most frigid politeness to his sovereign, remarking at the same time that as Diarmaid had been good enough to notice and comment upon his own and his parents' absence, he then called to inform him that their absence was not due to any inadvertence or accident, but solely to indicate their denial of Diarmaid's right to their allegiance, and their contempt for his defunct authority. King Diarmaid listened to this outrageous insult like one in a dream. He could scarcely believe his senses, and was only recalled to them by the prompt action of Banban who, when the first shock had subsided, collared the rebellious noble, and shook him vigorously, as he shouted in his ear :

"How darest thou make use of such language to thy sovereign lord ; and in my house too ? How darest thou, I say ?"

"Hold," said the nearly-suffocated Aedh Dubh, "I dare say and do, too, just what I choose, and Diarmaid Mac Cearbhall here is not my sovereign lord, and none who have been cursed by Ruadhan of Lothra ever shall be ; as for thy house, I do thee honour by entering into it ; and moreover, I did not select it, because it was thine, but because it is the temporary abiding-place of a cursed king—stay! do not choke me, O Banban."

"Ay, that I will, for well thou deservest worse than that."

"There was a time," now said the unhappy Diarmaid, "when not even my greatest enemy would dare thus to address me ; but now having, in the simple discharge of my duty, fallen under the displeasure of an abbot, I am the butt for the insults of every rebel and hypocrite. Oh! woe! woe! why am I, the anointed High King of Eire, the only hapless being for whom the Church of the God of Mercy hath no protection and no mercy ?"

"I will tell thee, O Diarmaid," said Aedh Dubh; "it is because thou thyself had no mercy for Aedh Guaire, the chief of Ui Mainé."

"What! no mercy! had I not more mercy for him than the Abbot Ruadhan had for me ? Aedh Guaire committed murder and treason, and by the laws of the country he forfeited his life. For refusing to grant him his worthless life, because he was the relative, and had sought the sanctuary of the Abbot of Lothra, that vindictive religious and his brother abbot, Brendan of Birr, committed the greatest outrage known in history, not only on myself and my children, but on the hapless citizens of Teamhair. God alone knows what the future will bring forth, or how many thousands of lives the cursing of Teamhair shall destroy. Then, when I spared the life of Aedh Guaire, accepting a ransom, Ruadhan and Brendan refused to revoke their malediction. Thus, while I, the representative of the State, showed mercy to a rebel and a murderer, Ruadhan and Brendan, the representatives of the Church, had no mercy for an ill-used King, or his children, nor for the innocent population of Teamhair, or the still more innocent babes, who will be the real sufferers from the downfall of Teamhair."

" It is fearful to contemplate," said Banban.

" I understand not such fine logic," said Aedh Dubh ; " all I know is that whatever the Abbot Ruadhan does is right. Ruadhan has cursed Teamhair, therefore the malediction is just."

" Well, perhaps thou art a better theologian than I. All I can say is that if such work continues, and if future abbots and prelates imitate the conduct of Ruadhan, there may come a time when there shall be neither cities nor kings in Éire to curse. Then, perhaps, the Church will reign triumphant, and perhaps not. It may be that the Church, or rather those who call themselves the Church ; for I distinguish between the Church as a divine institution, and those individual ecclesiastics who call themselves the Church in order to further their own personal ends or political ambition."

Here Diarmaid, forgetting his infirmities, warmed into his subject, as he continued :

" It may, perhaps, some time or other, suit the policy of the ' *Church* ' in the last sense of that word, to curse, not one king, or one city of Eire, but the entire population, from the highest to the lowest, and every city, village, and acre of ground in the whole country ; and as Ruadhan and Brendan have done with Teamhair, so some future ecclesiastics may do with Eire itself, declare that no king or queen should ever again reign in that cursed country. Ah ! but it may be that all these things will bring their reward. If the Church will not tolerate Irish kings, who love, and to the utmost of their power, benefit and endow the Church ; if the Church will preach disloyalty and disobedience to Irish laws and institutions, famed for their justice and clemency, then, perhaps, at some future time the successors of the men who do these things will be satisfied with their work, and will preach to the descendants of the present

population loyalty, obedience, and service unto death, to whatever foreign masters they shall appoint to govern the land; and
instead of lording it over native sovereigns, they will only be
too proud to be allowed to kiss the feet of their foreign masters,
and be thankful for small remissions of perpetual punishments."

"Thou art not over respectful to the Church, O Diarmaid,
that thou speakest so," said Aedh Dubh.

"I tell thee, O son of Suibhne, that I mean only particular
members—dignitaries, if thou wilt—who prefer their own private
interests or public party or political strife to the real interests
and glory of the Church; and who merely use the latter to give
prestige and sanction to the former."

"To whom dost thou allude, O Diarmaid?" asked Aedh
Dubh.

"To all to whom it applies, whether they are yet in existence or whether they have yet to be born."

"Well, I neither know nor care aught for those who have
yet to be born; but if by those who are yet in existence thou
includest Ruadhan of Lothra, I tell thee to beware," said Black
Hugh, growing blacker still.

"I include all who deserve it," said the Ardrigh; "and now
I would know how long is it since thou didst become so loyal
and devoted a son of the Church?"

"Well," answered Aedh Dubh, "much as I detest thee, O
Diarmaid, I will answer thy question. I care not a screapál* for
the Church, according to thy first definition of it, that of a divine
institution; but thy second definition of the Church is another
matter. I care very much for the Church as a political body
and for some of those ecclesiastics whom thou so much abhorrest.
Ruadhan of Lothra is my best friend, and I will not tolerate his
actions being brought before thy bar of justice."

"Were Ruadhan of Lothra in his proper place he would
stand before me a supplicant for pardon and mercy."

"Darest thou speak thus of my personal friend; then take
that, and with it learn that the curses of so holy a man are not
an empty sound."

Uttering these words, Aedh Dubh, like a flash of lightning,
raised his sword and with it pierced the unfortunate monarch,
who fell into the arms of Banban.

Banban had been all the time standing listening to the foregoing dialogue, but himself scarcely uttering a word. However, on hearing the last words, and perceiving the quick action

* A threepenny piece.

of Aedh Dubh, he instinctively rushed between the monarch and his assailant, but only succeeded in preventing the sword from piercing the heart. But as Diarmaid fainted away and fell back upon the nearest imda, despite Banban's support, the treacherous assassin, dreading that Diarmaid should now live, again lifted his sword, this time directing it at his neck, and nearly severed the head from the body.

The assassin fled, but Banban, laying the fainting Ardrigh on the imda, ran out of the hall, and fortunately encountered Diarmaid's physician—one of the "*Ten*,"—whom he sent in to his master. Then he raised his voice and called loudly for assistance. Diarmaid's anam-chara, or soul's friend, and all the other members of the "*Ten*," as well as Banban's servants, were soon around the dead monarch. The physician declared that not a spark of life was in him when he examined him. The anam-chara knelt down to recite the prayers for the dead, and all present followed his example. When they arose, he addressed a few feeling words to them, asking their continual prayers for their late dear sovereign, who, he assured them, had for a considerable time past been a model of every Christian virtue, and he concluded by expressing a hope, that as he was sorely tried in this world in his capacities, both of a man and a king, that his happiness and glory would be the greater now in heaven. The words of the priest consoled those present, but it could not entirely silence the lamentations with which they bewailed their king. Someone asked Banban had he taken any steps towards the arrest of the assassin, but he replied that he had escaped before he could do aught to prevent him, but that he had set the officers of justice on his track.

ᴀɴ ᴄ-ꍈᴇᴀᴄᴛꍈᴀᴅ́ ᴄ́ᴀɪᴃ́ɪᴅɪʟ.

CHAPTER VII.

Ꭺᴅ́ʟᴀᴄᴀᴅ́ Ꭺꝉᴅ́ᴩɪᵹ̇ ɴᴀ Ꭼᴩɪᴏɴɴ.

THE FUNERAL OF THE MONARCH OF IRELAND.

WHEN the Fianna returned in the evening their surprise, grief, and horror may be imagined. They could scarcely realise the terrible woe that had fallen upon them. The *mna caointe* soon appeared and chanted over the late king the wild, weird songs of woe and glory. When the news got abroad great were the crowds that flocked from all parts to Magh Line. As succeeding days spread the news through every part of Eire, the populations of the five kingdoms sent deputations to attend on their behalf the funeral of the Ardrigh. Those deputations accordingly began to arrive day after day, and amongst them one day came the greatest of all, the deputation from Teamhair, the capital city itself, and with it the two sons of Diarmaid. But we will not dwell on the heart-breaking scene which then took place, nor upon the description which these Temorians gave of the effect which the terrible news produced in that city. Suffice it to say, there was weeping, groaning, and lamentations in every house in Teamhair. The following days brought deputations from the more distant portions of the country. At length when all who were expected had arrived, the arrangements for the funeral were brought to completion. The great and grand, though sombre, funeral car, drew up before Rath Beg. The white marble coffin, containing the body without the head was placed thereon, amidst universal lamentation. All the ensigns of royalty were there ; all the flags of the nation were there furled— the Gal Greina surmounting them all.

All the nobility, clergy, gentry, traders, merchants, farmers, ollamhain, and all sorts of people, rich and poor, assembled to pay the last honours to the remains of the Ardrigh. All the grand chariots had their gorgeous coverings covered over again with black silk or satin edged and otherwise adorned with silver lace. Diarmaid's own carbad thus arrayed was drawn unoccupied in the great procession. The clergy and monks from several monasteries, including that to which the remains were being brought, also Cluain Irared, Cluain Mac Nois, Ardmacha, Inisfallen, Ceananus, Scryne, and hundreds of others, walked four abreast, and chanted the Office for the Dead through all the streets, roads, &c., through which the procession passed. On and on it crept for seven miles northward, until it reached Conchobhar,* when it stopped at the Church of St. Macnisese, the oldest foundation in Eire. Here King Diarmaid's body was interred, amidst prayers, psalms, and lamentations. Great, however, as was the grief and woe of the people, they could not but feel for the much more natural and genuine sorrow of Diarmaid's two sons, Aedh Slane and Colman Beg. However, there is an end to all things ;

* Connor, in county Antrim.

so the sad ceremonial over, all again returned, some of the
people of Conchobhar and surrounding country to their homes,
and others who had come with the funeral returned with their
companions to take part in another ceremony—the funeral of
Diarmaid's head—which according to his own oft-expressed
desire that his body should be buried in Cluain MacNois, was now
to be brought thither, as the most that could be done under the
circumstances.   Accordingly a silver shrine was ordered, and
into this Diarmaid's head was put, and in a few days afterwards
all set out again, this time passing the northern banks of
Loch n-Eathach,* and travelling southward through the heart
of the country to Cluain Mac Nois.   At every point along
the route they were joined by fresh contingents of nobles and
people : the Righ Cuicidh, or Provincial Kings; the Righ
Tuathas, or Tribe Kings ; the greater part of all the various
classes of aires, or flaiths ; all the agricultural, literary, me-
chanical, trading, and military classes of all the five kingdoms
were there in great force, on foot, on horseback, and in chariots.
All the churches and monasteries of Eire—save those of Lothra,
Birr, and a few others, who sympathised with these latter—sent
as many of their monks and priests as possible.   The abbots
themselves and the bishops were there.   Myriads of students, .
native and foreign, also came in their hundreds of thousands to
do honour to the memory of their late monarch ; but the poor
were loudest of all in their lamentations for their friend and
benefactor.   •

Increasing in bulk as it went along, the sad procession was
likewise lengthened by accessions from all the rivers, which
brought mourners from Alba, Britain, the Isles, Gaul, &c.,
including priests, bishops, and monks from Irish foundations in
those countries, former pupils of Irish colleges and schools, as
also the Galli, Brittani, and Albani themselves.   The multitudes
of monks and clergy chanted Offices for the Dead in turn all along
the whole route.   This was relieved by the cepoy, or funeral
dirge, which recounted the descent and exploits of the dead.   It
was chanted by the mourning bards, assisted by their pupils and
the family mourners, while the professional mourners sang the
accompaniment in melancholy strains and in measured notes to
correspond with the metre of the dirge.   Then the Fenian army,
who turned out with all the honours, contributed their share in
paying the last public mark of respect to the deceased monarch.
All the military musical instruments were put in requisition, and

* Lough Neagh.

played now the Camhadh, or Lamentations (without words); again the Gol-truaighe, or melancholy music, exciting sorrow; then the Cuigrath, or Lamentations (with words), sung by the bards, dirge time; then the Calloid, or funeral elegy. Though numerous groups from Teamhair had gone to meet it at almost every point of the journey, when they reached the part of the Boinn, nearest to Teamhair, and again when they arrived at Mullingearr,* nearly the entire population of that city appeared to have congregated at those points. At the latter place, also, the Colleges of Cluain-Irared and Cluain Mac Nois, which had already sent deputations to Magh Line, now appeared in such force as to have it remarked that they had left those monasteries empty. From the time the funeral left Magh Line it halted at all the churches and monasteries on its route. Proceeding still south-westward, they at length arrived at their destination, and poured in their hundreds of thousands into the termoinn lands of St. Ciaran. People had already congregated here, and the rivers Sionnain and Brosna were black with corachs and larger vessels as far as the eye could reach. The furled flags and banners of many colours and myriad devices on the river and in the grounds, now joined the multitudes of similar ensigns which accompanied the funeral, headed by the more important banners of the provincial kingdoms, and the predominating Gal Greine. All the vehicles and horses being left without, the multitude, or all who could, entered the monastery gates. Soon every inch of ground of that large demesne was covered with closely packed masses of human beings.

Many of the foreigners, perhaps schoolfellows of Diarmaid and of Ciaran, or others who remembered the Eaglais Beg, or Little Church, which Diarmaid had, after bestowing the land, helped with his own royal hands to build with Ciaran Mac an t-Saoir, were now astonished to see the noble pile of buildings which Diarmaid's continued bountiful benefactions and munificent patronage up to his death had enabled Ciaran's successors to erect. The Eglais Beg, was now the centre around which were grouped no less than seven churches, two cloigetechs, or round towers, great school-rooms and lecture-halls, and all the other necessary buildings to such an institution, innumerable monastic cells, as well as an already large and important town.† As soon as crowding would permit, the shrine

* Mullingar, in Westmeath.
† The ruins of those now form a picturesque object on the banks of the Shannon, seven miles below Athlone.

containing Diarmaid's head was brought into the principal church, the doors and windows being left open, and here and in the other churches and without, hundreds of Masses were offered up, and thousands of religious chanted the divine offices, the abbots, priests, and monks of Cluain Mac Nois and Cluain Irared taking lead. This over, the shrine containing the monarch's head was interred with his first and second queens, and his brother, Maelmordha Mac Argatan, and his own son, Colman Mór, amidst the heartrending cries and inconsolable grief of his people. Then Amerghin Mac Amlaigh, the Ard Fileadh of the late Ardrigh, amidst universal silence, delivered the paneric, or funeral oration, recounting the genealogy, deeds, and virtue of the departed sovereign, and the loss sustained by the city of Teamhair, the kingdom of Midhe, and the empire of Eire and the colonies. When he had done, the Abbot of Cluain Mac Nois delivered a religious address, praising the virtues, charity to the poor, munificence and bounty of the late monarch to the Church, his encouragement and patronage of education, and wound up by asking of the assembled multitudes and all their friends, who either could not hear him or were not present, to remember the late beloved, but unfortunate sovereign in their prayers to their dying day.

All being now over, the vast throng began to disperse, having been refreshed in the proinnteach, or else in the biadtachs without; friend met friend, and acquaintance greeted acquaintance, and everybody condoled with all whom he met, anent their mutual sorrow. Our old friend, Aristophanes, now professor of Greek in Cluain-Irared College, who had come with the rest, now met two of his old schoolfellows there. Cannach (Kenny), Abbot of Cill Cannaich (Kilkenny), and Coemhghein (Kevin), Abbot of Gleann da Loch (Glendalough), who had also come with the people of their respective parts of the country to pay their last token of respect to their old companion and late sovereign. The three friends shook hands and expressed their grief for the loss of so dear a friend.

" What thinkest thou now, O Aristophanes, of thy old friend, Ruadhan ?" asked Cannach.

" I am disappointed in him, O Cannaich; but after all, when I think of his old grudge to Diarmaid, perhaps it is not so surprising."

"But surely " asked Coemhghein, "thou dost not approve of Ruadhan's revengeful conduct ?"

" Nay, most certainly not. In fact his conduct is inexplicable. I have loved him ever since my arrival at Cluain-Irared; but though no Eirenac,* I cannot express to ye the grief and the sorrow his act has occasioned me. Is he really an Eirenac, or is he of foreign extraction ?"

" No, he is no foreigner; he is one of ourselves. It takes a true Eirenac to hate and injure Eire. Every Eirenac prefers himself to his country."

" Strange, most strange," said Aristophanes.

"Thou oughtest to know us by this time," said Coemhghein.

" Yea, ye have a glorious country and a glorious history; but how can it continue if your people—otherwise superior to the inhabitants of any other country—are so selfish and unpatriotic ?"

"These are hard words," said Cannach, " but I fear too true. The words used by Diarmaid before his assassination in Banban's rath, may have a prophetic meaning."

" Ah ; I heard of that ; but he could not know, he could only surmise from what had passed under his own eyes."

True ; but is not that enough for a less intelligent man than the late great king ?"

" But why does the Church insist upon such extravagant power; why, no country could long survive what I have seen done in Eire since I came hither."

" Oh, believe me, Aristophanes, it is not the Church ; every individual monk or abbot is not the Church. I am an abbot, so is my friend Coemhghein here, yet neither of us would do the deed that Ruadhan had done for all the murderers in the world."

" I believe that," said Aristophanes ; but I am sorry for Ruadhan. If ever the churches and monasteries suffer from foreign invasion, Ruadhan's monastery and his successors of Lothra will not escape. But tell me, please, why should there be any notice taken of the curse on Teamhair. Why should not Diarmaid's son reign there as if nothing had happened ?"

" No; in the first place, Diarmaid's sons will not reign at all, either at Teamhair or anywhere else, at least for the present. They are too young, and besides the law of alternate succession requires a prince of the Northern Hy Niall race to reign now, as the late Ardrigh was the head of the Southern Hy Nials.†

---

* Irishman.
† The Irish monarchs continued to take their title from Tara till the Norman Invasion, and held conventions there for some time, but it was never

"Ah, I had forgotten ; but might not they dwell in Teamhair."

"They might if they liked ; but here our internal dissensions come in again. Fergus and Domhnall, the two sons of our former Ardrigh Muirchiertach Mac Earca, are the political foes of the Damnonian dynasty, of which Diarmaid was the representative. They are, moreover, the fast personal friends of the Abbot Ruadhan, and they will take pride and pleasure in showing triumphantly to the nation that his sentence on their late rival shall be carried out. Fergus and Domhnall, who as thou knowest fought successfully many battles against Diarmaid, will be crowned jointly Ard Righa na Erionn, and Teamhair shall most certainly be deserted during their reign."

"I see it now," said Aristophanes; "but will not the sons of Diarmaid be eligible to succeed them ?"

"Most certainly, if they live ?"

"Then might they not return to Teamhair ?"

"It is hard to say. No one can tell how long it will be till they come to the throne. Then, our people are so religious, that perhaps, much as they grieve over the fall of their ancient capital, they will have a scruple in attempting to save it in spite of the Church."

"Well, well, I know what *I* would do, if I had the power ; but perhaps your people are doomed to destruction. Let Fergus and Domhall do what they will ; let them reign where they please ; but if they would hand down their names with

afterwards used as a royal esidence. They never had any fixed place after, but each chose for himself a residence most convenient or agreeable, usually in their own hereditary principalities. Thus, the Northern Hy Nials resided at the fortress of Aileach, near Derry, and those of the Southern Hy Nials, first at the Rath near Castlepollard—now called Dun Torgeis, having afterwards become the residence of the Danish King, Turgesis—and subsequently at Dun na Sciath, on the margin of Loch Ainninn, now Loch Ennell, near Mullingar.

Diarmaid's son, Aedh Slaine, reigned when his turn came, and his posterity reigned down to the English Invasion.

Moore says : "This desertion of Teamhair must have gradually led to the disintegration of the Gaelic nation. Its tribes can no longer be said to have had any common bond of union between them, any Pan Gaedalon where they could meet in harmony and be reminded of their common origin. Patriotism, if it ever had existence amongst them, dwindled down to mere personal or family ambition, and henceforth they were the predestined prey of any warlke rovers that might choose to mix themselves up in their intestine quarrels. Thenceforth the Ui Niall or Ui Brian had as little sympathy with the Eoganachts or the Dal-a-Gais as they had with the Saxon or the Dane."

honour to posterity, they must imitate, as far as they can, the valour and chivalry, the justice and mercy, the ability, learning, munificence, and virtue of Diarmaid Mac Fergus Mac Cearbhall, THE LAST MONARCH OF TARA.—ARD RIGH DEIGHIONACH NA TEAMRACH.

CRÍOĊ.

Printed by H. M. Gill & Son, 50 Upper Sackville-street, Dublin.

www.ingramcontent.com/pod-product-compliance
Lightning Source LLC
Chambersburg PA
CBHW060538030726
47498CB00004B/1244